A DESERT SONG

BOOK ONE OF THE ROCK AND ROLL ANGEL TRILOGY

AMY M. YOUNG

AMY M. YOUNG

~

This is a work of fiction. Names, characters, businesses, places, events, locales, and incidents are either the products of the author's imagination or used in a fictitious manner. Any resemblance to actual persons, living or dead, or actual events is purely coincidental.

~

For Rosemary, Gary, Gregory and Autumn

For keeping me writing when I wanted to stop.

And my squid squad - who gave me a laugh, constructive criticism, and encouragement.

CHAPTER 1

*T*he hot summer sun had long since set on the arid desert sands of Arizona. I was on my way home, returning from a visit with my daughter Kristen, her husband, and their newborn daughter, Kathryn.

The clear night sky was beautiful—diamonds scattered across black velvet. I had been traveling for a week, taking a roundabout route back to my home in California. Seeing my newborn granddaughter had reminded me of how old I was. In the rearview mirror I saw a man from whom the blossom of youth had departed. The once past-my-shoulders strawberry blond hair was now cut short, and a face that used to be considered handsome had become "distinguished," with crow's feet and laugh lines.

It had been another tedious day of paying too much at little half-assed gas stations for fuel and junk food to get me through the day. I was exhausted and just wanted to pull off the road for the night. As I drove on, I noticed the usual signs of civilization slowly popping up around me—the increase in houses and other road signs, until eventually a large and tacky billboard read: *Vision Lake, Population Two Thousand Five Hundred*. Pushed on by the hope that I would find some place decent to lay my head for the night, I shifted down and sped into town.

The place was asleep only the way a small town could be, with all the lights off and the main street's pavement pretty much rolled up and stored securely on the curb for the night. Not even a stray dog roamed the streets. In the distance, on the proverbial horizon, a light shone on a neon sign. Thinking it might be a hotel, yet again I sped up through the narrow streets like the Magi following the star through the desert.

About five minutes later I pulled up in front of what was clearly a 1950s-era neon sign that beamed *Skylark Inn*. The entire area was dark—even the streetlights were off— and the only light in the place was a flickering candlelight in the office, but I decided to try my luck and see if they were open and had a vacancy for the night.

Pulling into a parking spot near the entrance, I got out and removed my suitcase from the trunk. I walked to the glass door that had a chipped and faded Office sign, and knocked. When I received no response, I decided to try the door. To my surprise it was unlocked.

Behind the front desk was one of the most beautiful women I had ever laid eyes on.

She leaned over the desk, working intently on something I could not see. Her long dark hair curled playfully over her shoulders, and that ivory skin made her a study in night and day, because of the contrast between dark and light. When she peered up with a startled expression, I could see gorgeous brown eyes, wide with fear.

"H-h-hello?" she called out timidly.

"Hi … um … I saw your lights on and wondered if you perhaps had a room available?"

She sat for a few seconds, confused, then stood up. "I-I don't handle anything like that. I'll have to go get Sarah. Wait here. Don't touch anything."

With one last frightened look at me, she tore off down a hallway to the right.

Her exit gave me a chance to take in my surroundings. The lobby was exquisitely furnished, if somewhat old-fashioned in style. The building itself seemed to be about the same age as the sign, but from the small amount of the place I could see, it had been well maintained over the years and didn't show its age too badly. The walls had a few large paintings on them—mostly watercolors—which were quite good. A local artist, I supposed. The paintings were all simply signed RNT.

After standing a few minutes, I decided to take a seat in one of the plush chairs. I heard the sound of two pairs of returning footsteps— one hurried and the other confident and slow.

"I don't know what I'm going to do with you, Rebecca," a stern female voice said as the footsteps approached and stopped just before the lobby.

"I've let you have your little *indulgences* like your music, your cat, and your drawings and writing, but if things like this keep on happening …"

The voice died off and the footsteps resumed. The dark-haired girl, who must be Rebecca, was followed by a tall, thin, and tanned "California" blonde, who, by process of elimination, had to be Sarah.

"Hello, I'm Sarah Williamson," she said, extending me a hand with perfectly manicured nails. "I hear you are interested in staying here."

I nodded, shaking her hand. She turned to the desk, and pushed Rebecca rudely aside to check what appeared to be an old-fashioned register.

"Well, you're in luck, Mister …" She waited for me to finish.

"Walsh, Jonathan Walsh."

"Mister Walsh. It looks like we have a vacancy." She turned to Rebecca. "Show him to room 210, and make sure you *don't* bother me again." With a fawning smile at me, she turned and stalked indignantly back down the hallway, into the night.

This left me with a rather nervous Rebecca gathering up her things from the desk. I noticed the sketch pad and various pencils and chalks she hurriedly shoved into a bag before she faced me again.

"I-i-if you'll follow me," she said, then went into the same hallway that Sarah had come down. I picked up my bags and followed Rebecca.

She led me down a winding corridor, past a picturesque courtyard with Roman style pillars covered in vines, leading down into what could have easily have once been a swimming pool. A floor-to-ceiling glass wall separated me from the beauty of the courtyard.

I must have paused, because Rebecca cleared her throat softly.

I tore my gaze away from the courtyard, and she gave me the look I've learned that only women can give: *The Eyebrow.*

I blushed like a teenager and we headed down another series of seemingly never-ending, maze-like hallways.

"This is your room. Have a good night's sleep, Mister Walsh."

She spoke in quiet tones as she unlocked the door and handed me the key. I resisted the urge to grab her hand and kiss it gallantly.

As I turned to thank her for taking me to my room, she was gone; I could just barely make out her faint silhouette against the dark walls as she glided silently away.

Oh well, I thought, as a gigantic yawn nearly split my head in two. *It's too late and I'm exhausted.*

Opening the door without even bothering to turn on the lights, I tossed my suitcases onto the couch, and made my way to the bed. Tumbling onto the mattress, I fell asleep before my head even hit the pillow.

~

*T*he sun streaming through a chink in the window blinds and the sounds of laughter brought me from my first deep sleep in ages to the waking world. It was around noon the next day, and it was as it should be in Arizona—hotter than hell. Stretching to shake off the remnants of sleep, I got out of bed and rummaged around in my suitcase. I took out a change of clothes and headed to the bathroom for a shower. After I stepped out of the steaming hot water, I glanced in the mirror. I needed to shave, but it was only a five-o-clock shadow and could wait until later.

Not bad. Not bad at all, I thought. *Not as good looking as you once were, but still not bad.*

I got dressed and while brushing my hair, I looked out through the narrow opening in the blinds. A large group gathered in the courtyard at what seemed to be a wedding. I hid behind the curtains, watching everything like a voyeur until the people dispatched into smaller groups and music began to play.

Taking my key and sliding the patio door open to the courtyard, I noticed the air was filled with the sound of the most incredible rendition of Chopin's *Raindrop* that I'd ever heard.

Cutting my way through the crowd, I saw Rebecca at the piano. She wore a sky-blue dress, and her ebony hair cascaded over her shoulders as she played. The bride and groom—obviously, by their attire—stood off to the side with Sarah, the person who seemed to be the owner of this place. She saw me enter the courtyard and with a brief word to the happy couple, she made her way across to me.

"Good day! Glad to see that you could join us!" She sidled up beside me, taking my arm.

"Hello"— I smiled at her and politely removed her hand from my arm —"If you'll excuse me ..."

I made my way through the crowd towards the piano. As I pushed through the throng of people, the girl whose name had to be Rebecca stared up at me, her eyes filled with a mixture of wonderment and anxiety.

I stood at the baby grand for a while, watching and listening to her as she played.

"Where did you learn to play the piano?" I asked. She was quite talented.

"I taught myself ..." She paused to look up at me. "Are you who I think you are?"

"That depends ... who do you think I am?" I returned, with a slightly devilish grin.

"Jonathan Walsh, lead singer of Torrent?" she ventured, and I broke into laughter.

"Yep, in the flesh."

With that her eyes went wide, and she hit a wrong chord. The discordant sound rang throughout the courtyard. Everyone's focus went to her, and she flushed a vibrant red, then paused in her playing as she stared at me.

"Keep playing, Rebecca!" Sarah hissed from about ten feet away.

"Why are you here?" Rebecca asked quietly as she resumed, moving into Beethoven's *Moonlight Sonata* as the chatter of the people in the courtyard continued around us.

"Let me just say I got stuck here. I'm leaving as soon as I can."

Rebecca looked up at me suddenly, her eyes filled with shock. "You don't know, do you?"

"Know what?" I asked, but at that moment, Sarah called out to everyone that it was time for the reception. The courtyard emptied out slowly.

I turned around to ask if Rebecca would like to go with me, and she was gone.

CHAPTER 2

While wondering where Rebecca had disappeared to, I joined the crowd of people heading to what was probably the reception. In the corridors, Sarah found me yet again. She walked along with me to a large banquet hall. It was an open room with plenty of seating. There seemed to be about two hundred people, and the buzz of conversations and laughter filled the place. I scanned the crowd, looking for that enigma called Rebecca, who by all rights should stand out like a rose amongst thorns in this sea of sun-bleached redheads, blondes, and brunettes, but she was nowhere to be found. Sarah invited me to have a seat with her, and I accepted. As much as she might rub me the wrong way, she was the only person I vaguely knew in the room, and the prospect of trying to make idle chitchat with people out of the blue wasn't something I looked forward to.

Sarah kept up a babble of conversation while we sat and was practically dripping honey from every pore to get me to pay attention to her. She was quite attractive; however, I didn't have the heart to break it to her that between my ex-wife, which she reminded me of just a bit too much, combined with the many decades I'd spent in California, the overly-tanned bleach blonde look didn't do much to endear me.

The bride and groom sat at the main table, surrounded by flowers and their wedding party. When the food and drink were served out, Sarah turned to me, exposing a large amount of tanned thigh.

"So, Mister Walsh, what brings you to Vision Lake?"

"I'm just passing through, heading home. It's been a long drive."

Sarah smiled and took a sip of her wine.

"Surely, you're not going to leave us that quickly! We're always happy to have"—she looked me up and down appraisingly—"new blood around here."

The tone of her voice and something else about her bothered me. It went beyond the basic resemblance to my ex, but I couldn't put my finger on it. She just made the hairs stand up on the back of my neck—that prickly sensation you get right before something goes completely and utterly wrong.

Playing along and trying to push that feeling to the back of my mind, I smiled. "Well, I might stay for a little while. I've been driving for almost a week now, and a few days off the road would certainly help to recharge me for that last stretch home."

I took a large drink of my wine and had to try not to grimace at the sour flavor. They went for quantity not quality around here. Still, anything to make that itch at the back of my brain stop. I waved a waiter over to refill the glass, which he did with a smile, then left.

"That's great!" Sarah chirped. "You'll have to join us for our services on Saturday. We always love having new people there."

Again, something in her tone sent that niggling little shiver down my spine. Part of me felt like I should run and hide, and the other part said I was being appraised like a prize-winning side of beef, or a Kentucky Derby winning racehorse about to be put out to stud.

Careful, Jon, you don't want to end up drunk and telling tales of your Great Aunt Laura and the sheep again, the voice in the back of my head warned.

I looked down. In the last five minutes, I'd slung back more than a few glasses of that wine, so much so that the waiter had left the decanter to my left, with a large pitcher of water. I pushed the wine glass away and moved onto the water.

Sarah stood and made a toast to the couple, who were called Jeremy and Andrea. I raised my glass to them, keeping back the advice only 20 years of marriage that ended in a bitter divorce could bring.

That was a bridge I never wanted to cross again. Having given the best years of my life to some blonde harpy who turned around and ... well, that's a story for another time and place. This couple seemed to be happy and in love, and a I hoped it turned out well for them. The more cynical part of me felt that love and happy endings were things best left to Hollywood screenwriters and novelists—not the real world.

As the meal was served, the conversations died down. The food, unlike the wine, was quite tasty, and as the couple stood to cut the wedding cake, I excused myself from the festivities. A full bladder from the untold glasses of wine and water made things a little less than comfortable.

I found my way down the hall, fully aware that Sarah's gaze burned holes in the back of my head. That woman didn't seem to be the type who took no for an answer, and all ego aside, it was becoming quite evident that she wanted me—for whatever purpose, I wasn't sure.

I rounded the first corner and leaned back against the wall. It felt cool in the shade provided by the shadows here. Rooms full of people tended to get warm regardless of the number of open windows or air conditioning. While sweating buckets in a live show is expected, it's not right to be doing so at a wedding reception.

I decided to head back to my room rather than try to search for some facilities near the banquet hall. Chances were that if I went back I'd run into Sarah, who would probably keep me waiting until hell froze over before letting me go, and I didn't know if I could wait that long.

I walked back past the courtyard. It was now the early evening hours, and the setting sun cast the courtyard in shadows and light. As I passed and looked around, I noticed a familiar dark-haired being at the piano. I had to wonder why she was alone. However, at that moment I had more pressing needs, and hoped that she'd still be there when I got back.

Ten minutes later, feeling much refreshed, I headed back out to the courtyard. Sure enough, she was still sitting there, and when I opened the door, the soft and gentle sound of *Für Elise* greeted me. When I walked across the courtyard to the dais where the piano was situated, Rebecca looked up, gracing me with a small smile.

"Hello Mister Walsh," she said, not stopping her playing.

"Please, call me Jon."

I took a seat on the stairs that lead up the dais and watched her play for a while. She moved through several different classical pieces before looking up at me again.

"This helps me to unwind after a long day of performing," she explained as she finished off another piece and then closed the lid.

"Why are you here?" she asked. No one just stops for a while and then moves on."

I gave a laugh. "Yeah, I'm getting that impression. You seem to know what's going on here."

She gave a small smile at that and turned back to the piano, her fingers drumming idly on the lid.

"You'd never believe me if I told you."

I picked up a portion of the vine that had fallen down and twirled it between my fingers. "Try me."

She sighed.

"It's a long story and I-I really don't like talking about it."

She seemed well and truly apprehensive about telling me, which of course heightened my curiosity. "So, how did you end up here?" I asked.

She stopped drumming her fingers on the piano and stared out into the ever-darkening hallways around the hotel.

"I'm not here by choice," she said at last, with a heavy finality to those simple words.

"Yeah, I gathered that from the conversation I overheard between you and Sarah the other night."

Rebecca smiled knowingly. "Yeah, well ..."

She went silent again. You could almost sense the mistrust in the air around her. She looked at me questioningly.

"How do I know the minute I walk away you're not going to run to

Sarah and tell her everything?"

What could I say to that? *I promise?* That would be hollow and I never made promises. Why tell people things you're not going to be able to keep? 'You can trust me' rang equally as hollow. She didn't know me from a hole in the ground. What did you say to someone who you wanted to trust you but barely knew you?

"I wouldn't confide in me either if I were in your place. All I can say is that Sarah doesn't interest me or have any claims on me. Maybe you and I can work on learning to trust each other?"

Rebecca looked around again, and abruptly stood up.

"I'd better get out of here."

She turned and fled out one of the hallways. Something had spooked her. What is me? Then I saw people heading back to their rooms for the night, and amongst them was Sarah. I immediately found myself wishing for invisibility and fervently prayed she wouldn't see me sitting in the courtyard. A few minutes passed before I realized that I held my breath while keeping my eyes closed. Opening one eye to quickly look around, I realized Sarah was nowhere in sight and the only people around were from the wedding and reception earlier, talking in small groups.

I stood up, and felt the hair rising on the back of my neck again. Before I could turn around to see who or what was behind me, a hand touched my shoulder gently and I jumped and let out a yelp that attracted the stares of pretty much everyone. Feeling the heat of a blush rising over my collar, I coughed and cleared my throat then made like I was trying to stomp a large spider or mouse to cover the fact that someone had just scared a few more years off my life.

Once the attention of the people around had turned back to their conversations, I turned around to come face-to-face with

Rebecca, who almost doubled over in near-silent mirth. Tears of laughter streamed down her face as she held her sides to keep from laughing out loud.

"I'm so sorry"—she gasped—"I didn't quite expect *that* reaction."

"What the hell *were* you expecting? I thought you were Sarah!" I said irritably. "You scared the bloody hell out of me!"

She snickered again, and tried standing up straight, only to double over again.

"I'm sorry," she apologized again. "It's just ... funny."

I grinned at the mental image of what I must have looked like. It probably was pretty amusing, even if I had been scared out of my wits. We both stood there laughing for a while, until she got her giggles under control.

"I just wanted to tell you, meet me back here tomorrow night and we'll talk. I just can't take the chance of us being seen by Sarah."

Before I could ask her why, even though I was somewhat sure of the reason, Rebecca disappeared with a wave into the darkness of the hallways.

Shoving my hands into my pockets, I walked across the courtyard and then into the hallways toward my room. Maybe she'd be able to shed some light; maybe she'd be able to tell me what secrets this place hid well from the outside world. The halls were pretty much empty with only a few people walking here and there, and I made it back to my room without being accosted by anyone.

Most of that night I tossed and turned, dreaming of falling from great heights and being chased by faceless, nameless terrors. An equally disturbing nightmare featured me being chased while a voice I didn't recognize and a face I couldn't see asked me to trust them, so I'd be safe.

CHAPTER 3

The sun rising woke me from my fitful sleep. The aftereffects of having imbibed the night before meant a blistering hangover, which reminded me why I generally didn't drink anymore.

After opening one eye and being blinded by the sun, I closed it quickly and rolled over. I moved a bit too quickly it seemed, because I found myself on the cold floor clinging to a sheet and swearing I'd never drink again if someone would just make the room stop spinning.

As I sat there, I figured I'd better get up anyway, seeing as the ice-cold floor was not someplace I intended to spend the day.

Clawing my way back up the bed and walking unsteadily to the bathroom, I managed to have a freezing-cold shower and performed my morning routine with minimal problems.

When I prepared to exit the room to find breakfast, I noticed a note had been slipped under my door at some point in the night or early morning. Reaching down, I grabbed the small folded piece of paper and stood slowly, so as to not upset the delicate balances of everything in my head. I read the note.

Jon,

Meet me in the courtyard at around midnight.

R

I folded the note back up and pocketed it. No sense in leaving it out where someone could stumble upon it and possibly tip off individuals that didn't need to know or find out about this meeting.

Opening the door, I stepped out with a bit more spring in my step and made my way down to the dining area, according to the directions from a young lady I'd asked in the hall. It was the same room as the reception from last night. I looked down at my feet to check that I had tied my shoelaces, since I'd pretty much dressed myself by feel earlier.

Unfortunately, when I raised my head, I noticed I was on a collision course with Rebecca. She read a book as she walked, and carried a muffin and a cup of something in one hand, totally oblivious of her surroundings. I didn't have enough time to warn her; I could only try to lessen the impact.

We still rammed into each other. Rebecca was coated in tea, and so was the book.

She blinked for a few moments, then sighed.

"I am so sorry," I said, grabbing some napkins and attempting to help clean up the mess I'd created.

"It's okay ... it really is. I'm washable. Thanks for helping though," she said, shaking off the book and the muffin. "That'll teach me to not watch where I'm going."

"At least let me get you a new cup of tea," I said.

She smiled sweetly at that. "Thanks. It was white tea; you'll need to ask Jodi for that. She's the one who's third from the end."

I walked down to the person she indicated was Jodi, and explained the situation. Jodi quickly procured another cup of tea.

I brought it back down to Rebecca, who was still dabbing off liquid.

"Thanks," she said, taking the tea from me. "You here for breakfast?"

I nodded.

She looked me in the eye. "Talk to Jodi again; ask her to hook you up with her patented hangover cure." With a wink and a smile, Rebecca walked away, presumably to change her shirt and pants.

It must have been obvious that I was relatively hung over, even though I thought there weren't any apparent clues regarding my physical and mental state. I scanned the banquet area. People sat in groups, talking and having breakfast. Everyone seemed dressed for work, and I suddenly felt out of place.

I went over to Jodi again, and asked her about her patented hangover cure.

"You've been talking to Becca!" She laughed, a jolly sound. "It's nothing much, just gives you something in your tummy."

She wandered off, coming back a few minutes later with a plate of sunny-side-up eggs and hash browns, a large mug of tea, and a large glass of orange juice.

"We don't have any coffee, but I gave you some of the tea I usually save for Becca. That should get you going. There's enough grease on your plate to clog your arteries up good."

I thanked her and headed for an empty table in the far corner of the hall, the furthest away from all the chatter, which with the remnants of the blistering hangover, sounded beyond loud to my ears. The eggs looked bloody disgusting—sunny side up was just not something that I would indulge in willingly. I decided to forgo them. My stomach lurched at the sight.

Grabbing the salt, I started in on the hash browns, which were delicious and greasy.

As I was enjoying my meal, Sarah came up to the table and sat down.

"Mister Walsh, I hate to ask this of you, but would you be willing to help out a few of the men around here with some general repairs?" she asked in what probably was her sweetest voice.

I nodded my okay, and mumbled out, "As soon as I'm done this."

She still didn't leave. She sat there twirling her hair around one finger and staring at me. I smiled, wiped the grease off my face, and finished off what I could of the tea and the juice. I stood, as did she, and she showed me out into another area of the place.

It appeared that several of the old hotel rooms were being turned into one large room. A few of the guys I'd seen last night were working on it. She introduced me to someone named Kyle, who said he was her brother.

He handed me a huge sledgehammer and asked me to start taking down one of the walls. I took the sledgehammer and began, all the while thinking, *Jon, you're forty-four. You're going to sprain or stretch something too far, you blithering idiot.*

However, the time went quickly, and before I knew it, I was sweaty, had gotten quite a bit of exercise, and had managed to take down my part of the wall faster than the men half my age.

Not bad for an old guy, I thought, as we took a break for lunch down in the dining area again. By the time we got there, it was pretty much deserted. Rebecca was there, off in a corner, the same book on the table. She didn't even look up when we entered the room, and I didn't bother her. Seeing as she had mentioned the night before that she didn't dare be seen by Sarah in my presence, I thought it best to keep it that way for now. Lunch was quick—a few sandwiches and water—and then back out to the work. If nothing else, this gave me something to do to pass the time. Kyle called it a day at the start of sunset, and asked us all to wash up and then meet in the courtyard after supper for evening prayer. That was something I'd decline, but the washing up bit I could definitely use.

The crew split. I shook Kyle's hand and left for my room. Twenty minutes and a nice hot shower later, I was dressed and checking the clock. Seven in the evening; give an hour for supper and then it was four hours of reading or *something* to keep myself awake.

Grabbing my keys and tossing them in my pocket, I headed out to the dining area. As I expected, everyone was there and the place was bustling with activity. Sarah found me once again, with exclamations of how fit I was and how Kyle had bragged me up. She dragged me over to her table, where they were served food instead of having to get it themselves. This time it was roast beef, and it looked delicious. I wisely stayed away from the wine—at least I was smart enough to not repeat stupid mistakes. Sarah and company at the table kept the conversation light and constant, so I was able to stay silent for the most part.

Sarah mentioned that Kyle and Jodi were to be married in a few weeks, and the preparations for that were going along swimmingly. This shocked me; the two of them seemed to be complete opposites. From the little I'd seen of her, Jodi came across as a cheerful, jolly person. Kyle was all seriousness and the male version of his sister, even down to the way they looked. Also,

Jodi's friendship with Rebecca—I assumed from their interac-
tions—and Sarah's complete dislike for Rebecca didn't add up.
Something was definitely amiss.

Partway through dessert, Sarah took a break from being the
center of the conversation, and turned to me.

"Mister Walsh, I hear you're quite musically talented. Would you
be able to help us out with some of our services this weekend?"

I protested, saying that I didn't know much music appropriate for
that type of thing; what small amounts of church music I could
remember were from ages-old versions of the Book of Common
Prayer. However, she would not take no for an answer. So, there it
was. I was at least stuck there until Sunday night.

Supper seemed to go on forever. The place emptied out, except
for Sarah's table. I checked my watch. Eleven forty-five. Four
hours we had been at the table, with Sarah holding the conversation. *Four frigging hours.* For the last hour and a bit, it had been a
discussion with Sarah, when she admitted it was against her
better judgment to give into Jodi's request to have a dance after
the reception.

I didn't question that. Obviously, they were of the belief that
dancing went against their religion. Something at the back of my
brain tingled once again, and I felt this was going to end in
trouble for me.

I checked my watch once more. *Eleven-fifty.* I had to get out of
there. Luckily for me, the group broke for the night, and Sarah
made sure to escort me back to my room. Something about her
still rubbed me the wrong way, and it was beginning to make me
feel like I needed a shower after every time she was around. The
moment I was sure she'd disappeared, I headed back out.

The hotel was quiet and only the crickets and other nocturnal animals could be heard in the still, cold desert air. I walked down the hallways to the courtyard. Pushing open one of the heavy glass doors that lead outside, I noticed Rebecca was already sitting down at the end of the stairs that lead up on to the dais. She looked like she was daydreaming, with a far off and distinctive "mentally not there" stare. She placed her chin on her knees and her arms wrapped around her legs. As I came nearer, her eyes focused and she waved to me.

"With how long Sarah babbled on tonight, I was afraid you wouldn't make it," she said, moving over on the step to make room for me.

"Does she blather like that every night?"

Rebecca laughed, and I felt a slight shiver crawl up my spine, and goose bumps broke out on my skin.

"Yes. I don't know when she sleeps. She's up from dawn till nearly midnight, every day."

We sat there for a while in companionable silence.

"You wanted to know why I'm here and what's going on. I still don't know if I can trust you, but I guess I'll to have to try," she said, watching me.

"I came here two years ago. At that point, this place was owned by my grandmother. She was living on her own and things weren't going well with running this place after my grandfather died. I had been planning to go to the University of Arizona that year, so I could help her out. I left my family back home, friends, Matthew, and everything to come here and help out."

"Who is Matthew?" I asked.

"Matthew *was* my fiancé," she said, smiling at the memory of him. "They haven't heard from me in so long, he's probably moved on ..." she trailed off, her eyes filling with tears. She wiped them away with the back of her hand and sniffed, then stared up over the rooftop to the sky, where the moon was like a giant pearl. She sat like that, silent for what seemed like an eternity, and I didn't want to interrupt her train of thought. With a deep sigh, she began to speak again.

"Anyway, Grandma decided to sell this place shortly after my second term. It's a huge property, and with just the two of us running it, impossible to maintain. The only offer she had was from Sarah. So, she sold it with the condition that our suite was left alone and the two of us allowed to live here.

"Sarah readily agreed to that, and well, they moved in. She, her brother Kyle, and the rest of the people here." Rebecca sat up, stretching a bit before she continued with the story.

"At first, I didn't notice anything strange. They kept mostly to themselves, but Vision Lake is a small town; most people here are either constantly in your business or just leave you alone. It was about a year after they bought the place, after Grandma died, when I noticed things changing. Sarah started threatening me and ... well ... strange things happened."

"What type of things?"

She looked around, terror showing in her eyes.

"I don't really want to talk about it yet. I'll just say it was weird stuff."

"I understand. I've noticed a few odd things around here, too."

She nodded silently and gazed back up at the stars in the sky, contemplating.

"So, Jon, why are you traveling?" she asked, breaking another silence.

I explained about my daughter and her family and that I was currently in between projects—in fact, the last call I'd had was about a Torrent reunion from Chris. "I really don't know if I can do it with how I feel about the entire situation between him and me, thanks to Tricia."

"Oh, yeah, you two got divorced a few years back, didn't you?" she asked, her chin on her hand, finally in a more relaxed posture.

"Yeah; it was messy." I normally didn't talk about my divorce, but I figured what the hell, it wasn't as if I was interested in a relationship. "I'm no saint, but at least I was honest about the things that I did."

"Oh?"

I sighed. This was something that was a bit of sore spot for me.

"Tricia and I married young, before the band and everything took off. Any *indiscretions* that went on I was honest about. I figured why lie about the messing around; it would just piss her off more than not telling her. Honestly, I don't think we ever really loved each other. It always felt like more of a business transaction. Tricia wasn't exactly rich or from a great side of the tracks. My family was a step up for her, a step away from where she came from."

Rebecca appeared to be intently listening and nodded.

"She could have at least told me she wanted out to marry Chris," I continued. "She always had a "thing" for him. But serving me with the papers at our daughter's wedding ..." I raised my hands.

"That's just ... nasty." Rebecca made a face.

"Yeah. Lost half my money and my property, and with it, most of my self-respect. Took a while to get that back; and well, I'm just to the point where I'm still rather bitter over the whole thing."

"I can't blame you. If that happened to me, I'd never want to see another man for the rest of my life."

"Yeah, that's kind of the point I'm at. I'm swearing off women for a while until I can get my head screwed on straight."

She smiled. "I hope you find someone someday."

"Well, I'm not looking, but if that person existed, I hope we'd find each other."

She murmured an agreement.

"Well, Jon, all I've got left to say is *pay attention* around here. If you do, you'll start to see things. Once you do, then we can talk."

She stood up and pulled the sweater that she was wearing closer around her.

"I think it's time we headed back in. It's getting colder and you should get some sleep before the sun comes up."

I stood up and together we headed across the courtyard. "At least let me walk you to your room. What are the chances that Sarah will be around at this hour?"

She nodded and we went down the halls together in relative silence. She tripped at one point, and elbowed me in the ribs, which began a short lived, but good natured elbowing contest.

"Well this is it," she said, as we arrived at her door. "Thank you for walking me back."

We stood at the door for a few moments. She played with her keys and I cleared my throat, the air suddenly seemed to become thick with energy. After what seemed like a lifetime, she opened the door, with a pleasant smile, said good night, and went inside.

I stood at the door thinking about things for a while, and then with a wry smile, I turned around to head back to my room, and came face to face with Sarah. Her arms were crossed and if looks could kill, I'd have burnt to cinders on the spot.

"I want to warn you, Mister Walsh, that is a very dangerous girl you're talking to. If you were smart, you'd stay as far away from her as you can."

It was late, I was getting tired, and she'd just ruined a perfectly good mood, which of course put me in a rather nasty mood.

"Whatever," I said half under my breath and pushed past her.

I had a feeling I would to regret that moment of irritation, but I had no idea just how much.

CHAPTER 4

The next few days crept by with Sarah keeping me busy helping out around the inn, doing repairs and minor cleaning. I kept an eye out for Rebecca but caught only glimpses of her in the courtyard from time to time, and once in the hallway near her room. It seemed that Sarah was going to make sure I didn't talk to her.

However, as the days plodded past, I had plenty of time for working and not a lot of time for thinking about the circumstances behind Sarah's motivations.

Each day was much like the one before it—hotter than hell in the Arizona sun, performing whatever tasks Sarah or Kyle had asked of me. Usually it was something small, like sweeping up the dining area, helping that lovely girl named Jodi with the dishes and food preparation, or repairing and repainting the exterior of the courtyard. Jodi was quite a chatter bug, and we talked about a lot of things: her life before she came to Vision Lake, her upcoming marriage to Kyle, the weather, and other guests that lived here. Rather mundane topics that passed the time and were safe for discussing. It wasn't until about the fourth day we worked together that things decided to take a turn for the worse.

About halfway through the day, Sarah showed up. Jodi and I had been cleaning dishes from the brunch they'd served and talked about nothing in particular. Just shooting the shit, really.

I spoke to a few other people in the kitchens as well, and it had been a pretty normal day until Sarah showed up with Rebecca in tow. You could tell that Rebecca did not want to be in the same room with Sarah. Sarah took Jodi and a few of the guys, and departed in a hurry, without mentioning why or where they were headed, leaving the two of us alone.

"Hey," I said.

I continued washing the dishes. Rebecca stood for a few minutes and then, without a word, began to dry the dishes and put them on the shelves. We worked in silence for a while before Rebecca stopped and watched me.

I paused and looked at her, too.

"What? Do I have some type of crud on my face?"

She actually cracked a small smile at that and blushed.

"No, I just wanted to say thank you for listening to me."

How do you respond to that? I just smiled, and with a nod, went back to work. Rebecca sent back some dishes that had a few things still stuck on them and got some suds on her hands.

She then scratched her nose, and a huge clump of soap suds clung to the end of it. She laughed and tried to brush it off while going cross-eyed from staring at it. Finally, she managed to get the suds off her nose and started drying dishes again. Time seemed to move a bit faster than it had earlier. We finished the dishes, and she wiped off her hands after a job well done.

"Would you like to go for a walk, now that we're through here?" she asked.

"Sure."

I dried off my hands and we headed out the doorway to stroll about the place.

It was surprisingly empty for the time of day. The halls were deserted as if it were midnight. Rebecca didn't say anything as we walked, but that was all right; sometimes the best thing to say is nothing at all. The size of the hotel was rather staggering. It seemed that at one time, Vision Lake might have been more than just a pit stop in the middle of nowhere on the road to somewhere.

Rebecca looked preoccupied. I wanted to inquire as to what was on her mind; however, I decided it would probably be best if I kept my curiosity to myself.

We walked into the courtyard, and Rebecca finally spoke.

"I hear Sarah's recruited you to play for their Sabbath services." She arched an eyebrow as she watched me.

"Yeah, not like I had much choice."

She motioned to the piano.

"Well, you might as well practice, whether it was forced or not."

She pulled a chair from up against the wall, where someone had been re-painting earlier, and placed it off to the left of the piano. She then went into one of the hallways, where there was a door labeled "Storage." She came back with an acoustic guitar.

"Seeing as there is only one set of sheet music, you'll have to read off mine, so you'd better sit up with me. If I remember correctly, you can play this," she said, handing me the guitar.

"You remember right." I strummed a chord and grimaced at how out of tune it was. "Ugh ... this is going to take some work."

We both sat down, and with Rebecca playing out the proper notes for each string, I was able to tune the guitar so that it sounded pretty good.

She played a song I knew vaguely. It wasn't one of Torrent's songs, but it was a nice duet for guitar and piano. When the song had ended, we caught each other's eyes and smiled. She was talented and could improvise quite well.

The moment was ruined though, by the sarcastic "Bravo" and clapping from the other end of the courtyard. I looked up to see Sarah standing there, her arms now folded across her chest. It didn't take a mind reader to know she was supremely pissed off.

"Rebecca, what are you doing?" Sarah came striding across the courtyard. "Mister Walsh is our guest, you shouldn't be asking him to help you out with your job."

Rebecca sat there grasping at words to respond.

"Sarah, I wanted to help her. It's all good."

Sarah turned towards me, her eyes blazing with fire. The anger was so physical that I could almost feel the flames licking at my feet. There was something seriously wrong. I had never seen anyone with such an all-consuming hatred and anger towards one person, and that included how my ex-wife felt about me.

"Okay, Mister Walsh. Thank you." She said in a stilted tone, and then turned back to Rebecca. "Just remember *Becky*, we have study tonight, and you're supposed to play the hymns. *Don't be late.*"

She turned on her heel and left, her hands balled in rage, her posture stiff as a board.

As she exited the courtyard through one of the heavy glass doors, which closed automatically to prevent them from being smashed by someone closing them in a temper, I heard Rebecca mutter behind me:

"Don't call me Becky."

I turned back to her. This definitely rated high on my *weird-shit-o-meter*.

"Do you want to keep practicing or call it a night?"

Rebecca looked down at the keyboard, her left hand tapping idly on the keys as she thought it over.

"Let's keep on for a bit. We were doing so well before she showed up."

I strummed a few chords and decided to play a song I'd picked up years before when learning to play guitar. It was classical, and I knew that, but the name escaped me as I played. It was evident that Rebecca knew the song, as she picked up the harmony of it and we played through the tune, and into a few others. When we'd finished, she looked up at me with a huge smile.

"I never knew you had classical training."

I blushed. "Doesn't everyone's guitar teacher start out with the classics?"

She shrugged. "I don't know. No one's ever taught me how to play my instruments. I taught myself."

My jaw wanted to hit the floor. "Instruments, as in the plural?"

"Yes, I can play guitar, piano, flute, sax, drums, trumpet, violin, and oboe."

"Wow."

Now it was her turn to blush, and the soft pink flush climbing her cheeks made her look even more beautiful. She could be striking in sackcloth and ashes.

Clearing her throat, she cleaned up her sheet music, which seemed to be a combination of hand written pages and pre-done scores.

"If you don't want to risk the wrath of Sarah again, you'd best head out of here," she said, standing up and taking the guitar from me. "She'll be starting evening study soon, and I'm sure you don't want to have to listen to her expound on the Bible for hours on end."

I nodded. "I'll see you later." With a small wave I moved out of the courtyard. I was sure Rebecca didn't think that I could tell that she was crying, but I could hear silent weeping as I left. As much as I wanted to comfort her, I knew if Sarah saw me with Rebecca much more, something supremely bad would happen. I feared for both my safety and hers. Sarah did not come over as the most stable of people, and I didn't know what type of retaliation she might have had in mind for Rebecca—and possibly me.

A ball of fear to formed in the pit of my stomach when I thought of it all. I wasn't quite sure why the fate of Rebecca weighed so heavily on my conscience. She wasn't anything more than an acquaintance to me; however, I didn't want her to come to harm.

I headed back to my room to think and to relax for the night. After sitting a bit, I decided to pack my things and get out of here, if she wanted to come, Rebecca would be more than welcome.

~

I woke up with the rising sun and got everything ready to leave. I showered and dressed and headed down to the dining area, where I knew Jodi and the crew would be working. When I came in, the room was pretty quiet. The bustle in the prep area was pretty much the only noise to be heard.

I grabbed a cup of tea and some toast and looked around for a table. The place was mostly empty except for two or three people at different tables reading or writing. I noticed Rebecca sat there, in the same outfit she'd had on last night. She had her head on her arms, sheet music spread across the table, and she appeared to be fast asleep. I walked over quietly and sat down across from her.

She was dead to the world. I couldn't help but chuckle at the sight.

"Rebecca," I called, trying to wake her up "Rebecca ... wake up."

Finally, I yelled her name, and she bolt upright in her chair, knocking over the cup beside her with a confused expression on her face.

"Whaa ... I'm awake, I'm awake," she muttered, rubbing her eyes.

"Didn't you get any sleep last night?"

She stretched, picked up the cup—which had been empty, thankfully—and gathered up the stray sheet music that lay scattered around where she'd been sleeping.

"Three a.m.," she moaned. "Three in the bloody morning."

"They were studying until *three* in the *morning?*" I asked.

"Yeah, and she's got morning study in about"—she checked her watch—"thirty minutes. I don't know how I'm going to stay awake for this."

She yawned again, and then stood up. "I'm getting another cup of tea. You want anything?"

I shook my head and she left, but came back quickly.

"If you'd like I can help you out," I said, "As long as she doesn't take all day."

"Thanks, Jon."

She sipped her tea and made a face. "I think they gave me Earl Grey," she said, sticking out her tongue. "Yecch."

"When I head out today, would you like to come with me? I know you haven't been home in a while ..."

Her eyes widened and she blanched even paler, if that were possible.

"Jon, trust me, don't even *try* to leave."

"What could happen? It's daylight, there is no one here who will stop me, and it's about time I started back on the road to home. Plus, I haven't seen my car in about a week; I'd like to make sure it's all right."

"Okay," she shrugged. "If I were you though, I'd take some ibuprofen or something. You're going to need it."

"C'mon, we'd better get set up."

Finishing off the rest of my tea, I followed her to the courtyard. The sun was just barely creeping into the sky and the dew glistened on most of the leaves of the vines. As Rebecca moved ahead of me I noticed something she was trying to hide—dark bruises on her upper arms and near her neck.

Anger and bile rose in my throat. I had no doubt this was because of the fact we'd been innocently practicing together last night. Even if we had been wildly shagging on the piano, there was no need for what I saw.

Rebecca didn't notice my reaction. She seemed to be wrapped up in getting things ready for the day. My resolve had changed; I needed to find out what was going on here. Once I had done that, I'd be able to leave this place—both in mind and in body.

She sat down and I pulled up the chair that was still left beside the piano. I asked Rebecca to come closer, because there was something I wanted to tell her.

"Rebecca, I'm going to asking you to trust me about something. It's about to look like I'm trying to get in good with Sarah. I want you to know I'm not, but I want to know what the hell is happening inside this place." I heard the venom in my voice.

She nodded speechlessly, her dark eyes teeming with tears.

The courtyard filled with people. Most of them were carrying a Bible under one arm, and some had their breakfast in the other.

Rebecca motioned for me to follow, and she began to play a song I vaguely recognized. I picked up the string part with the guitar and kept an eye on the growing gathering of congregants. A few people moved a table to near the dais where we sat, and set up what appeared to be a small altar.

Sarah sauntered in like a queen into her court. From her bearing, it was becoming obvious that she was, as Rebecca had said earlier, used to getting her way. Being back far enough, I could not hear Sarah clearly as she addressed the gathering of about no more than forty people, but she definitely had charisma.

From what I could make out, the lecture or study today was on the Armageddon prophesy contained within the biblical books of Daniel and Revelations.

The study seemed a bit one sided, as Sarah provided her interpretation of the verses and people made notations. Sarah went on endlessly and never seemed to tire. When she did pause for questions, I noticed they were not the type where people challenged her interpretation, but rather looked for more explanations, which she provided with gusto.

I checked my watch. Rebecca swayed glassy-eyed at the piano. It was clear she was exhausted, but both of us knew if she fell asleep there would be a fate that neither of us wanted to contemplate. I reached out and put my hand on her arm, and she started, but not so badly that she hit keys.

"Thank you," she mouthed.

Sarah had not slowed down yet. I felt myself zoning out, just like I had in school when the professor had become boring. Not to mention at home when Dad would get on a long-winded rant about something from the world of academia.

Rebecca gently kicked my foot and I realized I'd been rocking back on the chair, about to tip over. I slowly leaned forward to a normal sitting position and tried to sit upright. I checked my watch. Three hours had passed. Rebecca kept an eye on what was happening, and I was able to follow her prompts for playing music.

Sarah finally ended the study. The place emptied out slowly. Sarah staying where she was, watching everyone like a hawk as they exited the courtyard in groups, talking with each other. Rebecca cleared up her music and indicated for me to leave the guitar on the piano. She waited for me, and not escaping the gaze of Sarah, I offered to walk Rebecca to her room, not taking no for an answer, as it was obvious she was not in a state to manage it alone.

We walked silently, Rebecca yawning widely every few moments, which was infectious and it was difficult to keep from yawning as well.

When we went further away from the courtyard, I was tempted to ask Rebecca about the bruises on her back and shoulders. For a few minutes I silently argued with myself over it. Finally, I stopped her in a doorway between two sections of the hotel.

"Rebecca, what happened with your back? You're coated in bruises."

She looked down at her feet and tried to keep walking. I gently grabbed onto her shoulder, enough to stop her from going, but not hard enough to hurt her. She refused to meet my eyes.

"Rebecca ... if someone's done this to you, you should tell me."

She shuffled her feet, suddenly interested in the pattern of the carpet. Eventually she looked up. "I really don't want to talk about it, Jon."

"Fine, but at least answer this: Did someone do that to you?"

She nodded.

"Is this related to me talking to you?" I asked.

Again, a nod in response.

I contemplated what to tell her. I didn't want to say, "Stay away from me," which was the safest for her, physically. "Screw them" didn't really sound any safer to me, nor did any other suggestion my brain came up with. For once, I was left with no roads to take could guarantee everything would be all right at the end. Each road lead to danger, pain, and suffering.

I felt like letting out a guttural growl and punching the wall; I wanted to hurt the person who had done this to her. No one should ever hit a woman. There was and is no reason for it. Instead, I sighed deeply and gritted my teeth. After a few moments, we continued on. She seemed so frail, which didn't seem to be her usual self. From what little I had come to know about Rebecca, she seemed to be a friendly, somewhat introverted, highly intelligent, and talented woman. The woman I before me now didn't seem to fit with any of that.

We arrived at her room, and again, she thanked me for walking her and suggested I get some rest as well. Part of me wanted to stay with her, to make sure she actually did get sleep, and to make sure that no one else harmed her. The other half of me thought it was time that I looked around for some answers to the questions formed in my head.

The first person I thought of was Sarah. Everything in this place seemed to lead back to her in some way.

Wandering back through the hotel, I found Jodi sitting in one of the small lobby type areas that were scattered around the place. I asked her where I could find Sarah, and that I needed to talk to her urgently. She told me Sarah had gone out with a few of the residents to get supplies in Phoenix, and they'd be back in about two hours. I thanked her and headed to my own room. I unpacked what I'd packed and settled in for the long run. My curiosity was piqued.

Before I dropped down to talk to Sarah, I decided to check on Rebecca. I knocked on the door to her room and received no response. Calling her name didn't get any result either. I tried the door. It was surprisingly unlocked. I cautiously opened it, calling her name, and when I didn't hear anything I warily stepped into the room.

I saw Rebecca curled up on the couch, half falling off it, but sound asleep none the less. I quietly walked over and finding an afghan draped over the edge, I laid it over her. She stirred in her sleep, rolling over to face the back of the couch, and pulling the afghan tighter in around her. It seemed she'd simply passed out from exhaustion, and from how she had a pillow and blanket handy, she'd done it often enough.

Making sure she was all right, I quietly left the room and locked the door behind me. I laughed and shook my head, thinking of how tired she must be.

I headed back to the main lobby. I wanted to check on my car, just to be on the safe side. I'd owned it less than three months at this point. As I came in, I noticed two young gentlemen from the place standing and sitting around, respectively.

"Hey guys, just going out to check on my car!" I said cheerily as I went for the door, showing them the keys hanging off a finger by the ring.

"Sir, I need to ask you to step away. I can go check on it if you'd like," the one closest to the door said to me.

"Nah, I'd prefer to check it myself, thanks." I said, pushing forward towards the door. I tried the door. It was double-bolted and locked, which it hadn't been the night I'd showed up.

"What the fu—"

And with that, the world went black.

CHAPTER 5

*P*ain.

Pain worse than the most severe migraine I'd ever had, almost on par with the time I'd done a flying leap off a stage and had broken my leg in several places.

The world was still dark. I couldn't open my eyes, or—as I found out when trying to inspect my aching head with my hands—move with any degree of accuracy.

I attempted to call for help, but it came out as garbled nonsense. I felt a cool hand on my head, followed by a wet washcloth.

"Hold still, will you?" a seemingly feminine and annoyed voice said. "They messed you up pretty damned bad."

I did my best not move a muscle.

"You're lucky we went looking for you," she said.

I heard the woman call for another washcloth and something to clean up the wounds. I could also make out footsteps and another person explaining that this was all she could find.

"Oh well," said the voice closest to me. "Hold still, this is going to hurt like a son of a bitch."

They weren't kidding. If it were possible, the pain seared far worse than five minutes before. I screamed, which, while not the manliest of things to do, was the instinctive reaction to that much torture.

Again, the world went black and silent as I passed out.

When I came to again, I slowly opened my eyes. I could barely move, and my head ached like I'd been kicked by a horse. Blearily I looked around as much as the pain would let me.

I was back in my room, on the couch. I could see two people in the room with me, but I couldn't zero in on their features. One was curled up sleeping in a chair, the other sitting alongside me on the floor, which made focusing an impossible task. I moved my head too far and groaned.

The face of the person swam into clarity as she shifted her position. It was Rebecca.

"Hello," I croaked.

"Well, it's obvious they didn't beat you so badly you've lost your memory." She let out a small and wry laugh, then stood up and checked to make sure I hadn't dislodged any of the bandages. "Doesn't look like they broke anything, but they did ding you up pretty well. Jodi and I found you in the hallway after we went looking for you. She wanted to let you know that the person you needed to talk to had returned."

Rebecca wandered off then, and came back with a few pills. "Naproxen. It'll help with the pain." She placed them into my hand and grabbed a cup of water off the coffee table for me to take them with. I swallowed the tablets and the water gratefully.

"They bashed you pretty hard across the back of the head. That probably needs stitches, but the likelihood of us getting you out of here is slim to none."

"What the hell is going on?" I asked, my throat still cracking with dryness, as I tried to sit up on my own and failed.

"I told you before and you wouldn't believe me," Rebecca said, glancing over at Jodi. "But I think you're beginning to see this isn't someplace normal."

"I think you just won the award for Understatement of the Year."

Rebecca helped me stand up. I was dizzy and my head still felt like someone had cracked it with a hatchet. My vision was blurred, so I couldn't see well enough to get across the room on my own. Putting my weight on her and allowing her to guide me where I wanted to go seemed to work. I got to the bathroom, and indicated I was fine as long as I hung on to the counter and wall while I walked. I flipped on the light and looked in the mirror.

The sight that I was greeted with completely shocked me. My face was bruised and swollen. It appeared someone had nailed me in the jaw and I'd cracked the side of my head against the floor as I fell. I could see a few areas of dried blood coming from the wound on the back of my head. I felt the raised bump and with a hiss of pain, came away with a bit of blood on my fingers.

I knew there were other bruises on my body, and after seeing what I looked like, I didn't want to know. The stiffness and soreness told me where they were anyway. I sniffed and smelt something of a pretty high proof.

"What the hell did you two use to clean the wounds?"

"The only thing Jodi could get her hands on—Vodka." Rebecca said from the other side of the door. After I cursed she added, "Would you prefer we didn't do anything and just left you there?"

I opened the door and lurched through it. "No, but that explains why it fucking hurt like hell."

With Rebecca and eventually Jodi's help, I made it back to the couch and collapsed again.

"You're going to be dizzy and disoriented for a while. Jodi has agreed to bring some food down for you and run interference with Sarah for a while, if Sarah doesn't know what happened already, which isn't very likely."

Rebecca moved around the room like she was used to taking care of people who had the shit beat out of them on a regular basis. Then I realized she might be, considering she currently wore something that completely covered her own bruises.

"We'll both drop in as much as we can over the next bit, but the fact that you're conscious is at a good sign, at the very least. You were out cold for about two hours."

There was a knock at the door.

Rebecca froze. Jodi looked around for a place to hide.

"Who is it?" I called out.

"It's Sarah."

I cursed, as did Jodi and Rebecca. Rebecca quickly and quietly moved to the bathroom and closed the door. Jodi walked over and opened the door after making sure Rebecca was safely stowed away.

Sarah entered the room and when she saw my condition on the couch, then began fawning over me like I was a child who had just skinned his knee. She kept flitting around so much it was making me nauseated, seeing as I could barely focus on things that stayed still.

"Sarah, I really need you to leave, please." I gritted my teeth against the waves of nausea that flooded my senses. "I'm feeling like hell, but if I'm okay later on, I'll definitely make a point to see you."

She looked hurt; however, she took Jodi and left, leaving me in relative silence. After a few minutes, Rebecca opened the door to the washroom and stepped out again.

"Um, I guess I'd better go, too. Sarah's going to start her evening Bible study in a bit," she said as she opened the door to leave.

"Rebecca ..." I called out as she move through the doorway. She turned around.

"Thanks for taking care of me. I'd like it if you'd check in on me later. I'm not in much of a state to be going anywhere right now." I smiled weakly.

A bright smile lit her face. "Sure, Jon."

She left the room, closing the door behind her with a quiet click.

Now alone and feeling very lonely, I had time to think, which— due to the banging my brain had received earlier—wasn't exactly easy.

I knew that to find out more I would have to work past my mounting disgust of Sarah. It could possibly be dangerous, for other people *and* myself, but I had to try. I doubted Rebecca could help me get to the bottom of things, so I wouldn't involve her. I didn't want to endanger her life. She'd become one of the few people I believed I could trust around here—a friend and confidante. Then once the batshit was over, I wanted out. I'd stayed long enough to feel like I was going stir crazy. Every time I envisioned being out of this place, though, I saw Rebecca with me and I wasn't sure why. She had a life and a fiancé outside who she would probably go back to once she could get to them, and what interest would someone like her have in me—even friendship?

I shrugged mentally and relaxed into the pillows on the couch. All this thinking and plotting gave me more of a headache, and I felt tired again. I closed my eyes, figuring I'd just rest for a while, then maybe try doing something on my own.

I came to with Rebecca standing over me and shaking my shoulder. It was quite dark in the room, and she had only turned on the light by the door.

"Holy Jesus, Jon!" She exclaimed when my eyes opened. "I've been trying to wake you for the last twenty minutes. Didn't you hear me knock and come in?"

"Uh ..." I managed, and she started off on a tear.

"Don't do things like that. Holy shit! Do you think I enjoyed imagining I'd have to drag a body out of here and tell Sarah that her favorite little pet is dead? I don't have that much of a death wish!"

She was scared, flustered and frustrated. She sat in the chair where Jodi had been earlier and sighed deeply, calming down, realizing that she was out of trouble in that area, at least.

"I brought you supper. Sarah is getting very suspicious of my coming here, you know," she said, getting up and bringing over a tray of food. "I'm pretty sure she's convinced I'm shacking up with you."

She laughed, and I joined in.

"She's a wee bit paranoid, isn't she?" I asked.

Rebecca nodded, sitting back down. "I should check that bandage on the back of your head before you start eating."

I put the tray down on the coffee table and made room for her to sit on the couch behind me.

She sat down and I could feel her fingers gently trying to remove the bandage without hurting me. Unfortunately, there was a lot of dried blood cementing the material to my hair quite firmly.

"Jon, I'm going to have to—"

"Just pull it. I'll be okay," I interrupted, and reached down to take hold of the couch cushions just in case it would be painful.

I felt her put her hand up on one side of my head and then the pulling of the bandage from my hair. It hurt quite a bit, but it was clear she took care to be as gentle as she possibly could. I felt her tug, and the pressure on my head increased, then finally it was free. I also felt her get closer to inspect the wound, and it sent a little shiver down my spine. The sensation was quite different from the tremors of disgust that Sarah had generated. I hadn't felt like this in so long, I'd forgotten what I was feeling.

"Well, this looks better than I thought. Seems you're one of those people who bleed like stuck pigs when you get a head wound." She ruffled up the hair in the area. "You definitely need to wash your hair though."

She stood up and I sat back, taking the dinner tray off the table. "Care to join me?"

She nodded and moved over to a chair of her own. "I ate already, but I'll keep you company If you'd like."

"I'd like that very much."

After I'd eaten, we sat and chatted for what seemed like hours about random things, nothing important, just talking to talk. Rebecca became more and more interesting as the conversation took form. However, it seemed she preferred to hear me speak.

"I love listening to you talk. Your accent—where is it from?" she asked at one point.

I laughed. It was something people had commented on most of my life.

"Well, I grew up in New York, but both my parents were from England—my mother from Doncaster and my father from around Abingdon. I guess I picked it up from both of them. Dad was a professor, so he had that upper-class accent. Mum always balanced him out there though; she had that definite Yorkshire accent." I turned the tables. "You're not from around here; your own accent gives that away. You're definitely from the New England area."

She smiled. "I'm not telling where I'm from, but you're close."

"Why aren't you telling?" I asked, teasing.

She laughed this time. "If I tell you everything then there will be nothing to talk about."

She had a point. I was enjoying this little chat about nothing. It was an excuse to get to know her better and I liked the company.

She looked at her watch. "Almost midnight. I'd better get going," she said with more than a little bit of regret in her voice. "Good-night, Jon."

"Good Night Rebecca. See you tomorrow?"

She nodded as she left the room. Getting up slowly, I managed to make it over to the bed, which was more comfortable than the lumpy couch.

~

*I*f I had any delusions about how old I was, the supreme stiffness of every joint in my body and the dull ache in my head the next morning sent that home with a bullet. Moving slowly, I managed to make it to the washroom and shower out the blood stuck in my hair. Water hitting that area hurt like a son of a bitch; I wished I'd suggested the night before that Rebecca assist me in washing my hair. It was embarrassing for me to admit I needed help. As I finished up dressing, there was a knock at the door, and Jodi stood there, a large pile of my clothes and some new linens in hand.

"Someone thought you could use help with some laundry," she said, and handed the things over to me with a smile, before scurrying down the hallway.

I wasn't sure who had suggested I needed laundry done, but I had my suspects in mind, or at least one person who I hoped was the culprit. I took the things into my room again and put them on the bed. While I sorted out what was what, a small note fell from one of the shirts. I picked it up and read it. *Hope you're feeling better. You know where to find me.* It was unsigned, but the handwriting was a dead giveaway as to its author. With a smile, I tucked it back into the shirt where it had fallen out of and walked, stiffly, out of the room.

Jodi had mentioned that Sarah had a usual daytime routine she followed. At 6:00 a.m. she taught the morning study, and went off for a meal afterwards. Then she spent time in her office, taking care of various things. Jodi had kindly provided the room number and what time Sarah would most likely be there.

Checking my watch, I saw it was about an hour early before Sarah would be in and when I'd have to put what I'd jokingly come to call "Plan A" into effect. Not hungry due to the lingering nausea and still slightly blurry vision, I headed for the one place I

knew I could find some solace, and maybe some companionship
—the courtyard.

I walked up onto the dais and sat down at the piano. The area was
nicely hidden from the elements by the overhang of the roof.
Lifting up the cover on the keys, I decided to try my hand at
playing again; the last time had been many years before, and I
knew I would be rusty. Hesitantly, I played some random song
that entered my head, nothing special, or so I'd thought, until I
heard a familiar voice singing along.

I looked up to see Rebecca standing at the other end of the
courtyard.

"Doing pretty well for someone who had the crap beaten out of
him less than 24 hours ago," she said with a smile. She stepped
down the stairs and across the wide area of the courtyard.

I grinned sheepishly and closed the lid on the piano as she came
up onto the dais to stand beside me.

"Sorry. Repressed musical frustration I guess," I said, starting to
stand up. She motioned for me to sit down and took a seat in the
chair that had been there for the past few days.

"So, I guess this is the last time we're going to get to talk freely for
a while."

I nodded. It wasn't something I wanted to do. However, distance
was the best thing for both of us, for safety's sake. Sarah's distaste
for Rebecca was clear, and considering the events of the last
while, I didn't want to tempt the demon and risk bringing down
the wrath of the beast herself on anyone but myself.

We talked for a while, discussing in what seemed to be mutually
understood code words about what I was getting myself into. The
next bit that lay ahead of me was something I dreaded. I felt I was
walking into the bowels of hell. The only consolation was that it

was highly likely there wouldn't be too many people to miss me if I were gone. Tricia certainly wouldn't. Kristen, well, yes. Beyond that, I didn't know.

"Keep yourself safe, okay?" Rebecca said as I got up to leave, putting a hand on my arm.

"I'll try." I said, hesitantly placing a hand on hers and giving her what I hoped was a strong smile.

Then, not looking back. I walked down to the room and steeled myself to face Sarah.

There but for the grace of God go I, rang through my head.

I knocked on the door of what Jodi had told me was Sarah's "office."

"Who is it?" she asked curtly.

"Jon. Jon Walsh."

There was a silence, and then hurried paper shuffling and things being re-arranged.

"Come on in!"

I put my hand on the handle, and pushed the door open.

CHAPTER 6

Once inside, I was greeted with the sight of Sarah sitting behind a desk. She had a stack of papers off to one side and worked on something with a huge dog-eared Bible sitting in front of her. I don't know how she managed it, but there had to be more skin showing than clothing would account for, and it was highly distracting.

She fixed her blue eyes on me with apparent concern.

"How are you feeling, Mister Walsh?"

"For having seven shades of shit beat out of me, okay I guess."

She never apologized for it; not a word was mentioned about the reasoning behind it. I sat down and began to discuss things, reluctantly agreeing to help her out, and trying to seem like I wanted to join in whatever she was doing.

"And what about you and Rebecca?" she said, leaning back in her chair, an eyebrow raised and a pencil to her lips.

"What about Rebecca and me?" I asked, a ball of *something* forming in my stomach.

Plausible deniability. A wonderful thing in this instance, but after saying that sentence, I wanted to throw up. "There isn't anything between us."

"*Good,*" she cooed and leaned in closer, which afforded me a view of her more than ample cleavage.

"Why don't you join me for dinner tonight and we'll discuss things further?"

I gulped. "Sure."

Oh God, anything to get the hell out of here, my brain pretty much screamed at me. The walls felt like they were closing in and the air felt too thick to breathe.

She sat back again, and looked at me appraisingly.

"Well, we'll see you then. Six-thirty, don't be late."

I nodded as I stood and made my way to the door. I was shaking like a leaf—whether that was simply on the inside or if there were any outside clues, I was unsure. I closed the door and made my way around the corner before I collapsed on the floor. I'd never had a panic attack in my life until then. My heart wanted to leap out of my chest, my lungs didn't want to cooperate with my brain to help me breathe, and my legs altogether refused to support me. I felt I'd just sold my soul to the devil, and the cost of the transaction had yet to be fully determined. I sat on the floor trying to get my racing heart and hyperventilation under control. I leant my head back against the wall, and swore when the still tender area on my skull came in contact with that wall.

Get up, you old fool. It'll be a great thing if Sarah comes round that corner and sees you as an emasculated twit having a panic attack in plain sight of everyone.

My breathing barely under control and heart still racing a mile a minute, I slowly pushed myself up the wall and back into a standing position. Trying to take a step, my legs wobbled but finally cooperated. I had to resist the urge to sprint the hell away from where I was and take one deliberate step after another.

As I walked back down the halls with my hands in pockets and my gaze firmly planted on the floor, I passed the courtyard. I looked up, but it was empty. With a soul-shuddering sigh, I resumed staring at the floor again and kept walking back to my room, passing people as I went along. For some reason, I found myself taking the long route back to my room, down the opposite end of the place, near Rebecca's room. This end was quiet, with only few people around. I was about to round the last corner just before her room when I heard the sounds of a struggle and stopped short. Slowly easing my head around the corner, I saw Rebecca being accosted by Kyle.

He had her by the throat, held up against the wall with one hand. She wasn't struggling at this point—I couldn't blame her, being against someone who had at least twice the strength she possessed and struggling would just have made the situation ten times worse. I strained to hear what he muttered to her in low tones.

"You just stay away, you hear? Stay the hell away from him. He's Sarah's and there's no way I'm going to let you ruin it for her. You got that?"

She nodded as best she could with being held that way. He then forcibly kissed her and threw her to the ground. "You fuck this up, you'll regret it."

I swung myself back around the corner and plastered myself against the wall. There was no way I could run and get far enough away in the condition I was in to have made it believable that I didn't hear the entire exchange, and I couldn't physically take Kyle on. The man was built like a brick chicken house, and I didn't know how many people it would take to beat me senseless, but I was pretty sure he did.

I heard his footsteps retreating in the other direction and breathed a sigh of relief. Peeping around the corner, I saw him turn the other corner of the hallway. Rebecca still lay on the ground, coughing and sputtering.

Inching forward, I came to her side. I didn't bother to ask her if she was okay, it was evident to anyone with eyes that she wasn't.

She looked up at me, terrified, and recoiled in fear from my touch. She curled into the fetal position on the other side of the doorway as tears streamed down her face. I reached out for her again, and this time she responded, clinging to my shoulders and sobbing. I cradled her in my arms as she cried, the two of us sitting on the floor outside her room. I wanted to tell her everything was going to be okay, which would be a lie. I wasn't even sure I was going to make it out of this place alive. Instead, I just comforted her the best way I could. After a while, her crying slowed to large gulping sobs and she sat back, her face red and tear-stained.

"I am so sorry about that, Jon." She said, wiping away the tears with the back of her hand. "I'm just so scared." Fresh tears fell.

So am I, I thought. *And I'm wondering what the hell have I done ...*

"Ugh. I look like a fool," she said, getting up unsteadily. I stood with her.

"Jon, as much as I don't want to say this, I think we should keep apart for the time being." She looked me in the eye. "You're a great guy and everything; I just don't want to end up, well, I don't want to end up dead."

"I understand," I said, feeling suddenly very much alone.

"If you need me, for safety's sake, please get Jodi to do it. She attracts less attention than a six-foot-something blond guy," she said with a smile.

I smiled back. She had a point. Jodi tended to blend into the background better than I ever could.

She hugged me, then opened her door and headed inside.

I went back down the hallway where I'd come down. It seemed like in order to find out the mystery behind Skylark Inn, I would have to sacrifice more than I ever wanted to.

The dinner hour came quickly and at six-thirty I found myself in the dining area with Sarah, seated at her table.

Sarah had been quite conversational, talking about how they came to Vision Lake and bought the building they were currently in. Apparently, she and Kyle were from Oregon. They were brother and sister, and the middle children of a family that totaled six children, including themselves. About half way through dinner, Jodi and Kyle joined us at the table. Jodi was uncharacteristically silent, and Kyle had the smug smile I'd come to associate with him over the past day or so, which I wanted to wipe of his face. I had no doubts he'd threatened Jodi as well.

At this point, Sarah turned her discussion to Jodi and the upcoming wedding plans. They were about three weeks from getting married, and for the first time, Sarah was allowing them to have a dance, at Jodi's request. The one objection Sarah had to the entire process, as did Kyle, was Jodi's choice of maid of honor. Jodi had picked Rebecca, against both their wishes. Inwardly I cheered for her making an independent choice of someone who she wanted, but outwardly I offered no hint of my opinion.

The conversation droned on and on, and I tuned out until I felt something crawling slowly up my leg. Attempting to find out what it was without attracting any attention, I knocked my napkin off my lap and bent over to retrieve it. I had a hard time believing what I was seeing when I peeked under the table. Sarah had her shoes off and was running her foot up and down my leg. With a start, I sat back up straight and moved my chair back far enough that I hoped she'd stop trying to play footsie with me all through dinner. That alone was enough to earn an irritated look from Sarah as she kept on a steady stream of conversation with Kyle and a few others at the table. I kept to myself, having nothing to add to the conversation, and focused on the food.

As dinner drew to a close, Jodi asked me if I would help her with some things for the wedding. Sarah had taken the other girls who would normally assist Jodi to work on other tasks, but the bride-to-be said she trusted me to help her out.

We left the table and headed out to a room marked "Arts and crafts." Jodi opened the locked door and walked in.

"I just need someone to act as another set of arms for me." She said as she pulled out a dressmaker's dummy with a partially finished dress on it. "Plus, I like having company when I do this."

She loaded my arms up with bolts of fabric and tended to the gown. While she worked she spoke about how she was not looking forward to the upcoming wedding; it hadn't been her idea and she wasn't really sure if it was a smart move. My two thoughts about it were to keep my mouth shut and to wonder if she was acting as an agent for Sarah—baiting me to reveal if I was up to anything. Then Jodi let drop a statement I never thought I'd hear.

"I don't really want to be here, but how the hell do you get out of something when the last person who left here went in a body bag?"

That caused me to drop the bolts of fabric. They hit the floor with a muted thud and I stood there staring at Jodi, completely shocked at what I'd just heard.

Altogether unperturbed, she picked up the fabric and then leaned in close.

"Jon, if you really want to discover the truth about this place, you'd better be prepared to make a gamble where you might lose everything that means something to you. Sarah, she doesn't take no for an answer. She's got an eye to add you to her stable, and well, bad things happen when she doesn't get what she wants."

She put down the material on a table and looked at me seriously.

"I've risked everything I have to keep my friendship with Becca. She seems to think you're a nice guy and I'm inclined to agree. If you hurt her, though, I swear I will bring down the wrath of hell on you."

This was totally out of character for Jodi, who normally came across as someone who you wouldn't think would hurt a fly. However, it was an effective threat. She was serious—Hades *would* break loose.

"Jodi, I'm trying to keep her out of it. Last thing I want to do is hurt someone innocent in this."

She nodded, her features still clouded with concern.

"She trusts you, Jon, and coming from Becca, that's a leap not to be taken lightly. She's stronger than you think."

Jodi packed up, handing things to me with instructions about where they went. When we exited the room, she pulled me close to her again to quietly whisper:

"Rebecca is a threat to Sarah. Keep that in mind. Make your choice as to who you're going to stand with, or don't take a stand at all."

She locked the door and said goodnight. I headed back to my room, once again through the courtyard, where I wanted to sit for a while to think on what had been said and how I'd ended up in this mess. From what I could tell, that front door was normally locked. Hell, the crack on my skull that still hurt was some evidence of it. But why had the light been on when the entire place was dark? I didn't believe in coincidence, neither did I believe in fate.

Sitting on the stairs closest to the hallway from where I'd walked, I shook my head as I thought about both what Jodi had said and why I'd come here. This place created more questions than answers for me, which made me uncomfortable. I was usually the person with the answers and now my world had turned upside down where other people supplied them. I was the one with all the questions.

The moon was full and still barely illuminated the courtyard. Everything remained in shadow. I looked up and could have sworn I saw a figure down the other end, sitting, but when I blinked and looked back; it seemed to have been a trick of the dim lighting.

The cold night air didn't do much for my thinking. My head ached as millions of thoughts wrestled for attention. I got up with a groan and headed back to sleep for the night.

Lying in that semi-conscious time before falling asleep, things became clearer to me. However, they were answers I didn't want to hear or acknowledge. With the rising sun the next day, the thoughts disappeared, but I was still left wondering if I'd ever feel quite alive again.

CHAPTER 7

The day dawned hot and early. Even though it was late September, it was still "the uncomfortable end of warm." A knock on the door shortly after 5:00 a.m. had awakened me. I called for whomever it was to come in. My eyes were still bleary with sleep and I could only make out the female form holding up a tray.

"Breakfast in bed," the voice attached to the figure said, and through my half-sleeping brain, I didn't recognize who it was. She put the tray down, then sat on the bed with me. I attempted to blink and rub my eyes clear of the sleep that clouded them, but wasn't entirely successful.

I could see a bit better but could barely make out the person's face. All I could really focus on was the fact I wasn't a morning person and having someone I wasn't involved with in the room with me—before I was awoken and dressed—bothered me.

The person leaned in closer and offered me a strawberry. I blinked, and my vision finally cleared. I was able to see it was Sarah, dressed in a skimpy nightdress and housecoat.

I yelped and tried to jump backwards as much as I could in the situation, which simply resulted in my falling off the opposite side of the bed and taking the tray with everything on it with me. Pulling the sheet around myself, I stood up and tried to get back any dignity I had left while addressing the situation at hand in a normal tone of voice.

"Wh-what the hell are you doing here?"

"I thought you'd enjoy breakfast in bed," she said with a pout.

"Not much of a breakfast person," I said, walking backwards from her, merely ending up in a corner.

She followed me over into the corner, trying to be seductive.

"Well, at least join me in the dining room for something?"

That at least gave me an out—ten or fifteen minutes to get dressed. "Um, yeah, sounds like a better idea. Give me a bit to get ready, you know, showered and shaved and all that, and, umm ..." I trailed. I did not like surprises of this nature one bit.

"See you there." She left with a wave and a wink.

As the door closed and latched behind her, I let out a sigh of relief.

"Thank God," I muttered under my breath, and proceeded to clean up the mess I made.

Once that had been done, I began my morning routine and in twenty minutes I was dressed and heading out the door. I decided to take the long route to get to the dining area, hoping Sarah would have left by the time I got there. Unfortunately, she was still in discussions with Kyle when I arrived. Jodi was also there, looking bored and sleep deprived.

I took the only seat at the table, beside Sarah, and was promptly served waffles and orange juice by one of the kitchen staff.

Seemed that being on her good side had its perks when it came to the food in the place.

"So, what's on for today?" I asked, attempting sound cheery, which I never have been before at least one cup of coffee.

Sarah thought for a moments, then gave a pointed look to Kyle.

"Well, I'm working on tonight's study and I'd like you to help me with the music."

"Doesn't Rebecca normally do that?" I asked and regretted saying the name the second it left my lips.

"Yes, but she's currently taking a break. The stress, you know," she said making the standard "she's nuts" gesture near her temple.

"If you'd help out it would be *appreciated*," she added, telling me just how much it would be, in ways I really didn't want to think of.

I agreed to meet Sarah in the courtyard around noon. When I got up to leave, I remembered Kyle had asked if I'd help with some basic maintenance around the place, so I stopped and asked Jodi what was going on and to find out where had Rebecca gone.

Jodi responded in hushed tones that she hadn't seen her since last night, and Rebecca wasn't answering any knocks on her door.

I walked out following Kyle, but my mind wandered back to what I'd thought was a trick of the light last night. Had that been Rebecca? My brain dismissed it and I didn't think much about it as I worked.

When lunch came, I grabbed a quick apple and headed off to the courtyard. Kyle had acted more smug and superior than usual today, and I was glad to be out of his presence, if even for a few minutes.

I arrived in the courtyard to be greeted by Sarah and a large group of people—mostly women. Sarah wasn't rehearsing; this looked like a study in progress. I felt like I was on display again as I greeted the group, and was handed a guitar by Sarah.

There was murmuring that someone new was doing the music and people wondered where Rebecca had gone. I tried to ignore it as it only fueled my own curiosity. Sarah handed me some sheet music, saying I should be able to pick up on it pretty quickly. It had been years since I'd last looked at sheet music and at first it appeared to be a mess of illegible squiggles. After a few looks I noticed the heading, *Guitar Chords,* and saw the chords written along with the music notation. I breathed a sigh of relief to whoever had done that.

The first songs were ones I knew from childhood, but it was nice to have the chords there anyway, as some people's interpretations differ on the same song. Sarah conducted a study on what seemed to be the place of women in the church, and it was evident to see why Jodi had mentioned that Rebecca was a threat to Sarah.

Sarah was charismatic when she wanted to be. Even though I detested her on more than one level, I was held spellbound at certain points when she expounded on one topic or another. She knew how to hold and motivate an audience, which was definitely powerful. Rebecca seemed to be this type of person's worst enemy: the self-reliant, idealistic, down-to-earth type who formed rational arguments and actually thought for themselves. I had no delusions that Sarah didn't like her for those reasons, and probably for many more I didn't yet know.

So far, I'd not seen more than a few things to raise my suspicions, but hopefully that would change. I knew Sarah intended to get me in one or several compromising positions. I was also fully aware there was more going on than met the eye, from the reactions of both Rebecca and Jodi. The problem had been figuring out the enigma this place represented. And from Jodi's statement earlier, I wouldn't be able to play both sides against the middle. Eventually I would have to make a choice as to where my loyalties lay and go from there, consequences be damned.

Sarah finished up the Bible study with a hymn I didn't know, but had her singing solo for most of it. I had to resist the urge to cover my ears from the physical pain of her off-key caterwauling. Instead, I focused on the sheet music and tried to ignore the growing headache sneaking up on me with every note.

Once she was done, and the courtyard cleared out quickly, she came back to me and took my arm.

"Mister Walsh, would you like to come with me? I'd like to show you some areas around here, seeing as it looks like you're going to be staying for a *long* while."

The sinister finality in that one sentence bothered me. Sarah guided me out of the courtyard slowly, talking about nothing in particular. It did seem I rested on the edge of her trust enough that she was willing to at least speak to me about what her group was doing at Skylark Inn and what plans they had to move out into the local community. She also mentioned some of the other people around the place, and how they'd come to be there.

I learned that Jodi's actual name wasn't Jodi; it was Judith. She had arrived from Phoenix after a pretty terrible breakup with her fiancé, who had left her at the altar. She had known Rebecca prior to coming here with a few friends, and had made herself useful in the kitchens as an experienced cook. Her refusal to segregate Rebecca had cost her, and that was evident. Sarah spoke of her more as an employee than a member of the group, and her upcoming marriage to Kyle was mainly due to Kyle's interest in her, for what purpose Sarah wasn't saying. Kyle himself didn't strike me as the type of person to settle down with one person in life. I made mental notes to keep an eye on him. As we walked, Sarah mentioned she'd like me to continue working with Kyle, and that would definitely afford me a way to keep tabs on him.

Still, not much so far had really caught my attention other than the distinct impression that things weren't exactly right. They felt a little off to the side and perhaps somewhat upside down compared to normal.

After Sarah had shown me around the place, which truly seemed massive, I headed back to the courtyard. The sun was just beginning to tip down the slope of the sky into evening, and rather than eating supper with Sarah, I decided to forgo food for sitting out in the fresh air with a guitar, which I hadn't done since my junior year of university. Then I'd been inspired by what I thought was the love of the woman I'd marry, when really it was nothing more than a physical attraction that would last a few years and then fizzle out.

It had been her idea to bring a child into the relationship, and as much as I loved Kristen, she hadn't been a wanted child on my behalf. I had missed the important firsts with her—the first step, first words, first day of school—by being away on tour. By the time I came home for good, she was already headed to junior high, and we were like strangers rather than father and daughter. The fights between Tricia and myself hadn't helped the situation any, even though we tried to keep them civil and under wraps. It had been clear the end was near many years before either of us actually admitted it. Kristen had been truly remarkable, and as an adult she had reached out to me to build the bonds I hadn't done the years before. She had even asked me, against her mother's better judgment, to walk her down the aisle when she'd married a few years ago. And now with my granddaughter, I was getting to play the role of grandfather. I didn't quite feel old enough to be a grandfather, but it was fun to spoil Kathryn in the way I'd not been able to with Kristen.

Sitting on the stairs with the guitar, I reflected on my love life. Divorced not even three years, a handful of romantic entanglements—nothing lasting or serious—I could definitely say I'd never experienced what people called being in love. Every relationship had been physical, whether a one night stand, of which I'd had a grand total of two, or an on-again-off-again relationship that managed to stumble on for a few months. There was no drive for me to stay longer than the fun lasted and no desire to see a person every day for the rest of my life, or make sacrifices for her. For the last two years I'd decided to step back from that arena for many reasons. If nothing else, the rampant sexually transmitted infections were enough of a fright, even to someone who'd lived through the sixties and the seventies when there was shagging aplenty, especially for those on top of the charts. If I was going to kill myself, then I'd do it leaping from a perfectly serviceable airplane and trusting my life to a sheet of cloth rather than face endless months of treatment for something I could've prevented. As well, with the resultant bitterness over the divorce, I hadn't found anyone to be truly attractive. Sure, a beautiful woman could still get my hormones running, but what was the point of even trying? Women wanted the young strapping males, not the middle aged, past sell-by-date guys, no matter how good they looked.

Strumming random chords and deep in thought, I was far away mentally from where I was physically. I felt inspired, and I couldn't put my finger on why, but I knew it felt good to feel like this again, and that's what I concentrated on. I had stumbled onto a random chord progression that sounded good, and tucked it away, seeing as I was no lyricist. I remained content to sing words especially written for my compositions.

When I came back to myself, I noticed a crowd of about ten people standing and listening. Once I stopped they applauded and I blushed while thanking them for their kindness.

"A work in progress," I said, putting the guitar back and making my way out of the courtyard to the area Sarah had referred to simply as the "Garden."

It was a high, walled-off zone, about the size of a soccer field, planted with whatever vegetables or flowers would grow in the soil. Someone had obviously worked hard to get the ground to produce what it did, and even the smallest success was celebrated on a chalkboard by the entrance. I wandered around for a bit, enjoying the smell of the flowers down one end of the garden. The earthy scents were a pleasant reminder of my house back in California, where I had a large landscaped lot and had put in a garden this past summer. Nothing on this scale; it was mostly an area I could go to be by myself and think, create, and plan.

I found a stone bench in the garden and took a seat. For some reason it felt strange to be alone there. I felt there should be someone with me, sharing the simple act of sitting in the natural beauty that surrounded me. It honestly bothered me, as I'd never felt quite that way before. I loved being around people in large groups, but one-on-one people situations often bothered me, and I preferred to be alone rather than come off as an irritable bastard.

I sat alone for a while, thinking again, something I seemed to do a lot of since I had been informed I'd be here a while. Introspection was something new for me; I'd always been a person who looked more to the future and didn't dwell too deeply on the past. That attitude had probably cost me, but with my life, the thought of looking backwards held too much trouble.

The sun had finally set, and I went back in to the dining area where Sarah had asked me earlier to meet her for the evening study. It was a change of venue, as she usually held it in the court-yard because of the piano. However, the person who normally played that instrument was nowhere to be seen, and that allowed Sarah to move things to the dining room, where she had more control over the proceedings.

When I came in, a small crowd had already gathered, drinking tea and hot chocolate and lounging around. It was a little less formal than usual, now that they were indoors. It held an atmosphere I could enjoy. Jodi handed out the tea cups and chatted away. She smiled as she saw me approach, and gave me a larger than average mug of tea. I sniffed it, pleasantly surprised to note that it was the white tea I'd managed to knock all over Rebecca earlier.

"White tea, yeah," she confirmed, "sweetened with honey. It'll do your voice good." She winked and moved through the crowd, talking to the others and doling out their preferred drink.

I could see the area where I was supposed to sit was already set up, along with Sarah's podium and books, but she was nowhere to be found—which probably accounted for the more lax-than-usual atmosphere. I wandered over, drinking my tea and took a look at the planned music for the night. Nothing new there; seemed she was sticking to the tried and true classics rather than relying on me to provide the mood music, which was good. I was more likely to lapse into a poor cover of something like *Twentieth Century Boy* than to be able to play old musty church standbys, not for lack of my parents dragging me to church most of my life.

The moment I sat down, Sarah finally breezed in the door, about thirty minutes late, acting like nothing had happened. However, if you were watching, her tone and actions gave off a tell that something had happened, and she was none too pleased about it.

She called everyone to order and asked me to play and lead the first hymn. Now it became obvious as to why Jodi had made her comment about the white tea. I wasn't sure I'd be able to handle the tune, having not sung it since I was in junior high, but from the looks of several of the women, I was managing at somewhat decently.

A smile came to my face when I remembered the original teenage angst and hormone-driven reason I'd started playing guitar in the first place. I'd been turned down by my first crush as she was into the "sensitive artist" type, and I'd been playing junior varsity hockey at the time. Over the years, the reason had proven true. Women seemed to go for this type, though you could be too sensitive and artsy for some of them. It was a very fine line to walk—maintaining sensitivity while being masculine.

Instead of her usual Armageddon prophesies and Seconding Coming tirade, Sarah instead turned back to the first books of the Bible, to the story of Cain and Abel, the world's first case of sibling rivalry. I guessed it was likely Kyle had done something to precipitate this; however, he was sitting, unscathed, in the second row with Jodi at his side, the two of them quietly talking to each other.

I listened to what was being said with half an ear, my brain randomly wandering through things I'd thought about during the day, and settling rather interestingly on Rebecca. It had been about a week since we'd first met, and she had managed to work herself into a lot of my headspace. The fact that she was a stunning beauty probably helped. While I'd decided to keep my pants zipped at this point in my life, I was still alive, and had a—shall we say—*appreciation* of good looking women, of which she fit the bill more than perfectly.

However, present the baser urges might be, this seemed more than that. I was acutely aware of the feelings of physical desire and lust, the latter of which was an enabler for the first and I'd often confused the second for that elusive emotion called love. That's not to say, given half the opportunity, I wouldn't want to throw her on the piano in the courtyard and do things to her that were probably illegal in some states, but in this case, there was something else there. I shook my head and smiled. There was no way I was falling for her. None whatsoever.

"Something you'd like to share with us Mister Walsh?"

The question brought me back out of my reverie with a bit of a start.

"No Sarah, nothing that needs to be shared with the rest of the class."

"Good. If you could lead us in our closing hymn for the night, then?"

I shuffled through the sheet music and came to where we were, and began to play and sing. As much as I loved singing, if I had to belt out stuffy church tunes for the rest of my existence, I'd slash my wrists.

Once the song had ended, Sarah sidled up and spent a good deal of time talking with me. She kept touching my arm during the conversation, which I found really annoying. She was much too physical and forward, and she creeped me out. I had no issue with equal rights in every stage between men and women, but I was a bit of an old fashioned romantic when it came to relationships. It took a special kind of personality to hit on a guy and not come off like a rampant slut. Unfortunately for her, Sarah was not that type of woman. I half expected the next time I saw her she'd be parading down the hallways naked in search of me. I shuddered at the thought.

Sarah offered to escort me to my room, and I didn't think I should dare decline. So, we walked down the hallway with her pretty much hanging off me, and me trying not look like I was bothered a bit. This was going to be one of the most difficult acting jobs, ever.

When we arrived at my door, I turned to thank her for the walk, and just about ran into her face. She was waiting for me to kiss her. I pulled back immediately, thanking her for walking with me and slipping inside my door as fast as possible without making a scene or injuring myself further than the events of the last week had already done.

I leaned against the wall and thought karma was a bitch who took way too much pleasure in kicking me repeatedly in the nuts.

CHAPTER 8

My internal alarm clock woke me shortly after the sun rose. So far nothing out of the ordinary happened—no visits from Sarah and no notes. I wanted to get back on the road, but this place kept me anchored. Curiosity got the better of me.

Lounging in bed for the first time since I'd arrived, I had time to clear my head of the cobwebs that sleep had coated my thoughts in. Once I got up, I did my usual morning routine, and took good look at myself in the mirror. Overall, not bad. I appeared and felt a bit younger. The hair was getting a bit long, but what could I do about it? Plus, it didn't look half bad for once—not half as curly as it had been years before, which made me resemble a bloody poodle every time it got to this length. Figured I'd let it grow and see where it went from there.

I got dressed and I headed out to the dining area. I was famished. As I came in, I nearly ran full force into a familiar face.

"Good Morning!"

"You're chipper," I commented, heading inside. "Care to join me for breakfast?"

The invitation seemed to make her a bit uncomfortable; however, after a few moments she agreed. After I'd gotten my breakfast of tea, toast, and jam, I selected a table for two off to the side of the room.

"So, where have you been hiding lately?" I said, stuffing my face with a bit of toast.

"Nowhere," she said in a noncommittal tone.

"Rebecca, don't try it. You were out of circulation for four days. Jodi was beginning to think you were dead."

And so did I, I thought, but did not say out loud.

Her expression clearly stated it was none of my affair what the hell she'd been up to over the past few days.

"Where I've been to over the past few days is your business *how,* Jon?" she said, staring straight into my eyes.

Well, I called it. "I was just a bit concerned, that's all."

Now she had a bit less of the "screw off" face as she sipped her tea. Something had definitely happened; there was more of an edge to her than usual.

"I really just don't want to talk about it, Jon. Maybe later, but with Sarah breathing down my neck and yours, I'd rather just not ..."

"Sarah's involved in your disappearance?"

Rebecca shook her head. "I shouldn't have told you anything."

She quickly made to stand up. "Look, thanks for the talk, but I think I'd better get out of here before trouble gets stirred."

She froze while staring over my shoulder, and I had no doubts as to who was making her way across the dining room area.

Rebecca reached out half-mindedly and put her hand on my arm.

"I'll talk to you later."

Then she bolted out of the dining area, stopping only to say something briefly to Jodi before leaving.

No sooner had she turned the corner when Sarah flitted into view. Sitting in the spot recently vacated by Rebecca, she smiled and talked to me about the day, and what she'd like me to do. I decided now was the time to try and see if I could make inroads here to discover what the hell made some people nervous and downright frightened around Sarah. Otherwise I'd be here for life most likely, without knowing what was happening.

"Sarah, would you like to join me for a walk?" I said, sipping the last of my tea.

You would think I offered her a million dollars or a lead role in a movie, because before I was even up from my seat she took my arm and pretty much dragged me along with her. As I followed, she continued talking to me, in more excited tones, of things I had no clue about.

When we came to the garden area, I asked the question that hopefully would take me further down the road of understanding how this place worked.

"So, Sarah, what do you do here? I mean, I thought this was a hotel, but I'm obviously mistaken."

She hesitated for a moment, then let go of my arm to move forward and smell the flowers draped over a trellis. She lingered a few moments and then turned to face me.

"Mister Walsh, Jonathan ... all we are is just a small group of people worshiping God the way the Bible instructed. That is all. Nothing strange or unusual."

I raised an eyebrow in disbelief. That simple statement did

nothing to explain either Rebecca's fear or Jodi's comments. Either I was surrounded by irrational, phobic people, or there was still something Sarah hadn't revealed yet. My money was on the latter.

"No disrespect, but I've seen things that make me question your answer," I said, as a-matter-of-factly as I could. "I just want to know more. Call me curious."

She went back to studying the flowers and ground around her, debating on what to answer.

"How familiar are you with the Bible, Jonathan?" she asked, using my first name for only the third time since I'd been there.

I had a passing familiarity with Bible stories. Having grown up Church of England and very laxly raised with religion, I was familiar with the basics, but had never really felt called to learn more.

"I'm not totally unfamiliar with it."

"Well, join me for Bible studies. We'll see if we can bring you up to speed on what our little group believes."

She smiled and left me standing there, thinking on what she'd said. Since there wasn't much to do when you weren't working around the place, I had two choices. Sit in the summer sun and bake in the courtyard or go back to my room. Of course, I could always swing by Rebecca's and see if she was up for an impromptu jam session or even just a walk. I doubt she would desire the company of someone easily twice her age, but in this place, there wasn't much choice in who you could speak to.

I could also grab the book my daughter had given me, *Headhunter*, which despite its size was turning out to be rather interesting. In what little time I'd had to read, that is. Despite being from a family of academics, I'd gone to university only to please my family, and had chosen journalism rather than anthropology, as my father had done. He had eventually become a professor on the subject. The decision not to follow in his footsteps had caused some issues in the family, but studying moldy old cultures wasn't exactly something that caught my interest. I'd always been encouraged in the artistic pursuits I'd taken up as a child—guitar lessons, piano lessons and violin lessons—but no one ever expected me to make a career of being a musician. While I enjoyed well-written literature, I wasn't one to actively seek it out. Luckily, I had passed those genetics to Kristen, who had completed her degree in English Literature before she was married. I had no doubt in my mind she'd go back to school as soon as she could to continue her education, and her husband, who was a doctor, would fully support her. Some days I really wondered who her mother was, as she barely seemed to have inherited any traits from Tricia.

Deciding on the second choice of roasting in the sun, I grabbed the book and my sunglasses and headed for the courtyard.

I sat on the stairs and was so thoroughly engrossed in the book, I didn't notice someone had come up to sit alongside me, until they sneezed. Of course, I jumped a mile and dropped the thing.

It was Rebecca, who once again took pleasure at scaring the everloving crap out of me. She reached down, grabbed the book, and handed it back to me.

"Jesus, put a bell around your neck, will you?" I said, taking the book with a half-serious smirk on my face.

"You should be wearing sunscreen. You'll get old and wrinkled if you don't."

"I already am, so what's the point in just delaying what further decay there is to come?"

She shrugged and handed me a bottle of sunscreen. I took it, and without another word, slathered it on what areas were available to be burnt to a crisp, then tossed it back to her.

"You missed your neck," she said, offering to put some on. If I didn't know better I would have sworn she was subtly hitting on me but dismissed the notion. This was simply her being nice.

I leaned forward, and she gently massaged some onto the back of my neck, then checked the area where I'd been hit earlier in the week. "You're healing up well," she said as she moved back over to the other side of the stairs.

She curled into an impossibly tight ball, wrapping her arms around her legs, and resting her chin on her knees. She looked out over the courtyard, her gaze dreamily drifting far away.

"Thought you were terrified of Sarah running into the two of us talking?" I asked, curious as to why she was here.

"I am, but Sarah has a routine she rarely ever misses. She's in Phoenix right now with a group from here, getting supplies for the next month."

"How does this place make enough to stay afloat?" I asked, putting down the book. She turned her head to look at me.

"Sarah allows a select few to go to work. The rest of it even I don't know."

She turned back to watch the sky, mentally a million miles away. I watched her for a few moments and then went back to reading. Even without talking it was nice to have companionship.

The next time I looked up, she had a book as well. *Faust* by Johann Wolfgang Von Goethe. She was more than just a pretty face. The story of Faust was not light reading material, by any stretch of the imagination. If nothing else, it was dark and twisted, and took most people years to get through it.

She noticed me looking after a while and smiled.

"What, didn't expect someone like me to be reading such *deep* literature?"

I shook my head no and went back to reading. Part of me thought she'd be the type to gobble up fluffy romance novels, but the other part thought she'd be the type who wasn't afraid of epic novels and the classics. We spent what seemed like forever in quiet companionship in on either side of the stairs of the court-yard. As the sun tilted towards the late afternoon, Rebecca got up and stretched. Walking down to the other end of the courtyard, and opening the lid of the piano, she began to play.

She started out with some simple classical, moving through into more difficult baroque, then into jazz, and finally, music that could only be called rock. She was enjoying herself thoroughly, which was clearly evident from her smile and the way she pounded out the tune on the piano.

"Hey, I have to get my fun time in while Sarah's not here. If I had to play stuffy church tunes every day I think I'd commit suicide," she said when I gazed at her.

I laughed; she had expressed the same sentiment I felt a few days ago. It was nice to see someone enjoy playing the piano, because I always got stuck doing it every time Torrent played a song with keyboards or piano in it, which I made sure was mercifully a rare occurrence. I wished I had access to an electric guitar, as it would have been nice to have a jam session.

"Why do I feel like playing *The Golden Age of Rock and Roll*?" she called out to me. "All I'm missing is a guitarist or two!"

"Hey, at least I know the lyrics to that one," I called back, putting my book down and sitting up fully on the stairs.

She laughed. "Well, c'mon over then, let's give it a go." With a gesture of her head, she indicated she wanted me to come over to the piano.

I went to her, and she played the intro. Feeling a bit foolish, I did my own introduction, it had been years before, then we launched into the song. She sang backup vocals and I managed to belt out the melody like I hadn't in a long time. All that was missing was an electric guitar to make it perfect. I was amazed at her vocal ability for someone who didn't seem to have ever taken voice lessons or sung professionally. She had quite the range and handled the lyrics well.

When she finished off the song, we both took a few deep breaths and then broke down laughing.

"Oh, that was more fun than I've had in a while," she said, still laughing.

"I know! I haven't sung like that in *years*," I said, leaning against the piano lid and trying to catch my breath.

"When we get out of here, I'd love for you to come record it with me," I said, somewhat absentmindedly.

She stopped laughing.

"You would want *me* to record this with *you*?" she asked, disbelieving. "I'm just a nobody who can play piano."

Wow, her self-esteem was low. I'd rarely heard anyone her age play piano so well, and her singing ability soared above average.

"Rebecca, you're one of the most talented people I've run into. Why you haven't been playing professionally is beyond me. I'd love to bring you out to the studio and have you play on a few tracks."

She still stared at me with shock and surprise. Her mouth hung open, and despite the probable incorrectness of it, I reached over and gently pushed her jaw up. She still sat there, eyes wide with surprise, not moving.

"You look stunned."

She shook her head. "I am. Most people, mostly men, only see me for my looks."

The surprised expression still remained, but a brooding darkness had settled in over it as well. Whatever had happened in the days she'd been missing had involved a lot of bad things. Lingering at the edge of my mind was the suspicion that Kyle had been part of them.

She closed the lid on the keys and checked her watch.

"Sarah will be back in about an hour. Probably best we don't stay here too much longer."

I nodded and went back over to the stairs to get my book. I picked up hers as well, and handed it to her, with the sunscreen.

"You want to go for a walk, then?" I asked. For some reason, I felt like I was fifteen again, and the déjà vu was unsettling.

She nodded, a slight blush climbing her cheeks and I led the way out of the courtyard. Seeing as I didn't know more than where the courtyard and the massive garden were in this place, I headed to the latter. Silent as usual, Rebecca walked alongside of me. She wasn't much of a talker, which was nice. Sarah always babbled, probably fearful of awkward silences, not realizing that some-times the quiet was the best thing, and more could be said in a pleasant silence than not.

We turned the last corner and entered the garden and Rebecca's face broke out into a large smile.

"I haven't been here in ages," she said, moving ahead of me and spinning around to take in the sight of the flowers blooming, and the vegetables of all colors, in different cycles of growth or ready to be harvested. "God, it's *beautiful*," she added, sitting down on the bench, her head still swiveling to take in everything.

I nodded, reluctant to say anything. At least her somber mood had somewhat disappeared and she was smiling again.

"So ... where were you the past four days? Inquiring minds want to know," I said, sitting alongside her.

"Jon, I don't want to talk about it, okay?" she said, looking away. "I'm a big girl and I can manage. I don't need a white knight to come rushing into a situation he knows nothing about, only to make it worse."

Well, Jonny-boy, if that doesn't say, "Fuck the hell off," nothing does.

I just sat there, somewhat dumbstruck.

"I understand. I just hoped we'd arrived at the point where we could trust each other with things like this," I said, trying not to sound hurt, which was difficult, because the sudden lack of trust did hurt.

"Look, Jon, yes, I'm a damsel, yes, I'm in distress, but I can handle it." She got up and slowly walked away. "You just don't need to get roped into this. You don't have any ties or obligations to me, and I'd rather not involve you. It's got nothing to do with me trusting you at all."

She stopped at the trellis and reached up to pull a bunch of flowers closer to her to inhale their perfume. Then she came back to the bench and sat back down.

"Jon, you're a great guy, you've become a really good friend to me lately, and I *do* trust you." She reached out and put her hand on my leg. "But there are things you don't want to be a part of here. I know you'll rush in and try and solve the problem, which will just make things worse. Let me handle this, please. Like I said, I'm a big girl. Don't worry about me."

How did I tell her I would worry about her no matter what she said? How do you say that without coming off like you're a control freak?

"Just promise me if you're in trouble, please get me, or ask Jodi to get me, okay?"

She smiled up at me. "I promise if it's something I can't deal with, you and Jodi will be the first two people I call, okay?"

That was going to have to be good enough for me. She didn't want me interfering, and despite the fact that my curiosity over the situation would drive me mad by one means or another, Rebecca wouldn't talk about it.

Again, there was silence. We just sat there in the sunlight as it filtered down, and it felt right to be together. Rebecca was still absorbed in her surroundings, but seemed to enjoy the silence and tranquility of the garden.

I turned to tell her that we probably should head back in before Sarah tried to find me and I came face-to-face with Rebecca, mere millimeters apart. The tension in the air felt pretty heavy, as this was one hell of a charged situation. We sat there, unmoving, for what seemed to me like forever, before Jodi came at a full run into the courtyard.

"Becca, she's back"—she panted, leaning against the wall —"You'd better get going."

Rebecca grasped Jodi's hand, and with just enough time to grab her book, Rebecca was pulled away as fast as Jodi could manage.

She looked back over her shoulder, and I couldn't help but wonder what might have happened in that moment if Jodi hadn't shown up when she did. I smiled and then shook my head.

"Heatstroke," I muttered under my breath. "You're hallucinating because you've got heatstroke, Jon."

Running my hand through my hair, which felt quite hot from the sun, I decided I definitely had some condition related to the heat, so I headed immediately for the dining area to get some ice-cold water. Making my way through the halls, I noticed the influx of people who hadn't been there earlier. Sarah had designated select people, mostly women, who were kept here at all times, but there also seemed to be a good chunk of men about.

Jodi, as I thought, worked in the kitchen. She directed a bunch of other people in making supper, which for the amount of people here, took a good deal of preparation. She looked up, and hurriedly waved me a hello before running off to deal with a mess that someone else had made. Heading to the fridge at the back of the prep area, I grabbed a bottle of water and went back out. Before I made it out the door, however, Jodi called my name and ran over to meet me.

"Has Becca mentioned to you about what went on?" she asked, leaning up against the door frame.

"Nope. I got the 'I'm a big girl' speech," I replied, cracking open the water and taking a long drink.

"Same here. Something must really have gone wrong." Jodi shrugged. "I figured she might have told you something that she didn't tell me."

I raised an eyebrow while taking another drink of water. That statement was a little odd.

"Jodi, why would she confide in me instead of you? She trusts you with her life. I don't think she'd trust me with her car keys."

Jodi looked at me with what could only be described as a sly smile.

"Jon, she—"

A large crash radiated from behind her in the kitchen.

"Damn it. Jon, I've got to go deal with those putzes. I'll have to talk to you later."

She rushed off, and as she disappeared into the crowd I heard her yell at whoever had messed up. Being on the wrong side of Jodi was not an experience that I ever wanted to have first-hand, from the invective coming from the kitchens.

I decided to finish off the water and then find somewhere a little shadier to finish the book. However, nowhere came to mind other than the dining area where I already was, so I decided to take a seat down the far end, away from the chaos of the kitchen prep area, and at least try to finish off where I read last.

I flopped down into one of the seats and putting my feet up on the empty chair across from me, opened the book to read. As I flipped back to the page I'd bookmarked by bending over the top of the page, a note fell onto my lap. I knew it wasn't from Kristen, because she wasn't the type who would write notes and randomly stick them into books. It left only one person. For once, my curiosity didn't get the best of me. I put the note back into the book and finished off the chapter I wanted to read.

Once I had finished the chapter, though, I surreptitiously pulled the paper back out from beneath the last pages of the book.

Feeling again like a schoolboy, I looked around to see if there was anyone else besides me in the room, and when I confirmed the coast was clear, I unfolded the note and began to read.

Jon,

I know you and Jodi both want to understand why I've not been around for the past few days. I wish it was something I could talk about with both of you, but I don't want to get you more deeply involved than you have already been. I also wish it had been something as simple as a raging migraine.

Please understand, there are things neither of you want to learn about this place. Jon, I know you might think *you want to know about them. If I were to tell you, probably get both of us killed while trying to fix the situation.*

If you trust me at all, please listen to what I'm saying. You've seen enough to realize certain people here don't have much love for me. Please don't give them reason to go the last mile.

R

I felt torn between anger and compassion. I directed my anger at the people who tormented Rebecca only because she had simply possessed an independent spirit, and my compassion for her stemmed from feeling that no one deserved to live in such horrendous fear. She was right; I wanted to know more, but I also didn't want to endanger her. I had no doubts about who the people she was referring to were—by process of elimination, they had to be Kyle and Sarah.

I thought about showing the note to Jodi, but figured she probably had received a similar one. So, tucking it away inside the book, I closed up the novel and walked back to my room, to make sure I kept the note out of the prying eyes of certain "someones." Even then, I couldn't guarantee that it'd be safe from their grasp.

At least I felt a little more secure putting it somewhere other than on my person.

Once I'd hidden it somewhere in the room that only I'd remember, I checked my watch. It was 6:00 p.m. Time for supper, then Sarah wanted me to actually read the material for Bible study. Like that was going to happen. Hopefully, 24 years after my last university class I would still be able to bullshit my way through her questions.

I trundled back to the dining area. Jodi threw off her apron and heading to the table. She saw me and immediately walked over.

"Sarah's sick. There's not going to be a study tonight. Kyle had to drag her back to her room. Heatstroke," she muttered.

"What do you guys do around here when there isn't a study?" I asked as we sat at the empty head table in the dining room.

"Usually I go find Becca and we just shoot the shit for a while," said Jodi, dishing out some of the food she'd been working on earlier. "A girl's night in."

I nodded, and started in on supper. It was interesting to note that with Sarah absent, no one had a glass of wine. I wasn't the only one who wanted to drink when she was around.

About midway through supper I decided I'd ask Jodi if Rebecca had given her a letter as well. When I asked the question, Jodi squinted and looked at me funny.

"No. Why do you ask?"

I explained about the note I'd gotten from Rebecca earlier. This caused Jodi to put down her fork and pick up a glass of water. With a pensive expression, she sipped the water and remained silent for a few minutes.

"Before I jump to any conclusions, what did this letter say?" she asked.

I gave her the Cliff's notes version. She nodded throughout it all. When I was done, she sat again and thought for a few moments before saying anything. When she did it was a one-liner:

"I think you should join me for the girl's night in, Jon."

Evidently that settled that, and she went back to eating her supper. She still brooded as she ate, and it was noticeable that the gears churned in her head, because things hadn't exactly been making sense.

Towards the end of supper, Kyle showed up, quite worn out. He greeted Jodi with a kiss and asked her what the plans were for the night. She let him know that it would be the same as every night Sarah was sick; Jodi would visit the girls and just have a talk. I noticed that she safely stayed away from mentioning Rebecca to him. He seemed okay with that, and we left without a further word.

Jodi still had the contemplative look on her face that she'd had since I mentioned the letter to her earlier. Something was definitely eating at her, and hopefully she would talk about it sooner or later.

We walked through the halls down to Rebecca's room and I noticed everyone seemed to be out enjoying themselves. There were families with children wandering around, and the courtyard appeared to be pretty full of people socializing in good sized groups.

"When the cat's away, the mice will play" ran through my head, and it was true here.

Jodi knocked on the door of Rebecca's room. Music played

blasted loudly, and Jodi had to bang on the door quite hard to be heard.

The door swung open and Rebecca stood there, her hair pulled up into a long ponytail, wearing what had to be the world's oldest tour t-shirt.

"Hi Jod—" She stopped short when she saw me standing there, leaning against the opposite wall. She turned the most amusing color of pink, from the roots of her hair right down to what little skin was visible. "Um ... hi," she said to me, and I waved silently from where I stood.

"C'mon in," she said, gesturing to us while giving Jodi a look that clearly read: "What is he doing here?"

Entering the room, it was obvious this wasn't your average suite, but more like a small house all unto its own. I reckoned that what used to be the hotel had been built off it. The small hallway led into a large sitting room with a full kitchen off one end, and a hallway that by probable matters of deduction, led to the bedrooms and the loo.

Rebecca walked over to a stereo system and turned down the music. It was evident that it was rather new, as she was listening to CDs. I saw some of her collection, and yes, there were Torrent ones among them. However, I also saw bands who I did and didn't recognize—Def Leppard, Barenaked Ladies, Our Lady Peace, and Moist, to name a few. She indicated that we should take up residence on the sectional that had been set up in the living room. I glanced around as we walked to the sofa, and it was evident this had been her grandparent's suite. Rebecca had added her own touches over the past while, but it was definitely not something that completely matched with her style.

Jodi and I took up seats at opposite ends of the sofa, and Rebecca disappeared into the kitchen area. I heard cabinets thump and glasses being collected. A few minutes later she returned with a large pitcher of lemonade and three glasses. Putting in on the coffee table, she poured out the lemonade, then flopped down in the chair across from us.

"So, what's up for tonight?" she asked, taking her glass from the table and curling her legs underneath her.

Jodi looked at me and then back to Rebecca.

"Becca, I think you need to tell us a few things," Jodi began.

You could almost see the waves of panic coming off Rebecca like fog on a bay. She gulped audibly and fidgeted in her seat as Jodi continued.

"You've been assuring both of us you're a big girl and can handle what's happening to you, but you're not telling us what's actually happening. We both want answers. I know about the note that you gave Jon, and I think that you owe us both the courtesy of informing us what the hell's going on here."

Rebecca fidgeted some more, and turned away. "You would never believe me if I told you," she said with defeat in her tone.

"Try us," I said, trying to sound confident.

"Fine, but when you don't believe me, you can't say I didn't warn you."

CHAPTER 9

*R*ebecca assumed the classic storyteller's pose and began telling the story that would change how I felt about everyone and everything within the Skylark Inn.

"When this all started, it was '97. I'd been down here two years at that point.

"Grandma and I knew she couldn't keep running this place all alone, especially with me in university and her getting into the upper years. So, she shut down operations and put up the inn for sale. There was only one condition to the sale: we had to have this home"—she gestured, taking in the entirety of the house we were in—"left alone for at least three years, preferably for life. Of course, by this time, Vision Lake was really a ghost town. No one was coming through, and the offers we'd received all wanted us out, mainly because potential buyers planned to redevelop this place into a car park or something. The only ones willing to agree to our terms were a couple of people my age, Sarah and Kyle. The conditions basically stated that if I were to stay here after my grandmother passed away, they would not evict me or otherwise ask me to leave. This is part of the reason I'm still here today. The other part, well, we'll get to that in due time.

"When they first arrived, I knew they were with some sect of Seventh Day Adventists who had been de-fellowshipped by their church, and this raised questions in my mind. I wondered why should I bother with them, but *chacun à son goût*, right? Anyway, they bought the place and started doing their renovations, which Jon, you have been a part of. During that time, more and more people arrived, most of them from California and Oregon, where Sarah and Kyle are both from. Still, nothing too much out of the ordinary; I mean, what church doesn't want its own property and, in this case, a place for their followers to stay? We figured it was just temporary and they'd be moving into the community with other people. Well, Grandma passed away last year. I'm not even sure if Mom and Dad know, or if Grandma's will has been read. She was eighty-nine, so it wasn't a complete shock. After the funeral, when I came back here and got ready for the new school year, things began to go wrong. And what I mean by wrong is that everything just went upside down. Sarah and Kyle ..."

She began to cry at that point. This was obviously difficult for her to speak about. Jodi reached out for her, but Rebecca put up a hand, signaling to be left alone. Rebecca took a few minutes and composed herself. My heart was in my throat. She was a good friend, and I desperately hated watching anyone I cared about suffer. She looked up with teary eyes, and continued, focused on me.

"Sarah and Kyle. Huh ... how to start on that? I guess with Kyle. Kyle is nothing more than a womanizing bastard. He's not a good man. The minute my grandmother passed away, knowing full well I had a fiancé back home, he made advances on me. We're not just talking harmless flirting. I could handle that. We're talking unsolicited back rubs, getting in a not-so-inconspicuous feel of assorted body parts. I told him to back off, but that just intensified his interest in me."

Anger rose within me, and I balled my fists to keep from walking out and punching Kyle for just those few things. However, I had a strong feeling there was more to come.

"He'd grab me and dry hump me repeatedly, and he seemed to get some sick twisted kicks out of me trying to fight his advances —the harder I'd fight, the more he'd do it. The "highlight" of all this was the night I played for his sister in the courtyard. As I cleared my things away after the service, he attacked me. If Jodi hadn't come along at that point, he probably would have raped me right in the courtyard." She turned to Jodi. "This was that night about a month ago Jodi, where I disappeared for a while. I'm so sorry, I don't want to tell you this about your future husband, but you said I owed you both an explanation, and as much as I hate it, this is the explanation for a *lot* of the things that have been going on lately."

Rebecca stood and paced the sitting room. "The last thing that happened, well, I'm pretty sure Jon witnessed." She turned again to face me, as if drawing some strength from me while I sat there. "And it also leads me into talking about Sarah."

Jodi turned to me, and raised an eyebrow, somewhat surprised at all this, but also not so much.

"Yeah, I did see it, Rebecca," I began, "and I'm sorry I couldn't do anything."

"Don't be sorry, Jon. He would've kicked your ass and mine had you come rushing in. At least you were there for me after he left."

It was Jodi's turn to speak up. "So, what exactly happened?"

"Well," I said, "I was coming back to my room after having a little chat with Sarah, which led nowhere, I might add. I decided to go the long route and swung by here. When I turned a corner, I managed to walk in on the end of I'm not sure what, but Kyle had

Rebecca held up against the wall by her throat, and was telling her if she fucked this up for Sarah, then there would be hell to pay."

Jodi's eyes widened. She looked from me to Rebecca. "What the hell?"

Rebecca sat back down again, and began the next part of the story.

"Well Jodi, I know you came here after the entire fiasco with Roger. I know that you don't believe as these people do, but you needed some solace, and they took you in. But we'll talk about that later. You both wanted an explanation ... and this is turning to a long one.

"Now then, Sarah came along with Kyle. They're about six years apart in age. Kyle is the older one. They arrived together with this strange set of beliefs. They also brought many of the people you'll find here. Sarah and I have never gotten along, ever. She wants me to break and give in to her, and I just can't. She's hated me since the first moment we met. People seem to think she's this great prophet who actually believes what she's telling them. She doesn't believe a single word. Why do you think there's wine on her table and no one else's? She's a hypocrite of the highest order.

"Before I move on to anything stranger, I want to know if you still want me to keep going, because I'll tell you things I'm positive are going to make you look at me funny."

She watched Jodi and me expectantly. Jodi appeared pretty amazed already from what I could see. I myself remained taken aback by the actions of Kyle. No civilized human being acted the way he had with Rebecca. Sarah of course, played a role in all of this. I felt sure of it.

I leaned forward. "Go on, Rebecca. We want to know more, and I promise I'll be there for you, no matter what."

She gave a small smile and sat back. "Jodi, do you remember Miss Whyte?"

Jodi nodded.

"Do you remember her leaving here at all?" asked Rebecca.

Jodi thought for a while, and then shook her head.

"Of course you don't," said Rebecca. "If you recall, she questioned the points Sarah made in her sermons, and, well, you didn't hear too much of Miss Whyte after the day Sarah called her into her office, did you?"

Rebecca stood up and paced again. "No one ever has left this place of their own free will. Miss Whyte—she pretty much disappeared, and anyone else who has had the balls to challenge Sarah immediately turns into an endangered species. This brings me to why you haven't seen me for the past few days."

She paused, then pulled down the neckline of the shirt she had on. There were clear bruises around her neck, down by her shoulders, and after pulling up the sleeves, more bruises were evident. My blood boiled, and I got up from my seat. I had to do something. I felt like a powder keg, and I wasn't quite sure why this all got under my skin as much as it did.

I wanted to punch the wall, or more honestly, I wanted to punch Kyle, and as much as violence against a woman went completely against my nature, I would dearly have given my left nut to be able to clear Sarah's clock. Unfortunately, it seemed like she was the only way out of this place and back into the "normal" real world.

All I could think to do to get rid of the stress I felt was to go over to Rebecca and hug her tight. I sort of gestured a question if that would be okay and she nodded. I put my arms around her, and with a grunt, she returned the hug. We stayed like this a while, and she whispered in my ear, "Thank you, Jon."

I finally let go and moved to the seat beside Jodi. Taking a sip of lemonade, Rebecca continued with her story.

"Jon, you might recall the night you were beaten pretty senseless ... or you may not; I'm not sure. You've healed up pretty well over the past week, so you might not remember. I know you saw the bruises on my neck then. I figured most people would probably take it like I'd been fooling around with someone. Most of the people here don't know about Matt back home, so they'd assume that first. Well, some of the marks are from the time you saw Kyle in the hallway. The others are from Sarah herself.

"See, she doesn't like you being around me. She really, really, *really* wants to get in your pants, Jon. There's something about you, and I'm pretty sure she's not aware that you're a rock star. She seems to come from that "granola crunchy" type of family, you know the type—those who live off the land and ignore the outside world? Oh, what's the term for them? It's on the tip of my tongue ..."

"Fanatics?" Jodi offered.

"No, but that will do for now. Anyway, Jon, she seems to think there is something going on between us. You can try telling her we're just friends, but she's convinced I'm behind your pretty much ignoring her. Every time she sees the two of us together, it's hell on earth for me. The past four days she's held me in what can only be described as a torture chamber. The only thing she's missing on making it fully hell for me would be twenty-four hours of continuous Anne Murray music."

I laughed, as it probably would have been my vision of hell as well. I caught the sparkle in her eye as she watched me before continuing.

"First, Kyle was the one who came to my room. I thought it was you Jodi, because we were supposed to be working on the dress fitting, so I opened the door. There he stood, and then grabbed me by the throat again. When I fought back, he gagged me and dragged me along by the back of the neck until we got to Sarah's room. Once we got there, it was pretty much the Spanish Inquisition: Jonathan Walsh Edition. When I didn't give her the answers she wanted to hear—and to be blunt, I don't know quite what she wanted from me—she had Kyle take me someplace around here. I don't know where it is; I was seriously on the edge of blacking out. All I can remember is that it was dark, and there were no windows. It seemed larger than a broom closet or any closet I've been in, and it smelled—oh, Lord, how did it smell. They kept me in there for three days without food, water or facilities. By the time they let me out that night, I was so thankful I would have done almost anything for my freedom, and I think they knew it.

"So, yeah, that's where I'd been. I wish I were making all of this up, because when I say it aloud, it sounds like I'm stark-raving loony-tunes."

Rebecca laughed nervously, looking back and forth between Jodi and me to see which one of us was going to react first.

It was me. I stood up to walk out of the room. Rebecca followed as I got to the door.

"I knew you'd think I was nuts," said Rebecca. "Now you don't want anything to do with me. Way to go Becca, tell people all the things that make them think you're a total nutbar."

I turned around to face her.

"Rebecca, I don't make promises I can't keep. I promise you I believe you. Every. Word. I'm just going to take a little walk and certain people had better hope I don't run into them." I went back down the hallway and heard her cry out as I nearly went round the turn.

"Don't you realize, Jon, they *expect* you to do this? They want you to go to them and act like you are right now. You'll try explaining to Sarah there isn't anything going on between us, but you'll only confirm her suspicions and she'll *never* believe we're just friends."

Rebecca called it. I would go rushing in like I was about to, trying to set everything straight, and my doing so would only create more problems.

"You're right." I said, turning around with a gesture of defeat. "Last thing I need to do is make this worse when I'm trying to make it better."

I came back into the room, where Jodi sat, silent and stony. She saw me enter, and stared at Rebecca, who closed the door behind me as I walked back to the sofa.

"Becca, if you ever find a man who is willing to do things like that for you, don't let the opportunity for love pass you by," Jodi said simply.

Everyone sat back down. Now that we'd heard Rebecca's account of why she'd been missing for days, it was time to take it all in and decide what to do next. My first urge was still to go completely ballistic on Kyle and Sarah. I wanted to hit something, hard, and by nature, I generally wasn't violent. Jodi appeared to be in shock, and it took a long time for her to speak.

"I *knew* Kyle was an asshole. I knew there was no way he was interested in me for me. But I'm in too deep to get out now. I never realized how much of an abusive prick he truly is."

"You're not still going to marry that bastard?" I asked, appalled at the thought.

"What can I do, Jon? If I end everything now that we're heading down to the wire, my life will be hell. You don't turn down a Williamson without paying a steep price."

It was Jodi's turn to pace the floor. "It's too late for me, but by the grace of God I will get you two out of here, if it's the last thing I do."

Rebecca and I exchanged looks. Both of us appeared to be thinking the same thing. "Jodi ... it's not too late ... you can come with me," Rebecca said.

"No, you two will get out, and I'll make sure of it. Me, I'm stuck here."

Jodi's finality about it would accept no arguments from either of us.

"Well then. Where do we go from here?" I asked, as Jodi sat back down. Hours had passed; it was creeping up on the middle of the night.

"I don't know," answered Jodi and Rebecca together.

"We have to think of where we're going to go from here," I said. "Just bumbling about isn't going to get anyone anywhere in this situation." I finally took a sip of lemonade. "I know the only way I'll have any effect is to play into Sarah's wants and needs." I shuddered visibly. "And I'm not looking forward to it."

"I still think it would be best if we're not seen together in public for the most part," Rebecca said. "You're aware now that she's after you—and just how much she'll do to get me out of the picture."

"You two not seeing each other after talking to each other for so long is going to make Sarah just as curious as if you two were talking," Jodi interjected. "You have to strike a middle line, make it look like nothing has really changed between the two of you. Plus, having someone to commiserate with will make this time more endurable than if you were both trying to go it alone."

She was right. Rebecca and I had grown used to having the other to talk to. It was a nice arrangement, and I enjoyed it. I couldn't speak for Rebecca, but the lack of dissent from her seemed to indicate she enjoyed our time together, in some way at least.

"So, just keep on keeping on?"

"For now, yes. And Becca, you're going to have to keep a straight face when Jon's with Sarah. I'll run interference as best as I can between everyone. Just bear in mind that this sham of a wedding of mine is coming up in about four weeks, and if things get out of hand, I swear I will kill you both with my bare hands."

I laughed at the mental image, and even Jodi had to smile, despite her seriousness. I had no intentions of making anything worse for anyone, if I could.

"You do realize, Jon, Sarah's going to ask you to accompany her to the wedding," Rebecca said.

"Yeah. I get the feeling she'll be taking up all my time."

Rebecca yawned then, and I noticed it was about 1:00 a.m. Sarah would be starting her morning Bible study in about five hours, and we'd all need some sleep. I spoke up and it was agreed that we should meet again tomorrow. Jodi offered cover for us in the guise of completing the wedding dresses she had me help her out with a while back. And with agreement from everyone, we split up the group for the night. Rebecca saw Jodi and me to the door, and as I left, I couldn't resist the urge to give Rebecca a kiss on the cheek. She colored a bright red when I did, and as she was closing the door, she wished me a warm, good night.

Whatever it was about her, she'd cast quite a spell on me. I wandered back to my room with a goofy grin, whistling a tune. Rebecca had become one of the best friends I'd had of any gender during most of my life. The only person I could put on the same level was Ryan, Torrent's bassist. Ryan had been the peacemaker during the meltdown in '82 that had resulted in the dissolution of the band. Over the past 18 years, he and I had kept in contact, even though we resided in opposite ends of the country. I had been there as his best man in 1980 when he had married Heather, and I was also Riley's Godfather. Ryan was the shy, reserved type, who rarely spoke. If he actually vocalized what was on his mind, you knew it was important. I just wished I could introduce Ryan to Rebecca. The two of them would likely hit it off; they so were similar. I could imagine the them ridiculing me already—sharp wit, and well-meaning humor at the ready.

I got back to my room, and with a smile, I opened the door and stepped in. Tossing my keys on the dresser, I headed into the bedroom area. Because I'd half-expected to find Sarah naked in the bed, I flicked on the light quickly and breathed a sigh of relief that the bed was empty. Changing into my usual PJs, I headed back out. There was a knock on my door. Without thinking, I opened it. Sarah stood in the hall with a parcel in hand. She smiled appreciatively at the sight of me in my T-shirt and PJ bottoms.

"Jonathan. Hi," she said, giving me a third or fourth look-over. I closed the door partially, hiding myself from view.

"Hey Sarah. What's up?" I asked, wishing I hadn't opened the door; it had been such a nice walk back without her interruptions.

"I just wanted to drop this off with you. Hopefully I'll be feeling better tomorrow and we can have our first study over dinner at my place. Say, five in the afternoon?"

Jodi had nicely given me an out with the wedding party dresses thing earlier. I told Sarah I'd be helping Jodi because Jodi had asked for my assistance earlier in the day. Not taking no for an answer, Sarah relaxed when I agreed to an earlier dinner as long as I was out of there by five, so I could give Jodi a hand.

Taking the parcel and bidding her goodnight, I closed the door as politely as I could. Inside the packaging lay a leather-bound Bible. I groaned and put it on the table. This did not bode well for me in any way, shape, or form.

Exhausted from all the excitement of the day, I decided to give everything a bit more thought the next morning, when I would be fully awake and had at least a cup or two of tea in me. I turned in for the night, reflecting back to the conversation Rebecca, Jodi, and I had had earlier. Rebecca must be a strong character to have survived what she'd been through and not break. I envied her willpower and endurance. More than that, I hoped once she got out of here, the man in her life would treat her the way she so richly deserved.

I fell asleep. The last thing on my mind was Rebecca. For the first time I could recall, I felt peaceful and slept a dreamless sleep.

$\sim$

The next morning, a quiet rapping on the door woke me. I rubbed my eyes and rose—this time being smart enough to grab the dressing gown I'd brought with me—and opened the door. It was Rebecca, tray in hand. She was already dressed and looked a hundred times better than she had the night before.

"I'm not coming in," she said, "But I wanted to thank you for believing me last night. Jodi did these up special for you." She handed me the tray, and then with a small wave and smile, she headed off down the hall. I lifted the cover on it and found light, fluffy pancakes covered with strawberries and whipped cream. The girl had either done her research or she'd just lucked out that strawberries were my favorite fruit and pancakes ranked high up my breakfast list. I took the tray back into the room and settled down to enjoy the breakfast, which also included tea.

Once I'd eaten and dressed, I brought the tray down to Jodi and the crew in the dining area. Jodi, as usual, had to deal with someone making a mess of things, and could only spare a few moments to say good morning before she was called off to deal with the emergency of the hour. This left me, as usual, with tons of time on my hands on not much to do with it. I knew Kyle would find me if they needed work done, and for the sake of Jodi and Rebecca, I'd resist the urge to lay him flat out because of his past actions. I knew Rebecca usually she spent the free time she had engrossed in the arts–I'd typically found her playing piano in the courtyard–but Jodi had said Rebecca also could be found in one of the many high-walled areas that were set aside for growing vegetables and flowers. Even Rebecca's suite had a large garden attached to it, which had been her grandparent's private garden, and she spent a lot of time there drawing and writing.

I decided it was best just to take a wander around the place to see what was up and hopefully find something to do. I purposely avoided the courtyard for the time being, as that was most likely where I'd find Rebecca, and I didn't want to arouse anyone's suspicions by looking like I sought her right off.

Sure enough, as I wandered, Daniel, one of the guys from Kyle's work crew, found me and asked if I'd like to help them out with a minor project.

"Not much work, but the more hands we get on it, the faster we get this done and get back to our regular projects," he said, shrugging as we wandered off to the workshop area, which really was a set of converted rooms at what seemed to be the back of the inn. When we got there, I could see the guys were busy building a trellis. "For the wedding," Daniel muttered, rolling his eyes as he instructed me on what needed to be done. It was clear that most people felt the wedding of Kyle and Jodi was more of a sham than even Jodi herself did. However, as she had so succinctly put it the night before, it seemed no one refused a Williamson and lived to tell about it.

The work went swiftly with five guys helping on it. By noon we had the thing built and the women came in to decorate it. We all headed out as a group then, to accost Jodi and friends for some refreshments. She must have known we were on the way because a table had been set out with drinks and sandwiches for us. We devoured everything but the table, the work having made for some rather large appetites.

Jodi herself came out and joked around with the guys. She gave no indication about how she truly felt about the wedding. Daniel was Kyle's best man, and he wasn't too happy about Jodi's choice of maid of honor. Jodi brushed him off with a few comments and went back to her work. As we were heading back out, she pulled me to one side and asked me if I would play the music for the ceremony. Of course I said yes, as this was Jodi asking, not Sarah, and we agreed to discuss it that night while she and Rebecca worked on the dresses.

With my morning now spent and nothing else that needed doing, I was back to being on my own, and I resumed my wandering about. I stopped for a while in the garden and just sat, basking in the sun. Once the boredom of counting grains of sand set in, I headed out. I hadn't taken the book from my room, not expecting to be left to my own devices for long. Sarah normally had a way of finding me that seemed to be more on target than radar, and long most days I didn't have long to wait before I'd been roped in to something.

Today however, I could walk without being accosted, and by 1:00 p.m. I'd found my way to the courtyard. As I had hoped, Rebecca played the piano. A guitar leaned up against her instrument, waiting for me to show up. When I came in, she greeted me warmly, and I noticed she had a slight blush every time I showed up these days. It made more beautiful, if such a thing were possible.

"Waiting for me?" I asked gesturing to the guitar.

"Actually, no. I was working on a new piece for Jodi's wedding. Based off of *Jesu, Joy of Man's Desiring.*"

She picked it up and began to play, and once again, I was amazed at her ability. She finished off and I applauded. She coloured deeper and put down the guitar.

"I just hope whoever Jodi finds to play for her can handle it. Most of the people here don't know their ass from a hole in the ground, musically."

When I told her I would be playing the music, she smiled and laughed. "Well, there go my worries. Just no lapsing into any songs from Torrent, okay?"

I laughed with her and picked up the guitar. "I promise nothing." I strummed a few random chords.

We sat there for a few minutes, her at the piano and me with the guitar, both of us saying nothing. Then we both tried to speak at the same time. We laughed, and she spoke first.

"Enjoy your breakfast?"

"I was just going to thank you. It was great. Strawberries and pancakes. Mmm. Very good."

She coloured even more.

"Well, you're welcome. Jodi had picked a bunch this morning, and I thought you might enjoy them."

I felt like a teenager—tongue-tied and awkward. This wasn't a sensation I was used to, and it made me highly uncomfortable, even though I enjoyed being around Rebecca. I normally felt confident in pretty much any situation, but she caused my knees to turn to jelly and my mouth and brain to lose connection. I knew this would get me in trouble one of these days, but right now I managed to keep it under control.

She closed up the piano and asked me if I'd like to take a walk. I was always up for one, so I accepted, and we left the courtyard, heading in what seemed to be a completely random direction. Rebecca was silent for the first part, as usual. When we got to one of the many gardens, she commented on the flowers, and veered off to smell them.

I meandered around, following her loosely, thinking to myself. She finally waited up for me, and we resumed our jaunt around the place again in companionable silence. When we stopped, we were in front of her place. She opened the door and headed in.

"Well, what are you waiting for?" she asked, as I stood out in the hallway. "C'mon in."

I stepped inside, but asked, "Rebecca, are you sure you should have a guy alone in your room?"

She stared at me, completely amused.

"Jonathan Walsh, are you suggesting you're going to take advantage of poor, little old me?"

I had to admit she was right. I would never do that to her or any other woman for that matter. I cared what she thought of me, and the last thing I wanted was to throw away what we had for one quick and hollow moment of physical passion.

"Not at all," I said while taking a seat on the sofa. She wandered into the kitchen and came back with two glasses of cold water with ice. I thanked her for the one she handed to me, and then she sat opposite me on the other half of the couch.

"So, I figured we could talk here." she said, tucking her legs up underneath herself and putting the water down. "I enjoyed it when we chatted in the courtyard. It's nice to get to know you more as a human being rather than a superstar."

It was my turn to blush. "I wasn't in any way a superstar, Rebecca. I had my fifteen minutes of fame; they just lasted a bit longer than some other people's."

"I'd have to argue that, Jon." She sipped her water. "You don't live in a small three-bedroom bungalow in the sticks. You're still out in California, aren't you?"

I nodded. One of the few things left from the divorce was the house in Los Angeles. I had sold that shortly after Tricia had gotten married to Chris and moved into a new house out in Oakland. It wasn't your Average Joe's house; it was in a gated community where a few select people tended to live. Rebecca was in part right. I wasn't your average person. I hadn't come from a lot of money—my parents lived comfortably, but not with the amount of wealth my daughter Kristen had benefitted from as a child. Fame does change us all, though, and I doubted if I were to run into my twenty-two-year-old self today, I'd even recognize me.

"Yeah, I still live out in California. I'm not hugely rich, but that's what everyone seems to see. They hear "recording artist" and dollar signs immediately flash in their eyes. Yes, there is a bit more money in it than working in a nine-to-five job but I paid my dues to get here."

"I know," she said. "It's not like I come from a poor family. For some reason, people around here seem to think I did, but my family lives comfortably back home. I don't think I would have been able to move out here to help my Grandmother if they'd been poor."

So, she came from a similar type of background. I wanted to ask what her family did for a living, but I was interrupted by the chirping of a clock on the wall. It was four in the afternoon and that meant I was late for Bible study with Sarah. I groaned, and Rebecca gave me a look of sympathy.

"Time to march into hell," I said, getting up.

"Good luck. I'll be thinking of you," she said as she saw me to the door.

I'll be thinking of you, too.

I jogged down the hallway back to my room, grabbed the Bible Sarah had dropped off the night before, and taking a deep breath, headed down the hall towards Sarah's quarters.

I slowed as I came nearer to Room 478, which had glass French doors and stood alone by itself, the other rooms that surrounded it having been renovated into this one suite.

Knocking on the door, I heard Sarah tell me to come in, and I braced myself for the slow descent into what I was sure was the road through Hades.

CHAPTER 10

When I pushed open the door, I half expected to see Sarah laid out on a table completely naked and just waiting for me to take advantage. Instead, I found myself shocked and surprised to see her modestly dressed in a white dress with her hair pulled back into a studious braid, and wearing very little makeup.

"Hi, Jonathan. If you'll come with me, dinner's ready. Once we've eaten, we'll move onto the study for the evening. You should be out of here to help Jodi by five."

If her aim was to confuse me with this current presentation of herself in comparison to the other times she'd spoken to me, she'd achieved her goal. However, because the numbers didn't add up, something in the back of my brain kept nagging me. I wondered if Sarah's assumption that Rebecca and I were an item had precipitated this emulation of the way Rebecca acted and dressed. Was this was Sarah's attempt to lure me like the sirens of a Greek legend?

I followed her into the dining area and noted her place was rather opulently decorated, including the dining area. I took the seat she indicated across from her at a long table. The meal was already on the table, served on china with gilt edges. There was of course, the ever-present bottle of wine she graciously poured into both glasses. I promised myself I'd stay with one glass throughout the dinner, as being totally blotto wouldn't be any help to anyone.

The meal itself had been prepared by Jodi—roast chicken and vegetables—and dessert was already present as well. Strawberry shortcake.

Sarah asked me to bow our heads for a brief blessing on the meal, and after she had said a few words, we ate. I stayed away from the wine as much as possible and simply drank water. Sarah kept up an almost steady stream of conversation again, and I tried to listen to what I could and commented when it seemed appropriate.

The dishes were cleared off, she grabbed two Bibles, and brought them back to the table. Before we were able to get into the study, she surprised me with some questions.

"So, Jonathan, is there anyone special in your life?"

This came out of the blue, and I gaped like a goldfish for a few moments.

"Um, well, I'm not in a relationship at the moment, if that's what you mean," I said. I didn't mention the same things I'd talked to Rebecca about before, that there hadn't been anyone in my life since before the divorce to Tricia had become final. I didn't trust Sarah as far as I could throw her, and I wasn't going to show my cards to anyone until the dealer had called.

"Surely a handsome man like you must have a different lady by his side every night?" she asked, getting her Bible open and looking at me for a reaction.

"Sorry, Sarah. I'm just a bit too old for that. My days of multiple women at once have been long over for years. I'm not even looking to settle down at this point in my life. I 'm happy to be a bachelor right now."

I could see she wanted to ask more of me, but she dived into the study of the New Testament, and we spent the next half hour pouring over it. She answered any questions I had, which were few.

It neared five o'clock, so she wrapped up her study, and decided to arrange a time for another. This was definitely going to put dampers on a lot of plans I might have wanted to make, but I arranged for it to be right directly after her morning study—ten in the morning, to save on things that would need to be done after lunchtime and supper. She let me know that once we had sufficiently covered the Bible we'd move into their doctrine. I figured this was when things would get interesting.

As the clock on her mantle chimed five, she showed me to the door, and had the same expectant look on her face as the last time she's walked me to my room. *You can't change the spots on a leopard,* I thought and once again, I politely excused myself. I headed down the halls to my suite, and after dropping off the Bible, jogged back up to the Arts & Crafts room where I knew Jodi would be working.

I knocked and when she called for me to come in, I was greeted with a surprise. On the little stool Jodi used for fitting the dresses stood Rebecca, her hair piled high on her head and her body clad in an exquisitely made, full-length sapphire blue dress. The dress was cut enticingly low in the back, but not enough to make it lewd. Rebecca looked over her shoulder at me, and smiled widely at my reaction.

"I take it you like what you're seeing?" she said as she turned to step down.

The front of the dress was quite modest, with an off the shoulder neckline, and the skirt of the dress flared out from her hips down to the floor. I was rendered speechless, and it was her turn to come over and push my jaw back up.

"Wow. You look ... gorgeous," I said when I my ability to speak returned. She smiled again and did a small twirl, making the skirt flair out around her.

"I feel like I'm playing dress up," she said, getting back onto the stool as Jodi came over with chalk to mark an area of the skirt. "I feel like a princess waiting for my prince to come along."

Jodi didn't give me the chance to respond, handing me a large basket of things and telling me to follow her around. I felt like one of the mice in Cinderella, but the rewards of watching this dress take shape was worth it. Once Jodi finished marking the areas on the dress she needed to alter, Rebecca stepped down and out of the room for a moment. When she came back, she had draped the dress over one arm and wore her everyday clothes. She handed Jodi the dress, which immediately went back on the one empty dressmaker's dummy in the room.

We began working on the next dress, which was in less of a state of repair than the one Rebecca had been wearing, and was obviously designed for someone a lot shorter and less able to carry off a stunning design like Rebecca had worn.

"You have to see Jodi's wedding dress," Rebecca muttered as we worked together, pinning up the hem of the dress along the chalk line Jodi had drawn before. "She's actually going to look like a fairy-tale princess."

Sure enough, Jodi appeared a few minutes later in her dress. Rebecca held onto the fitter's pincushion this time, and Jodi did indeed look like she'd stepped out of the pages of a children's book. It brought back memories of my daughter's wedding two years before. She had decided to get married in Jamaica, on the beach. It had been a small wedding, family and friends. Of course, there had also been the infamous incident where Tricia served me with divorce papers, but it was also a gathering of people I hadn't seen in a long time—Ryan and Heather; Mike and his girlfriend Liz, who I had met only briefly; and Chris, with Tricia draped over him like a cheap rug. I hadn't brought a date with me, even though Tricia and I had been separated a few years at that point. There wasn't anyone in my life then either, and I'd wanted my daughter's wedding to be special. Chris and I had spent the entire wedding shooting each other nasty glances, and Ryan, ever the peacemaker, had tried to keep the entire thing from going sky high. Luckily, he'd succeeded in keeping Chris and I apart and the day went pretty well, aside from the papers being served, of course, but Kristen got married the way she wanted to a man who I could see would sacrifice everything for her.

We worked on Jodi's dress, just adding the finishing touches, and as she came back in with the gown in her arms, Jodi said she wished it were for a wedding that actually meant something.

"Like yours will someday, Becca," she said sadly as she smoothed the dress.

Rebecca shot Jodi a look.

"So, when are you and what's-his-face planning on getting married?" I asked while Rebecca communicated with Jodi in a fast-moving series of hand gestures I couldn't decipher.

"Oh, we haven't gotten that far. All he did was slip the ring on my finger and that was it. We haven't discussed anything since I left for university," Rebecca said distractedly. I noticed the ring finger of her left hand was bare, and there was no indication she'd worn whatever ring he'd given her in a long time. She didn't even fiddle with the finger like those of us who had worn a ring for a while and had stopped wearing it for one reason or another. I had stopped the habit shortly after I took the wedding ring off from my own marriage. It amazed me how taking off a simple gold band I'd worn for almost twenty years could feel so freeing.

"Do you think you'll ever get married again, Jon?" Rebecca asked as we cleaned up the fabric and supplies we'd been working with on the two dresses.

I hesitated for a few moments. I hadn't been asked that question in the almost three years Tricia and I had been divorced.

"Well, if I were to ever find the right person, I'd consider it," I said simply, throwing some of the scraps I had in my hands into the garbage. "You have to keep in mind I'll probably never find that person, so the likelihood is pretty slim you'll ever see me with a wedding band on this hand again," I added, wiggling the ring finger of my left hand.

It was Jodi's turn to ask a question. "What would the ideal person for you be, Jon? Humor us girls; the guys around here rarely talk about what they're interested in."

I sat down, and the two of them grabbed chairs as well.

"I feel like I'm being interviewed," I said with a laugh. "Well, she'd have to be smart, I can't stand stupid people. She'd have to realize she's not getting the better end of the deal when it comes to me. I'm stubborn, and I tend to get a bit obsessive when I'm working on something, so she'd have to be able to be her own person when I'm in the recording studio or whatnot. She'd probably have to have the patience of a saint to put up with me when I'm in a mood and it would be a nice bonus if she were a creative person herself. It would be great to have someone around who would understand what the other is going through, even if the other doesn't take the spotlight themselves. Try explaining why you're going over hours of recording session footage to someone who has no interest or understanding of what and why you're doing it. Plus, if I were to take her on the road with me, she'd have to live the life of a nomad for a few months at a time, and most women I've met can't handle it. Living on a tour bus for months at a time with three to four other people gets on your nerves and by the time the tour is over you just don't want to see them for a few months."

The two of them watched me intently, and every so often Jodi would nail Rebecca in the ribs, to which Rebecca would gently kick her.

"So, now that you've probed me for those answers, what about yourselves?" I asked, turning it back to them. Rebecca coloured, but looked right at me as she answered.

"Okay, I'll bite. My ideal man ... hm ... kind, understanding I'm not going to be the "barefoot and pregnant" type, he'd have to know music is like air to me and I can't live without it. He'd have to stand by me when things got tough and be able to put up with the stubborn streak that Judith says I have." A bit of friendly elbowing ensued between them. "He'd have to be honest with me; I couldn't take being cheated on and if I ever found, out I'd likely show him his heart while it was still beating and then shove it down his throat. He'd have to be able to put up with my family, especially my kid sister, and being a smart, good looking guy wouldn't hurt his chances any either."

Jodi sat there between us looking back and forth. Rebecca glared at Jodi, and before she could open her mouth to speak, Rebecca cut her off.

"Don't even, Jodi. Do not even say it."

Jodi looked at me and shrugged. "I won't then," she said simply, and got up off the chair to wander away. "One of these days I'm going to take a trip down this river in Egypt," she muttered as she walked away. "Becca, Jon, you might have heard of it. *De Nile.*"

When Jodi returned she had a plate of cookies and tea on a tray. She put it down and we dug in, talking about general things that went on around the place. Jodi inquired as to how the study with Sarah had gone. I couldn't help but roll my eyes and say that it hadn't gotten far at all.

There was a knock at the door then, and when it opened, there stood Sarah and Kyle.

"I just wanted to see how the preparations were going, Jodi," Sarah said in that sickly-sweet voice. I thought it was likely she had ulterior motives as well. "Hello, Jonathan. I hope Jodi's been keeping you busy."

I nodded and made like I was still cleaning up. Truth of it was we'd finished for the night shortly before they'd arrived. The only dress still out on the dressmaker's dummy was Rebecca's. Jodi and Rebecca went back to work on it, adding what appeared to be a bustle.

Sarah hung around for a few moments longer, and then whispered something to Kyle before leaving. Kyle stayed around for a bit longer, and then left, taking Jodi with him. Rebecca and I were alone once again.

We both sat back down, unsure of what to do. Everything had been tidied, and I was pretty sure someone stood just out of sight beyond the door, waiting for something to happen that would prove Sarah right. Of course, I could be paranoid and second guessing things, but I figured better be of the mindset that they were talking about me than to be unprepared.

"So, any grand plans to get us out of here?" Rebecca asked, breaking the last cookie in half and offering me the other half.

"Nope, you got any?"

"Nope. We're boned, aren't we?"

"Pretty much, I figure."

Again, we sat there, with not much to say. Most of the topics for polite conversation had been used up, and neither of us wanted to venture into more personal territory.

I cleared my throat and stood up, offering her a hand. She waved me away and got up, and we left the room. Rebecca locked the door behind us, turning off the light and then heading towards her room.

I decided to go back to mine, and before I'd gotten thirty feet, I heard a voice call quietly, "Hey, are you going to join me for coffee or what?"

I turned around, and she was standing there with a smile, waiting for me to follow her.

"Well, you could've said something," I called back as quietly as I could, and walked with her towards the dining area.

"I thought I had. Sorry, I don't expect you to be a mind reader," she said as I caught up with her.

There were a few scattered people, Sarah's study having let out a few moments ago, and everyone presently enjoyed a tea or hot chocolate. Sarah was nowhere to be seen, neither was Jodi. I went over to the prep area and made a quick pot of tea and headed back out to the dining area with it and two mugs for the tea.

Rebecca sat in the very back, as far away from the main area as she could get without attracting attention.

I sat down and poured out the tea. Most of my time with Rebecca was spent silently. I didn't mind, as this was easiest. Neither of us had to find words to fill the silence and it was comfortable to be with someone who felt at ease in their own skin. She thanked me for her cup of tea and sipped quietly. I felt something on my leg and looked down. Rebecca had her legs stretched out and her foot was resting gently just below my knee. I was pretty sure she wasn't trying to play footsie with me intentionally, so I just let it be. She seemed to be used to stretching out her legs underneath the table, and it was understandable a habit like that would be something she'd probably keep up even when sitting with someone else.

"So ..." she said, toying with her tea.

"So ..." I said back, not sure at what she wanted to discuss.

She shrugged and looked away. "Do you have any clue what Jodi was going on about?"

"What, with the 'de Nile' comments?"

She nodded.

"I'm not sure. I think they were directed to the two of us, but don't hold me to it."

"I'm really not sure what she's trying to hint at," Rebecca said. "Well, no, I'm pretty sure she's trying to set the two of us up, but that's just crazy."

Not so crazy, a part of my mind said, which I quickly tried to shush. The last thing I needed was my brain trying to tell me it wanted things I wasn't remotely interested in. Some days I was beginning to doubt my own sanity. The last thing I needed was a fling—too much baggage, and it just wasn't something I could handle.

"I suppose if things are meant to be, you can't force them," I said simply, advice I'd learned from being married once already.

No matter how much Tricia had tried to shove our relationship down my throat, it never should have been. She'd always been more attracted to Chris, and those two complemented each other in ways we didn't. Tricia was always insecure and insanely jealous. She was also a grasping greedy bitch, and the divorce had driven it home. I was just happy she'd married Chris pretty much as soon as the ink was dry on the divorce papers, and I had been smart enough to get that travesty of a marriage annulled within the church as quickly as possible. It wasn't that I ever intended to remarry, but I wanted to make sure the separation between us was as legal and binding as it could possibly be.

Rebecca seemed to be reading my mind as she asked, "So, you don't ever think you'll remarry, then?"

I shook my head. "No, I don't. There's not a woman in this world who could put up with me and my quirks." I took a sip of my tea, and out of the blue blurted, "Plus, I don't think I've ever loved anyone to the extent where I'd want to be with them for the rest of my life or theirs."

She nodded and took a sip of her tea. I watched her. Just being with her felt natural. I couldn't put a name on what this was as I'd never felt the way I did now.

She poured another mug of tea and asked if I wanted more, to which I waved a "no thanks."

"Has Jodi talked to you about what music she wants played yet?" she asked.

"No, but I've got a few things in mind. If you want to go to the courtyard I can show you."

She nodded, and we took off.

Once outside, in the cool desert night breeze, I picked up the guitar, hopped up onto the piano, and began to play a song that had come to me while we'd been talking.

Rebecca sat there and listened as I sang. It was a song Ryan had written during the final year of Torrent, one that had been voted down in those last days. No one had ever heard it other than the guys in the band, and Rebecca was the first outsider give it a listen. I wasn't sure if I was doing the song any justice, but I gave it a try. Ryan had written it in the weeks leading up to his wedding to Heather, and then I didn't get what he was talking about, as my own marriage was starting into its monumental downswing. Now I was beginning to understand some of what he'd written—I guess my age mellowed me somewhat.

When I finished playing, all Rebecca said was, "Wow." I smiled and suggested she sing something at the wedding. She had a beautiful voice, and it would be a shame to let it go to waste. Rebecca flushed a bright red and refused point blank. She'd never sung in front of the group here and part of me couldn't blame her for not wanting to.

As the midnight hour neared, both of us decided to head home, and I offered to walk her to her door. She accepted and we talked about Jodi's wedding, which seemed to be rushing up on us like there was no tomorrow. There seemed to be something she wanted to ask me just before she went inside, but she must have thought better of it, because she just bid me a goodnight. I wondered what it was, but just as quickly dismissed it. Trying to figure out what went on inside a woman's head was the quick way to insanity, as far as I was concerned.

I headed back to my room, and for once, looked forward to the next day.

~

J woke from a restless sleep, haunted by a feeling of dread and dreams of falling all night long. As the sun rose, I dragged myself out of bed and thought of what to do for the day. There wasn't much choice, and I felt again torn between discovering what was going on here and getting back into the real world. I tried my window, to find it locked shut. It wasn't under lock and key; there something glued it shut so I couldn't pry it open and escape. The beating I'd endured the week before had informed me that the front door wasn't the way to get out either, and I couldn't think of any other means to escape. The gardens were walled in, the courtyard was central to the place, and there couldn't have been any route to freedom from there, or I assumed Rebecca would have already taken it.

I showered, dressed, and headed out for my morning walkabout. If nothing else, between working with Kyle on the odd days they needed me and the amount of daily cardio, I kept fit. It was also early enough to run into Jodi on her way to the kitchens, and she invited me to join her to help get breakfast underway for everyone. I protested at first, but she insisted, and I followed her in. Donning an apron, I was put to work with Jodi preparing potato pancakes, and we talked like we had before. Jodi was her chipper usual self, and after about a half hour, she went off to, "Grab other help," as she put it. She returned after about twenty minutes with Rebecca in tow, and threw her an apron, telling her to give me a hand with puréeing the potatoes. Jodi took off into another part of the kitchen, and I had a feeling she discreetly kept an eye on the two of us from a distance.

We worked alongside each other without talking for a while, me with my potatoes and Rebecca adding in an egg and flour every so often to the mixture, along with some onion, before sending the large bowl down the counter to the cooks, who ladled it onto the griddles, flipping them every so often.

"Just me or is Jodi trying extra hard to play matchmaker?" I asked at one point as I handed Rebecca another bowl for the ingredients.

"Definitely," she said, turning to me with a smile and rolling her eyes. "She likes doing this. Everyone has to be paired off in life for Jodi; salt and pepper, ketchup and mustard."

I laughed. "Will she ever give up on it?"

Rebecca joined in my laugher and shook her head no. "She won't give up until she's either been smacked by reality or someone shoots her."

We went back to working silently for a while, and as I turned to ask Rebecca to pass me a utensil she flung a small handful of flour in my direction while asking for something, covering my entire face.

I stood there in shock, and so did she for a few moments before breaking down into helpless giggles.

"That's it. This is war," I said, grabbing a handful of flour and throwing it in her face.

She squealed and lobbed more flour in my direction. I retaliated with some pureed potato, and soon it was an all-out food fight with missiles launched equally between the two of us. I grabbed her around the waist at one point and dropped a soaking wet, cold potato down her shirt ... which resulted in a massive amount of screaming and me getting repeatedly brained with a whisk before I let her go. Rebecca got even by tipping a small bowlful of the puree over my head and then bolted at high speed across the prep area. I took off in short order after her and cornered her in one corner of the prep area, with only a handful of flour and an egg in hand.

"Give up. You're cornered and you're not going to win this one." I lapsed into a horrible Dirty Harry impression. "You have to ask yourself, do you feel lucky? Well, do ya?"

I closed in and then grabbed her about the waist, which resulted in the egg getting smashed over my head and a lot of high-pitched squeaking as I pulled her from the corner. As I held onto her, I had the urge to kiss her, and not resisting or questioning it this time, I did. She stiffened for a moment out of sheer astonishment and dropped the handful of flour she had onto the floor. Then she returned the kiss and I felt her arms around my neck.

A cough from the rear of the room surprised both of us, and I let go of the hold I had on Rebecca, who promptly fell to the floor. Jodi stood, hands on hips, shaking her head back and forth in both dismay and amusement.

"I can't leave you two alone for two minutes without things going awry, can I? You should see yourselves. What a mess!"

I had no doubt what I looked like. I could feel the puree and egg running down my neck and I knew I was coated in a good amount of flour. The prep area was rather similarly coated. Rebecca had flour everywhere and globs of puree in her hair.

"You two go get cleaned up. Rebecca, make sure *you* wash the egg out of his hair, the last thing I need is for one of you to smell like eggs three days from now because someone used the wrong temperature of water to remove it and accidentally baked it into your hair." She shook her head again, her seriousness being undermined by the laughter in her voice that she couldn't keep out. "I don't want to see you back here until you've thought about what you've done, and you're dressed in clean clothes for breakfast. "

She shooed both of us from the prep area out into the service hallway leading around the dining area. Rebecca led the way, glancing back at me every few moments, alternately smiling and looking deep in thought.

"Let's go to my place," she said. "I at least have the kitchen sink, so I can rinse the egg out of your hair." Rebecca hung a right and pulling her keys from the pocket, still looking pensive.

Once we were inside, she disappeared into the hallway, and came back with a few towels and a bottle of shampoo. Pulling a chair from her dining table, she instructed me to kneel on it so I could lean over the sink. She hopped up onto the counter and twiddled with the faucet for a few, then filled a bowl with water before pouring it over my head without warning, leaving me sputtering. She wet down my hair, gently rinsed the egg out, and proceeded to add the shampoo.

"Your hair looks nice, Jon," she said as she rinsed it out. "You look better with longer hair."

"Thanks," I said as she handed me a towel. "I usually wouldn't think of letting it grow, but what can I do about it here?"

Rebecca shut down the water and motioned for me to take a seat. Then she disappeared off into the hallway again, and I heard water running.

"I'm just going to shower this stuff off before it dries into cement. Stay put."

She must have trusted me more than enough to shower with me in the place. I stayed where I was told, and a few minutes later she emerged dressed in clean clothes, her hair wrapped up into a towel.

"Time for you to get cleaned up; let's move down to your room."

I finished drying my hair, and we headed down the hallways across the place to my room. Once there, I gathered clean clothes and disappeared into the bathroom. I took a few minutes extra before I came out, dressed and ready to go. Rebecca was sitting on the couch, towel drying her hair, waiting for me.

"Why did you do that?" she asked out of the blue as I put my shoes back on.

"Do what? Put on my left shoe first?" I asked, playing stupid.

"Kiss me."

I shrugged. "It felt like the right thing to do."

She laughed heartily. "That's the best response I've heard to this question. Don't worry; I'm not trying to read too much into it," she added, getting up from the couch and joining me over by the door. "Just trying to figure out if it meant anything."

I didn't quite know how to respond. I knew I didn't want anything short term. On the other hand, I wasn't sure I wanted to a long-term relationship unless it was with someone who would be willing to go the long haul with me. I finally realized I was attracted to Rebecca, and I cared about her in more than just a platonic sense. Beyond that, though, I didn't know if what I felt was love or just basic physical attraction.

"Well, why don't we just take things one day at a time then," I said.

"Ah. It did mean something, but you're not sure what. I'm okay with that."

We headed back down to the dining area; the mood had changed perceptibly between us, for the better. Acknowledging there at least was a basic level of attraction had lowered the tension in some ways, and Rebecca behaved less restrained about being in physical contact with me. We practically flirted with each other. The people around us noticed something had changed as well; Rebecca normally didn't eat any meals in the dining area. Her presence there raised eyebrows and the fact that she sat with me and laughed at what I said definitely got the attention of the denizen.

Normally I would not have given someone her age a second glance. Women that young were often too flighty and self-absorbed, wanting to be seen with someone like myself as a status symbol—and I wasn't interested in playing that game. Despite her youth, Rebecca had been through enough to have created a maturity that generally wasn't seen until later in life.

Jodi came out and with a huge grin on her face, walking over to our table.

"You two certainly are the talk of the hour. If you don't watch out, Sarah's going to rain on your parade."

Rebecca's face grew serious. The last thing either of us needed was Sarah finding out about this. It would go over as well as a lead balloon for both of us, and would seriously hamper me from getting any further information about the true goings-on of Skylark Inn and how to escape.

I checked my watch. Seven in the morning. Sarah's study would be starting soon, and both Rebecca and I had to be there. I finished off the remainder of my breakfast and got up, offering my hand to Rebecca. She looked at me with a certain amount of amazement but took my hand.

"She's going to find out sooner or later," I said, shrugging.

We headed to her room to pick up the sheet music she'd need and went to my room to get the Bible I knew Sarah wanted to see on me at all times. Then we slowly wandered down to the courtyard, hand in hand. For once, everything felt natural with Rebecca. There wasn't any forced display of affection. I didn't have to constantly be fawning over her and her over me. We just *were,* and it felt normal.

When we got to the courtyard, she dropped my hand and whispered that she'd wait a few moments before heading in. Sure enough, Sarah was there already, starting to prepare for her usually marathon length sermons. I trotted down the stairs with what I knew was an unusual level of happiness and even greeted Sarah with a cheerful "Good Morning!" before settling into the seat I normally took in the front row.

"Well, well, we're chipper this morning," she remarked with a smile. "That's good to see."

"I've had a good morning," I said honestly. No need to tell her why I was having such a good morning.

Rebecca came in and slunk down to the piano without attracting much notice. She set up her sheet music and began to play, giving me the occasional glance with a smile on her face and a sparkle in her eyes.

The usual crowd slowly entered into the courtyard in groups. I could discern from the general buzz that the two of us in the cafeteria area were the main topic of discussion, and privately prayed it would take its sweet time getting back to Sarah. As much as I wanted to throw caution to the wind, I didn't need to raise the ire of an already unsteady personality I was sure would bring down the fire and brimstone when given the chance, or order said things to be brought down through her brother Kyle.

Sarah waited about fifteen minutes for most of the people to filter in, then began on her sermon for the day. She promised to keep it short, as she had other things and other lessons to attend to.

She spoke about one of the parables. True to her word, the discussion took less than a half hour, and once Rebecca had finished up the closing hymn, everyone was dismissed. The crowd moved out in groups, those who had to work went out faster than the others who stayed behind. I could still pick out bits and pieces of the discussion about the appearance of Rebecca in the dining room with me, but thankfully it seemed the appeal of that particular story was waning, and people went on to more mundane topics. I had no doubt this would rear its head again, and that we would be watched by the entire population for further signs of a budding relationship between the new guy and the strange girl.

Sarah came up to me before I had a chance to do anything, and taking my arm, walked with me out of the courtyard and down the halls.

"So, you had a good morning."

I nodded my agreement. "Yes, yes I did."

"Anything I should know about?" she asked with a raised eyebrow.

"Sarah, I can safely say there is nothing you should know about in my life."

We were at her suite again, and this time she set up in the living room. I took a seat in the love seat and tried to take up as much space as was possible. Today, she continued along with the same line of study, and introduced the basic beliefs of her group. I understood the basics that she spoke of—the Sabbath, the state of the dead, the great controversy, the Apocalypse, and spiritual gifts. None of this seemed entirely out of the ordinary; even with my limited knowledge, I knew these things were backed up by many verses within the Bible itself.

Before we got into the teachings that differed from their parent church, Sarah shut down the study for the day, and disappeared off into her kitchen. She came back with two glasses of something to drink and proceeded to take up the line of questioning she'd begun the other day.

"Have you ever been married, Jonathan?" she asked, watching me over the rim of the glass.

"Yes, Sarah. I've been divorced for about three years now. She's remarried."

"No one in your life since then?"

Not until this morning. "No, there isn't anyone in my life. I think I've said before that I'm happy being a bachelor right now."

"What about you and Rebecca? I know I've asked this before, but I just want to make sure ... Nothing going on between you two?"

"No, there isn't anything going on between the two of us." *That you should be aware of.*

"Good."

I checked my watch, making sure she saw me. I felt uncomfortable. Not that anything other than her attitude had changed. She still dressed like the last time—modestly, with her hair braided back. Her body language seemed different, as well as the way she responded to anything I said.

"I think I'd better get going. I know Jodi wants to talk to me about music and she probably still wants me to help out with getting those dresses done." I stood, ready to leave.

"Oh, I'm sure Jodi can wait a few moments," she cooed and followed me to the door.

"Yeah, I don't think she can. I'll see you tomorrow," I said, slipping out the door just before she got there.

In the hall, I breathed a sigh of relief. Yet another close call without finding out anything new. This couldn't keep up much longer. I needed to making progress in figuring out more this place, or, I needed a miracle. It semmed unlikely that either would happen.

a few days passed without any major changes in Sarah, Rebecca, or Jodi. We inched closer to Jodi's wedding and planned out the music. Rebecca volunteered to play a piano solo; I'd handle the rest on piano and guitar and lead the guests in singing. The reception would have a DJ, hired from outside the compound—this was a rare occurrence—and there would be a dance. Jodi mentioned it had taken a lot of bargaining, begging, and pleading to get one.

"The entire place will be on edge that night. Don't even try to upset the status quo or I know for certain Kyle and Sarah will bring you to your knees," Jodi said on the last night we worked on the two dresses. The other girl worked nights most of the week, so she came in to be fitted when she was off work in the early hours of the morning, around the time Jodi headed to the kitchens to prepare breakfast.

I didn't see much of Rebecca, because Kyle had asked me to help him keep the renovations on time again, as they'd lost a few men to random injury. I had my doubts as to how random the injuries were, but I joined the guys. They kept me busy tearing down and rebuilding walls, carting things from point A to point B, and finally working in the burning sun in the courtyard, repainting the concrete floor with four other guys, so it would look presentable for the wedding. This repainting forced Sarah's studies inside and actually canceled the morning studies, due to Jodi's reluctance to give up her dining area between breakfast and lunch. I caught glimpses of Sarah darting from place to place, and when I ran into Jodi, Sarah was normally there, but I never did meet with the so-called prophet alone. I was unsure if Rebecca would mind me dropping by her place randomly now that things were, well, more out in the open, so the days dragged on like weeks from not being able to see her.

One day after work, I decided to throw caution to the wind, and stopped by her rooms. It was Friday, so people were running around doing what they needed to get done before the sun fell, and most of the compound was deserted. Kyle had let us out early, and I purposefully went down the end of the complex where I knew her room was. Knocking on the door, I heard loud music, probably too loud for my knocks to be heard. I knew Jodi would probably pop by later in the day after vespers, but until then, usually no one would be here. I tried the handle. The door was unlocked. I carefully pushed it open and went inside. At first glance Rebecca was nowhere to be seen. I turned to face the kitchen, and there she was, dancing around like a fool to the song played, head in the fridge, looking for something buried in the back.

Deciding to return the favor for the many times she'd snuck up on me and scared the wits out of me, I snuck up behind her, which was quite easy as she was engrossed in listening to the song and finding whatever it was in her fridge. I grabbed her by the waist, which caused her to scream loudly and kick me one in the crotch—hard.

I crumbled to the floor like a sack of oatmeal, and if I'd thought my muscles hurt from working, I was pretty sure they wouldn't be protesting after this pain.

"Oh my God, Jon, are you okay? I am so, so, so, so sorry," she said, kneeling on the floor beside me. "I thought you were Kyle."

"Note to self: Never, *ever* do that again," I squeaked.

Once the majority of the pain had passed, she helped me hobble over to the couch.

"What brought you by?" she asked, sitting down beside me.

"I just wanted to see how you were doing. I haven't seen you since that morning, you know."

"Well, that's sweet of you," she said with a pat on my leg. "I figured you were just avoiding me."

I flashed her a look of incredulity. "Why would I want to avoid you?"

She shrugged. "I figured something had happened with Sarah to change your mind about the "take it one day at a time" thing."

"Rebecca, I wouldn't have come looking for you if that were the case. I was wondering if you'd like to have dinner with me. Jodi says Sarah's gone to Phoenix for the day and won't be back until later tonight. There are things for the wedding she needs to pick up that she wouldn't allow anyone else to go get."

"Are you going to be able to walk?" she asked, concerned. "I really am sorry. I seriously thought it was Kyle."

"I'll be fine ..." I managed. "No permanent damage done."

"So, dinner in the cafeteria?" she asked, with a sour look. "I mean, I love Jodi and all, but she does deliver groceries to me, you know."

"You, the domestic type?" I asked, and instantly regretted it.

"I *can* cook," she replied indignantly, getting up off the sofa and heading into the kitchen after turning down the music.

I tried to help, but was told to sit down and relax. Rebecca insisted she would be *domestic* enough for the task. It was pretty hard to miss the sarcasm on that word. I didn't win any points on that one. Still, Rebecca kept up a good conversation while she cooked, and each time I got up to assist her, I was shooed back to the couch. I could barely see the dining area from where I sat, but it looked like she was going all out. About an hour went by before I was allowed to leave the sofa and join her in the dining room.

When I came into the room, the table was set with nice china, and she'd prepared a candlelight dinner for two.

"I'm sorry I don't have any wine, but ..." she shrugged. "I've never been a big drinker myself."

I assured her it was fine, that I wasn't a huge drinker either, and generally only had a drink or two socially.

We sat down to a meal of chicken and risotto. She was right; she was more than able to cook well for two people. We ate silently, and I once again thought how beautiful she looked in the play of the candlelight. The soft glow highlighted the contrast between her lily-white skin and her dark-as-coal hair and eyes.

I must have been staring for a while, because she looked up at me with a grin and asked if there was something on her face.

"No, no. It's just ... You're just ... Well, you're rather ravishing in this light."

She blushed, which did nothing to detract from her beauty, and quietly thanked me for the compliment. The more time I spent with her, the more I found I was captivated by her in so many different ways.

When dinner was finished, she cleared up the table and I chivalrously offered to do the dishes, but she insisted on helping.

"I know where everything goes," she explained as I washed and she dried.

*O*nce that was done, she asked if I'd like to sit in the garden. When I inquired as to what she was referring, she pointed to two large French doors off the living room. I had known there was a garden off her suite but didn't see the doors until she mentioned it. I'd also assumed it was probably a postage stamp of greenery.

She opened the doors, and presented me with a full view of the garden. Of course, it was surrounded by the high walls that ringed everything except the front facade of the place, but the obvious care and landscaping that had gone into it predated that. There was flagstone laid on the ground and a terraced area with several different types of flowers growing in them. The central feature of the area was a wrought iron patio set, and what appeared to be a fountain in the earthen wall nearest to the large retaining wall situated on the far side of the garden.

"Wow. This place is gorgeous," I breathed, stepping out into the area. The sun was setting over the western horizon, and colour embraced the walls—hues of orange, crimson, and yellow. I marvelled at the sight while Rebecca stood back at the doors, smiling as she leaned casually up against the frame.

"It's where I go when I need to get away from it all. Just take my CD player, maybe a book, and sit out in the garden by myself."

I could see why. Whomever had created this place had made

something beautiful where you could get a break but still not be away from home.

She eventually joined me in the dying light, standing by my side, enjoying the beauty of the sunset in the garden. I looked over to her, and when I caught her eye, she moved closer to me. Wrapping an arm around her, we watched the light slowly fade from the sky, going from a brilliant crimson to a deep violet as the stars speckled the night. I didn't want the moment to end. I wanted to catch it and hold it in time—just the two of us and the breathtaking sunset. I wanted to cherish times like this before they vanished, which they tended to do quite quickly, in my experience.

She cuddled in even closer, and I noticed she seemed a bit cold. "Maybe we should go back in?" I quietly suggested. She shook her head no, seemingly content to just stare at the sky.

"When I was a bit younger, my sister and I used to lie outside in the backyard at night and see how many constellations we could name," she said, her voice just barely above a whisper. "I haven't done that in what feels like forever." She turned her head to look at me. "Do you have any brothers or sisters?"

"Nope. I grew up an only child. Ryan's like a younger brother to me, but family-wise Chris is the closest to me. I never got to do things like this. Went on tons of boring lectures with Dad, but nothing like sitting out in the backyard watching the stars. Not like I could, with New York City being so close."

As the night cooled down past the comfortable level, we headed back inside. She wandered around a bit aimlessly.

"There's not much to do here at nights. I usually just read, draw, write, or just sit and veg," she said, finally coming to light on the couch. "Not quite sure what you were imagining when you dropped by."

"I actually came by just to talk. Nothing in particular in mind, other than that."

She shrugged. Part of me wondered if she wanted me out of there, and the other part of me wondered if she expected me to bunk up with her right away. I wouldn't lie, being around her made my blood sing, but I had moved beyond wanting a one-night stand with any bit of fluff a few years before my divorce had become final. Hitting forty had definitely driven home the reality that I should act a wee bit more mature than my twenty-some-year-old self had been.

"If you want me to leave ..." I said, resignedly, heading for the door.

"Not really. I enjoy being around you."

I stopped and turned around. She knelt on the couch, so she could see me over the back of it.

"Should I stay or should I go," I sang with a smile, knowing full well I was quoting an overly-famous Clash song.

She smiled back at me. "Are you just going to spew song lyrics at me all night? I mean if you are, you could at least share your own."

I couldn't help but laugh. She was comical and sweet as well as beautiful. I sat down on the small love seat across from her and we talked about general things, like how my day had gone and what new things were happening. I found that even though I rarely saw her around the place, and she wasn't favorably regarded by the people around her, she actually kept up to date on most of the gossip. She spoke of the music she worked on and the visit Sarah had paid to her earlier in the day before leaving for Phoenix. I found myself losing track of all sense of time while listening to her. It was intoxicating.

Eventually, the topics turned more personal.

"How did you and Chris end up forming the band?" she asked, stretching out and resting her head on the pillow of the sofa, watching me intently with her dark eyes.

"Oh, you want a history lesson?" I said laughingly.

"Hey, I've got a captive audience with Jonathan Walsh. Do you think I'm going turn down the opportunity to know little dirty secrets about one of my favorite bands?"

"You have a point. I'd do the same in your shoes."

I settled back into the loveseat, throwing my arms over the back of it and preparing to drudge up history.

"Chris and I both attended UCLA. I was there because family was close—Chris' mum is my Dad's sister, my aunt. Chris went there for acting. I took journalism. Can you imagine me working for a newspaper or something like *Rolling Stone*? That's a laugh, isn't it? Anyway, we had been playing guitar since, God, I was maybe ten, and he was about eleven when he picked it up. So, there were the two of us.

"We ran into Mike at one of the jam sessions they had at a student bar, I can't remember what the hell the name of it was, it was so long ago. This would have been in 1974, I think. Yep, Chris was 21. Just legal, and I still wasn't, which was pretty funny. Mike joined us for a set on drums one night, and we just were in awe— that boy was a virtuoso on percussion. Chris looked at me and went, 'We need to get a band together. I think we could kick ass.'

"Back then we played covers. Problem was, we needed a bassist. I think we had at least five of them for random periods of time before we settled on Ryan. Ah, little Ryan. He was 15-years-old when he joined the band in '75. I was in New York on summer break and posted an ad in the papers around the area. He'd been playing for a couple of years and was incredible. I mean, it takes most bassists a few years, sometimes a few decades to move from the four-string to the five-string bass, and he was already on it. His parents had to sign the contract when we got our record deal that year, and I promised them I'd make sure he'd finish his education. He did. With my Dad's help, we got private tutors and Ry finished high school a year ahead of his old classmates. By Christmas of '77 we had a platinum album within two weeks of release and things just went from there."

"Didn't you marry Tricia then, too?" she asked, sitting up and leaning forward, eager to hear more.

I sighed. "Yep. I was 20 when I made that mistake. One of the things I'd do differently if I could live life over with the knowledge I have now. She married me not because she wanted to be with me, but because my family had more money than Chris' did, and then she thought bringing a child into the mix of the two of us was a good way to try and save the relationship."

I shook my head in disbelief over the events of my life. "It didn't. I spent most of my time out on tour. By the time I got home permanently, Kristen was in junior high, and it was like living with a stranger. If she hadn't been born, Tricia and I would have been divorced within two years. Instead, the fighting went on for almost 20 years. Sad, isn't it?"

She nodded. "So, if that hadn't happened you would've stayed unmarried?"

"Hell yes, knowing what I know now, I'd have stayed a bachelor for life. Kristen would have been Chris' daughter—if he'd actually decided to have children. Considering the randy asshole he was in the '70s, I wouldn't be too amazed to find out he has at least three kids with three different women."

Her eyebrow just about hit her hairline. "Really? From all

accounts I've heard, *you* were the one who was the "randy asshole" in the group. Not Chris."

"I'll be honest with you Rebecca; I've had maybe ten women in my life. Ten. Don't even need to move to toes to count them. I could probably name them all if I wanted to. Truth be known, it wasn't all sex, drugs, and rock and roll for us. There's the huge perception it was, and for some of us it might have been that way. I certainly can't comment on what Chris, Mike, and Ryan did when the shows were over, but I know for myself it was usually a few drinks with the boys to wind down after the night was over, and then I crashed. Usually Ry went with me, so I can say it's highly unlikely some of the things you've heard about the group are true. I don't think any of the shit Chris and Mike ever got up to had been on the level of the Terror Twins, or remotely close to Led Zeppelin and the fish incident. There was some sex, some drugs, and a lot of rock and roll, but nothing on the level of tabloid news reporting."

"Seems like a lot of groups are saying that these days," she said with a skeptical sigh. "Next thing I know you'll be reciting the "Don't Do Drugs" public service announcements to me from memory."

"Hey, I'm not going to do that. Most of the people who do have gotten roped into it in exchange for certain things not being mentioned legally, if you know what I mean. Sure, I did my share of shit in the '70s, and I'm not proud of it. I'm not going to tell anyone not to do it, because it's their frigging life and role model or not, they're going to try it if they want to. I did, I'm alive, and I stopped because I didn't like the way half the crap made me feel. Trust me, you don't want to watch me coming down from a high. It's not pretty, and I'm not much into self-destructing."

She sat back, apparently satisfied with the answers she'd received. "I think you're the first person I've ever heard admit they did drugs, other than the people who you *know* did their and everyone else's share of the hard stuff." She looked me directly in the eyes. "Now, before you can ask, no I haven't done drugs. People think I'm insane enough as it is."

"Aren't all us creative people just a bit off-normal to begin with?" I asked, standing up with the intention of sitting beside her on the couch, now she'd left me some room.

She tucked her feet under her and nodded, while murmuring an assent as I sat down.

"Creativity is insanity to the 'normal' person," she said. "If you tell a person who doesn't have a creative bone in their body that you've got music running through your head, and the only way to get it out is to write it down or play it, they think you're nuts."

It was my turn to nod with understanding. "Yeah, it was like that with my Dad. He never understood why I wanted to play. Mum did, though."

We sat silent for a while, before she raised an eyebrow and asked, "So, what *does* it feel like to come down off a high?"

I sighed. "Really like shit. That's the short and sweet of it. The slightly longer story is that I wanted to kill myself every time I came off cocaine, and it took Ry's physically restraining me to prevent it from happening. Can you picture it? Ryan, who at the time had to be ninety pounds soaking wet! I don't remember much else about the other drugs I've done, except that I felt like abject shite while using them, most of the time. I can remember thinking, 'What's the fun in this?'"

She nodded and leaned up against me. I wrapped one arm around her, and she yawned—a head splitting yawn—as she checked her watch. "It's after two in the morning," she murmured sleepily, putting her head on my chest.

"If you want me to go, I certainly will," I said, leaning down to rest my head on hers.

"Nah. Stay as long as you want. I like having you around. It just … feels right," she said, the drowsiness clear in her voice.

I yawned, and the room swam in my vision. After a few minutes, I looked down, to find her sound asleep, snoring ever so quietly. I didn't want to disturb her by getting up, and I ended up falling asleep not long after, still on her couch, with her curled up against me.

~

The gleaming sunshine in my eyes woke me up the next morning. I rolled over and found myself on the floor in short order. I wore the same clothes as last night, and the room was not at all familiar. I looked back up at where I'd fallen from, and it sunk in that I was still in Rebecca's suite and had been asleep on the couch. She'd awakened at some point in the night for her own bed and covered me with a blanket rather than wake me up. I checked my watch. Eleven in the morning. I was late for any number of things, and none of the repercussions would be good. This was the latest I had overslept in the longest while, and I actually felt rested for once.

Getting off my ass, I spotted a note on the coffee table. Apparently, she'd woken up around 7:00 a.m. and gone to do whatever had been asked of her by Sarah the day before. Rebecca hadn't wanted to wake me up because I looked, as she put it, "peaceful." She said she'd be back around noon, and if I was still there, she'd make lunch for the two of us.

I had to wonder if Sarah stormed on the warpath or if Rebecca had been able to get Jodi to run interference for me. Both of them knew I was supposed to be at Sarah's for study about an hour ago, and from what I knew of Sarah, there should have been a small army of people out looking for me, ready to drag my carcass back to her, alive or dead. Though knowing Sarah, it would be preferably alive and ... my mind recoiled at the thought that ran through it. The things Sarah might have wanted to do to me sat on my list of "Don't need to know, don't ever care to find out."

I heard a knock on the door and froze in place, trying not to make a sound or move a muscle. The door slowly swung open, and Rebecca's head peeked in. When she saw me, her face broke into a smile and I began to breathe again.

"Why didn't you answer the door?" she asked, holding a basket on one arm.

"I thought you were Sarah. I was supposed to be at study with her an hour ago, and I didn't show up."

She laughed, putting the basket on the counter in the kitchen.

"Well, you're lucky. Jodi's got her convinced you're puking your guts up right now—food poisoning. So, you're off the hook for at least twenty-four hours. I have lunch in the basket. I went down to help Jodi with a few things, and she sent up something special for the both of us."

"Excellent." I got up from where I'd been crouched on the floor and made my way over to Rebecca.

"You'll probably want to change and stuff," she said. "It'll take me about fifteen minutes to get everything ready, so you might want to head back to your room. If you run into Sarah, just try and look ill, okay? Try picturing Kyle naked. That does it for me."

"Has anyone told you that you're completely evil lately?" I said with a smile. "I like it!"

She smiled back and waved as I headed out the door to my

room. I luckily made it there without running into anyone, and twenty minutes later—showered, shaved, teeth and hair brushed, and dressed in some clean clothes—I worked my way back to Rebecca's room. At about the halfway mark, the worst thing that could have happened to me happened, short of my ex-wife deciding to remarry me on a spur of the moment decision. I ran into Sarah.

She looked genuinely surprised to see me.

"Jonathan ... nice to see you out and about. Feeling better I take it?"

I prayed for the ability to throw up at will, to lie through my teeth, for the ground to open up and swallow me whole. Of course, none of those things would happen, except maybe the lying through my teeth part.

"Oh, just a minor respite from the W.C. Just wanted to get a breath of fresh air before the retching and shitting kick back in."

Her face revealed how disgusted she was at that statement; however, she kept trying to take my arm. I had to think quickly.

"In fact, Jodi's not sure if it was food poisoning at all or some type of flu. Best not to come near me right now. I don't want *you* catching it."

She stopped in her tracks, and then took two steps back.

"Thanks for thinking of me. I'll see you, um, when you're feeling better, I guess."

And with that, she took off down another corridor at high speed, trying to get away from this potentially infectious person.

Once she'd disappeared out of sight, I said a silent thank you to the big guy upstairs and kept on my way to my original destination, only a few minutes later than I had hoped to arrive.

Checking both ways to make sure I couldn't see Sarah anywhere in sight, I knocked on Rebecca's door and she answered.

"You're late, you know," she said with a stern face, but the amusement twinkled in her eyes, seriously undermining her attempt at being stern with me.

"I ran into Sarah. You're lucky to have me here at all."

Shock flickered across her face, but to her credit, she quickly hid it away, replacing it with the smile she'd had on her face a few moments before.

"Well, c'mon," she said, taking my hand and pulling me inside. She led me through her suite out into the garden, where a large blanket was laid out on the ground, and a picnic lunch was set out for both of us.

"You have Jodi to thank for this," she said, putting a hand on my arm before letting go of it to sit down on the blanket. I joined her, and she began laying out the stuff from the basket. The small feast included a veritable mountain of fruit, finger sandwiches, and what looked like some type of macaroni salad.

"Tuck in," said Rebecca, handing me a paper plate.

Twenty minutes later and feeling quite stuffed, she cleared off the blanket and lay down in the sun. I reclined as well, and we sat there watching the clouds in the sky.

"Do you know how many fangirls would give their left arm and leg to be in the position I'm in right now?" she asked, rolling onto her side to face me. "Alone in a secluded spot with Jonathan Walsh."

I laughed. "Not many, likely. C'mon Becca, I'm going to be forty-five in a few months, divorced, and bitter. I've had a lousy career. I'm a has-been."

She sighed with a combination of laughter and exasperation. "You're way too humble about yourself, Jon. There are plenty of women out there who still find you attractive, smart, and think you're dead sexy."

I had to smile. She was honest in pretty much anything she said. I found it sweet and enchanting. Every moment I spent with her I enjoyed. Was *this* what falling in love with someone felt like? She complimented my personality in ways that made me a better person when I was with her. When she wasn't around, I actively sought her company. Is this what finding your soul mate was supposed to feel like? I knew even though I never meant for any of this to happen, it wasn't in my hands to control, and I recognized it was something I didn't want to let go.

"I'm not sure why one of the guys here hasn't snapped you up in a heartbeat," I said, reaching out to brush a lock of hair that had fallen forward over her face back. "You're gorgeous and sophisticated. You should be surrounded by hot young guys all vying for your attention."

She rolled back onto her back, staring up into the sky, watching the clouds roll slowly by for a few moments.

"Yeah, you'd think that, wouldn't you?" she asked, her voice somber. "Except I'm too brainy for the guys here, and I'm not built in any way like Sarah, which is who they all go haywire for, if you haven't noticed."

"Actually, I hadn't." *You're the one who has held my attention since the first moment I stepped into this place.*

"Then you're either crazy, blind, or possibly one of the few sane people in this place," she said with a sardonic laugh, as she rolled back onto her side. "Is it okay I'm choosing to believe it's the last one?"

"It's perfectly fine with me. I personally like it the best out of the options given."

She laughed again, this time with no trace of sarcasm or annoyance, and leaned forward to give me a gentle kiss before settling back, her arm underneath her head, watching me as I watched her.

"I'm not sure why you're interested in me, Jon, but I'm not going to question it," she said, her dark brown eyes searching mine. "I think I'll just enjoy it for however long it lasts."

I hope that's a long time. "Yeah, me too."

CHAPTER 12

The next day rolled around slowly. I'd left Rebecca's at about five in the afternoon, after we'd spent most of the day talking about this, that, and a bit of the other. We walked about in areas where she knew Sarah rarely went. It was the kind of quiet, peaceful afternoon I'd always wished I had someone in my life to share with—where you're not concerned with how you look, or even if you're talking. You're just with someone who makes you happy.

We met up again after Sarah's evening study, and spent the remainder of the night helping Jodi with the finishing touches on the dresses. In my mind, we weren't acting any differently than normal, but twenty minutes in, Jodi said the two of us were giving her cavities from being so cute together. The night progressed pretty quickly with all three of us talking and working, and before I knew it, I was saying goodnight to Rebecca at her door, and debating whether or not to give her a kiss goodnight. She ended that mental discussion by kissing me, leaving me standing there, happily stunned for a few moments, before she closed the door with a quiet laugh.

I headed back to my room, as it was well past midnight, and I happened to pass by Sarah's room. The lights were still on. Something caught my attention from the amount of noise made, and I stood just out of what I felt to be visible range, to see what I could see. I couldn't make out what anyone said, but I could tell Sarah wasn't thrilled, and the level of unhappy reached about ten times what it had been the night I'd shown up at this strange place.

I could make out Kyle's voice as well, and another two voices I knew, but couldn't put names to them off the top of my head. I could have sworn I heard my name mentioned, but footsteps headed towards the direction of the door, and I knew it wouldn't be to my benefit to be around to find out who it was and what exactly was being spoken about. I took off at a quick walk, and broke into a jog as I rounded the corner away from there. With my heartbeat echoing madly in my ears, I headed back to my room, and once the door was shut, I leaned back and took a deep breath. That had been excruciatingly too close for comfort for me. The last thing that probably would help my situation was being caught red handed eavesdropping on Sarah. The entire— dare I say—relationship with Rebecca walked that fine line of being publicly known and being a question in most people's minds. Jodi could keep up pretending we were just friends, albeit quite close friends, only for so long. It was inevitable Sarah would find out how things had moved beyond merely being a friendship. Sarah's reaction would be bad, beyond any doubt. The question remaining in my mind was how epic the explosion would be, and how many people would be taken down in the blast radius when it happened.

My instincts told me to protect both Rebecca and Jodi from what I could. Jodi had been a good friend to both of us, especially for having known me a very short time, and anything I could do to get her the hell out of the danger zone would be a bonus. Rebecca, well, as far as I was concerned, she was coming with me when I left this place. Her remaining with me afterwards was a question I didn't feel like contemplating right this moment. I wanted to stay as close to the here and now as I could; thinking about the future was only a time-sink and something I tried not to do.

My mind still going a mile a minute, I got ready for sleep. I moved on autopilot, and before I knew it, I lay there, lights off, staring at the ceiling and trying to convince my mind to stop running through constantly worsening possibilities of what would happen when Sarah found out about Rebecca and me.

The only thing that continually came to mind was the plan I had aborted earlier—work my way into Sarah's better graces. This would mean acting a role I wasn't sure I was capable of, and to date, hadn't been able to stomach long enough to be effective. It would put a wedge in between Rebecca and me in public, and most likely, between us in private as well. It was something I didn't want to do, even though we were taking things one day at a time. The thought of everything we had crashing down around me terrified me to my core.

I closed my eyes, and what seemed like a mere second later, there was a knocking on my door. The room was still dark, but I could see from the chink in the blinds, it was morning.

Rubbing the sleep from my eyes, I groggily stumbled to the door and opened it. Sarah stood there; face as innocent as an angel's and a smile a mile wide on her face.

"Good morning Sleepyhead!" she chirped.

I couldn't help but think that overly-cheery morning people should be gathered up *en masse* and shot, just for the sanity of people like me.

"I was wondering if you'd like to join me for breakfast, and then maybe we can talk a bit. You seem to be feeling better today, if your looks are any indication. There are a *ton* of things we need to discuss."

She was way perkier than normal, which of course, set off the alarm at the back of my brain again. But at Skylark Inn, who knew which way was up, down or sideways? Everything skewed enough off the real world that I didn't know if the mind sirens were going off in vain, or if they legitimately wailed for a reason.

"Sure Sarah, just give me about fifteen minutes to get dressed, and I'll meet you at your table in the dining room," I said, yawning the entire time.

She seemed to take this as an acceptable answer, and with a jolly wave, she wandered down the hall in the direction of the dining area. I closed the door and leaned up against it and sighed. Wasn't the old maxim: "Out of adversity comes triumph?" Who was I to complain at having to suffer a bit of inconvenience to help myself and my friends get the hell out of this place? Perhaps it would bring something better into everyone's lives, like living freely in the outside world.

With a resigned sigh, I began the process of getting ready for the morning. This would be one of those days where I wished I could get over my paralyzing fear of flying. It wasn't so much a fear of flying, but rather a fear of a sudden and fiery stop at the end of it all. Hell, when Torrent had gone on European tours, I'd made sure to book enough time to get across by boat rather than the shorter, usually around nine-hour plane flight. The only time anyone had managed to get my ass on a plane successfully was when I was doped out of my tree on Valium. Enough of that in my system and I didn't care where I went or how I got there. The dreams while I was knocked out were some of the most horrifying ones I'd ever had and outstripped any acid trips that I could recall.

There'd been reasons I'd laid off the drugs very quickly. Things tended to make my mind go bonkers, and with the strange crap my brain churned up, it was better I just stayed the hell away from it.

Taking one last look into the mirror, I closed my eyes and prayed this wouldn't be the worst morning of my life.

When I walked into the dining area, it felt like a million eyes focused on me at once. Now, this would have been normal when I stood on stage, but having pretty much everyone look at you during breakfast felt an unnerving. Something was definitely up and it genuinely made me uneasy.

I went over to Sarah's table, and as soon as I was seated, the silence that had greeted my appearance in the dining room returned to a dull buzz. Sarah remained her same cheerful and happy self as she'd been when I had answered the door earlier, holding a large mug of coffee in hand, and wearing a smile on her face. Jodi appeared from the kitchen area and stopped short, giving me a quizzical stare as she resumed her walk out of the dining area.

One of the people who worked in the kitchen prep area came out with Belgian waffles and a large mug of tea for me.

"You said you wanted to talk to me about something important, Sarah?" I asked as the server set the food and drink in front of me.

"Not so important as to disturb your breakfast. Eat! We'll talk after you're done," she replied, leaning back in her chair and watching me guardedly as I dared try the food.

I wished I had a food taster, because I didn't put it past Sarah to slip something into the food or the drink that would make me spill my guts and say things I didn't want her to know. Scenes from old movies with the sodium pentothal injections that "made you talk" ran through my head. I didn't want to think of the topics I'd likely talk about. For a reporter, I would be Pop Culture pay dirt. There were stories from the days when I was a hell of a lot wilder and lot less wise that could probably ruin careers at this point, or at least cause major embarrassment. I cut into the waffles and dutifully took a large bite, hoping she hadn't stooped to that level of trickery yet. It tasted fine, but I knew you couldn't put stock in how food tasted.

Sarah waited patiently while I worked my way through the food and downed the tea. Sitting back in her chair, she watched me like a hawk, the smile ever-present on her face. It was alarming. I wondered what things she wanted to talk about. My brain screamed to deny anything and everything about any relationship between Rebecca and me, even for my own safety.

Once I finished, I pushed the dishes away and looked directly at her.

"Well, what was so important that you wanted me to have breakfast with you?" I asked, knowing the irritation could be heard in my voice. I didn't like being strung along, and that was precisely what she was doing. It felt like sand in the proverbial swimsuit.

"I only wanted to know if you were feeling better, which I can see you definitely are. I'm so glad it was just a bit of food poisoning, rather than a virus of some sort."

I nodded and crossed my arms across my chest, waiting for her to continue.

"I wondered if you felt ready to move to the next stage. From what I can see, you've got a good grasp of the basics, and I'd definitely love to introduce you further into what we do here."

So, there it was. My chance to level up.

"Sure, what do we need to do?" I said, trying to sound eager to learn more, which took no effort. I needed to know why both Rebecca and Jodi walked on eggshells, why I had been beaten senseless, and what had been the big secret behind everything. I was also as fearful as all hell about what I would see, what I would hear ... and what I'd be forced to give up.

Sarah outlined her plan over the period, which after calculating quickly in my head, took almost two weeks, up to and including Jodi's wedding. It would involve a lot of time spent in Sarah's presence, and not a lot with Rebecca. That would be difficult to pull off without damaging the beginnings of what seemed to be something that could go either nowhere or be a long lasting and rewarding relationship. Rebecca understood I was trying to get out of here. Even though she might view it as a senseless endeavor, she still knew there would be times that charades like this would have to happen.

I nodded and tried to keep everything straight in my head. The room had pretty much emptied of people, and only a few late-risers sat there, enjoying what was left of the tea. I noticed Jodi had returned sometime during the discussion. Lunch preparations were in full swing. Jodi normally didn't do a large lunch, because about two thirds of the place seemed to be allowed out to work, but there were those who remained behind who needed to be fed.

Kyle breezed in, popping quickly into the kitchen and then over to Sarah, whispering something in her ear. She made the "in a minute" gesture before turning back to me.

"Well Jonathan, I guess I'll be seeing you at our study later tonight then?" She rose from the table and I stood as well, glad to be finally let out of purgatory.

Sarah and Kyle both stormed out of the dining area, and I saw

Jodi trying to attract my attention from the doorway of the kitchen. I waited until I saw Kyle and Sarah disappear out to the lobby, and went over to Jodi.

"What the hell were you doing?" scolded Jodi. "Sarah suddenly come to her senses and invites you for breakfast? Rumor has it she knows about you and Becca."

Her last words left a ball of ice cold fear in the pit of my stomach. The last thing we both needed was for Sarah to have found out about the two of us before "the two of us" even really got off the ground. However, it did explain the late night talking I'd overheard last night. If I wasn't just being paranoid, and they *were* talking about us, then that would imply Sarah kept it as a trump card, close to her chest, in case something happened where it would be to her advantage to use it.

All I managed to say out loud was, "Shit."

"Look, I'll keep up the white noise as long as I can. This is the first time I've seen Becca happy in over two years, so if I can help it stay that way, better for everyone. Especially her."

Jodi turned back to the kitchen, making sure no one was listening. Everyone who worked there stood quite a far bit back except for one person, who appeared to be Rebecca, but with their back to me and hair pulled up under a hairnet, I couldn't tell for sure.

"If you're up to doing some stuff, I know I could always use a hand," Jodi said, walking in. "Plus, some of the people here like having you around."

Jodi nodded in the direction of the mysterious person who I felt pretty sure was Rebecca. They turned around, and sure enough, it was her. She smiled at me.

"Now, if I leave you two together again, am I going to have to worry about food fights? No hanky-panky in the kitchen, got it?" Jodi asked, laughing despite trying to keep a serious face.

"Yes, Boss." I said, saluting her, for which I got slapped on the arm.

"You two can work on making the sandwiches. Jon, you're a quick study and I'm willing to bet you've made sandwiches before. Becca, you can help him out should he suffer a senior's moment or two."

Jodi then flew off to another part of the kitchen, yelling out orders to the less competent people. I went over to the wall where the aprons hung, all white and clean for once, and got suited up to help Rebecca.

"So, this is what you do for fun during the day when I'm not around," I teased.

"Oh, shush you." She swatted me as she continued working on the sandwiches. I watched her for a few, and mimicked the same assembly pattern.

"I swear, Jodi keeps setting us up so that we'll be alone," I said, picking up the tray of sandwiches she had arranged. I picked up mine and followed her, going into the walk-in cooler.

"Does she know something I don't?" she added.

That I'm pretty sure I'm falling in love with you? "How about that both of us don't know?" I said with a grin, handing her my tray.

Rebecca put it with the other one in there. "Well, it wouldn't be difficult to do, seeing as Jodi's marrying Kyle and she pretty much has her ear to the ground with everything around here. Honestly, though, I don't think we need excuses to be alone with each other, do we? That is *so* sixth grade."

She looked at me with a smile that dared me to tell her yes, indeed, we did need excuses to spend time with each other.

"If you think I'm going to answer with you within reach of a few different types of vegetables to throw my way, you're crazier than I am," I said with a wink.

That at least got a laugh and a tomato gently lobbed at me, which I caught with no problem. I tossed back into its bin.

"And even so, the answer is no," I said as I pushed open the door and stepped back into the suddenly too warm kitchen prep area, nearly knocking over Jodi, who came down the hall from the kitchen proper to the prep area.

"Gee, thanks, Jon." she said, the irritation evident in her voice. "Just what I needed, to be squished by someone who outweighs me."

"Sorry, Jodi! I didn't know you were there," I said as Rebecca slid out from behind me. She quickly checked Jodi over, and after only finding a few minor scrapes and a few areas that might leave bruises, pronounced Jodi fit to resume bitching and complaining at me.

Jodi smiled at that and laughed it off.

"I'm sorry, too," Jodi said. "Just getting a little steamed at all the silly requests Sarah's given me for things leading up to the wedding. As if I don't have enough on my plate managing this incompetent bunch of boobs."

A crash from the kitchen area seemed designed to prove her point. With a sigh, Jodi rolled her eyes and headed back in find out what they'd done this time. Rebecca and I waited for her to return.

Sometimes hanging around Rebecca felt awkward. I never knew

what she really expected of me. It was like being a kid all over again. Most of my past relationships had been superficial, entirely based on physical attraction rather than any lasting connection. I couldn't care less if I had had a bad day and ripped into them over whatever little thing they'd done that annoyed me; it wasn't like it was going to matter down the road.

But this. This actually meant something to me. What exactly, I didn't know. All the denial I'd been wallowing in over the past few weeks was over. Just the thought of Rebecca made me smile and ignited my heart, which was something I'd never experienced before.

On impulse, I checked my watch, as days seemed to meld into each other without much differentiation between them other than the sun rising and setting. We were now in mid-October. One more month until I got another year older, if I managed to make it that far. Forty-five years old. Rebecca couldn't be much more than 21.

"How old are you?" I blurted without thinking.

"Old enough to know better than to answer the question without asking why you're asking me!" she said with a laugh. "How old do you think I am?"

"I'd say you're about 21."

"Guess I should be flattered. I'm 23, Jon," she said with a grin. "Which means there is an almost twenty-two-years' difference between us, if that's what you're thinking about."

I swear, she could read my mind. Not that age really bothered me. Hell, Mike, Torrent's drummer, was married to someone fifteen years his junior and they got along just as well as Ryan and Heather did. Of course, this was Mike's second attempt at marriage—the first one having gone the same way as my own.

Was this relationship an attempt to prove I could still attract the younger set? I didn't like to think so. This felt different, like I didn't need to prove anything. She wasn't with me because I was Jon Walsh, rock superstar from the seventies, washed up recording artist. She liked for me, or at least I thought.

"Why are you interested in me, Becca?" I asked, leaning up against the table behind us. "I'm really kind of curious."

She leaned back against the table as well and sighed. "If you're thinking I'm with you because "Oh my God, he's a *rock star!*" then you're really mistaken. When you first came here, I was terrified of you. I mean holy shit, who would think they'd ever meet one of the people they thought were amazing when they were kids? But then you took the time to talk to me to get to know me, and I got to know you. Guess what? You're an ordinary person. Sure you live a little more extravagantly, but you're a regular everyday person like the rest of us. Your job is just not ordinary, but you yourself? You're a great guy."

I looked at her, amused. "Oh? How? I've been called an asshole for so long it's beginning to become the word I most associate with myself."

She rolled her eyes. "Tricia, by any chance? Let's see ... Assholes wouldn't have helped Jodi out; they would've tripped her, called her fatso or other names, and pushed her around like Kyle does. You're incredibly kind and you're usually smart. You've always treated me like my father taught me women should be treated. You don't act like I haven't got a brain and can't make up my own mind. You treat me with respect, and dare I say a bit of affection." She moved in closer to me. "I know I'm important to you because of how you behave. I like your sense of humor, how you actually seem interested in what I'm saying, and you take me seriously. I like the fact that I can sit down at the piano, play you a bit of a song and you can improvise with it. I like feeling I can be myself around you; I don't always have to be dressed up and smiling. I can have a bad day with my hair looking like crap, and to you, I'm still beautiful."

She leaned in and gave me a peck on the cheek. "Of course, I'm not going to deny that you're being damn hot doesn't add to it, but even if you were in a car accident tomorrow and were never good looking again, it doesn't change how I'd feel. It's what's in here—she poked me in the chest with her index finger—"that attracted me to you. And it's what keeps me thinking that if we're taking this one day at a time, let's see where today takes us."

I liked that philosophy: *If we're taking this one day at a time, let's see where today takes us.* It lifted some of the relationship pressure off both of us. If things didn't turn out, it wouldn't be anyone's fault, or it could be both of us. Either way, it acknowledged there were two of us, and we needed to make the choice as to what each day would bring.

"So," I said, casually wrapping an arm around her waist, and pulling her in next to me, "Where should today take us?"

Before she could answer, Jodi came barreling into the room at top speed.

"Jesus Murphy, you two get out of here!" cried Jodi, trying to be as quiet as possible while making sure the urgency of what she said came through clearly. "Sarah's coming through any second.

I looked around. We could exit out the back door, but what were the chances that Kyle would be there, just waiting to spring something on us? I could hear Sarah's voice as she walked through the kitchens, alternately complimenting and chastising people as she came through.

Jodi and Rebecca both panicked, and then Jodi's eyes lit on the door to the walk-in fridge. Opening it hastily, she pushed the two of us in, and shut the door tightly. The door was thick, but I could just hear the voices outside.

Sarah asked Jodi what the issue seemed to be, why she'd come running ahead of her to the prep area. Jodi said she'd wanted the place to be spotless, plus they were having a bit of trouble with the walk-in door; it was sticking. She jiggled the door knob to illustrate, and I saw there was a part inside, in case someone entered in and the door didn't function properly from the outside. I put my fingers into it so the door would appear to be jammed if Sarah tried to open it herself, which was highly likely, considering that by the tone of her voice she barely believed a word of the tripe Jodi had fed her.

And Sarah did try the door. Little did I know it would trap my fingers in a pinch of death. I inhaled sharply, trying not to cry out from the pain. Rebecca, who had been standing behind me the entire time, put her hand on my shoulder, and once Sarah had stopped trying the door, assuming it was broken, I promptly stuck my hand into a bucket of something. I wasn't sure what it was, and quite frankly, as long as it wasn't related to any bodily function, I didn't care. It was cool and my fingers felt like they'd had both coals and knives on them at the same time.

"Whatever possessed you to do that with your hand?" Rebecca whispered into my ear, standing as close as she could to prevent her voice from being heard by Sarah, who by my reckoning was less than a foot away from where we stood.

"I don't know. My brain said, 'Jam the damned thing so Sarah can't get in here.' I really wasn't putting too much thought into *what* to jam it with."

"Evidently," she said with an almost silent laugh.

She pulled my hand out of whatever it was in and examined it. Nothing was broken, no lacerations to my hand, but a few of my fingers would to be bruised for a while. Some magnificent story-telling would have to take place to explain the injuries on my hand. I tried flexing the fingers. They were a bit stiff, but that would go away as long as I tried to keep them moving.

"Well, that's going to hurt in the morning," she said quietly, bending each of the fingers herself to make sure they weren't as damaged as they could be. "But I think you'll live and still be able to play guitar."

"Good news, seeing as I kind of make my living doing that," I whispered back to her with a wry smile.

I noticed she was shivering. We'd been in the cooler now for about fifteen minutes. I couldn't hear anything outside the door, but I didn't want to leave until Jodi returned with the all-clear, lest Kyle and Sarah waited outside the door to brain either of us with a baking pan.

"Are you cold?" I whispered, asking the obvious question, but I wanted to make sure she felt it. The last thing she needed was hypothermia.

"Y-yes. I'm frigging freezing in here," she said, teeth chattering, as she rubbed her hands up and down her arms, trying to regain some warmth.

I on the other hand was still warm, though cooling off slightly from the lack of movement. Reaching out with my non-goo-encrusted hand, I pulled her close to me, trying as best I could to share what warmth I had with her, to keep her from getting too cold. She quickly wrapped her arms around me and rested her head on my chest. I leaned down, my head on hers, and wrapped my other arm around her, keeping Rebecca as close as I could, without getting my gooey hand on her. Her hair smelt of wild-flowers, like it had been dried in the sunshine. Intoxicating. She held me tighter and looked up with a smile.

"I love listening to the sound of your heartbeat," she said quietly and closed her eyes. "So calming."

I laughed quietly. It was the first time anyone had ever said anything like that to me.

"So, where should today take us? You never got to answer that question."

She lifted her head up again, still not moving from my chest. "I don't know. There isn't a hell of a lot to do around here. It's not like I can say, 'Hey, let's take in a movie.' I mean, I think I might have a few old movies on VHS, but it's not the same, is it?"

"Well, it's either that or sit around and do nothing. I mean, it's not a smart move for the two of us to be together in the courtyard right now. I'm pretty sure Sarah doesn't need any more fuel to the fire. She already suspects something; we don't need to be the red flag for that particular bull."

I felt Rebecca nod, and then the door rattled. Not letting go of Rebecca, I grabbed the handle, and was promptly yelled at by Jodi and to let go of the door. Taking her at her word, I released the handle.

The door swung open, and a bemused Jodi was standing there, taking in the sight of Rebecca and I huddled together in the cooler.

"Why didn't you two come out after Sarah and Kyle left?" Jodi asked, pulling the two of us out into the prep area.

"W-w-e wanted to know it was safe," Rebecca stammered, still holding onto me and chattering.

"Jon, what the hell happened to your hand?!" Jodi grabbed it and inspected the massive bruises. They were already turning a spectacular shade of purple-red beneath the quickly drying goop.

"I jammed the door with it," I said, cringing as she moved the fingers gingerly.

"Oh, aren't you two just perfect for each other? Not a drop of common sense between you." Jodi shook her head in dismay as she rushed around the preparation area getting things together, then disappeared into the kitchen proper.

She came back with two cups of hot cider, a small pail of ice, and a blanket. Handing us each one cup, she took my injured hand again and stuck it in the ice, then draped the blanket around us.

"You two are under orders to go back to Becca's place, sit down on the couch, keep the hell out of trouble, and try not to injure yourselves. I'll bring supper down for you, so you don't have to worry about Sarah finding out anything."

She shooed us off down the service hallway, which lead right near Rebecca's suite. We must have looked a fright, the two of us draped under one blanket, one holding the other up. She held a cup of cider in one hand and I had my hand in a small metal bucket of ice and managed to hold the bucket and a cup of cider with the other hand. I imagined we both looked frozen through and somewhat unhinged as we staggered down the hallway.

We found our way back to her room with no problem, and once she managed to open the door one handed, we almost tumbled inside.

Rebecca guided me over to the couch, and when I was seated with the bucket of ice between my knees, still with my hand in it, she took off for the kitchen. I heard the whir of a popcorn popper, and a few minutes later, she returned with a large bowl of popcorn and a VHS tape in one hand.

"Well, seeing as we're under Jodi's orders of house arrest and to stay out of trouble, I thought we could watch this." She shook the tape. "It's a Harrison Ford movie. Should be pretty neutral." She wandered over and put the tape in the VCR.

"Is there something wrong with other types of movies?" I asked, taking the bowl of popcorn from her as she sat down and threw the blanket around herself.

"Well, I didn't think you'd be up to watching a total chick-flick. Come to think of it, I'm really not up to watching a chick-flick, either," she said, making a face, and pressed play on the remote.

We settled in to watch *Indiana Jones and the Last Crusade*. I hadn't seen it in a while, not being a huge movie buff, but it kept my attention.

By the time it was over, we'd warmed up, the popcorn had been demolished, and the ice in the bucket had melted to water. The swelling in my fingers was mercifully less than it had been when we'd exited the cooler. I checked my watch, it was only mid-after-noon, and the hours stretched ahead of us. I didn't have anything that required my presence until the evening worship, which was in a few hours still, and both Rebecca and I had to be there. Afterward, Sarah wanted me to join a small group study, which involved herself, Kyle, Jodi and, a few other people who I wasn't familiar with.

Rebecca lounged on her side of the couch, and I couldn't help but think of where this was heading, once again. It seemed like she was bringing me into her life while keeping me at a distance. I couldn't blame her; I didn't want to get hurt either, but still, the most we'd done was sit and talk. There hadn't been much phys-ical contact between us, and when there had been, I usually initi-ated it. When she was in my arms, however, she seemed content to stay there, but whenever we spoke about where this relation-ship headed, she didn't see it lasting more than over the next day's horizon. Or was that my own insecurities talking? I had been so used to instant attraction, short courtship, intense passion, and a fizzling out into nothing. What was between Rebecca and me had been so gradual.

I must have been staring, because she asked what was up.

"I'm sorry, I just, well, I was just thinking. About you. About me ... about us really." I shrugged and looked away.

This at least grabbed her interest. "What about us? I thought we were taking this one day at a time." She turned to face me, surprised. "I didn't think you were after a commitment of any type right now, which you know, suits me fine."

What to say to that? Were we even together? The lack of definition of "us" was actually beginning to bother me, and it bothered me that I was bothered by it. Yes, it was a relationship, but what type of relationship? I shook my head. Normally this type of thing didn't affect me at all. Why it had suddenly creeped into my mind was beyond me, but I knew one thing—I didn't want what we had to end any time soon.

"I really don't know what to say right now. I, I just, well ... oh, I don't know," I said throwing my hands up in frustration at not being able to express what was on my mind in a coherent fashion.

Everything I wanted to say ran through my mind. I was too afraid of opening my mouth and having gibberish come out, making me look like a prize idiot.

"What, Jon? If something is bothering you, just say it. I'm a big girl; I can handle pretty much anything you can throw at me."

I sighed, and sat back. What could I say? I didn't upset the delicate balance of whatever we had.

"Okay, listen. I'm afraid of looking like a total twit while trying to push out what's running around inside my head and have it make sense. You make me feel like I'm 15 again. I don't know how you do it, and it's not really a bad thing, but you just make me feel like I'm learning everything all over. I mean, I wouldn't try anything I've ever done before on you. I don't want to lose what we've got, but I'm not sure of what we've got, and where it's going. I mean ... oh God, I'm rambling again." I shut up, running my hands over my face, feeling mortified and asinine at the same time.

When I removed my hands, I was greeted with laughter. If I'd felt like crap mere moments ago, it was rubbed in hard by how she appeared highly amused by my discomfort.

I groaned and buried my face in my hands again.

"Oh, Jon ... You are adorable when you're trying to be sincere," she said, still giggling. "You're normally so cool and collected. When you get all flustered and lost it's so cute. Here I am thinking you're going to say you want to call everything off, and it's the exact opposite. Oh my!" She snickered again.

I didn't quite know how to take that. I was still mortified and wanted to disappear into the floor.

I felt my hands being pried off my face. Rebecca knelt on the couch beside me, and looked directly into my eyes. I tried to avoid her gaze, but she reached out and moved my face back to hers.

"You are just too sweet to be true, you know that?" she said, smiling broadly.

Before I could respond to that, she kissed me. I was shocked and sat there for a moment before realizing that I should probably respond at the unexpected show of affection.

I reached up, careful to avoid using my injured hand, and brushed her hair while returning the kiss. Her lips were like velvet and still a bit salty from the popcorn earlier. It was a pleasant surprise. She pulled away to look at me again, and tried to say something, but before she could, I silenced her with a kiss, returning it with some intensity, before moving to pull her tighter to me. She tumbled forward, landing gently on me with a laugh.

"Now, where were we?" I said teasingly, then showered her neck and jaw with gentle nipping kisses, which elicited a few soft moans from her. This was definitely not what I had pictured for where things were headed today, however it was most welcome.

As Rebecca shifted her position, there was a pounding knock on the door. Rebecca lowered her head to mine and quietly swore under her breath.

"Whomever the hell decided *now* would be a good time to visit ..." she trailed off as she moved over to the side of the couch she had been on, pushing her hair back and straightening out her clothing. I sat up and we quickly tried to look like we hadn't been having a good snog, which it seemed that both of us had been greatly enjoying.

"COME IN!" she bellowed, the irritation directed at whomever still knocked on the door.

Jodi entered, bearing two plates of what most likely was our supper.

She looked back and forth between us several times quickly. It was obvious she was aware that she had not come at a good time. Rebecca's cheeks were still somewhat flushed, and she had the general disheveled look, which gave away that *something* had been interrupted. I knew I was just as reddened as Rebecca, and I was pretty sure my hair showed the signs of being tousled by hands other than my own. Neither of us breathed normally.

Jodi put down the plates on the dining room table, and again, stared at the two of us.

"I brought supper as I promised. Jon, I'll drop by after the service if that's okay with you and you can come with me to Sarah's study. Sorry if I intruded," she said uneasily.

Rebecca thanked her stiffly and walked with her to the door. There was a muted exchange I couldn't make out between the two of them, and Jodi blushed to the roots of her hair before quickly excusing herself and exiting the room.

Rebecca turned back to me, and I got up from the couch and crossed the room to her.

"If this isn't what you want, we don't have to go any further," I said, wrapping my arms around her. She leaned back against me, her head resting on my shoulder. "We don't have to do anything that you don't want to, and this relationship doesn't have to go any further if you don't want it to."

She sighed. "It's not that, Jon. I'm just a bit scared. Where do we stand? I mean, are we a couple or a brief fling? I know we're taking this a day at a time, but I'm terrified of Sarah finding out that there is something going on between us, and ..." She sighed again.

I turned her to face me. She hung her head and refused to meet my gaze, until I lifted her head up gently, so that I was able to look into her arrestingly dark eyes, which were full of fear, worry and a few other emotions I couldn't put names to at the moment.

"Rebecca. This is *not* a fling. If we were anywhere but here I'd say we were definitely an item. Hell, I'd probably have gone out and spent extravagant amounts of money to impress you by now." She laughed at that. "As we're stuck here, all I have is myself. I want to be with you, and quite frankly, if Sarah finds out, she'll have to come through me to do anything to you. Crickey, she'd have to come through Jodi and I to get to you. I care a lot about you. I don't want you to get hurt, and I want to be there for you. Nothing is going to change that. You got it?"

She nodded in response. I kissed her tenderly, then her let go. My brain screamed at me to tell her that I loved her, but I didn't want to rush to saying something I wasn't entirely sure she wanted to hear right now.

Rebecca took my hand and we walked over to take our seats on the opposite ends of the dining room table. The meal was some type of roast beef, served very thin, with assorted vegetables that I didn't recognize. It tasted delicious, and we finished it quickly. We both sat there for a while, not looking at each other or the meal, feeling a bit unsettled. Neither of us felt certain what the next steps should be, and the current situation at hand with Sarah and having to keep everything under wraps didn't help it any.

Rebecca finally broke the silence. "So ..." she said, toying with her napkin.

"So?" I responded, hoping this conversation would evolve beyond one word pleasantries.

"Well, we have about an hour before we're due to be in Sarah's presence, separately of course," she said, still toying with the napkin on the table. "What are we going to do until then?"

I chuckled, as I could think of a few things, none of them appropriate to suggest, and all of them meant jokingly. Quite honestly, I couldn't think of much to do other than to sit and talk or to sit and read, just being around each other.

"Why don't we go out in the garden? It's a beautiful evening, and it gives us a chance to be out of this place as much as we can," I suggested.

She nodded at that, and we both stood to leave. I took her hand in mine before heading out into the brisk night air. It was, as I'd thought, a beautiful night out, the sun just starting to sink below the horizon and the insects and birds singing their night song in the far-off trees. We stood there for a while, taking it all in.

I decided to stop wondering where this would take us. No matter what I could call it, I wanted this to last.

"Do you ever think we'll get out of here?" I asked, as Rebecca leaned her head on my shoulder.

"I don't know," she responded.

"If we do, will you stay with me?" I asked, turning to look down at her.

"I can't say. Why don't we cross that bridge if and when we ever get to it?"

It was amazing how things had gone from bad to good to damn good to completely ambiguous within one day.

The intervening time went too quickly and before I knew it, I headed down to the courtyard alone. Jodi met me at the stairs that lead down into the middle of the floor, and suggested I sit with her and Kyle throughout the sermon. I accepted and we moved over to the left-hand side of the place. Rebecca came in silently and meekly just before the service, and quickly moved into position behind the piano, never looking at me, Jodi, or anyone who gathered there. Rebecca stared off into space, a joyless look on her face, as if too many things wore her down.

Sarah breezed into the area with Kyle behind her, just prior to when she was supposed to start. Everyone who had been invited had arrived, and as she came near where I sat with Jodi, Sarah gave me a nod of approval as she continued along to the podium from where she usually conducted her nightly studies.

Tonight, after the opening hymn, she decided to do some prayer requests, and then opened the floor to discussion. I had no illusions this was for my sole benefit, a way of showing me how she ran this place, and that this was an "open discussion." It also served to allow her to exert her influence over the group itself without lifting a finger. I knew from Jodi that the group would rarely ever challenge Sarah's interpretations, which people had assumed were a gift from God.

I stayed silent during the discussion, I didn't need to expose the real reason that I played the intent listener to this discourse. Jodi stayed silent as well, keeping her eyes down and on her Bible the entire time. As Jodi had been the one who had informed me of the very basics of how this place worked, it wasn't a shock that she played the part of the quiet, unquestioning wife-to-be of the apparent second-in-command of this place. Having spoken with her alone and with Rebecca on any number of occasions, I knew the opposite was true. Jodi lead a double life, a very dangerous one at that.

After about an hour of unspeakably tiresome debate between the assorted groups, Sarah called the evening to an end. Rebecca played again, this time a haunting melody that echoed the darkness that surrounded us in both the sky and in the people who were there. Jodi reached out with her hand and indicated that I should stay seated as the others left. I looked up, and Rebecca slowly gathered her things together to leave. She caught my eye, and surreptitiously waved as she put her things away. I returned it as best I could without attracting the attention of Sarah, who watched my every move.

Soon enough everyone filtered out of the courtyard, leaving only a small group that included Jodi, Kyle, and myself.

"So, ladies and gentlemen, should we adjourn to my study?" Sarah said, leaning over the podium.

There were murmurs of agreement from the crowd, and we all rose slowly. Sarah found her way directly over to me, and insisted I escort her back to her study. She wrapped her arm around mine, and with a bright smile that I tried to return—by the way, I'm sure she forced hers, too—we walked down to her room as a large group. She kept on talking the entire way, but I tuned out after the first minute or two. I nodded and feigned interest in what she said, but my mind wandered to when I'd be free, and how I could work with Jodi and Rebecca on the next steps of getting out of here.

We arrived at Sarah's suite in a short time, and she finally let go of my arm to open the door. Entering into the place, she directed us to go down a hallway on the right; the study was the large room on the right at the end. We made our way there, Jodi and Kyle taking the lead, and Sarah, once again attached to my arm, bringing up the rear.

Kyle pushed open the door, and I was astonished to see the lavish study filled with dark wood and books lining the walls. A large heavy looking wood table and assorted chairs occupied center of the room.

"Take a seat. Sarah sits at the end. Jonathan, she'd like you to sit right there," he gestured to the chair to the right of the end of the table, and he sat down on the other side. Jodi took a seat beside him. I casually tossed my Bible on the table as I sat down, garnering looks from the people who were seated down from me. Apparently, that was not a good thing. Jodi coughed, and introduced me to them and them to me. There were two couples: Sasha and Martin, and Kelly and Paul. The other two that made up the group were Linda and Phil, brother and sister. My inclusion created an even number, once you included Sarah in the mix.

Sarah came in after me and took her seat at the head of the table.

With a quick glance at me that said, "Behave," Jodi took off and came back just as quickly with a tray of glasses for everyone and a pitcher of something. Sarah, as was her custom, had a glass of wine. So did Kyle. Sarah offered me some wine, but I politely declined. I felt sure that something was up, and I wanted to be as clear in my thoughts as possible. Hopefully, the niggling little itch at the back of my brain wouldn't be going off in vain, and this would be the night I'd get some answers.

Jodi took a seat, and Sarah sat back, watching everyone at the table. Sarah gave me a smile before she spoke.

"Well, ladies and gents, here we are. We have a new initiate to our group—Jon. I want you to treat Jon the way you would treat me. He's our guest here and deserves the same respect as I do. Anyone who doesn't offer him the best of care and I find out, well, there *will* be consequences and they *won't* be pretty." Sarah issued a steely glare to anyone who dared question her on that statement.

"Now, things we need to discuss," she continued. "First off, we all know that Jodi's wedding is coming up shortly. I think it's two weeks, isn't it dear? Yes, two weeks left, and you're all encouraged to go. Kyle's finally settling down with our dear Jodi. Although I wish you'd find someone else to be your maid of honour, dear, but I know that you and that simpleton have been friends for longer than I've known you, and I doubt anything could change your mind." She sighed resignedly. "But on to other things, shall we?" She pulled some papers out of a portfolio that rested on the table.

About a half hour of standard business talk followed, and I tried not to allow my eyes to glaze over. She finally finished up and put away the portfolio. The brother and sister announced that they had to leave, and Sarah bid them a brief goodbye, then watched me intently, with a look of desire.

"So, Jonathan ..." she said, reaching out and running her fingers languorously up my arm. "Will you accompany me to Jodi's wedding? I'd very much appreciate it if you did." She leered at me with her blue eyes surrounded by short, stubby blond lashes.

"Well, um, I'm going to be performing the music, Sarah, so I'll be there regardless," I said, clearing my throat and trying not to agree to anything that would bind me to her in any way.

She pouted just a bit at this evasion of her question, but seemed to interpret my response as a possibility that she would accompany me to what seemed to be the event of the year.

"Then you'll definitely need to save a dance or two for me," she said sweetly and winked. "Now, there is the matter of inductions into the faithful. We have a few coming up over the next few weeks, and we need to plan how to handle them. I hoped Jonathan would volunteer to play music for the events that aren't his own, but as he's still pretty new, I'm not sure he knows what to expect."

My brain fully set off the alarms, and shouted, "Danger, Will Robinson," flailing its hooks like the Robot in *Lost in Space*. Jodi must have noticed the shock and alarm on my face, because she gently kicked me under the table to remind me to keep it together.

"Sarah, I don't think Jon's familiar with how everything works," said Jodi. "You should teach him a bit more about how this place runs before asking him to do things like that for you. Don't want to shock the poor man into a heart attack."

Jodi had provided cover and a bit of a delay with that statement. Also, she paved a way for me to get all the facts before they moved to bring me into the fold in the truest sense, which was something I didn't want.

"Of course, Jodi. I got ahead of myself. Jon and I have a lot planned over the next week and some, and by that time he should be better able to understand what we do, so he can help us out fully."

She flashed a smile at both of us, then turned back to the rest of the group. "I think that's it for tonight, folks. Not much to discuss; however, I think we'll have more next time. Say, Thursday night?" Heads bobbed an affirmative. "Good. We'll bring Jonathan a bit further in at that time. Let us bow our heads in prayer before we go our separate ways."

We all bowed our heads, and Sarah said a prayer that rambled on forever. Once the amen was said, the group split up quickly, leaving Jodi, Kyle, Sarah and me alone in the room. Kyle was the first to stand to leave, and following his lead, I picked up my Bible and hoped to head out of the room.

"Jonathan, would you mind staying a minute?" Sarah asked, rising from her chair. With an inward sigh, I stopped my exit and turned to face her. She waited until Jodi and Kyle had left the room, and then took my arm, guiding me to the door.

"Scuttlebutt has it that you've got something going on with one of the, well, *less desirable* people within the group."

I gulped, she must have heard something about Rebecca and me, and tried to see how much I'd relinquish under pressure.

"I do hope it's nothing too serious," she continued. "I'd hate to see you throw away something worthwhile for a quick fling." She ran her hand lightly up my shirt, her fingers tracing a pattern on the cotton.

I tried to resist the urge to shudder, and simply smiled.

"Sarah, I'm not sure what you're talking about," I stepped back, to put some distance between us and to regain my personal space, which I hated to have invaded unwillingly. "I can safely tell you that there isn't anything going on with anyone *less desirable*."

Sarah sighed, displeased with the answer she'd been given. "Hm. Then I guess I'll see you tomorrow after morning study. We'll work on getting you up to speed on what goes on behind the scenes."

She let go of me. I opened the door and left. I could feel her watching me as I retreated down the hallway.

Well Jon, this is what you've wanted. Welcome to the danger zone.

CHAPTER 13

For several days nothing interesting or noteworthy happened when I was in Sarah's presence. Rebecca and I had taken to meeting on the sly; usually we'd connect around lunchtime, on my break from helping out Sarah or Kyle. Even then, it wasn't anything outstanding—usually she'd have a lunch packed and we'd eat it in one of the less frequented garden areas, enjoying a picnic and each other's company. It felt good to be a part of a couple, and we spent a lot of time just sitting and talking. We spoke about our respective childhood experiences and I mentioned things that had happened "on the outside," to which she listened with great interest, having been pretty much cut off from the rest of the world for almost two years. She talked of things she'd been working on musically, and what she had found out from being in the right place to overhear all the gossip of the day in the compound.

As Jodi's wedding rapidly approached, we had an excuse to be seen together in public without arousing anyone's suspicions that there was something going on. She walked me through the piano solos and ran through the pieces that Jodi wanted played at the wedding. It had been a few years since I'd had the opportunity to play piano for more than a brief bit. I was out of practice, and it showed. However, after a few runs through each piece, the knack came back, and according to Rebecca, I improved quickly.

If anyone had bothered to pay any attention beyond the barest of glances in our direction while we were working through the music, they would have noticed Rebecca wasn't simply giving instruction to a friend. She spent most of the time with her arms draped over my shoulders and her head resting against mine. When she sat beside me on the bench, one of my arms would be around her—definite signs of two people who were beyond friendship.

I hadn't thought much more about what we were. I'd been married long enough that the woman in my life was either my wife or my mistress—depending on the situation—and there hadn't been a lot of the later in recent years. I was glad at this point not have the former. Chris could keep her. Rebecca and I were definitely more than simple friends, but did adults use the terms boyfriend and girlfriend for each other? Even there, it didn't accurately describe us. We could be best described as "significant others." Yes, there was a romantic relationship, but it wasn't easily labeled into any particular slot. Which, with my life, was typical. Nothing ever fit neatly into the slots.

I spent most of my free time helping Jodi get everything ready for the wedding or assisting her with tasks around the kitchen areas. When I wasn't doing that, I read in one of the gardens or courtyards. Tonight had been one of those nights where I didn't have a lot to do, and I was near the end of my book. I decided, as it was a rainy day, to forgo trying to sit in the courtyard or gardens, and just relax in my own room. I had thought about going to see Rebecca; however, we'd been practicing earlier, and I figured that she'd probably had enough of seeing me for one day.

Pulling out some paper and a pen from one of the bags I'd

brought with me, I began a letter to Kristen. I had no real hopes of it getting to her while I stuck in here; Sarah would probably have someone inspecting the incoming and outgoing mail like a spy, checking everything to ensure no word about *Skylark Inn* got to the outside world. This place struck me as Waco just waiting to happen all over again, and I wanted to write as much of what I could to my daughter, in a way that wouldn't arouse too much suspicion. I also told her of the burgeoning relationship between Rebecca and me, well aware of the fact that she and Kristen were probably within a few months of each other in age. If and when I ever got out of here, and if Rebecca decided to stay with me beyond the mere miracle of escaping this place, introducing the two of them would probably be on par—pain-wise—with having Rebecca run into Tricia. Yes, it did feel a bit strange being involved with someone roughly the same age as my daughter, but she wasn't my daughter. I knew the relationship would definitely raise some eyebrows in the outside world; however, it wasn't as if I were eighty and she in her mid-twenties.

I took a seat at the desk and continued to write, outlining what had happened so far. My handwriting was horrible, as usual. Mum had always sworn I'd been destined to become a doctor. Of course, the quick signature looked completely different from the rambling stilted script that filled the pages. After years of being in the public eye, signing my name for an autograph had become second nature, and my handwriting there became fluid and almost feminine-looking. I had had very little time for writing in the last few years, and most of that I'd typed on word processors, which made my life a hundred times easier. Otherwise, all correspondence went through my management team and I'd just review the thing and sign my name to it.

I read halfway through what seemed like the tenth page when I heard a quiet knock at my door. So quiet, in fact, I didn't even pick up on it until whomever it was knocked again, a little more insistently. Having been at the inn almost a month, I could pretty well identify Sarah by the strong, confident rap she used on any door that she didn't want to bust down using someone's head.

"Just a moment," I called, finishing off the last sentence on the page, recapping the pen, and placing the written pages out of direct sight.

I got up and leisurely made my way to the door. Unlocking and tentatively opening it, I was surprised to see Rebecca standing there.

"Hi." I was more than a little shocked to see her out in the open like that. Something didn't add up.

"Hi"—she kicked restlessly at the carpet—"You going to invite me in or do you really want Sarah to see me? I mean you're not that far away from her place ..."

"Oh shit. Where are my manners? Just a little surprised to see you."

She came in rather quickly, and I closed the door behind her. "Sorry about the mess." I quickly cleaned up and turned back to find her still standing there, looking somewhat ill at ease.

"C'mon in, sit down, relax, and make yourself at home. I'm afraid I don't have the conveniences that you do. It seems that Sarah stuck me in one of the larger rooms that fateful night."

I sat down on the large couch and gestured for her to join me. "So, what do I owe the wonderful pleasure of your company tonight?"

If she could look any more uncomfortable, she managed it. "Just rather bored, and I hadn't seen you in a while. It feels kind of like you're trying to avoid me."

"Becca, we'd been practicing together in the ruddy courtyard this afternoon, and it's not like we haven't been seeing a lot of each other. We're pretty much together at least once or twice a day!"

She gave me a look that could've burned holes into ice.

"Yeah, but ... oh never mind. How about I leave then?" She got up from the couch, but then changed her mind and sat back down. "I just haven't seen you alone, out of the public eye, for about a week, and it's been a hell of a day."

Her behaviour seemed a bit off kilter. Whatever happened today obviously bothered her and she wasn't sure how to process it. I wished I'd possessed Ryan's charm and charisma with women. He could come off to most men as a stereotypical homosexual man, but he was straighter than an arrow, and had women falling off him in droves.

"Okay, tell me what's upsetting you. I don't like seeing you all rattled like this." I took her hand, trying my best to let her see that I did want to know. She turned to me with a smile and sighed deeply.

"Sarah's been riding my ass over anything and everything. You'd think I pissed in her cornflakes just by existing. Mind you, I'm pretty sure I do piss her off just by existing. If she could get rid of me with a pen stroke, she would. But she can't, so she's on a bitching rampage. The music's too slow, the music's too fast, the music's too secular, it's not this, it's not that. Then when I help Jodi out, she gets on Jodi's ass, and as if Jodi doesn't have enough on her plate with this stupid wedding coming up and dealing with that idiot Kyle to begin with. And Kyle, well, let's just not go there." She pulled down the neck of her shirt, and the dark bruises on her shoulders stood out against the paleness of her skin. I involuntarily clenched my fists and inhaled sharply.

"Yeah, so that's been my week without you. Not that your presence during anything that I've mentioned would make things any better ... I'm sure it would have probably made things a hundred million times worse. I mean, Sarah wants you. Kyle knows there's something between the two of us but he's not sure what, and it's really pissing him off. You being highly visible with me would just, oh, probably get us killed."

Rebecca sighed and leaned back into the couch, emotionally spent and physically exhausted. There were a million things I wanted to do that ran through my head, most of them involving some form of violence on Kyle and Sarah, which I knew would not aid the situation in any way. So, I did the only thing that I could think to do. I moved closer to her and wrapped my arms around her. She rested her head against me and held me in return.

"I don't know how we're going to get through this, Jon," she said quietly.

"I don't know either, Becca."

If I'd been terrified before about of what would happen, the prospect that I involved another person—who should be innocent of all the strange and evil things that happened here—frightened me even more.

"How many days left until Jodi's wedding?" I asked, as time seemed to blur one day into the next. I had lost track of the day again. I knew the wedding was soon, but at the same time it seemed to drift ahead of me far away enough so I could forget about it.

Rebecca sat up. "Four days left. We're getting into the serious crunch zone. This week is going to be hell."

I had no doubts that this week, as well as the time from here on out would be critical to many things, and to both of us.

There was a knock at the door and the insistence of it alerted me right off that it was Sarah. Why she dropped by at this time was beyond me, our meetings generally weren't until later in the day, after the evening worship. I must've tensed involuntarily, as Rebecca's eyes went wide, as she mouthed silently, "Sarah?" I nodded in response, and the knocking got louder.

"Get into the loo," I murmured into her ear, and she moved as quickly and quietly as was possible towards the washroom.

I got up and made my way to the door, making sure to shut the bathroom door on the way past so that it would seem that I had just come from the facilities.

"Be there in a moment!" I called. The knocking stopped and I could hear the impatient sigh clearly from the other side of the heavy wooden door.

I opened the door and Sarah stood there, agitated and tetchy at being kept waiting.

"Jonathan. I was beginning to think that you weren't home," she said, the irritation evident in her voice. "We've got an emergency meeting scheduled to address some serious things that have come to our attention, and it was thought that it would be a good idea to have you there."

My heart sank and my stomach did a quadruple somersault.

"Okay," I replied.

I could hear my heart hammering in my chest. She took me by the arm and yanked me down the hall without waiting for any other response. I protested that I had to lock up, and Sarah told me it didn't matter, where she'd take me was much more important. My thoughts went to Rebecca, probably still hiding out in the bathroom. I knew she could hear the exchange that had gone on and hopefully would extricate herself from there after a safe amount of time had passed.

I trailed behind Sarah like a flag in a strong wind. I could barely keep up with her pace and continually tripped and just about fell at one point. She weaved through random corridors on her way to wherever we were headed. I totally lost track of the number of corridors and twists and turns she took me down, never letting go of my arm. Finally, we arrived at another room, one that I's not seen before. She knocked on the door, and to my surprise, Jodi answered. That explained why I had no idea where I was, I'd never been down this end of the compound. Jodi gave both Sarah and I a perplexed stare, but before Jodi could say anything, Sarah pushed the door open, and barged in with me still in tow.

Kyle sat at the dining room table with several other people, most of whom were from the group that had been at the last few meetings. I looked around as much as I could while being dragged inside. Kyle and Jodi's place seemed almost as expansive as Sarah's suite. Rebecca's living quarters were the largest in the place, basically being a small home that had been added onto the main body of the hotel many years before.

Jodi and Kyle's flat was decorated much in the same way that Sarah's had been, except Jodi added her own touches. I could tell that Kyle had been the person who lived here alone before Jodi had moved in with him, because the place still had the air of a bachelor's apartment, even with the brightening of Jodi's influence.

We reached the table and I was invited to take the seat beside Sarah, which put me directly across from Kyle, with Jodi on my right.

"Okay, everyone's now here?" Sarah looked at Kyle, who nodded his head, his dark blond hair catching the light.

"Well, as the Council of Elders, I've asked you all to come here to discuss a matter of some importance. It appears that we have a heretic in our midst. It has come to my attention that one of our own has been spreading a message that is contrary to what is taught here. We have two choices in this: to de-fellowship this person and ask them to leave, or to continue on until we have further evidence and then ask them to come before us in a tribunal of sorts, where they can explain their behaviors. Either way, this is going to end in sorrow." She shook her head.

I could see no emotion on her face, not even regret or anger. It was like watching a puppet show, as if she were controlled by an external party. The expression on her face never changed, like it had been permanently painted on.

She looked back up at the others. "I am assuming you know who this is. Votes please?"

She turned to Kyle first. "Tribunal." he said gruffly.

Jodi was next "Tribunal."

And so on down the line. There were four votes for tribunal and four for de-fellowship. I abstained because, as I said to Sarah, I had no clue who it was and wasn't versed enough in their comings and goings to make a decision in this. Sarah was, of course, not pleased in her fellow elders, which made the next turn of events less shocking for most of them than it should have been.

"So, onto the problem called Rebecca Taylor."

My head and Jodi's snapped up in unison. Both of us were surprised to hear Rebecca's name. It was also the first time I heard anyone mention Rebecca's surname.

"Sarah. You have an agreement that says you'll leave her alone," said Jodi, looking alarmed. "There isn't much you can do to her besides torture her like you have been. The girl is bloody-well terrified of you and Kyle, you know that."

"Yes, Judith, I am aware of that"—the annoyance clear in her voice—"However, she has been a thorn in our side for too long and there are things that we *can* do. I'd say we have a line into her world, seeing as both you and Jon are friends with her."

That last sentence was accompanied by a very pointed look at me. I felt reasonably sure that Sarah knew something. She wouldn't tipping her hand as to what, but it seemed clear she definitely held something back.

"Sarah, what are you playing at?" I said, crossing my arms in irritation.

She smiled smugly.

"Let's not get into details. Let's just say we'll slowly smoke her out. Once we do, she will be in my hands like a rabbit out of a hole."

I shivered involuntarily. This put both Jodi and me in an awkward situation. Should we mention anything to Rebecca and risk her acting rashly and revealing she knew something was up, or did we keep silent and suffer a guilty conscious the entire time?

"Sarah, please tell me you aren't going to pull any stupid stunts before the wedding," Kyle said, just as enthused as the rest of us were about this suggestion.

Rebecca might not have been popular, but it appeared that even though she had been considered the strange girl, people generally didn't want her to come to harm, if the uncomfortable glances and shifting around in their seats were any indication.

"Kyle, do I look that damned dumb?" She nailed him with a glare that could've melted steel.

He shrugged, and leaned back in his chair, intent on studying the ceiling, since it appeared Sarah would in no way answer that question. My own hope was that she'd not cause a fuss until after the wedding, as I could only imagine the hell that Jodi would raise, even though she felt that the nuptials were as much a charade as my own to Tricia had been over twenty years before.

An unenviable silence followed that comment, then Sarah dismissed everyone, asking that we show up the day before Jodi's wedding to further discuss the issue with the first person, whose name I still didn't know. I had a feeling that it didn't bode well for them, and I wasn't looking forward to seeing the results of anything that might happen. Sarah announced that she would stay with Kyle and Jodi for a while, and I managed to escape without being dragged into anything further.

I headed back to my room. I wondered if Rebecca was there still. I checked my watch. It had been about an hour since I'd left. She probably headed to her own room; I doubted she'd have stayed at my place without anything interesting going on. I tried the door. It was still unlocked, meaning she'd left it that way when she vacated the premises, or, she was still there. I pushed it opened and noticed immediately the light was still on. Softly tiptoeing into the room, I saw Rebecca curled into a corner of the couch in the living room portion of the suite, the book *Headhunter* in her hands. She looked up from the book, and smiled when she saw me.

"Hey, what was the commotion all about?"

My stomach did a triple flip. I could edit the truth of what had been said, or I could tell her out-and-out what a portion of the meeting had been about and risk her going off half-cocked, the same way I'd wanted to whenever she mentioned whatever Kyle or Sarah had done to her. I weighed the options. One was pretty much a fib. While I might have had no compunctions about doing that in prior relationships, this one was different, and I knew straight away that lying now would have massive repercussions down the road. Of course, telling her that certain things coming down the tubes for her weren't exactly on the up and up would have long reaching repercussions as well.

I must have had quite the expression on my face as I stood there contemplating the potential outcomes in my head, because she got up and came over to me. She looked me directly in the eyes and put a hand gently on my shoulder.

"Jon, what is it? Obviously there's something on your mind and I'm willing to put money on it that it has to do with me. So, please, tell me?"

Staring into those darker-than-the-night eyes, which searched mine, looking for a hint of whatever went in my head, I knew that I couldn't lie to her. I decided that telling her the truth, the consequences be damned, would have to be the route I took. Removing her hand from my shoulder, I held it and glanced down at it. I was again reminded while I held her left hand that there really was no sign that she'd ever worn an engagement ring. Before I told her anything discussed in that meeting, there was one thing I wanted to get out of the way.

"Rebecca, I want to know something. Matthew—you mentioned before that you are engaged to him. Now you know how I feel about you, and I don't want to be strung along or have you stringing anyone along. The one thing I can promise you is honesty, and if I'm going to give you that, I expect the same in return."

She sighed deeply. "Listen, for all intents and purposes, it's over between Matt and me. I mean, we're thousands of miles apart, it's been years since I last spoke to him. As far as I'm concerned, I'm ..." She looked at me and my mind finished what I wanted her to say: *Your girl.*

"Well ... I'm in another relationship now," she said. "If I ever get out of here, I'll definitely be telling him it's over. It's going to be hard, because it's going to hurt, but it is over."

She gave me a sad smile and squeezed my hand. I took her at her word, and for once in my life had a little hope in reading between the lines. It sounded like my question, "Would she stay with me once we left this place?" had an answer. I'd have to wait and see once we did get out of here if the two of us could make it in the "real world," as relationships formed under circumstances like this tended to deflate like a flan in a cupboard once they hit the outside.

With her hand in mine, I brought her back over to the couch and we sat, facing each other. I told her first about the call for a tribunal, and she supplied the name of the person that had not been mentioned—Mary Collins. Mary had been questioning Sarah's motives and interpretations. This, as Rebecca and Jodi had both mentioned before, put her in Sarah's crosshairs. The vote for a tribunal had been a way to give Mary a chance before the axe fell.

"Jon, you don't want to be here when that comes down. Trust me. I've seen enough things here that would make your hair whiter than snow. I have nightmares, horrible nightmares, because of the things I've witnessed. If half the "elders" voted for a tribunal, then that was to give Mary time to either smarten up or die right. Another option would be if Mary could find the way out that you and I are looking for. I'm sure there has to be a way out. I mean, I haven't seen Kismet in forever."

"Kismet?" I asked, eyebrows raised.

"Kismet is the name of the cat that lives around here. Sarah keeps insisting he's mine, but he's as much a part of this place as I am. Kind of a big gray grumpy ass of a cat."

"Okay. Just keep that thing away from me. The last thing I need is to be itchy, sneezing, and have my eyes feel like the Gobi Desert."

She gave me a surprised look. "You're allergic to cats? I never knew that."

"Well, it's not exactly something I like to broadcast."

She relaxed a bit, looking off into a corner, her mind working away. "So, what else did they discuss? I get the feeling there was more than just that one issue."

I sighed. This was the part I didn't want to talk to her about. The part where I revealed that Sarah had some insidious plan to get Becca the hell out of here in one way or the other, but she hadn't revealed the details of it—yet.

"Rebecca, I can't lie to you. There is something else." I sighed again, deeply. She watched me intently. "Sarah wants to drive you out of here. I don't know how, but by God I intend to find out what the hell she's got up her sleeve when it comes to you."

Rebecca sat there for a few moments, her face not betraying whatever went on behind those dark eyes. Then she shrugged and leaned back, breaking contact with me, and pulling her feet up under her.

"Well, then there is only one thing I can do about it," she said in a matter of fact tone.

"What's that?"

"Get the hell out of here while I still can."

I wanted to ask her if she was frightened, if she really thought that she could actually make it out. Then I realized she had to have been terrified. Sure, we talked about breaking out, but it was like talking about winning the lottery or striking it rich—something you dreamed about, but that you never thought would actually happen.

We sat silently for a while. Rebecca stared into nothingness with a determined expression. I watched, waiting for her to do or say something.

After a while, she stood and faced me. "Look, it's about high time we tried to figure out how to escape. I'm sure there has to be a way out that doesn't involve leaving with a toe tag and inside body bag. We just have to find it."

"*We* have to find it?" I repeated.

"Yes, *we*. Unless you want to get out of here on your own all of a sudden?"

She headed for the door. I stood and followed, unsure of what to do next.

"I'm going to talk to Jodi. There has to be something that we can do to get the ball rolling," she said by the doorway. "Stay out of trouble, okay?"

"I'll try." I said.

She stood there for a few seconds, before pulling me in for an impulsive and passionate kiss, which surprised the hell out of me. She then left the room, and as the door swung shut, I could see her taking off down the hallway at a quick run, headed across the compound to where Jodi stayed. I hoped for Rebecca's sake that Sarah had left Kyle and Jodi's place by now. The last thing that either of us needed was closer watching by Sarah and Kyle. I worried for Rebecca but knew at the same time she could handle most things that came her way; after all, she'd managed to make it through two years living here and still be alive.

Locking the door, I wandered over to the window that overlooked the courtyard. The dais on the other end of the place was bathed in shadows as the sun set. I tried the patio door and found it sealed shut, allowing me to only look out on where I'd probably spent most of my time here, and some of the happiest moments in this place. The rain had finally stopped, and everything seemed to have that freshly washed feeling things got just after a rainstorm. It had poured for most of the day, and there were scattered puddles on the concrete of the courtyard. Rainwater that had collected dripped off the overhang, which protected the piano.

I knew I'd stood a while, thinking and taking in the sun setting in the west, where home was for me. I longed to be out of here, to be back where I knew how things worked. I also wanted to bring Rebecca with me, if she'd come along. I wasn't 100% sure that she'd stay with me, but for once in my life I felt willing to work through any problems that might crop up, rather than move on to the next new thing that caught my interest.

I must not have heard the initial knock on the door, as my attention became distracted by the door knob rattling, and a highly insistent pounding on the door. Crossing the suite as fast as I could, I opened the door.

Rebecca watched me with concern. "Didn't you hear me knock?" she asked, looking like she wanted to either cry or smack me with a frying pan, I wasn't sure which.

"No, not until you rattled the knob. I'm sorry, I was off in another world. I-I just wasn't listening for anything."

She didn't even wait for me to invite her in; she just blew right past me.

"So, I talked with Jodi. She's agreed to helping us get out, as you probably guessed. The only thing she's asked of us is that we don't try anything until after the wedding; that way, the place will be less on edge, and she says that you'll have time to find out more about what Sarah's got up her sleeve."

The entire time she spoke, Rebecca paced back and forth, her long dark hair pulled up in a ponytail that whipped around as she gestured. I closed the door and watched her as she dashed about, and felt shocked by the sudden intensity of the drive she had to leave *Skylark Inn*. After she finished speaking, she paced for a few more moments and then stopped, looking at me.

"Well, aren't you going to say something, Jon?" She tilted her head a bit to the side as she awaited a response.

"Um, okay. I'm really not sure what to say to all that. Just, well, kind of stunned."

She sported a quizzical grin. "About what?"

"I don't think I've ever seen you this animated. It's ... nice to see." I said, with a huge smile.

"Look Jon, I need to be out of here. The last thing I want is to die in this compound. I want to go home; I want to experience life again! I've ..."—she looked at me shyly—"I think I've found someone who I actually want to be with, and I'd like to see if, well, if we can make it on the outside of this place. I really want to see the sky from a different place, to do the normal things that I've been denied for the past two years, to be free again." She smiled, with warmth in her gaze.

Rebecca moved around the room again. "Jodi will be coming over to my place in about"—she checked her watch—"half an hour to discuss some things. Sarah felt a bit tired after you left and headed off to bed." She rolled her eyes to indicate what she thought of that. "I doubt it's really true, so if I were you, I'd watch out if you want to join us."

"Of course I'll join you two tonight. We're planning on finding a way out, right?"

She nodded.

"Your place?" Again, she nodded. "I'll be there with bells on, then. I promise I'll not be late. Sarah or no Sarah."

"I'll see you in a half hour," she said, attempting to project a level of confidence in her voice that she truly didn't feel. Rebecca headed out the room, and I called her name just as she reached door. She stopped and turned around.

I walked over to her and gave her a quick and tender kiss. I never knew in this place when could be the last time that either of us would see each other. She smiled and took off into the maze of hallways.

The door closed, and I headed back over to the letter I'd been working on for Kristen. Picking up the pen and sitting down at the desk, I continued where I'd left off, omitting mention of any plan—the information in the letter was damning enough. Should it fall into the wrong hands, I was assured a not-so-quick and not-so-pleasant end.

I hadn't gotten more than three cramped paragraphs that detailed my days as of late, when there was yet another knock at the door. I put everything away again. This time it was Sarah, who, as Rebecca and I had assumed hadn't been sleeping at all.

"Hi, Jonathan. Just wondering if you'd like to come with me for a stroll. There are a few things that I'd like to discuss with you." She tilted her head slightly, watching me like a bird of prey, probably just waiting for a moment of weakness to pounce and make her kill.

"Sure, Sarah. Jodi and I have a get together in a half hour that I can't really be late for, just firming up the last few details of the music for the wedding."

I locked the door behind me, and as per her usual custom, Sarah took my arm. She spoke of the things she worked on, of which she wanted to make sure I was part. When we got to what appeared to be our destination, she turned to me.

"So, can I ask for the pleasure of your company in two-days' time at Jodi's wedding? I know you're doing the music, but I'd really appreciate it if you'd accompany me to the dance afterwards," she said, tracing her way up the front of my shirt with a finger.

I had to resist the urge to shudder. The answer I knew she wanted to hear—and wouldn't stop until she got it—made me want to retch, and I couldn't bloody well tell her that I had plans for the evening without putting both the person and those plans at risk.

"Sarah, I'm going to be there. I'm really not committing to going with anyone in particular right now. But, I'll save a dance for you, okay?"

The look of anger and disappointment that flashed across her face let me know that she wasn't happy with that response. To her credit, she buried it quickly.

"Well, if that's the best I'm going to get from you, I'll have to take it," she said.

It really didn't feel like it should be two days until Jodi's wedding. It felt like the four weeks had pretty much flown by. I had known Rebecca for over a month, give or take a few days. We'd been together as a couple for a few weeks, and still managed to keep it from public view for the most part. From what I could figure, I'd been here about a month and half. This was one of the slowest moving relationships I had ever been in, and at the same time, highly fulfilling. I never would have considered a relationship with someone of her age before. If it hadn't been for this unusual place, I never would have gotten to know her for who she was. We were from two different worlds—worlds that rarely ever connected.

Rebecca had mentioned her family to me. Her father was a lawyer, I knew that, and her mother a teacher. Her sister was in a pre-med program at university, and Rebecca had been working on her own degree. Her mother's family was from Arizona, but I didn't know where her father's family was from. I had spoken about my own family: my father the anthropology professor, and my mother his administrative assistant. How we'd come over to Canada before moving to New York, and Chris' family had come over the year after. I had traveled a great deal as a child, which probably lead to my fear of planes. I'd mostly used the rail and boats these days.

Sarah watched me and spoke about what Jodi's wedding would mean. Sarah and Kyle had put a lot of time and effort into it. Kyle had finally picked someone to settle down with, and Jodi was the perfect complement to his still freewheeling ways. Jodi was, and I could not disagree, the rock in this place, a strong woman with deep beliefs and a truly caring person. Kyle had chosen Jodi out of all the women here, which duly shocked both Sarah at the time, and myself at this moment. Kyle didn't seem to be the type who would willingly romance a woman like Jodi. Evidently, he had, and they'd been engaged for about a year now. The only thing that both Sarah and Kyle wished was for Rebecca to depart the scene. Of course, they couldn't just *let* her go, as she knew (through Jodi) too much to be allowed on the outside. Sarah didn't out and out say that, but I felt clearly able to be read between the lines.

I checked my watch. It was coming up on the half hour mark. I had to find a way to get out of here. Luckily, Jodi came by at that moment, probably sent by Rebecca to ensure I showed up on time.

"You're late, you know? How am I supposed to depend on you for anything, Jon?" Jodi said, taking me away from Sarah by the arm. "Sorry, Sarah, I need to borrow him. Probably be late-late tonight before he's available again. Sorry!" she called back over her shoulder, dragging me back down the hallway, not to her own room, but in the direction of Rebecca's.

Sarah shrugged, still resentful over the answer that had been given to her earlier, and made none the happier by Jodi's well-timed arrival to take me away.

"You come at Becca's bidding?" I asked quietly as she continued to pull me down the hall.

"No, Kyle let slip Sarah's plan tonight, after ten too many glasses of wine. She wanted to get you alone tonight, and well, have her way with you. If I allowed that to happen I'd have to kill him, her, and you, then I'd have to explain the entire thing to Rebecca. This is just me saving time and your ass. The last thing I need is Rebecca being upset because the man she"—Jodi looked at me, smile on her face—"cares for was in Sarah's clutches, or dead because of it."

We arrived at Rebecca's room, and Jodi finally let go of my arm, sure of I where I was supposed to be at the right time. Jodi knocked loudly on the door, but there was no answer, so she knocked again. The second round of knocking was greeted by the door opening and Rebecca drying her hair.

"Sorry Jodi, Jon. Had a little run in with supper. Got it all over me. Had one hell of a klutzy moment. C'mon in."

We entered and Rebecca had tea set out on the table, already brewing. She walked over to the couch, still drying her hair, and sat down, indicating that she wanted me to sit beside her. Not that I wouldn't have, but for a moment I was worried it would bother Jodi. An unfounded fear it seemed, as when I sat down, and instinctively put my arm around Rebecca, Jodi automatically took the seat opposite Rebecca and smiled, saying it was good to see two of her friends so happy together.

"So ... how are we going to get out of here?" Rebecca said, leaning forward to pour everyone a cup of tea.

"Well, the front door method is right out. My noggin still hurts when I think of it," I said, taking the cup she handed to me with one hand and rubbing the spot where I had been knocked on the head during my attempt to check on my car a few weeks' back. The wound had healed, but the memory of the blow brought back the pain.

"The windows are sealed to the outside. The only ones that are generally unsealed are the ones that face into the courtyard." Jodi said. "The laundry is done in here; the cooking, as you know, done here; and the children are schooled here. There's not much opportunity to secret you out of this place."

"Then how are we going to leave?" asked Rebecca, crestfallen. "There is not much I can think of short of a catastrophe that could help ... and even then, it would probably take us down with it."

Jodi reflected while staring out the large French doors, her mind a million miles away. She eventually noticed both Rebecca and I had stopped talking. With a bittersweet smile, Jodi looked at both of us.

"Don't you two worry, we'll find a way. Just leave it to me. I know this compound really well from combing it over when I first lived here. Becca, there are probably places not even you are aware of!"

Jodi stood. "You know, I don't think I've ever seen you so happy, Becca. It's been years since you've smiled like this. I think maybe back in University. Jon, I've not known you as long as I have Becca, but when you came here, you were a broken-spirited and sorry person. Since you two have gotten together, both of you just complement each other and make the other better. It makes me glad to see people who were meant to be with each other finally end up together."

She gave us a slightly teary-eyed smile and headed out the door, saying she just needed to get something and she'd be back shortly.

Rebecca leaned back, cuddling into my side. I rested my head on hers.

"So, we still taking things one day at a time?" she asked, wrapping her free arm around my chest.

"Well, is that what you want?" I asked reaching up to take her hand in mine.

"Yeah, no pressure that way. No expectation." She lifted her head to look at me. "What do you call what we have?"

"I've thought about that. I consider you my significant other," I said. "I'm not sure the terms boyfriend and girlfriend work here."

"So, this is more than a fling, then. "

"Definitely. Much more."

She put her head back down. I wanted so much to tell her what was running through my heart and my mind and what I felt for her. This *was* so much more than a casual affair. It had the potential to be something lasting and significant. However, I just couldn't find the words. When I was around Rebecca, I lost all ability to translate thought into speech without making a total ass of myself, putting my foot into my mouth and saying something that could unintentionally cause pain. I knew she'd been hurt enough in this life already, and I didn't want to go through a reopening of past wounds that had finally healed.

I didn't want to rush things, but I also didn't want it to drag its feet, slowly crawling on to its death. I had never been this uncertain about what to do at what time in a relationship, ever. Even with the farce that ended up as my marriage to Tricia—which for me had really been an excuse to get laid on a regular basis without people throwing a benny over it, and for her, a step away from her roots to a higher-class family—I hadn't been this uncertain. Of course, by this point, Tricia and I had been well-acquainted under the sheets. With Rebecca, that aspect would come when it was right for the two of us, and I didn't want to pressure either her or myself into a situation that wasn't right. She'd let me know when things got to that point, and I was more than willing to wait. It wasn't that I didn't desire her—quite the opposite. I'd walk on broken glass, hot coals, or through jellyfish tentacles if she asked me to. Her simple presence stirred up feelings I hadn't felt for years that made my blood sing, my heart dance, and every cell in my body vibrate with a sensation that I'd never felt before.

We sat there for a while, and just "were." I held her hand in mine and noticed the contrasts between ourselves. She was light and dark—almost black hair and eyes against alabaster skin—with a beautiful countenance, which hid a hurt and abused heart. I was the ruddy golden boy— reddish blond hair, blue eyes, and a warm skin tone. She had the long fingers and slim hands so typical of pianists, which I had always admired. I, on the other hand, was completely average. The only things I had been blessed with were musical talent and height. They were what had pretty much ended my hockey career before it got started. I was four inches taller than Chris, and while I was athletic still, there was no way that I could take the hits that hockey dished out. If I could go back in time, I'd thank Anna for turning me down because she was attracted to musicians rather than burly hockey players. Her rejection had set me firmly on the path of music, much to my father's dismay, for he foresaw hockey scholarships to the northern schools, and instead I chose the life of a bard, taking the much-reviled journalism program.

To my family it was one of the lower careers, which people from families like ours didn't take to. Despite emigrating from the class-system-bound United Kingdom to the free-for-all United States, my parents still clung to "certain degrees for certain types of people" until they passed away. Mum wanted me to be better than what she'd come from, and both my education and marriage to Tricia had dismayed her.

I could still remember her sitting down with me and advising me that yes, even though hers had been a lower-class family than my father, they still derived from the relatively same social circles and shared the same interests. She had had the unenviable task of dealing with the fact that she had been a young secretary and he a young university professor, and her boss. She'd left his department when she had realized that things were progressing down the romantic path, and I knew it was a part of why they'd left the United Kingdom. I knew I still had family in Abingdon, Reading, and Oxford on Dad's side, and a few of Mum's family still were kicking around Yorkshire and in London. I hadn't seen them for years, not since Torrent's last European tour in 1980.

"Rebecca ..." I said, bringing my right hand up into her hair.

"Yeah?" she said quietly.

"Something I want to ask you."

She lifted her head. "What's that, Jon?"

I looked deeply into her eyes, and my heart soared, and I couldn't help but smile.

"*Are* you happy being with me?"

Before she could answer, there was a tap knock on the door, and Jodi came back in. She had in hand a large sheaf of paper and what appeared to be architectural drawings of some sort.

"I thought that these might help you guys out," she said, coming over to the living area.

Rebecca got up and cleared off the coffee table and both of us got down on the floor with Jodi, rolling out the documents.

"Jodi, where did you get these? My grandparents built this place, and I've never seen those!" said Rebecca with obvious interest.

"I found them while Kyle and the guys were gutting the old northern end. The drawings were in one of the rooms. I'm guessing it used to be an office of sorts. I got to them before Kyle and the guys could, and kept them. I was in an architectural sciences program at university, so these just amaze me."

I studied the drawings. They seemed to outline the place, with some obvious differences. There were two courtyards, one of which—the current one—was originally a swimming pool. The other was where the current dining area. The place was larger than it appeared from the road, and yet seemed small at the same time.

"Here is something I found out," said Jodi, tracing a route with her finger and pulling a sheet of paper out of the huge bundle of papers she'd brought with her. "Take a look. There's a hallway that isn't really there. Well, I shouldn't say that. It's there, but they didn't mark the actual one that's being used today."

She sketched out the hallway. "We'll have to check it late some night and see if it still might go out to the outside world. I haven't had the time to get to the end of it." She put down the pencil and looked at me. "Jon, are you afraid of spiders?"

I laughed. "If it's got six or more legs, it's going to get squished. I don't like them, but I'm not scared of them."

Jodi laughed. "Okay, well, that's good. This place has a few infestations of various types in the service areas. That and mice."

At the word "mice" I twitched visibly.

"What do you think Kismet was brought here, for Jon? Kismet hunts the mice," Rebecca said, unsuccessfully stifling a laugh. "You're afraid of mice and allergic to cats. Oh, that is priceless."

Even Jodi was snickering at that revelation.

"Okay, I'm afraid of mice. Terrified. Absolutely terrified of the wee things," I said, shivering.

The two of them chortled for a while, and then with a few coughs, we got back to business. It was agreed that we should get together the day after the wedding, when things had calmed down around the place, to further explore the tunnel. Jodi indicated that she had previously gotten about half way down before losing her nerve, as she had been going it alone.

"I think this might help you get out of here," she said. "Failing that I have another plan. I'm going to keep that one to myself, just in case something goes wrong, and well, I'd rather be the only one who knows about it." Jodi once again stared at the garden, lost in thought.

She then gathered up her things. "I hope I can help you two to get out of here."

Rebecca looked sadly at her friend. She reached out and took her arm. "Jodi, you're coming with us."

Jodi shook her head, and finished collecting her things. "Becca, I love you like a sister, but I won't be able to leave, no matter what. I hate to think I'm pretty much here for life, but you and Jon will be okay. One day you'll be married and have little children together."

I wasn't sure what Jodi was thinking, but marriage was nowhere near my mind. Yes, I cared for Rebecca deeply, and wanted us to be together for as long as possible, but marriage did not figure in my plans with her. Call me what you want, but marriage was something I never wanted to indulge in again. Should Rebecca come back with me to California, I would more than willingly share my life, my home, my finances, my family, such as it was, with her.

Jodi got up gave a quick hug to both of us. She said that she should get back before Kyle was suspicious of where she'd gone with such a large amount of paper. Apparently, she had told him she was working on wedding plans, the last-minute things like seating arrangements and outlining the tasks that her maid of honour—Rebecca—would do. She dashed out of Rebecca's place quickly and with her head down, and despite her attempts to hide it, I could see the tears streaming down Jodi's face.

Rebecca and I were left there in her room, sitting on the floor. She didn't move for a while, and seemed pensive. I could only begin to imagine what was going through her mind. If Jodi was correct, there was an exit people weren't aware of. If it didn't work, there was still an ace up her sleeve. I had no idea what Jodi might have held in reserve to get us out of here, but she was an intelligent woman, and knew this place like the back of her hand, or probably better.

"Rebecca, it's well past midnight. Sarah's going to want to have me for a study tomorrow. I don't want to leave, but I'd better before Sarah suspects anything more. I know she knows something, but I'd rather not give her any more reason to hit on me than she already does."

Rebecca nodded, her mind still elsewhere. She stood without thinking and saw me to the door. As I leaned down to kiss her good night, she put her hand up and looked into my eyes.

"Yes, Jon, I am happy with you," she said, answering the question I'd asked at least an hour before. She then kissed me gently and ran her hand through my hair with a brooding smile.

"Good night, Jon. See you in the courtyard tomorrow for practice okay?"

I nodded and left. When the door closed behind me, I leaned against the wall and thought it was getting harder and harder to leave her every night. She had become a part of me in ways that no one ever had been. I wanted to protect her, I wanted to be with her every waking moment that I could. What was this? I never had felt this way about anyone. Not anyone ever that I could recall in my life. It wasn't anything that I could put a name to. I wished that I could call Ryan; he was my counsel in things like this. If someone I was dating didn't get the nod from Ryan and Heather, it usually wasn't something that would last too long.

It had unfolded that way since the beginning of the time I'd known Ryan, pre-Heather in his life. Ryan hadn't gotten along with Tricia; they'd fought like cats and dogs. Mike hadn't gotten along with her either. The only one who did get along with my ex-wife was her current husband, which wasn't any type of shock. It didn't take hitting me with a plank over the head to drive home that there was more than just friendship between them. My own indiscretions aside, the night that I had come home from a tour unannounced, the last date having been canceled due to extreme weather in Florida, I had happened to come upon my then wife and Chris in a romantic tryst in Tricia's and my house at the time.

It gave me the actual physical proof that I needed to get the process of separation, divorce, and annulment through the church. That very night I'd moved out and began to search for a place of my own. The next day I'd called my lawyer and initiated the process that would end my marriage.

I stood up from the wall and headed back to my own room. I passed several people on the route back, and each one nodded and smiled. It was nice in some ways here—no one really knew who I was aside from Rebecca and Jodi—and it was a refreshing change to know I was appreciated for just being myself, not the dollar signs that flashed in people's eyes whenever they heard "recording artist." It was great to just be plain Jonathan Walsh again.

When I got back to my room, there were no surprises such as Sarah or Kyle waiting to question me there. I sat and finished of the tale of *Headhunter*, then took a relaxing shower before climbing into bed for the night. I fell asleep quickly, and my dreams were peaceful for the most part. Rebecca was in them, we were somewhere I didn't recognize, but we were happy and together. I wasn't sure if it was an omen or a random bit of flotsam that my brain churned up, but it was a good dream—something that hadn't happened for ages.

Little did I know what the next day would bring.

CHAPTER 14

*I*n the morning, I awakened to the sound of insistent knocking on my door. I checked my watch; it was 7 a.m. and I was late for Sarah's study. With a curse and a groan, I pulled my still half-asleep body out of bed and stumbled towards the door, pulling on the t-shirt I normally slept in as I fumbled about, tripped, and just about fell over things that had been left on the floor. I cursed everything and its existence at this point. I hated mornings. I'd never been a morning person and being woken up from a peaceful sleep added to my annoyance.

I flung open the door with a half-awake and extremely grouchy: "WHAT???"

Only to come face to face with Rebecca, who blinked wildly for a moment and then stepped back.

"Woah. Mister Cranky Pants," she said, taken aback by the snarling beast at the door.

"Sorry, Becca. Didn't know it was you." I said, running a hand through my hair, which felt like it was sticking in twenty different directions at once. "C'mon in."

The room was still dark, and once again I tripped and stumbled across the place, heading for the blinds, which I opened part way to let some light in. Rebecca took a seat, neatly moving aside my shoes, which were wherever I'd kicked them off last night.

"So, what brings you here this early?" I said, yawning and trying to flatten my hair into some semblance of normality. I must have looked like the result of someone attaching jump leads to my mane overnight.

"Just wanted to say good morning and let you know that Jodi ran interference for you again. Told Sarah that you'd been up most of the night helping her, and to just let you be for a while."

"You didn't have to come all the way here to do that. I'd have met you in the courtyard at ten." I said, yawning again and collapsing onto the couch.

I looked at her from the angle where I'd landed on the couch. Goddamn she was beautiful. She was also a morning person. Not an irritatingly happy morning person, but one of those people who still drove me mad. Should this go any further, I'd have to either work on being less of a crank in the morning or she'd have to try being less of a chipper, cheery soul.

"Well, I felt like it. I like being around you, even when you're grumpier than hell," she said with a smile, getting up and coming over to me. "You look like someone just shocked you with a couple of hundred volts."

"I know. My hair has a mind of its own today. Now you know why I kept it cut short."

She made what probably was a vain attempt to make my hair go one way or the other. "Well I like it longer. You look handsome with it this length. I just never knew you had wavy hair."

I couldn't help but smile. Leave it to her to see the bright side of a hair disaster.

"So, what's up for today?" I asked, taking her hand, and pulling her down onto the couch beside me.

She settled into my side and looked thoughtfully out the window at the clear blue sky.

"Well, we have to practice for Jodi's wedding, and we need to do it in the order that we're going to play it for the service the day after tomorrow. Then Jodi said Kyle wants you to help out with painting for a while, probably until supper time and after, and tonight is the rehearsal dinner, and well ... after that we could, I don't know ... go for a walk or something. Sarah's pretty wound up with the plans for the wedding, and the only other thing on her mind is getting you in a compromising position, so she's not likely to be wandering around my end of the place tonight, or tomorrow."

"Okay, give me a few minutes to get this mop of mine under control and get dressed in something that is suitable for public. I'll meet you in the courtyard," I said, and she stood with a nod.

"See you there in fifteen minutes." She bent down to give me a kiss and with a smile and a wave over her shoulder, she headed out the door and down the hall in the direction of the courtyard.

My brain argued with me as I went through the motions of getting dressed and ready for the day. *Jesus, Jon ... Why don't you just tell her how you feel? This is love, damn it, and you're throwing it away because you're scared to lose it entirely. She probably feels the same way for you that you do for her, so what the fuck are you waiting for?*

How could this be love if I never knew what that really was? Was I expecting some type of Hallmark card sappy shit as love? *Prob-*

ably, I concluded, as I stepped out of the shower and stared at my reflection. Someone I barely recognized looked back at me, and it occurred to me that I'd not gazed in a mirror for about three weeks. I appeared happy for once and the bitterness that had been there for as long as I could recall, making me look older than what I truly was, had disappeared. I looked healthy and about ten years younger than when I'd come into this place. My hair was remarkably darker than it had been when I'd come here, probably from being out of the sun for most of the time, bordering more on the reddish end of strawberry blond and the piercing steel blue eyes that watched me shocked even myself. I doubted that most people I knew could easily recognize me.

Getting dressed quickly, I headed out to the courtyard, hair still damp, and a smile on my face. If this really was love, I didn't want it to end. When I arrived, I saw Rebecca had already set up for the two of us—guitar for me at the ready—and she warmed up with scales on the piano as I came up the stairs onto the dais.

"You're late," she said in a singsong voice, continuing her routine on the piano.

"I am not," I said back in the same singsong voice that she used with me.

"You're five minutes late, Jon," she continued playing, never missing a beat.

"And you have no sense of time then. I've only been fifteen minutes!" I said, pointing out the time on my watch.

Rebecca looked at my watch and back at her own. Hers showed that indeed, I was five minutes late. By mine, I was right on schedule.

"Oh well, never mind," she said. "Let's start with the music for before the processional, when everyone's being seated."

She dug through the large amount of sheet music she had on the piano, coming up with a neatly written list of songs in Jodi's precise hand. Without much comment, I picked up the guitar and counted the time for the song, and we began the rehearsal. There wasn't any use in arguing with her. She seemed worse than me for not admitting when she was wrong and stubborn as all hell. As much as I cared for her, it was times like that, which had been mercifully few and far between, that irritated me.

Did I want to end the relationship over them? No. I was no picnic to deal with myself. We all had our faults and today was one of those days where some of hers grated on my nerves. Having been woken from a sound sleep after a late night didn't help matters any.

We finished the first set of songs, a classical set, and moved into the processional. Rebecca made sure I knew the signal to change from the preview music to the processional, and we went over it several times, to the point I actually had to put down the guitar and say something.

"Becca, I'm not senile yet. I'm only forty-four. I can still remember when to change music without having it drilled into my head."

She hung her head a bit and flushed red with embarrassment.

"Sorry I'm so uptight about this, Jon. I just don't want to fuck up and give Sarah any more reason to come down hard on me. It's been hell around her lately, and I ... well ... I guess that I've been taking it out on you. Again, I'm sorry."

She resumed playing, her cheeks still scarlet and her eyes watering. I didn't mean to be so fractious with her over it. Everyone's nerves were on edge and tempers were raw. No one wanted to mess up and have Sarah ream into them over it.

As we practiced, I noticed Sarah and Kyle walking about and

talking as they wandered. In a show of brotherly affection, he grabbed Sarah and turned her upside down. She was screaming and pounding on his back to put her down and yet laughing like a fool the entire time. I was duly shocked. In the time that I'd been there, I'd never seen the two of them acting like a normal brother and sister. He eventually put her down, and she proceeded to return the favor to him by pulling his shirt up over his head and then taking off, a gale of laughter following her down the hallway.

I didn't know when I'd stopped playing, however a polite cough from Rebecca brought my attention back to the present.

"You'd think you've never seen two people act like morons before, Jon," she said, resting her hands on the keys and looking at me with an odd expression.

"I've never seen *those two* behave like that. They're always so stuffy when I'm around. Just shocked me, that's all." I said, turning over my brain the revelation that Sarah might actually be a human being. Could it be that despite all evidence to the contrary, she did have a heart?

"Don't let that deceive you, Jon; she's only that way towards certain people. Now, can we get back to practicing?" The annoyance in her voice was apparent, even to me.

I was taken aback by it. If Rebecca were Chris, I'd be bracing for a diva moment which would be well in progress by now. Instead she simply sighed and began to play the piano prelude of the song that was the last guitar and piano duet before the processional. We walked through it, and when we finished, she stood and took the guitar from me.

"Okay, your turn, Jon. Let's see if all this practicing has paid off." She stood back, and I played the processional—*Jesu, Joy of Man's Desiring*. Rebecca stood there, her eyes closed and a smile on her face. From being irritable a few moments before, she now appeared simply angelic—calm and transported from where she was. The look was familiar to me. I had watched Ryan, Kristen, Mike, and even Chris be lifted by music. In the short amount of time I had seen Kristen grow up, we had spent a lot of it together in the studio I'd had in the basement area of the old house in Los Angeles. She was a wordsmith, which came from my father. I had inherited the gift of music from Mum's side of the family. My mother had hidden it well, but she was quite musical and enjoyed singing, mostly in church, but was known to launch into song while doing the most mundane things around the house.

I finished off the song, which was one of the more beautiful Bach pieces I'd learned to play when I was a child, and Rebecca returned to earth with a smile.

"That was beautifully done, Jon. Thank you."

She put a hand on my shoulder and squeezed gently. I moved into the hymns that Jodi had chosen, beautiful and sweet—perfect for a wedding. Rebecca sat down on the stairs in front of the piano, watching and listening. Jodi had asked for me to do a vocal solo, and before I launched into it, I noticed Rebecca tense physically. I looked up and saw Sarah standing there, watching the proceedings from the edge of the courtyard. I refused to let her presence take me away from what I was supposed to be doing, and with my eyes firmly fixed on the words and music in front of me, I sang through the song, and finished up with a flourish.

Applause echoed down the courtyard, and it came from Sarah, who had a genuine smile on her face and clapped earnestly.

"Jonathan, that was beautiful. Truly beautiful," Sarah said, making her way across the courtyard. Rebecca tensed visibly with each step forward. I tried to keep in mind the display I'd seen with Kyle a bit earlier, but Sarah still gave me that unsettling tingling feeling in the back of my brain.

"Will you be joining us for the rehearsal dinner tonight?" Sarah asked, walking right past Rebecca without even a second glance —her blue eyes locked on me.

I nodded.

"Good," she said. "Maybe you can provide some incidental music for us. You're wonderfully talented."

I ducked my head and blushed a bit at that. It still amazed me when I was complemented on my playing, especially on the piano, as it had never been my strongest instrument.

*S*arah came over and put a hand on my shoulder, a sincere, or what I thought to be sincere smile on her face.

"Well, I guess I'll see you there, then," she said. "Have a good afternoon." She leaned in and gave me a peck on the cheek and then took off out of the courtyard, giving me a sultry glance over her shoulder as she left.

Rebecca watched her as she left, and gave me a look that would melt steel.

"What?" I asked, picking up the guitar from her hands. "Becca, you know that there is no interest on my part with Sarah. I'm just playing along."

She shrugged. "Playing quite well I'd say."

Those simple words made sure that I knew she wasn't thrilled with the entire thing, and if I judged correctly, there rang a note of jealousy in there as well. This told me that the casual attitude she had towards the two of us lately was more of a ruse than my own. I couldn't help but smile at this. Neither of us wanted to be hurt if the other didn't feel the same way.

We finished up the practice, and not a word was said with regards to Rebecca's reaction to Sarah. She took the guitar from me and put it back into the storage area. The place was beginning to fill with people, talking and looking for food. I saw Kyle enter and with a brief wave and a smile over my shoulder, I headed off to meet him before he came to meet me.

The rest of the afternoon was spent knocking down walls in another part of the compound, and it kept me busy, providing some much-needed exercise as well. By the time supper floated around, I was tired, sweaty, and just wanted a shower, a quick bite to eat, and to relax for the rest of the night. The first on the list of things to do, the shower could be taken care of easily enough.

Kyle dismissed everyone, and I made a beeline for my suite, where twenty minutes under a blisteringly hot shower relaxed the knots in my muscles and allowed my head to clear before heading into the dining area. I knew as well as anyone that Sarah would be sitting there waiting for me to enter and, not content without being the center of attention, once I'd gotten into the place, she'd loudly call for me to join her, Kyle and Jodi at their table.

Stepping out of the shower and wrapping a towel around myself, I looked for something appropriate to wear. Tonight was the wedding rehearsal and dinner. This made going into the dining area even more of a danger zone. I thought to myself that I'd love to bring Rebecca with me rather than sitting separately, trying to pretend like there was nothing going on between the two of us. However, it was not to be. Other things had been ordained for the two of us, and they did not include being in public together at this event.

Getting dressed quickly and fixing my hair—a mass of curls that had grown to "complete pain in the ass" length—into some semblance of neat and tidy, I headed down to the dining area. The room had been transformed and was incredible to see. The lights were dimmed, and each table had its own floral centerpiece with candles providing a flickering glow that encouraged intimacy. Inwardly, I groaned. This would have been perfect for a *tête-a-tête* with Rebecca, but I knew I wouldn't be seated with her. I turned just in time to see Kyle, Jodi, and Sarah coming up the hallway towards me, with Rebecca trailing far behind.

Sarah was all smiles, and as usual, was styled impeccably, wearing in a black dress that hugged every curve of her body and made her tanned skin glow. She took my arm, and with the usual greetings and meaningless conversation she never seemed to stop spouting, we turned and met the bride and groom to be. Kyle actually appeared suitably dressed in a light grey shirt and pants. Jodi wore a white dress. Daniel stood beside Kyle, trying to look as respectable as he could, and Rebecca stood off to Jodi's side, wearing a beautiful dark green dress, her hair pulled away from her face. Rebecca refused to meet my gaze, instead looking away down the hall in the opposite direction. With a few comments, we headed to the courtyard, where chairs had been set up for the next day's celebration. The other two portions of the wedding party—a girl that Sarah identified as Marisa, and James, another guy from Kyle's work crew—joined us in the courtyard. There was a judge there, and a few of the random enforcer types that milled around the compound, trying not to be obvious as to why they were there.

I took my seat at the piano and played during the step-by-step rehearsal. Rebecca stood up half way through the ceremony and joined me at the piano, and I picked up the guitar that had been placed there. It wasn't the usual one that I was used to playing; it was a dark, almost black acoustic, and we went through the duet we'd planned. Thankful for small miracles, the guitar was tuned, and we played the piece which Rebecca had composed, based off the processional, with ease. Then the judge went through the final steps of the ceremony, Sarah stood and gave her benediction on the service, and I played the processional, which ended both the wedding and this rehearsal. The judge confirmed a few times, and when he said the date, I realized that the day following would be my forty-fifth birthday. He shook hands with everyone and then left, accompanied by two of the guards, under the guise of showing him to the door through the maze of hallways.

Joining up with the group as they headed to the dining area, but hanging back so that I could be with Rebecca, we all walked, most of them talking: Sarah and Kyle together, brother and sister; Jodi with the other girl and Daniel, who was her boyfriend; and James, who had taken off with the other gorillas to ensure the visitor from the outside didn't get into business that he shouldn't.

Rebecca and I stayed far away, yet close enough so we wouldn't attract attention and could chat at the same time.

"So, how are you doing?" I asked quietly, watching her.

"I could be better, could be worse," she said noncommittally, toying with a bracelet on her arm.

"Playing hard to get?" I asked, smiling. I caught the faintest glimpse of a grin, but her face went serious again just as quickly.

"No, but we just don't need Sarah coming after us, especially since she's interested in you," she whispered, looking up at me. Then her smile grew. "I do like the hair though, Jon."

I turned away, blushing. We came to the dining room, and as I'd pretty much predicted, Sarah flew up to me, took me by the arm, and dragged me off to their table, leaving Rebecca to sit with Marisa and the others.

Dinner was served by the kitchen crew, bedecked in suits and dresses, a change from the grungy free-for-all they normally wore around the place.

We ate in mostly silence, save the rare and festive speech by someone in the group. When the dishes were finally removed from the tables, Sarah stood and advised everyone to get some sleep, as the day would come early and be long tomorrow, and she reminded us that all things had to be completed by the time the sun went down on Friday. People got up to leave, but Sarah asked me to stay. Going against my better judgment, I turned to say I would, and Sarah grabbed me by the shirt front and pulled me down into a kiss. I tried to get away from her, but her grip was almost super-humanly strong, and short of pushing her off me, I couldn't easily escape her grasp.

When I became free again, I saw the familiar dark eyes of Rebecca, narrowed in anger. I made eye contact, she glared once more, and began to walk away.

"Chose who you're going to stand with or don't make a stand at all." Jodi's words echoed in my head. This was going to be that moment, the one where I'd either have to stand or fall, make a choice for good or evil. Sarah or Rebecca, a woman who was interested in me as another notch on a headboard, or a woman I could see spending the rest of my life with. One road was the easy path, the other would lead me through hell. All that said, the choice was easy.

Pushing Sarah away, I tore off down the hallway that Rebecca had entered, aware I'd just made my choice, and knowing full well it damned me. I could feel the fires of Sarah's anger burning on my back as I raced away from her, and felt alive for the first time in my life.

I finally caught up with Rebecca near to her room.

"Rebecca ... will you please wait up?" I panted as I caught up with her.

She stopped, turned, and scowled at me, arms folded across her chest. The expression on her face dared me to take her on in a war of words.

"What?" she snapped, a foot tapping as she waited for me to catch my breath after the sprint I'd made to catch up with her.

Just tell her, you stupid old fool. "I ... I ..."

"WHAT?" She barked, dark eyes flashing and a rosy pink flush on her cheeks.

"Damn you're beautiful when you're angry."

And that wasn't it ...

She slapped me hard across the face. Pivoting on her heel, Rebecca marched back down the hallway to her room.

Hand on my face, feeling the sting of the slap, I took off after her again.

"Rebecca, Becca, please ... wait! That's not what I wanted to say."

She looked over one shoulder and kept walking. "I think we're past talking, Jon."

I caught up with her and kept stride with her.

"You are most definitely the most headstrong, stubborn ..." She turned around, ready to slap me again. I grasped her wrist gently. "Feisty, sweet, kind, caring, and gorgeous woman I have ever met."

"If you think that's going to soften me up, you're highly mistaken."

She ripped her arm away from me and tried to open her door. In her anger, she had a hard time getting her keys and fitting them into the lock, which bought me some time.

"Becca ... Sarah means nothing to me."

Rebecca managed to get the key in the lock.

"That sure didn't look like a nothing to me." She opened the door, and went inside. "Goodbye, Jon."

"Becca, no!" I cried, walking over to the door, which slammed in my face. "I ..."

Just bloody well say it.

"I love you," I said quietly.

Turning around, I slammed my palm into the wall with frustration and cursed myself for being such an ass. Then I headed back down the hall, half-heartedly hoping she'd heard what I had to say, and would come running after me—but knew it wasn't likely.

Around the corner towards my room, I came face to face with Sarah, who immediately lectured me over what I'd done. I let her go on for a few minutes and just closed the door in her face. I didn't need to be told what I'd done wrong. My life seemed to be one big mistake. From joining Torrent to marrying Tricia, and everything on down the line—lousy husband, lousy father, lousy musician. A disappointment to my family, friends, and to myself. I couldn't even tell the woman I cared for more than life itself right now that I loved her, without inserting my foot in my mouth and swallowing hard.

Part of me wished I hadn't given up smoking years before. The urge to light up and sit in the dark with a beer, wallowing in my own stupidity, was overwhelming. Hell, I'd even mostly stopped drinking over the years. Tonight, I would remedy that. Leaving my room and heading down to the dining area, I grabbed one of the bottles that Sarah set aside for herself every day, and uncorked it. I came across one of the guys from Kyle's work crew out back of the dining area, indulging in a contraband cigarette. Bumming one and a light, I inhaled deeply and thanked him, heading off to the one place I knew of where I really could enjoy getting pissed—the courtyard. I sat down on the stairs, smoking, and drinking back the wine in large gulps, quickly getting leathered.

The door behind me opened and I heard a familiar voice.

"Thought I'd find you here."

I turned around; there was Rebecca. I could just imagine what I must've looked like, cigarette in one hand and three quarters of an empty bottle of wine in the other.

"Hey," I managed and took another large swig of wine.

"Jon, you're drunk," she said in a tone that booked no debate.

"No, I'm fucking blitzed. I passed totally pissed about oh ... twenty minutes ago."

I finished off the cigarette, then flicked it off into the darkness, exhaling the last of the smoke.

She still stood there, mouth agape.

"What?! Never seen someone totally fucking pissed before?" I asked with no shortage of sarcasm. "Or never seen a man make total fucking jackass of himself for you before?"

"Jon, I'm not talking to you when you're like this. Find me when you've sobered up."

She went away, out the door and down the corridor. I saw her shake her head in disbelief a few times before she disappeared down the hall. Now I never wanted to be sober again.

I stood up unsteadily, and decided to go back for another bottle of wine. If I was going to get drunk, might as well get completely out of it—the only way to erase the stupid from my memory. I staggered down the hall, a little amazed at what one bottle of wine could do. My tolerance level had dropped over the time I'd stopped drinking. I made it to the dining area again, only to be confronted with Jodi while I opened another bottle.

"Jon, you don't want that. Trust me," she said, trying to take it from me.

"Sod off," I said, reefing it back and taking a defiant swig in front of her.

"Fine!" Jodi raised her hands in surrender and backed away. "You can bet your ass I'm going to be the one who'll be stuck looking after your puking ass tomorrow, too."

"Whatever," I said, rolling my eyes as I left and headed down the hallway to my room. It seemed everywhere there was someone who wanted to lecture me about something.

When I got both halfway back and halfway through the second bottle, I ran into Sarah.

"Jesus fucking Christ!" I cried. "What the ruddy fuck do you want?"

"Jon, you're drunk," she said with disgust.

"And you're a whore, but at least tomorrow *I'll* be sober," I quipped, finishing off the bottle, throwing it on the floor, and reveling in the cracking of glass against the wood.

This prompted Sarah to ream into me about being drunk in public. In what I hoped was the middle of her speech, I felt a familiar stomach churning that meant puking was imminent. Sarah, ignoring my protests and insisting she could yell at me through a closed door just as well, held onto me. As she finished up a sentence, the wine and everything I'd eaten that night made a spectacular return, all over her. It was amazing and disgusting all at once. It was also the last thing I remembered before the world went dark.

~

*M*orning came. It felt like I had hosted the semi-finals of the Elephant Clogging World Championships on my forehead while my throat transformed into the Gobi Desert. I cracked one eye open, and immediately shut it from the onslaught of light.

I heard a voice, more of yell, saying, "The drunken asshole is awake."

Footsteps from at least two people moved around me, I felt a cold cloth on my head, and someone lifted my head off whatever surface it rested on to offer me water, which I gulped great fully.

"Thank you," I croaked, trying to roll over. The world spun, and I rolled back the way I was with a groan. Slowly I realized I lay on my bathroom floor in the recovery position. Someone had dimmed the super-bright lights, which seared into my eyes through my eyelids, and with some effort, I sat up on the floor with my back against the wall.

As my eyes adjusted to the lighting, I realized Rebecca sat on the floor across from me, cool cloth in hand, and a concerned expression. The other person in the room was Jodi, who stood back, glaring at me with the "I knew I was going to have this job" look on her face.

"Oh Jesus," I swore, and buried my face in my hands. "What the hell happened last night?"

"Before or after your stunning display of digestive pyrotechnics?" asked Rebecca.

"Oh God. That really happened."

"Oh yeah!" Jodi commented loudly from the hallway.

"Yup," said Rebecca. "Jodi brought you back here. She says you stopped vomiting around six in the morning, but didn't stop being an asshole until you passed out again."

I opened my fingers to glance at Jodi, who had the same look on her face as five minutes ago. "I am so sorry."

"Jodi called me to come keep an eye on you, seeing as she seems to think that some of your half-drunk ramblings were about me," said Rebecca. "Personally, I couldn't understand a word you said. When you get blitzed, your accent becomes indecipherable."

I groaned again, this time from embarrassment. I didn't want to think what I'd gone on about. According to the guys, I was a rambler of many things, mostly embarrassing little tidbits I should probably keep to myself and the outlines of a country song—or three.

Rebecca asked Jodi to leave for a few, and that if I got out of control, she'd call for her.

As the door clicked shut, I winced.

"Jonathan."

Oh no, she's pulling out the full first name ... never good.

"I'm not going to lecture you about being drunk. Hell, I'd like to applaud the fact that you managed to coat Sarah while she preached to you," she added, with a wry smile and laugh. "You're paying for last night now, and I know that. And boy-howdy, are you ever an asshole when you get drunk."

She switched positions and continued.

"I just wanted to let you know I did hear what you said last night."

I removed my hands from my face.

"And ..."

"And? You tell me this and then run off and totally get shit faced? What am I supposed to say?"

I sat up straighter on the floor, rubbed my eyes, which were burning like coals, and composed myself as best as I could, considering the situation at hand.

"I want you to know that wasn't how I normally am," I said. "I haven't gotten drunk in ages, and *that* drunk, well, I think I wasn't legally able to drink the last time I was that out of it. Also I gave up smoking years ago. I used to think it made my voice sexier, but it didn't."

She nodded, and I continued.

"I still mean what I said last night, though. I love you." I reached out and took her hand. "You are the most gorgeous, brilliant, loving woman I have ever met, and you make me feel like I haven't ... ever ... felt before."

Rebecca smiled and blushed. "Well, it's not every day I have someone repeatedly make a total ass of himself for me."

I laughed. "I'd make an ass out of myself every day for you, if you asked."

She looked down and grinned.

"I'll tell you what. Get yourself cleaned up, because you smell disgusting and you definitely need to brush your teeth." She waved her hand in front of her nose.

I had no doubt as to how gamey my breath was.

"Once you're cleaned up, meet me at my room," Rebecca added. "We'll talk."

She got up and left. I heard her and Jodi discussing something in hushed tones, and then two sets of footsteps receded into the distance. Standing up slowly and carefully, I stripped and wandered out into the main area of my room. Jodi had nicely left some ibuprofen and a bottle of cola there for me, which I gulped. I threw my soiled clothes in a pile and brushed my teeth. Taking a cool shower to wake myself up fully, I hummed quietly under my breath as I got ready. I made sure to look the best I could, considering I was still bleary-eyed and quite hung over.

With a bit of a spring in my step, about an hour later, I left my room and headed towards the unknown.

I arrived at Rebecca's door without being accosted by Sarah. Something told me that after throwing up everything I had on her the night before, it would be a while before Sarah was able to face me again.

I knocked and almost instantly was greeted by Rebecca, who looked more breathtaking than she had in the entire time I'd known her—from the first moment I'd met her to right before that second. She wore the bridesmaid's gown Jodi had created for her, and had her hair pulled back, with beautiful flowers laced throughout it.

"Hi," she said.

"Hello," I said returning the smile.

Before I could say another word, she reached up and pulled me into a passionate embrace.

Damn ... still got it, I thought as I felt her hands run through my hair. My hands found her waist. She stepped back, not breaking the embrace, and I followed, kicking the door shut behind us.

When we finally separated, what seemed like an eternity later, Rebecca lead me over to the couch and sat down.

"Before this goes any further, we need to talk." she said, reaching for a glass on the table.

"Okay."

"When did this happen?"

"When did what happen?"

"You and me."

I shrugged. "I don't know. I'm kind of glad it did though." I smiled and the smile was reflected back to me.

"Me too," she said.

Rebecca leaned up against me and laid her head against my chest, and I knew my heart was hammering. All I could think was, *What the flying fuck has come over me?* Rebecca in this proximity made me almost shake in my shoes. It was like being a ruddy frigging teenager again, terrified of girls and the mystery they were. Not that women were really much of a mystery—far from it. I'd been married, and hell, there were a few other women who I'd known intimately before and, I was ashamed to admit, during my marriage. But none of them had been quite like Rebecca. There was something about her, which told me this wouldn't be a one-night stand. If I was going to go all the way here, this would be something lasting.

"What are you thinking, Jon?"

I sighed. Quite a few things beyond what the flying fuck am I doing were running through my head. I lifted her head off my chest, gently.

"Becca, are you sure this is something you want to do? I mean I'm twice your age. You're young; you should be out there with someone your own age, hell, with a bunch of them. Not with a washed up old rocker who doesn't deserve someone as beautiful and brilliant as you are."

She squinted at me, as if trying to figure me out.

"Jon. I'm an adult. I know what I'm doing. This is a choice I'm making for myself. I really don't care how old or how young you are. I've never felt the way I do when I'm with you. I never even felt this way about Matthew; quite frankly, I was with him was mostly to make my parents happy. I loved him, but I don't think I ever was *in* love with him. That's part of what I wanted to talk to you about."

She moved back over to her own side of the couch again, taking my hand and I turned to face her.

"If, I mean, when we ever get out of here, are you still going to want to be around me? Am I just going to be another notch on your headboard or is this something that you're serious about? If it's the former, I'm not interested. You're a great guy, sexier than hell, and a person I'm willing to remain friends with if—"

I cut her off with a kiss.

"Rebecca Taylor, I would willingly die for you. I don't go getting all melancholy and pissed over someone who means nothing more than another piece of ass. If I wanted that, I could have had Sarah from the moment I walked in here.

"When I came here and met you, you should remember, I said that I wasn't looking for love, but that if that one special person came along, I hoped I'd find her. I think I have. I don't know how else to say it to you. I love you. I hope you feel the same way. If you're just out to get a washed up old rock star in bed, then *I'm* not interested, well, I am but ..."

She laughed with me on that one.

"I promise you, this isn't a fling," I continued. "I said things last night I normally wouldn't say. I promise you honesty—whatever you ask I'll answer honestly. I'm not going to promise you anything I can't keep and that I don't mean."

For once, I meant those words. I'd only known her for a brief span of time, but I would promise her what I could truly deliver: if she were to stay with me, I would only have her in my life, I would never intentionally hurt her, I would die for her, and I would love her for as long as I lived.

She studied me then, and I knew she was trying to think of something to ask. The question she posed hadn't been quite what I expected.

"Jon, I've just realized, I don't even know your full name."

I laughed. "That's an easy one to answer. Jonathan Christopher Walsh. I don't know yours either you know."

She looked down sheepishly, then answered. "Rebecca Nicole Taylor."

"That's a beautiful name. So, Becca, where do we go from here? I've told you that I love you, you seem to feel the same way, and there's no way at this point we're going to be able to hide this from Sarah, seeing as I ran off after you, puked on her, and—"

She shook her head. "I don't know, Jon. If I were to say I thought this was going to be easy and fun for the both of us, I'd be lying out my ass. We still have Jodi's wedding today, and I'm pretty sure Sarah's goons are going to be watching the two of us like hawks from now on. The only thing that could make everything better is for us to figure out how to leave this place. But we can't crawl out the windows, the doors are all being watched ... there isn't any obvious way out."

I stared at Rebecca, her hand in mine, and said the only thing that came to mind. "I'm not leaving without you. It's either the two of us make it out or we stay here together."

She smiled more brightly than I'd ever previously seen. Unfortunately, as it was close to Jodi's wedding ceremony time, I decided it would be best that I head back to my own room. As I headed out the door to get ready, I kissed her goodbye ... for several minutes. When we parted and the door had closed between us, I turned around towards my room.

I came face to face with Sarah. She carried a hurt expression, but despite how I knew full well I was heading into the calm before the storm, I couldn't wipe the smile off my face.

"I thought I'd find you here," she said in a rather flat tone. "I was wondering if you'd accompany me to the dance after my brother's wedding."

Wow, even vomit didn't stop this woman. I knew that even though Sarah had fully been made aware of the blossoming relationship between Rebecca and me, it wasn't wise to turn her down outright, even though I'd made my choice.

"Sarah, I'll be at the dance. I'm not going with anyone in particular." Which was true without being fully true. I wasn't specifically going with Rebecca, but I did hope to spend most of my time with her at the dance. Sarah knew I provided the music at the ceremony, and would be there for that.

"Well, I'll see you then." The air of defeat hung around her like a cloak as she walked down the hallway. I felt pretty sure this was the first time she'd ever been turned down by anyone in her entire life.

⌒

I arrived for the wedding dressed in the best clothes I'd had with me, which just happened to be a suit, because I'd attended the baptism of my granddaughter while in Colorado. Jodi was resplendent in the wedding dress, which made me proud in that I'd helped create it. Her two bridesmaids looked gorgeous—Rebecca being, of course, the one who held most of my attention. The music and ceremony had gone off flawlessly, even though the duet between Rebecca and I had garnered quite a few stares from both Sarah and Kyle.

Once the ceremony had completed and everyone was shepherded into the transformed dining area, Sarah found the courage to find her way back to my side and had managed to completely monopolize my time at the dance. Short of hanging a sign on me that said "not interested," she would not give up on whatever hope might have existed (slim to none) that I might change my mind about who I'd rather be with.

So, when the Master of Ceremonies announced that the next song was to be lady's choice, I grumbled inwardly, *Yet another dance with Sarah*. I began to contemplate whether or not I could slit my wrists with the butter knife.

As the song began to play and people paired off, I was surprised to see Rebecca standing in front of me. "May I have this dance?" she asked, holding out her hand with a broad smile.

"Of course!" I said, returning the smile and taking her hand.

We walked out onto the dance floor and I couldn't help but notice again how beautiful she was up close. The dark blue dress Jodi had made for her hung perfectly off every curve, her hair hung long and loose around her shoulders, rather than pulled up and away from her face the way it had been for the wedding.

A country song played, and Rebecca was more than able to dance with ease. I could feel Sarah's eyes burning with anger as we danced. No one had accepted her request to dance, and Sarah was left standing off to the side.

I looked down at Rebecca. I thought it funny that despite my vow that I'd never fall in love again, I'd gone head over heels for her. As the song moved onto the another slow tune, I held her closer, and her head found my shoulder.

You could almost hear Sarah explode as she watched from the sidelines. When the song wound to a close, we walked off the dance floor together, hand in hand, and out of the dining area. It felt like being at a high school dance. We settled on the stairs in the courtyard.

There was a wonderfully cool breeze blowing and the music from the reception could still be heard, muted in the background. I held Rebecca close and we watched the stars. After a few minutes, I could feel her watching me rather than the night sky. I leaned down and kissed her. I felt her hands run through my hair, and my hands instinctively found her waist as our lips met.

"Woah ..." I said as we separated, and Rebecca smiled and laughed. The dance continued on behind us, and I was pretty much only aware of Rebecca and the stillness of the night air. Rebecca laid her head back against my shoulder, and we sat that way for a while, until a song came on, that got Rebecca on her feet.

"Jon, may I have the pleasure once again?" she asked, standing and extending her hand. I took it. As we danced, just the two of us in the moonlit courtyard, the lyrics of the song came through clearly. The song was one I recognized by a young girl from Swindon, Billie Piper, *I Dream*. It seemed appropriate considering the circumstances. "I love you, Rebecca Nicole," I whispered into her hair as we danced.

She pulled back from me just enough to gaze into my eyes. "I love you, too, Jonathan." It was the first time that she'd ever said the words to me. My heart soared—I had never had those simple three words spoken to me with such sincerity. She laid her head back down on my chest, and as the song ended, we headed, arm-in-arm out of the courtyard and back into the dance. Jodi was getting ready to toss to bouquet and Rebecca wanted to be there for her friend.

When we returned, Sarah was nowhere to be found, and Jodi had called all the unmarried women over. On the count of three and a drum roll, she tossed the bouquet over her head and it landed squarely in Rebecca's hands. I laughed at the surprised look on her face and those of the other girls there. The garter toss was next, and at the urgings of the work crew, who knew I wasn't married any longer, I joined the guys. Kyle whipped it out into the crowd, and I lost track of where it went. The crowd laughed, and the guys stepped back from me, so I put a hand to my head. There, sitting squarely in the middle of my noggin' was the garter. I laughed and removed it, flinging the thing back into the crowd.

They pushed the two of us together for a dance, and Rebecca got to choose the song.

As we moved together to the center of the dance floor, she looked at me and laughed. "I guess we're just meant to be together, aren't we?"

I agreed with her, and as the lights dimmed back down, the song began to play. It was a Torrent song, *If I Hadn't Found You*. I laughed, she had picked the one song where Ryan was given the chance to take lead vocals, and the song was written by him, too. It was one of the last songs we'd done before the split, written for his wife Heather. For once, I understood the lyrics that Ryan had penned years ago.

We danced the first verse together in the small spotlight that the DJ had with him and then the other couples around the place joined in. As the song finished, I kissed her in front of everyone and the sea of *awww's* that came from the group made both of us blush. For better or for worse, it was now out in the open that there was something a bit deeper than friendship between us.

We left together and wandered in that eerie calm that comes right before the storm unleashes its full force on you. We strolled slowly down to Rebecca's room, and out through into the garden that her grandparents had planted years ago. It was beautiful in the moonlight, and secluded. We sat on one of the benches, and for a while, just looked at each other, not saying a word.

Finally, breaking the stillness, I leaned over and kissed her. Her lips were like silk, and she leaned in closer. Deepening the kiss, I pulled her to me, and ran a hand through her soft hair. I could smell the perfume of the flowers that had been in her updo earlier. Stopping her gentle explorations for a moment, she changed positions on the bench, moving nearer to me. Her mouth returned to my lips and then alternated between gentle nibbling and working her away across my jawline. I moved my way slowly down her neck and onto her shoulders. I was rewarded with a quiet, almost inaudible moan from her, which made me double my ministrations in the light of further rewards.

She worked off my tie, and loosened the buttons on my shirt, but before she could continue any further there was a pounding on her door. She cursed under her breath and rested her forehead against mine for a moment before getting up, still cursing under her breath.

She strode inside and threw open the door with a very tetchy: "WHAT?"

There were a few thumps that came from the room, and I heard Rebecca scream. This got me to my feet and into the room before I was even sure that I'd moved. I saw two of Kyle's goons grabbing onto her, and her fighting with all her might. She managed to get away from them by biting onto one and kicking the other squarely in the privates. She ran to me, and with what breath she could manage, told me to get the hell out of there, as they were coming for me next.

I refused to go without her, and consequently they decided to take out two birds with one stone. The last thing I could clearly remember thinking was, *Oh, no. Not again,* as the light faded from around me.

CHAPTER 15

I came to in the dark and there was a smell of rotten ...
something ... in the air. All I knew was that I wasn't
anywhere near Rebecca, and most definitely not around her
suite. The aching sensation at the back of my head that I'd
learned to ignore had returned with a vengeance, making everything in front of my eyes bob and weave in a nauseating dance. I
figured out I'd been laid out on the floor of some place big
enough for me to be curled into the fetal position, but when I
stretched, my legs touched the walls. My hands had been bound
behind me, and I wasn't the least bit comfortable by any shake of
the imagination. Everything hurt, and I had no doubt that these
thugs had taken the opportunity to make sure that any healed
injuries from the last beating I'd received were brought right back
the forefront of my mind. There was a good amount of new
bruising and contusions that would make moving a living hell.
What a great way to celebrate my forty-fifth birthday.

I tried opening my eyes, only to discover there wasn't much point
—I'd probably had them open for a while, anyway. My jaw hurt
like a son of a whore, and I was pretty sure somebody had tried
playing football with my head. For once in my life I was glad that

my phobias didn't extend to claustrophobia, as they put me in one hell of a small dark place. I tried vainly to sit but after a few tries I just gave up.

In complete darkness and without any way to tell time, my mind slowly wandered, and finally I fell into a fitful sleep, until a loud wail woke me. I pushed myself upright as much as I could and moved slowly towards the sound. It seemed to be in the same area, but without a frame of reference I couldn't make heads or tails of direction or sound. I felt like I was losing my mind, floating in some strange dark world, where I didn't know where I was, what was up, and what was down. Eventually I just gave up and laid back down. If this was designed to break me, it probably would. I wasn't that strong of a person, unlike Rebecca. With any amount of torture, I would break like a glass dropped on a marble floor.

Time passed—not sure how much— and I could barely feel my arms, my legs were on fire, and my head hurt with each small movement, so I tried to keep still. It might have been days, hours minutes, or months; I had no idea how long I'd been here.

Eventually a door opened, and familiar footsteps came into the room. Someone lifted me gently from the floor, though I could tell they were struggling with doing it. There was a bright light in the room, and I blinked hard against the unfamiliar feeling of it, which tore into my brain like a million knives. Finally, as my eyes adjusted, I could make out Jodi, who spoke to me in what seemed like a foreign language. I knew she was talking, but I couldn't understand a word of what she said. My head acted like a lead weight on a noodle, and kept lolling forward.

"Jesus, Jon, will you listen to me?!"

I understood those words, and looked up as best I could.

"What the hell did they do to you?" she asked, lifting my head and trying to get a closer look at me.

I tried to reply, but I was sure that what came out was gibberish. Jodi continued to hang onto my head, and stared at me with worried eyes.

Eventually, I spoke, slowly and deliberately.

"Where ... is ... Becca?" I asked, now able to hold my own head upright.

"She's not far from here. You're in worse shape than she is," Jodi said, trying to push my hair out of my face and checking me over for obvious injuries.

She then lifted my arms. They were still bound and hurt like the dickens when she moved them. Jodi pulled a small knife out of her pocket, and proceeded to cut the bindings off my wrists. I could move again, but barely felt like lifting my head.

"It took me about sixteen hours to find you both," she said, trying to get me to take a drink of water from a bottle that she had with her. "I had to bribe Kyle with his favorite things, sex and booze, and only then was he more than willing to talk." She once again, lifted my head. "Oh, Jon. Your poor blond curls are just covered in crap. You must feel like hell."

I tried to nod as much as my head would allow me to. I could barely speak, and my entire body, from every last hair on my head to my toenails ached like no tomorrow. Hell was an understatement for how I felt. My insides twisted with fear every time I thought of Rebecca and what they might have put her through. It was my entire fault, too. If I hadn't shown up at Skylark Inn, none of this would have ever happened. Sure, I'd not have met the love of my life, but to find her only to lose her so quickly would be far worse than never having found her at all.

I sat back, feeling very much responsible for anything that might have happened to Becca. I leaned back against whatever wall I was up against and began to cry, much to my own shock and Jodi's. Simply put, this hit harder than I ever would have imagined. No matter how I tried to look at it, I was to blame for this descent into hell for both of us.

After a while, the tears slowed and stopped, and Jodi had sat through the entire episode with a hand on my arm, trying to comfort me as best as she could. I wanted to melt into a crack in the floor and die.

"Jon, do you think you can walk, if I help you?" she asked. "I want to take you to where Rebecca is; that way, you two will at least be together. I can't guarantee what I'll be able to do to get you both out of this situation, but it's better for her to know you're okay, and for you to be with her."

"I ... can ... try," I said slowly, and with Jodi's help, I was able to stand for at least a few moments without tumbling back down.

It took three false starts before I could stand up with her bolstering me. In the dim light, I found myself covered with bruises, and whatever they'd bound me with had left burn marks on my arms. My jaw still hurt, and my vision swam again.

Jodi leaned me back against the wall, and quickly bent to pick up the small lantern that barely lit the place. I slowly moved my head and made out that I was somewhere in a small closet.

"Jodi ...where am I?" I asked as she allowed me to put some weight on her.

"You're in a part of this place you don't want to know about. It's by Sarah's suite, but not clearly evident to anyone who doesn't know where it is. You pissed off Sarah something good by turning her down. What did I tell you about this place being on edge last night?"

She pushed against the wall with her hip, moving the entrance to the side, then after sticking her head out to see if the coast was clear, she hobbled out with me. We took a few steps and then Jodi put me against the wall, where I was able to lean most of my weight, and I blinked like an owl at the intense lights of the hallway. Jodi pushed the portion of the wall that concealed where I'd been trapped back into place, and it disappeared from view. Only by staring at it for a long period of time could I discern where the secret door was.

Taking me over her shoulders again, Jodi set off at a slow pace, allowing me time to get my bearings, and stopped when I asked her too, lest I throw up what little I'd had to eat between getting completely shit-faced and now. The journey took about twenty minutes, but Jodi opened a regular door, one that led to one of the smaller suites around here. It was near to where Kyle and the work crew had been gutting rooms, and it was obvious that it was near to being gutted itself. Bare lighting fixtures hung from the ceiling, and when Jodi flipped on the light, I could just make out Rebecca's prone form on the floor.

She didn't move or make a sound when we came into the room, and with a whimper, I fell beside her when Jodi got me close enough. Crawling like a toddler over to Rebecca, I pushed the mass of dark curls off her face, and as best as I could, brought her limp, inanimate form to closer to me. I wanted her to open her eyes, and say something to me. I needed her to give me one hint that she wasn't dead.

"She's been in and out of consciousness since I found her, Jon," said Jodi. "They clocked her a good one; you can pretty much see that lump on her head." Jodi got down on the floor with us. "She's still breathing. Look."

I saw the slow movement of Rebecca's chest that indicated she was, thankfully, still alive.

"Don't make too much noise. I'll try to bring you food and water when I can. The facilities here still work, so you should be okay that way. I'll try to bring some things for both of you later tonight, when Kyle's gone to sleep. If Sarah finds out that I put the two of you together, well, getting out of here will be the least of your worries."

Jodi stood, and with a sad look, walked to the door. She'd brought some blankets and pillows for Rebecca earlier, and slowly, I laid Rebecca back down on them. With a huff of anger, Jodi turned off the light, and closed the door behind her with a click.

The stark moonlight filtered through a window, bathing us in its bluish glow. Physically, Rebecca was in better condition than I, for the most part, save the bump on her head. I couldn't tell if she'd suffered any brain damage from the hit itself, but the fact that she was alive gave me some relief. Making sure she at least looked somewhat comfortable on the makeshift bed of blankets and pillows, I curled up around her, holding her close. I'd just found the woman who I'd gladly die for, I wasn't going to let her go this damned easily.

I kept track of every little movement and breath that she took throughout the night, until the sun came up, when I fell asleep from exhaustion, still with one arm around her. The next thing I remembered was a blood curdling scream, which woke me up from that sound sleep. It was Rebecca, and she was clawing desperately at thin air, her dark eyes fixed on a point on the far side of the room. The blazing sunlight that entered the room told me it was past noon and that we were on the western side of the place. Fighting back nausea, I grabbed onto her as gently as I could, and tried to comfort her. She rewarded my efforts by clawing at my face, and pushing me away as much as she could, considering I outweighed her and refused to let her go. Eventually the screaming and thrashing subsided into sobbing, then once again into nothingness.

Jodi turned up shortly before the sun went down, dressed for the evening service that Sarah conducted. She had some food with her, and some clothes for the two of us. She checked on Rebecca and seemed worried as she listened to my recounting of the fit that Rebecca had earlier. Jodi's expression told me more than she wanted it to, but she promised to come back as soon as possible.

The next few hours went by slowly. I sat up and managed to eat and keep down a bit of the sandwiches Jodi had left for us, along with the bottle of water that was meant for me. The entire time I kept an eye on Rebecca. I wasn't up to trying to change clothing on myself or her, and elected to just keep clean by making as many visits to the washroom as I could, washing myself and hair with the soap that Jodi had left there. The sun went down and the moon began its slow climb up into the sky. Nothing much changed with Rebecca. There were no more screaming fits, but she didn't open her eyes or regain consciousness. Jodi came and went throughout the evening, bringing things that I requested and food, trying to be as helpful as she could with Rebecca out cold and me trying to take care of Becca while being remarkably injured myself.

About halfway through the second night, I woke up to the sudden intake of breath by Rebecca. I was wide awake within seconds and was almost reduced to tears by the fact she opened her eyes.

"Jon?"

She looked at me, and I began to cry. I couldn't help it. The happiness at one simple action was overwhelming.

"Jon, what the hell happened? Why does my head hurt? How long have I been here?"

She moved then, slowly turning herself over so she could look me in the face. She reached out slowly with one hand, tracing the area where she'd scratched me in the screaming fit she'd had, shocked to see the marks.

"What do you remember last?" I asked, helping her to sit up. She thought for a few moments and then stated the last thing she could remember was being with me in the garden, and that some of Kyle's goons had shown up.

"After that it's all a blur," she continued. "I can remember being in a dark room. Kinda like the place that Kyle threw me that last time, where I refused to answer any questions about you. Then I woke up here." She reached out her hand, gingerly touching my face, which was bruised from whatever Kyle and crew had done to me after they'd pulled me from Rebecca's suite.

"Oh, Jon. This is all my fault."

I took her hand away from my face and held it. None of this was her fault; if anything, it was my fault for being less than smart about keeping this out of Sarah's view.

"No, love," I began. "They caught us and your head hurts because they knocked you out, probably around the same time as they did it to me. I'm entirely to blame. All you did was fall for me, and it's my fault that I didn't handle this better."

The door creaked open and there was Jodi. She let out a squeak of joy that Rebecca was conscious and lucid.

Then she proceeded to give us news that neither of us wanted to hear.

"Jon, Becca. They know you're not where you're supposed to be.

Kyle and the guys will be going back to work tearing this place down, and they know that you're no longer in the holes. I'm willing to take the rap for it, but I've got to get you someplace safer than here."

"Where is going to be safer than here?" I asked.

"I'm taking you back to Becca's suite. It's the only place I can think of right now. They wouldn't look there, Becca's the only one with a key, and she keeps it well hidden."

She struggled to help Rebecca to her feet. I was able at long last to get to my own feet and help Jodi with Rebecca. Rebecca tottered and fell, complaining of dizziness and nausea. Jodi held her close, taking most of her weight. I kept my arm around Rebecca, and between the two of us, slowly and deliberately we made the long trip to Rebecca's suite.

Once inside, Jodi took Rebecca to her room, and I collapsed on the couch. I was exhausted from what normally would have been considered the short walk from one side of this place to the other. Jodi came out shortly, after dealing with whatever she needed to with Rebecca, and quietly threw a blanket over me before leaving.

Never in a million years would I have thought my life would descend to this level of insanity. Trapped in the middle of nowhere in Arizona, desperately in love with a woman half my age, beaten half to death. I would never have imagined I'd end up in what at best could be called a cult and at worst a madhouse run by an insane, insecure, and jealous bitch.

I fell asleep sometime in the night, to be awoken by Rebecca's whimpering. I slowly and stiffly unfolded myself from my berth on the couch, and made my way into her room. My eyes adjusted to the almost complete darkness, and I could see her, sitting up, fighting against something that wasn't there. It was evident that she was having nightmares, and knowing just a fraction of what had happened to her, it wasn't any surprise.

Having dealt with Ryan in the early days of the band, and his incessant sleepwalking, which made Chris and his never-ending sleep talking seem like a walk in the park, I was pretty sure Rebecca was experiencing night terrors rather than the run-of-the-mill nightmares. Deciding to comfort her while not trying to wake her unless it became necessary, I made my way over to the bed and sat beside her. Speaking in soft, gentle tones, I let her know I was there and that everything was okay. She seemed to calm down a bit and slowly fell back into a sound sleep.

Deciding to camp down in here for the night rather than having to trip back and forth between the couch and her room in the dark, I pulled the covers up over her and laid on top of the other side of the bed and tried to fall back asleep.

The rest of the night went by in a flash, and the next thing I knew, the sun was streaming through the windows right into my eyes. I groaned and rolled over, coming face to face with a very bemused Rebecca.

"Hi," she said, covers pulled up halfway over her face, snickering quietly.

"Good morning." I said, smiling and giving her a kiss on the forehead.

"Is there any particular reason that you're in my bed with me?" she asked, laughing again.

"You were having night terrors. I just came in to try and keep you safe from yourself. Decided to crash here rather than the couch. Nothing happened, if you're concerned about that."

She went serious at that comment. "Jon, I'd like to think you have more respect for me than to take advantage of me in a situation like that. Just wondered why you were in here with me. I trust you enough to know when the time is right for the two of us to move to that level."

"You're right," I said, giving her another quick kiss before getting up, stretching, and heading out of the room.

She stayed where she was, and I decided to return the favor of so many suppers that she'd made or arranged for the two of us, and planned to make her breakfast in bed. Going into the kitchen, I opened a few random cupboards until I found what I was looking for, and no stranger to gas ranges, I cooked breakfast. My only worry was that she wouldn't like the meal.

When I came into the room again, plate in hand, she was still in bed, reading a book. I noticed she kept moving the book as if she were having a hard time reading it, however it was soon forgotten as she looked up with a smile and noticed I held breakfast—waffles with what was left of the strawberries that Jodi had procured for us.

"Oh, breakfast in bed. How romantic!" she said, taking the plate from me.

I put down the mug of tea I'd brewed for her. I could tell from the way Rebecca moved that her head still bothered her, and she probably had the same problems I'd had: blurry vision, a loss of balance, and horrible waves of nausea that seemed to come from nowhere.

She tucked into the breakfast and I sat there, watching out the window, musing over random things.

"What are you thinking about, Jon?" She asked a few minutes later, putting down the plate onto the bedside table and leaning forward, watching me.

"I'm that transparent, am I?" I said with a laugh as I turned to face her.

"Only to me, I guess," she said, shrugging. "You look like you've got a few things on your mind."

I laughed humourlessly. "Yeah, I do. Just trying to figure out how to leave here before Kyle and Sarah find out we're gone from those hell holes they threw us in. I've got other things on my mind, too ... well, I'm not going to bother you with that right now."

I reached out for her hand. I still worried that because of my past transgressions, she'd take me for the cheating creep that I'd been years before and leave me the minute she hit the outside world. Or worse, that she'd stay with me only because I had a good amount of money. Both possibilities concerned me. I wanted Rebecca with me, but only if she were willing to stay with me for me, and not some idea of fame and fortune or being a rock-star girlfriend. I also agonized over how we would get out of the compound. I worried more than I ever had before, probably because I had someone in my life worth worrying about.

She took my hand and smiled. "Look, whatever it is, we'll work through it together, right?"

I tried to smile as bravely as I could for her. "Right." At this point the only thing that I was fairly certain of was that we'd most probably end up dead in the near future, roasting on a spit like pigs at a luau.

"So, where is today going to take us, Jon?"

Aside from the attack, nothing had much changed other than the fact that we were both aware that what we were feeling for each other was love and now we were confined to closed quarters. There was no way we'd ever be able to show our faces in the general population of this place again, unless something miraculous changed between now and whenever the hell we managed to escape. It was likely Sarah currently brewed some strange assault on both of us, and I feared for both of our lives. I'd always thought that falling in love with someone was supposed to be a joyous thing. While I was intensely happy to have found someone to love, the sacrifice it asked of me was something I hadn't been really ready for, and though I was willing to give up everything for her, the possibility of never, ever getting out of here weighed on my heart.

"Well, how are you doing?" I asked, reaching up to check the still prominent bump on her head. At least Jodi had changed Rebecca's clothes from the bridesmaid's dress to a t-shirt and shorts, clearly pajamas. Her hair still needed a good washing. So did mine. I probably looked like crap.

"I'm okay, I guess," she said. "I'm still having a bit of a hard time focusing on things, but it seems to come and go. Bit dizzy every now and then, too."

As if to make her point, Rebecca swayed a bit in the bed, putting her free hand up to her temple.

"Okay, why don't you go take a bath or something? It's been about five days since I know for sure that you've seen soap and water. Once I've cleaned up a bit myself, then we'll think of what to do, okay?"

She nodded, and with quick peck on the cheek, she slowly stood up and walked out of the room. I picked up the dishes and heard the water running as I made my way into the kitchen. If anyone had come upon us, they'd probably think that this was a scene of domestic bliss. Far from it.

A while later, she showed up again, this time her hair washed and combed out, and dressed in something a little more presentable.

"It's all yours, Jon. I think I left you some hot water. There are some towels in the linen closet, and you'd know better than I would if Jodi brought you anything to change into where it is."

She motioned towards the facilities, and I slowly walked in.

It was almost stereotypically feminine, without being fluffy and pink. There was no doubt a young woman in her twenties lived here.

Turning on the water, I waited for it warm up and casually glanced around. I felt completely out of place; I wasn't a part of her life to the extent that every personal detail was known to me. Yes, I was in love with her for what I knew of her, and I knew this was the beginning of the integration into each other's lives. I hoped it would go well and that we'd hopefully be together for a long time.

The water had finally heated up to a comfortable level, and I noticed that true to her word, there were towels laid out for me. Switching on the shower, I quickly stripped off and jumped in.

The refreshing warmth poured over me. I ran my hands through my hair, which having gotten long enough to be curly was also long enough to start knotting. There were reasons I kept my hair short. Fumbling around for a few moments, I finally found her shampoo and lathered up. The old habit of singing in the shower threatened to rear its ugly head again for me, and I decided to settle for just humming.

I could feel the muscles of my back and shoulders loosening in the heat. My head finally began to stop aching from the repeated bang on my brains, and every muscle in my body was beginning to feel less and less that I'd been put through the physical wringer by two people who were half my age and twice my strength.

I grabbed the soap that had been left there and reaching out blindly, I managed to find the face cloth she'd left. Normally I would have no compunctions about lathering up, but that was not my soap and I didn't need the last thing I'd probably wash connecting with the first thing she— in all probability— had washed.

Ten minutes later, rinsed off, I turned off the shower, and drew back the curtain. The humidity from the shower hung in the air like fog, despite the fan. Grabbing the towels, I wrapped one around me and dried off as I exited the bathroom.

"Becca, has Jodi dropped off ..." I began to ask, drying my hair as I came out of the bathroom into the living area to come face to face with Jodi and Rebecca. Jodi went red to the roots of her auburn hair and Rebecca just looked at me with a highly appreciative smile and laughed at Jodi's reaction.

I coloured a bit, and laughed, realizing that I was clad only in a towel and still partially dripping from the shower.

"Yes, Jon, Jodi's dropped off your bags from your suite. They're in the guest room at the end of the hall." Rebecca explained to Jodi that she'd show me where it was, and Jodi, still blushing like a maniac, made an excuse to flee from us.

Rebecca, snickering quietly, showing me to a room down the hall, opposite her bedroom. It contained all my belongings. I had to wonder how Jodi managed to get everything from one side of this place to the other without being seen, and without my key. Then I realized it had been taken from me sometime during the assault by Kyle's goons, and that Jodi seemed to be capable of doing damn near anything in this place. Now that she was legally and officially Kyle's wife, I didn't doubt that her power here would be second only to that of Sarah.

Rebecca shut the door without saying a word, and finally alone, I discarded the towel and rummage around to get dressed as quickly as possible. It was a bit embarrassing to be caught pretty-much naked by a close friend and your significant other, more for the former than the latter.

Once I was dressed, I looked around for my toothbrush. I couldn't find it so I headed back into the bathroom, only to find Rebecca already in there, retching up what little she'd had to eat that day.

"Sorry, Jon." she said, her voice rough and face pale. "It's not a comment on your cooking, I promise ... I just ..." she coughed and sat back on the floor. "The dizziness made me kind of sick."

I dropped the toothbrush on the counter, dental hygiene a secondary concern. Grabbing a glass, and a face cloth I presumed was hers, I turned on the cold tap and wet down the cloth, then filled the cup with water. Getting down on the floor with her, I handed her the cup of water, and lightly pressed the cold cloth to her face.

"It's okay. As long as you don't yack up your guts every time I cook for you, I won't take it personally. Now rinse out your mouth. I doubt the sick tastes good."

She nodded slowly, complied with the instructions, then spit into the toilet with a grimace.

I kept the cloth against her forehead and she leaned against the wall, her eyes closed. After a few minutes, she opened her eyes and smiled, seeming a bit stronger than before. I smiled back.

"Feeling less dizzy now?" I said, and she nodded again. "You have a quite a head injury, Becca. If we weren't trapped here, I'd have you into the hospital faster than you could blink. As it stands, as soon as we can when we leave, I'm getting you looked after."

"I'm okay for now, but I'll definitely take you up on that. I don't think things will be quite right for a while. Everything just keeps going blurry and off balance."

She stood up with that and slowly made her way over to the sink. Putting down the cup, she grabbed her own toothbrush and looked at me.

"Care to join me?" she asked.

I stood and the lapse in dental hygiene was taken care of swiftly.

Once we were done in the bathroom, we made our way into the garden. Despite the oncoming fall weather cooling things down, it was still beautiful out. Rebecca took a seat at the patio table and beckoned for me to join her.

I sat down; she took my hand.

"I know it's a bit late, but happy birthday, Jon."

I was surprised that she even knew when my birthday was, but I thanked her. We remained seated for a while. There wasn't much we *could* do in our captivity. I wasn't sure if we even dared to walk outside of Rebecca's suite at this time, and my guess was a very likely, no—if we wanted to live to see the outside of this nightmare. At this rate, though, I felt pretty sure I'd be taken out of here with a toe tag.

"So, is Jodi coming back today?" Rebecca asked somewhat absentmindedly, staring at the wall, probably daydreaming.

"I don't know. When I walked out of the shower Jodi was talking to you, remember? She was keen to get out of the suite, too. I can't blame her, I wouldn't want to see me half naked."

She laughed. "Yeah, I remember, it's kind of fuzzy though. It's ... hazy. I know she was here, but I don't really remember what she said." Rebecca put her head in her hands. "I think there's something seriously wrong, Jon. I shouldn't be feeling like this."

She glanced over at me, her eyes serious, and even someone as thick about health issues as I was, I could see she wasn't right. My only hope was that whatever was happening to her wouldn't take away the woman I'd come to know and fall in love with.

All this served to do was to further serve to fuel the fire of my hatred of Sarah and Kyle. There was no way that I'd let them destroy what I'd finally woken up to see I needed in my life. Becca was the one woman I'd ever felt I could spend the rest of my life with, and come hell or high water, if I was going to lose her, I'd go down fighting.

There was a knock on the door, and Rebecca stood to answer it. I asked her to sit down because in her condition, she should not be facing the unknown. I walked back inside and opened the door, partially expecting it to be the end of everything—Sarah or Kyle would be there, and what delicate peace we had in this micro-cosm once known as the Skylark Inn would be shattered like a mirror.

Thankfully, it was Jodi, tray in hand, carrying plates with silver covers.

"How's Rebecca doing?" Jodi asked, sliding past me just as a few people passed by in the hallway.

"She's not doing well, Jodi. She's already tossed everything once today, and she's dizzy and has a hard time remembering things. I'm just hoping it doesn't get much worse than it already is. If we can't her out of here for help, then"—I gestured helplessly—"I don't know what I'd do."

Jodi set the tray on the kitchen counter and put her hand on my shoulder.

"She's from Scottish stock, Jon. Head like rock in more ways than one. I have faith she'll be okay. Between the two of us, we'll make sure of it."

She gave me a hug, which I returned. Then I remembered Jodi

wouldn't be escaping this place with us, but she'd be the reason we'd get out at all.

"So, I guess we're delaying that trip through the passageway until Rebecca's able to at least remain upright without falling down?" I asked.

Something made me turned around then, and I found Rebecca trying to stand up and come in. She was as wobbly as a newborn foal. It was apparent that the dizzy spells had been coming in waves, as she had moments of perfect clarity and others of world turning, head buzzing dizziness. Jodi and I moved at the same time out to the garden, with me beating her to Rebecca's side by a few strides. Both of us—one on each side—helped Rebecca into the living room and made sure she was comfortable on the couch. Rebecca wouldn't be mobile to the extent that we both needed her to be for a while yet.

Jodi made sure both of us were seated with Rebecca on the couch and myself on the floor beside her, and then swiftly moved back and forth between the kitchen and living room, bringing food. When Jodi was done, she sat in one of the chairs across from us with a deep sigh, and leaned back, closing her eyes.

"You two are lucky you're in here. Kyle is completely avoiding answering me as to where you are—when he's sober—and Sarah is being a right twit over everything seeing as the musicians are gone and people are asking questions. Your absence is causing quite a stir around here, and I think it's more than what she anticipated. If folks aren't asking what happened to you, Becca, they're wondering what happened to Jon. A few of them miss your nightly little jam sessions in the courtyard," Jodi smiled at that, her eyes still closed. "And quite a few of them are wondering where "the two lovebirds" went. It's been so long since anything like that has happened here, it's kind of like a soap opera for a lot of the people."

Jodi opened her eyes, taking in the two of us: one on the couch and the other on the floor.

"Once Becca's feeling better, we'll tackle that passageway, Jon. Hopefully that won't take too long. I'm pretty sure Kyle or Sarah knows you're not in the pits anymore. One thing, though. Make sure each of you has a bag packed and you're ready to bolt at a moment's notice."

I knew the wheels turned in Jodi's head as to how to get us out of here as a last measure, and it troubled me what she might have up her sleeve.

She stood up and walked over to the kitchen to retrieve the tray and plate covers.

"I'd better go. Kyle and Sarah will want me to have lunch done soon and you both know how the bunch of incompetent boobs I've got to work with in that kitchen. I'll try and drop by later to see how both of you are doing."

She left and I turned to Rebecca, who, food untouched, sat with her head back and her eyes shut.

"You okay there, love?" I asked, and yet again, she nodded.

"Just a bit dizzy still. It'll pass; it always does."

She sat that way for a while, and then opened her eyes. "I don't think I should eat. I'd actually like to be able to keep something down, and eating this right now ... not a good idea."

I put down my own food, took the plate Jodi had brought, and put it into the fridge. When I came back, Rebecca had at least sat up, so I joined her on the couch and let her lean on me. I wrapped my arms around her.

"So, what are we going to do for the rest of the day?" I said, holding her as close as I could. "If you want, we can just stay here, like this."

"Mmm ... that sounds good for now. Maybe later we'll do ... stuff?" she said, snugging back into my arms and resting against my chest.

"Just want to sit and chat, then?" She nodded, head still against my chest. "What about?"

"I'd love to hear more about your childhood, Jon. You've heard so much about mine, indulge me, please?"

I could feel her head move so that she was looking up at me. "What do you want me to talk about specifically?"

"I'd love to hear more about England. I know you were there until you were about ten or so."

"Oh, I'm sure I'd bore you silly with that."

"Hey, Jon, I'm supposed to be a part of your life now, and I want to hear about it. Please, indulge me."

I sighed. It must be love if she wanted to hear the desperately boring details of my childhood, which was split between Abingdon and New York.

"Well, I was born on a typical British day, according to my mother, around ten in the morning in Abingdon hospital. I was the second Walsh to have been born in a hospital, Chris having been the first. I was overdue by about two weeks, and I've spent most of my life keeping up that fine tradition of being late for everything. I'd be late for my own funeral if it were possible. I went to nursery and primary school at the Manor Preparatory school with Chris until I was ten, as you know, then I moved to New York when my father got a teaching job there. We lived in Toronto for about half a year, before he got the paperwork straightened out to get all three of us into the States. I don't remember too much about Abingdon, other than I loved it. It's on the Thames, and it's very picturesque. You'd probably love it, too.

"Anyway, Toronto and New York were a bit of culture shock. I got picked on in New York for my accent. Being an ex-pat Brit as a child isn't the easiest thing to deal with. Dad made sure I went to a private school in New York—it was the closest thing he felt to me going to Eton, which is probably where I'd have been shoe-horned in if we'd stayed in England. I graduated from there in '73 and because family was close, I decided to go to UCLA with Chris. I'm not sure entirely as to why. Chris and I got along just as well then as we do now. We're fine in small doses, and as long as there aren't any women between us.

"Anyway, that's a bit ahead of where you wanted to hear isn't it?" I felt her nod again, and looking out the patio doors, I let my mind drift back to my childhood years again.

"Well, like I said, I'm not sure about a lot that went on in Abingdon, especially when I was quite young. I remember school was pretty boring, and I usually kept to myself. I was always the shy one. Chris was always the outgoing one of the two of us. We spent a lot of time together, his family living in Reading, which is about thirty miles down the road. We'd get together for every bank holiday and big holidays like Christmas. It was always the Walsh-James family and the Walsh family together at our place. Mum and Dad had a huge place in England. It's too bad they sold it when we moved. I'd love to ..." I stopped dead. I couldn't believe the sentence that I was about to say—move back there and raise a family. I had never considered dragging Tricia and Kristen halfway around the globe to my home town, mainly because Tricia would have died from the sheer boredom—even though it was not that far from London.

"You'd love to what?" Rebecca said, somewhat drowsily.

"I'd love to see it again. It's been so long since I've been home," I said, fiddling with long mass of dark curls that lay over my arms. Hopefully I'd managed to keep that thought to myself. That was something we'd deal when we got to that bridge. We had barely begun this relationship, it had just barely crawled beyond flirting and simple affection, and I didn't want to rush into it too quickly, lest I destroy what was there.

"Now I know you probably want to hear some schoolboy tales of things that Chris and I got up to, but I think I'll save those for another time."

She groaned her displeasure at that statement.

"Now it's your turn," I said, "and I get to pick the topic."

Another groan, this time of upset. Talking about her past was one thing that Rebecca didn't like to do a lot of. I was pretty sure that it was simply an issue of trust because she had been hurt quite badly by Kyle and Sarah, and trusting after that level of pain would be difficult. I felt quite sure as things progressed, Rebecca would open up to me more and more, but until she was willing, I'd have to make do with what she could tell me.

"Okay, I'll not pick anything too dangerous for you. You'd think the way you're going on, I'd asked you to play Truth or Dare."

"That would be more fun than talking about my childhood. It makes your slight little tale look like an epic, Jon."

I sighed and laughed.

"Okay, fine. Truth or dare?" I said, giving in.

"Truth."

I thought for a minute. It had to have been at least twenty years since I'd last indulged in this childhood game, and I had a hard time thinking of something to ask.

"Okay, how old were you when you had your first kiss?"

"Nine. It was my next-door neighbor at the time, Kirk. It was the worst kiss I've ever had. Now, Jonathan Christopher—truth or dare?"

"Truth."

She sat and thought for a bit, then sat up enough to face me. "First person you ever fell in love with?"

"I know you're expecting to hear some random name, but truthfully, the first person I ever fell in love with was you."

Rebecca laughed, then froze, realizing I was being completely honest with her about that one. She pushed herself upright and moved to the other side of the couch where she could watch me.

"You've never been in love before?!" she asked, the astonishment clear.

I shook my head. I'd had never been in love before. Lust, yes. Physical attraction, yes. Deep affection for a sometimes partner, yes. How I felt now, no. Nothing I could ever label as love.

"Wow. With how much you guys sang about love and all I figured ..." she trailed.

"If you noticed, I'd only been listed as a contributor of those songs. I'm more of a composer than I am a lyricist. Now, we're getting off the topic. Truth or dare?"

"Truth."

"Wildest place you've ever—what don't look at me like that!" I said, a mischievous grin on my face. "Okay, fine, geesh, no sense of humor today."

She curled up into a contented ball, staring at me from the other end of the couch, a huge smile on her face.

"When did you know you were falling in love with me?" I asked.

Her face went dreamy. "Truth?" she asked, her cheeks coloring slightly.

I nodded.

"Around the time you kissed me in the kitchen. Same question to you."

I thought for a bit, and the truthfulness of the situation came into my mind. "Around the same time. I'm just a little slow on the uptake, I guess."

She smiled and made her way across the couch toward me. "For someone who is a bit slow on the uptake, you're a damned good kisser, you know that?"

I was pretty sure that the game of Truth or Dare was pretty much over, or the next choice was going to be a dare, and I had a few guesses as to where that dare would be headed. Rebecca crawled back up to where she had been before. She looked at me, almost cross-eyed as she came closer and closer.

"Truth or dare." I said, a little more breathlessly than I'd intended.

"Dare."

Before I could say anything further, she closed the gap between us with an almost feline growl, and kissed me. I returned the kiss with equal passion; however, things didn't get much further than that as Jodi called out that she was coming in. That girl had to have the worst timing known to mankind. Rebecca quickly dropped back into the position that she had been in on the sofa for the past few hours, and yelled for Jodi to enter. Jodi did and with a sigh, flopped down on the love seat opposite us. By this time Rebecca had settled back into my arms, and was turned somewhat so she could look at Jodi. If this was going to be the closest I got to her at this point, so be it. When things got more intimate, it would be when it was right, and I wasn't going to force anything on her, and likely that she wouldn't try to push it on me until it was right for her as well.

"So, what were you two up to?" said Jodi, stretching in the chair. Rebecca and I shared a knowing glance and both broke down with laughter.

"Nothing much Jodi, just talking and playing a few old party games," Rebecca said once she'd gotten the giggles under control.

Jodi gave a look that underscored the fact that she probably didn't wholly believe that, but nodded, and updated us on what was happening in the compound. Sarah still hadn't gone on a search for the two of us, probably certain we'd come out of hiding on our own at some point, which would save her the trouble of mounting an all-out campaign to locate us. After all, it was an enclosed space; where would we conceivably run to? Kyle had been busy tearing down the suites, and didn't even have time to spend with Jodi most of the time, which she state was Kyle Code for getting some on the sly with one of the younger, more impressionable girls in the compound. Sarah had cut back on the food budget, so what was in the pantry in Rebecca's suite now was what we had to subsist off of, and whatever Jodi could manage to secret down here. Jodi and I both did quick mental calculations and came up with a figure of two weeks—until the end of the month. This meant that Rebecca had to be up and walking around well before she probably would be fully capable of doing so. Some slim hope existed in my mind that we might actually be able to get out of this place before Christmas. Jodi outlined her plan, and I sighed deeply. The chances that this would actually work were slim, but this passage seemed to be the only feasibly way we could try.

"So, like I said before," said Jodi, "both of you need to be ready to go on a moment's notice. That means have a small bag packed with only what you need. No trying to drag your entire wardrobe or anything like that. Got it?"

She looked back and forth between us until she had gotten two nods of understanding. I still didn't quite know how this would work out, but I clung to hope, however slim it might be.

Jodi discussed a few other things with Rebecca, and I zoned out until she bid goodbye to the both of us. Then we were alone again. By this time, the sun went down its westward track to night and Rebecca felt worn out. Disentangling herself from me, I helped her to her room, and she crawled sleepily into bed. I pulled the curtains and blinds as shut as I could, and with a kiss, I headed out of the room. As I went to pull the door closed, I heard her voice.

"Jon? Stay with me a while? I don't want to be alone."

I came back into the room and sat alongside of her on the bed, until she slowly fell into a quiet and hopefully dreamless sleep. Once I felt sure she wouldn't wake, I left the room, closing the door, and walked out into the garden. I sat, watching the sun set and wondering if we'd make it out and if Rebecca would ever be normal again.

CHAPTER 16

*T*he next few days went by without significant change to our situation. Rebecca felt a bit better, but still suffered through waves of nausea every now and then. She was at least able to keep food down for the time being, and walk by herself most of the time, but the knock she'd taken on the head still worried me. She acted more absentmindedly and forgetful than ever since I'd known her, and admitted things seemed consistently fuzzy. I made mental notes that if we ever got out of here, the second stop on my list would be the Loma Linda Heath Center to have her thoroughly checked out. By the fourth day of our confinement to the suite, Jodi and I judged that Rebecca should be able to make it, for the most part, through the passageway, and a date was set for that weekend, after the evening study on Sabbath.

We existed in Rebecca's suite doing pretty much the same things every day: getting up, showered, dressed, either sitting on the couch for a while talking or reading, going out into the garden off the living room and just sitting for a while. Once very late at night we snuck out into the courtyard, and just sat on the stairs, gazing at the sky and enjoying the few precious moments of stolen freedom that we had in the world beyond her door. It had been intoxicating—just the two of us in the crisp evening air, not a person about—like something from a movie. The night after that, we'd made another late-hour foray, this time into the large garden in the place, where we'd walked, almost getting lost amongst the vegetables and flowers. I'd picked a few flowers for her, and she'd gone so far as to put them in her hair. For being stuck in this insane place, with nowhere to go, there was no shortage of little romantic things that I could do for her. It was ironically the most romantic time I'd had with a woman in years, and I was enjoying that aspect greatly. However, a problem for both of us was that we were beginning to suffer cabin fever, from being in that small space with no one but each other to talk to, few things to talk about, and very little to do.

This, of course, led to the occasional fight, usually a short-lived yelling match that ended with the two of us at opposite ends of the suite, silent and steaming for a while, before one of us would find the other and apologize. Then things would go back to the way they'd been before. The difference here with her compared with past relationships was that I found myself more willing to work through the problems that arose rather than throw in the towel.

The third night, I slipped out after I knew the place should be sound asleep and headed to the storage area off the courtyard where I knew the guitar was kept. I'd been feeling particularly inspired that day and wanted to share with Rebecca the tune that had worked its way into my brain. Yes, I felt bold about taking such chances, but the likelihood that this place had someone awake was slim to none.

I made my way quietly down the hallways to the storage room, opened the door with the key Jodi had lent me earlier in the week, and picked up the black acoustic guitar stored in its case.

As I was closing the door, I heard a highly feminine giggle, followed by a moan.

I froze in place, my mind racing. Slowly I turned around, trying not to attract any more attention to myself than was necessary, and searched for the source of the noise, which continued.

I caught sight of Kyle and a young woman from the compound, down the other end of the courtyard, heavily involved with each other. There was no doubt in my mind that the woman he coupled with was not Jodi. As I turned to walk away, I caught the Kyle's eye, who with one glare dared me to tell Jodi about what he was doing with his hands all over the girl.

Shaking my head in disgust, I simply turned and walked away. I felt certain he wouldn't break off that intimate interlude to come chase after me. Of course, that didn't stop me from looking over my shoulder every few moments to make sure I was alone.

When I got back to Rebecca's suite, I put down the guitar and grabbed her in a tight hug.

"Okay, what brought this on?" she said, hugging me back.

I told her about running into Kyle in the area around the court-yard. She blanched a bit at that, but listened intently to what I said.

"I just want you to know, despite what I've told you about what I've done in the past; I will never, ever do anything like that to you. You have my word on it."

"I trust you, Jon. I think I mean more to you than any woman could ever mean to Kyle. Plus, you know I'll cut your heart out and show it to you while it's still beating if you ever did anything like that." The last bit of the sentence was accompanied by a large smile, and I knew never to test that theory as long as we were together.

I took her hand and picked up the guitar case, and we headed out into the garden. After being seen by Kyle tonight, I had no doubts that our enforced cohabitation would soon end, likely a very bad way, but I wanted to enjoy each moment as much as I could. I had felt inspired earlier in the day from the beautiful morning sunrise, which I had watched with Rebecca beside me, before we went back to our rooms to sleep for a few hours. Because the only times we could think of getting out of this suite had been mostly at night, we had slowly worked on adjusting our internal clocks to being more nocturnal—rising with the sunset and sleeping with the dawn.

Once she was seated in the garden, along the rock wall rather than at the table, I pulled out the guitar and began to strum out the haunting tune that had stayed in my head since that morning. If I'd had the freedom to write it down or record it, I would have. I hoped to remember when we got out of here. I had to use "when" and not "if," for my own sanity.

Rebecca sat and listened. I was not a lyricist, but words floated into mind with this song, and I put them to the music as best as I could, hoping they conveyed what I wanted them to. I closed my eyes eventually, playing and singing, blissfully ignoring everything outside of what I was doing musically.

When the song ended, I opened my eyes again, and expected to find Rebecca laughing and pointing. Instead I found her opening her eyes as well, an ethereal smile on her face.

"That was beautiful," she said simply. "You say you're not a lyricist, but that was lovely."

"I'm really not; I just felt motivated today. Everything seemed to have fallen into place for me to"—I shrugged—"feel inspired. Guess part of it is being around you."

Rebecca ducked her head and grinned. "I've never been someone's muse; it's a bit ... wow."

I put down the guitar and walked over. What I felt for her warmed my heart, and all the bad things, the habits that irritated me silly paled in comparison to it. I knew I wasn't any great ball of fun to be around twenty-four hours a day, seven days a week, but we'd made it through the last two weeks together without the option to leave, which made me a bit more optimistic about our chances in the real world.

I took her hands, and gently pulled her to her feet.

"Well, get used to it," I said, pulling her close. "I feel inspired around you, and I'm going to need my muse with me when I get back to California to work on that record with Chris."

The sun had fully set by this point, and the dark indigo of the night sky arrived with tiny pinpricks of starlight, the hazy veil of the Milky Way, and the waning moon painting the sky. Between being with the woman I loved and the beauty of the Arizona desert, I was sure I could write at least three albums' worth of songs.

I stood there with her a while, and just stared at her, silhouetted against the night sky. If I'd been a painter or photographer, I would have wanted to capture this moment in time, as I was sure the world would come crashing down around us shortly, and that any happiness I had would soon be erased.

"How are you feeling?" I asked as we walked inside. It seemed that she'd regained a bit of the ground she'd lost after being hit on the head, but I knew that the memory problems and headaches that she complained of would continue on for a while yet.

She held her hand in mine and reached up to push away a lock of hair that had fallen into my face. "Much better. I still get dizzy every now and then, but I've been able to keep food down for the past bit, so that's a good sign, isn't it?"

It was. Rebecca had been steadily losing weight from the inability to keep food down. It got to the point that I worried for her; she'd gone from healthy curves to gaunt since Jodi had brought me to her in the rat hole that Rebecca had been thrown into. I hoped that this small turn of events towards the good would reverse that trend.

"Yes, that's definitely good." I gave her a peck on the nose and she smiled. "You need to be able to keep on your feet for that big journey tomorrow night. You've got your stuff ready, right?"

She nodded, pointing at a backpack emblazoned with the University of Arizona's logo, hanging on the door to her room. My own small bag was packed with the basics—my car keys and the letter I'd been writing to Kristen—and also by the door to the room I'd been staying in. Not that I'd spent a lot of time there. Usually I'd fall asleep on the couch or sitting with Rebecca, who had, not surprisingly, developed a fear of falling asleep alone in the dark. By the time she usually fell nodded off, curled up around me, her warmth made me fall asleep easily. More days than not lately I'd woken up with her under the blankets, me on top of them, nuzzled together as if that was the way we'd always been meant to sleep.

Nothing sexual had passed between us; well, nothing beyond a few brief stolen moments and sessions of heavy petting. As much as I might want to take her out to the courtyard, throw her on the piano and do things to her that were illegal even between two consenting adults in most states—hell, probably in a lot of countries—I wasn't going to push anything before she was ready to move in that direction. Last thing I wanted was to shatter our fragile relationship and get myself lined up for a rape charge. No, sex would happen when it happened ... but it didn't stop me from hoping that it happened sooner rather than later. Personally, I felt that if it hadn't been for Jodi's horrible timing, we would have gone beyond brief make-out sessions long ago. Mind you, it had taught me that Rebecca had an extensive vocabulary of inappropriate language, some of it rather amusing.

We came back in, and Rebecca offered to make drinks as I took a seat, waiting. I watched as she headed into the small kitchen, dressed in a long, dark halter dress, her pale skin was made even more pallid by the fact that she'd been out of the sun lately. For once, her hair was down in long curls that rolled in languid waves down her back, stopping nearly at waist length.

She came back, holding two glasses of iced tea, with lemon in them. I was surprised she'd actually thought to do that. Rebecca handed one glass to me and sat down on the couch facing me, her legs tucked up underneath her. Taking a sip of the drink, she put it down and then turned to me with a sigh.

"Jon, I hate to do this, because I really love you, and I enjoy being with you, but ..."

Oh Jesus, she's giving me the relationship speech. This is not good. Ah well Jonny-boy it was good while it lasted, wasn't it? Nothing good ever contains the word "but."

"But what?" I said, gulping down the iced tea faster than I probably should have, trying not to sound either cross or worried.

"Well, I feel you act like I'm a porcelain doll. It's as if you're so afraid I'll break you rarely do anything but hold me occasionally and then put me back up on the shelf. I mean, it's great to be treated like I'm worth my weight in gold, but I'm human."

Before she could say anything further, I closed the gap between us, kissing her softly on the lips, and then deepening the kiss as she moved to straddle me on the couch. I reached up as we kissed, tongues intertwining, and ran my hands through her hair; it was so soft, like silk. She moved from kissing to nibbling on my neck and I moaned, enjoying the sensation. I turned my attention to her neck, and she gasped softly as I showered kisses down it and onto her shoulders. Her skin smelt faintly of perspiration and flowers, soft and almost not there but intoxicating. I could feel her pulse beating fast and hard against my lips as I continued to devour her neck.

"Entirely too much clothing," she murmured as she moved back from me and then pulled my shirt off and flung it somewhere in the room, then picked up where she'd left off.

"You do realize that there is no way I'm going to walk out of here without at least a novel if we keep this up," I whispered in her ear.

She laughed and pulled back enough that we could stare into each other's eyes. She took a quick glance down at my neither regions, then looked at my face.

"I'd say at least a newspaper," she said with a wink.

Standing up, she offered me her hand. I took it and followed her down the hallway. She opened a door and pulled me in. We were in her bedroom, which was almost entirely dark except for the small amount of light seeping in through the blinds. Dropping my hand, she reached behind her neck and undid her dress. It fluttered to the floor, revealing that she had nothing on underneath and was now clad in just a smile.

"Holy Jesus," I cursed and her grin increased. I moved over to her, and pulled her against me in another passionate embrace. My hands naturally drifted south, exploring every soft curve and hollow of her body. My hands found the small of her back, and rested there. Her hands were busy, one in my hair, the other lightly tracing down my back, her fingernails gently, almost not there, the ghost of a sensation running down my back that made me tremble with anticipation.

She broke the embrace then, her dark eyes dancing, and laughed —a heady, lustful sound.

"You like that."

I murmured my acknowledgment and set about tracing a path from her lips to her jawline and down her neck to her shoulders. I felt her return the attention by nibbling on an earlobe, and her hands moving ever downward, doing a light dance over my chest, stomach and stopping at the button of my jeans, which had become increasingly too confining for me. She paused there a moment, seemingly waiting for my permission to remove them.

"What are you waiting for?" I whispered into her ear.

She fumbled with the button, and I decided to save her the trouble, and taking my hands reluctantly away from her, I quickly removed the offending piece of clothing, letting it drop to a puddle at my feet.

"Damn ..." was all she could muster.

I decided to do the improbable thing then, and picked her up and carried her over to the bed, kissing her the entire way. Gently putting her down, I crawled onto the covers alongside her. Looking up at me with dark, fathomless eyes, she smiled, and I moved over her. I wanted this to be nothing short of spectacular for her. I'd never considered myself an extraordinary lover; however, experience had taught me to follow the woman's lead as to what she wanted and enjoyed, and even despite my withdrawal from the sexual arena over the past few years, there hadn't ever been any complaints I'd ever heard.

I bent down to kiss her again. Her lips were soft, and still had the taste of what she'd been drinking shortly before—faint hints of lemon and sugar. I felt her run her hands up my back and into my hair, pulling me deeper into the embrace. Her tongue gently explored and I returned the explorations in turn, and then moved from her mouth to her neck with a series of small nipping kisses that elicited a passionate moan from her as she arched her neck to expose more of it to me. I could feel her hands on my neck, fingers running through my hair.

I stopped for a moment, and she looked at me with surprise.

"Becca, if at any point you want to stop, just say the word. I promise you ..."

She put her finger against my lips, stopping me from talking. Then she rolled to the right, and rummaged in a drawer for a moment. Turning back, I saw what she had in her hand. Without saying a word, I nodded, understanding. In this day and age, it would be folly to engage in anything like this without some form of protection.

"Shut up, Jonathan, it's not like I'm a virgin," she said, voice heavy with desire, pulling me back down into the embrace. I had to admit, I had thought that for a while, but decided not to err in asking that question to her at an inappropriate time.

I could smell the faint smell of her perfume, mixed with the salty yet musky smell of her perspiration, as I worked my way down from her neck with gentle kisses to her breasts. Taking one in my hand, I felt her arch into my touch. I leaned down and gently took one nipple in my mouth. It hardened right away, and I heard the sharp intake of breath as I teased it with my tongue, before moving over to the other breast, and suckling gently on the other nipple. I could feel her hands in my hair, pressing against my head, pulling me as close as possible to her. I concentrated my attentions on her breasts for a few moments, until she pushed me back from her, so that I was sitting on my heels. She sat up, her ivory skin reddened with desire, Taking the condom back into her hand she ripped open the package with her teeth, and without announcement, reached for me. A few quick movements and the condom was on.

"Now, where were we?" Rebecca said a beguiling smile on her face.

She leaned in, kissing me tenderly again. I wrapped my arms around her and gently bore her back down to the bed. I didn't want this to go too fast. God only knew that I wanted this to be damned good for both of us, more her than me. Luckily for me, my brain was in no mood to argue philosophy, instead it kept reminding me to follow her lead, let her show me what she wanted rather than steam ahead like a freight train, no matter how much every square inch of my brain screamed that it wanted to "just do it now damn it."

I felt her hand on me still, moving with a rhythm that made me want to howl at the moon.

"Sweetie, if you don't ... stop," I said, trying to keep concentration on what I was saying, "things will ... woah ... be over before they begin."

Her hand left me then, and I felt it drift up and over my chest and down my arm.

"Well, are you going to do anything?" she asked mischievously, "Or do I have to knock you on your ass and do it myself?"

I couldn't help but laugh at that, which presented the perfect opportunity for her to take me by surprise and with one leg alongside my ribs and grabbing me by both arms, she flipped me over.

I laid there in shock, her straddling me with a triumphant grin on her face not unlike the lioness that had just scored a kill for her pride.

"Guess I'll have to take matters into my own hands then," she said, smiling as she bent down to kiss me again.

I tried to move one hand to touch her and was greeted with a gentle yet firm pressure from her hands on my wrists to kept them where they were. She worked her way down my neck across my shoulders and down my chest with gentle kisses, stopping every few moments to look up through the dark fringe of her hair, eyes almost black in the low light. She ran her free hand down my side and found the ticklish spots, which she teased mercilessly.

She continued to work her way down, stopping at my hips. The room was still and silent except for the ragged breathing of her and me.

She slowly crawled back up my body, showering me with biting kisses, which elicited an ardent groan from me, and a titillating smile from her in response. I'd never been one to be extraordinarily vocal in sexual circumstances; however, Rebecca seemed to know innately how to spark that deeply buried urge within me.

"So, you want me to stop yet?" she said teasingly, running her hand through my hair.

"God, no," was all I could manage.

She moved back down, and I once more felt her take me in her hand. This time, however, there was only the briefest movement, then I felt myself slipping inside her. She stayed still for a while, straddling me, and watching my reaction with satisfaction. For my part, I did complex mathematics in my head, trying to keep myself distracted from the sensations that threatened to prematurely throw me over a cliff.

She moved in a slow rhythm, her hands braced on my chest, keeping her eyes on mine. I had never been much of one for watching my lover's reactions, but watching Rebecca as she moved was electrifying. I leaned up to get closer to her, so I could touch her. She adjusted her position, putting a hand behind my head and pulling me in for a fervent embrace, and changed her pace. I'd never had a lover who openly enjoyed the female dominant position until now, and the change was invigorating.

"How are you feeling?" she whispered in my ear, voice barely audible and shaking with excitement.

"Well, I think I may well have figured out the square root of pi," I said with a laugh as I nuzzled her neck and reached up to cup a breast in one hand.

She laughed as well, the sensation being felt through multiple areas of my body caused me to tremble and cry out. I felt her stiffen and moan, her head thrown back in pleasure. She threw her head forward, her own eyes faraway and bright, dark hair cascading over her shoulders and down over her breasts. She then stopped and moved off me, coming to lie beside me, her head on my shoulder.

"Your turn," she said simply, watching me and playing with a stray piece of hair. I took her hand away from my hair, and gently rolled her over on her side, pulling her hair up to expose her neck and shoulders, I gently nibbled along where her shoulder and neck met, and was rewarded by her arching back against me with a muted sigh. The bruises that Kyle and Sarah's goons had left on her over the past while were faded to almost nothingness, and she wasn't against having that area touched, as long as it was gentle and by someone she trusted.

I pulled her back against me and entered into her, cursing at the sensations, lacking any words to describe how I was feeling at the time. The sensation pooled at the back of my brain and I knew this wasn't going to last much longer, no matter how much I tried. Riding the waves of sensation that ripped through my body like a knife, I became aware of only her and myself—sounds, touch, smells, all melded into one another—and before I knew it, I was hanging on the edge of climax, dangling on by a thread. Rebecca leaned back, seemingly sensing that teetering on the precipice of the void, and whispered simply, "Fall with me." It was enough. I pulled back once more, and with a cry that I'm sure was heard three states over, the blinding white heat took over my senses and I tumbled over that edge into the blinding oblivion.

After everything was taken care of and I'd come back to the bed, we lay there in each other's arms, basking in the afterglow that comes after good sex. Tensions that had been there before were gone, and I'd come to the conclusion that I could not love her without losing a bit of myself in the process.

She lay curled into my left side, long dark hair splayed across my shoulder and the pillow, dozing lightly. Her arm was across my chest, and hand intertwined with my own. I watched her sleep, peaceful and quiet, before succumbing to the lure of Morpheus myself and sliding into a restful and dreamless sleep.

When I woke up hours later, the bed was empty save for myself, but the warmth of the Rebecca shaped indentation told me she hadn't been gone for long, and once I'd gathered enough wits about me, I was able to discern that the shower was running. Getting up with a yawn and a stretch, I wandered into the washroom, where indeed, Rebecca was in the shower, a plume of steam rising over the shower curtain. I pulled out towels out for myself, throwing them with hers and then pulling back the shower curtain I joined a somewhat startled and steamy Becca in the shower.

"Good Morning, Becca-bear," I said, reaching around her waist to pull her dripping form closer to me, and planting a kiss on the warm and wet shoulder that was closest to me. She'd been in the process of washing her hair, and she smelled of the floral smell of her shampoo—sharp and sweet at the same time. She turned, washcloth in hand, soap suds from the rinsing of her hair sliding down her body.

"Good afternoon is more like it," she said, wrapping her arms around my neck and giving me a passionate kiss.

"Don't start something you're not going to finish," I murmured in her ear when we finally broke the embrace.

"I could fully finish anything I start," she said with a wicked grin and a wink. "However, I came in here to get clean, not dirty."

She turned back to rinsing out her hair. Once she was done that, she grabbed the bottle of conditioner and slathered it on her scalp. With a quick look at me, she grabbed me by the shoulders and switched places with me, pushing me under the hot spray of the shower, leaving me gasping and laughing.

"I've got to wait for this stuff, time for you to get clean, Mister Walsh."

The rest of the shower went as normally as possible for two people who shared it, and minutes later we both were out, dressed, and still somewhat warm.

Tonight was the foray out into the passageway that Jodi had been going on about, however, Jodi had not shown up the past two nights, and I was beginning to get worried that something had happened to her of the nefarious variety. Rebecca noticed my pacing and tried to comfort me by saying that it was probably nothing like I imagined, that perhaps Jodi had been busy, or a few other things had happened this week that had kept Jodi out of circulation. The last thing that Jodi wanted to do was attract more attention to her and us than necessary. In the last few days there had been no need for her to visit us, but from knowing Jodi's habits over the past few months, she usually dropped in on Rebecca daily. And Rebecca's well-meaning assurances did nothing to stop my concern that something had happened to the person who was probably our only way out of here.

By about five in the afternoon I'd worn a groove in the floor and Rebecca had moved out to the garden as a way of preventing yet another argument between us, as she had let me know in no uncertain terms without saying a word that I was annoying her seven ways from Sunday. If patience was a virtue, then it was one that had always been in short supply for me. I'd be one of those people who stood in front of the microwave yelling at it to hurry up.

The sun slowly slid down the sky, and after about an hour out in the garden, Rebecca returned and wordlessly worked on making a light supper for the two of us. She'd been feeling better today. There had been no signs of the usual headaches or over-whelming dizziness that usually took her from feeling fine to a curled-up ball, shaking and sweating a cold sweat. I left what had become my roost on the couch, and went over to offer my help with making dinner. She handed me two plates and the cutlery, and instructed me to set the table, adding that when we got out of this place, she'd expect me to hold up my end of the cooking, and not to expect her to be a Martha Stewart clone.

It was just easier, in her estimation, that she did the cooking here, as she knew where everything was, and with her current level of irritation, it was probably best that I stayed out of her way and didn't pester her with questions. I was beginning to think that I wasn't the only thing that was irritating her—Jodi's absence had to be on her mind as well.

I set the table and took a seat, keeping an eye on Rebecca. She stirred something on the stove, singing just under her breath, as she kept an eye on it. She'd braided her hair back out of her way after the shower and had dressed in pants and a shirt suitable for the possibility of getting massively dirty while we explored this unknown portion of the hotel. She looked up at me with a smile, and I realized that I'd been staring at her for a while.

"It'll be ready shortly, if that's what you're giving me that look about," she said. "Nothing hugely special tonight, just something easy so we can be fed and get out of here as quick as possible. I think Jodi said that she'd be over after evening services, so that leaves us about an hour."

Rebecca turned back to the meal prep and I checked my watch. She was right; Jodi had said that she'd be over then, but I still had that lingering, nagging doubt that Jodi would actually show up here at all. Knowing Kyle knew we were out and had seen me, my imagination ran over multiple and successively worse situations that could have happened to Jodi, which could prevent her from showing up and dampen any plans of escape.

Deciding that staring down Rebecca might not be a good idea— as much as I thought she was a gorgeous creature and worthy of being watched—and knowing that pacing like a caged lion would not do anything good for the situation except rile Rebecca and make my own agitation worse, I got up and headed out to the garden.

The sunset painted the sky in vivid shades of violet, blue, yellow, and red. The cool night breeze made me briefly shiver until I adjusted to it. I picked up the guitar that I'd left outside yesterday, and walked over to the small ledge of rock where Rebecca had been sitting when I'd played the melody that had lodged itself firmly in my brain.

I distractedly strummed a tune as I let my mind run over the possibilities that lay ahead after getting out of here. The first thing I would need to do is call Kristen, and let her know that everything was okay. Chris was next on the list; I had to give him the answer to the question he'd asked of me before I'd left.

Would it be a smart move to reunite Torrent? Ryan had tossed that idea around for a while, but he'd also suggested just the two of us put together a new band, maybe bringing Mike in on it as well. Ryan knew full well that even though Chris and I shared a family bond that by itself was thicker than water, the ambivalence between us over the affair he'd had with Tricia went pretty deep, even though I could not stand the woman and considered her a good part of what had caused the situation to begin with.

There had been some rumblings around the music community that we should reunite, despite how our genre of music was not exactly chart topping right now. After all, if The Eagles could put aside arguments, then why couldn't I bury the hatchet somewhere other than Chris' back and move forward? I mulled it over, wondering if it would be worthwhile to bring Mike from his teaching job back to drumming for something that might not even take off. Especially if Chris and I went at it hammer and tongs, the way we'd done in the years leading up to the day we'd called our manager Myles and told him that we'd finally had enough of the bullshit and we'd go our separate ways. I knew Ryan could be flexible enough with his scheduling and he'd be able to accommodate recording sessions—after all, I'd brought him in as both a studio artist and as a part of my backing band on solo efforts. That just left Chris and me.

I was between projects at the moment, not meaning that I was lacking for work, but that I was in the songwriting process rather than the recording and producing phase. Of course, now that I had someone in my life, it would probably be a pertinent idea to ask what her input was on the situation at hand, and plausibly to see if we'd be able to stand each other when the reality of the real world set in. There were just so many variables.

I sighed and looked up from what I was doing. My hair hung into my eyes, and I brushed it away to see Rebecca coming out from the French doors, a small smile on her face, beckoning me back in to the suite—dinner must have been ready. I put down the guitar and followed her. Sure enough, dinner was on the table. We both sat down and ate, neither of us talking and both of us worried. I put off discussing anything about the likelihood that Torrent would be reuniting, no sense in bringing up things that might or might not happen while we were still trapped inside this place. Once we finished dinner, I gathered up the dishes without speaking, and washed them.

"For a rock star, you're pretty domestic," Rebecca said with a laugh as she came up beside me and to dry and put away things.

"Hey, I wasn't born a rock star, and if you think my Mum would allow her only son to get away with being a lazy bum around the house, you're very mistaken, thank you very much.

"Oh, you're so cute when you get all uppity. The accent really comes out when you do."

I couldn't help but stop and look at her.

"What do I sound like normally then, huh?"

She thought for a moment. "Your accent is hard to really put a finger on. You sound British, but you've got a good deal of New Yorker in there. But when you get proud the Brit really comes out in your speaking. I'd never guess you were raised in the States."

"Oh, so it's just British, eh? Can't narrow it down a bit?" I elbowed her playfully. "I take offense to that, you know. Saying to someone from Abingdon that they're British when there are so many different accents in Britain ... it's like saying I sound the same as someone from Doncaster or Coventry. It's like me saying you sound like someone from Massachusetts, and you're from ..."

She turned to look at me. "Okay, okay. I'm sorry. Just to the average American ear you sound British, that's all. Most people here can't tell the difference between someone from London and someone from Reading."

The irritation in her voice was clear. I'd crossed a line with my teasing.

"Becca, it's okay, I was only joking, you don't have to get upset."

She put the last dish away and walked away, looking a bit distressed, and wandered in the direction of the door. Jodi was due to show up any moment, and the pressure of the wait was definitely getting to Rebecca.

"Is she ever going to get here?" she murmured under her breath, wrapping her arms around herself and staring at the door as if to make Jodi show up faster.

I resisted the urge to start pacing the floor again, and instead busied myself cleaning every last nook and cranny of the kitchen area, which, considering it was already clean, was a means of keeping myself from irritating her more and driving myself insane.

When it seemed like a rap on the door and the familiar voice of Jodi would never be heard again, there finally came a knock and the question: "Are you guys in there?" I just about jumped out of my skin, and Rebecca ran to the door to open it. I half believed Kyle played a trick on the us and someone would be ready to clonk Rebecca again on the head, but was pleasantly surprised— and relieved—to see Jodi enter the room.

After Rebecca had had her moment with Jodi, acting like a puppy that hadn't seen its owner in a fortnight, I managed to make my way over and give Jodi a hug. She returned it as best as she could, laden down with a bag that contained some things we were going to need for the trip down the passageway.

Jodi shooed us in the direction of the living room and threw the bag of things onto the table.

"Okay, people. Let's get our act together before we leave."

She tipped open the bag, and flashlights and other assorted things I couldn't quite make out fell into a jumbled pile on the table.

"We'll each need a flashlight, and I'd suggest taking one of these as well"—she handed out what appeared to be nightsticks. —"Just in case we run into one of Sarah's goons. No, Kyle's not really involved, you guys. He's kind of a secondary player in this drama. Most of what you've experienced has been Sarah's bidding. As Rebecca and I can testify, most of the men around here will do anything she asks just for the chance at one night with her. That's bred both loyalty and competition between them, and they'll do anything. Anything. This makes them twice as dangerous as the assholes that Jon ran into when he tried to check on his car."

Jodi took out the small hand-drawn map that outlined the corridor and we began to set up our action plan for that night. We decided to leave Rebecca's suite around midnight, as that would pretty much guarantee none of us would run into Sarah or any other ghoul.

The escape route remained concealed in a region near the dining area, apparently located behind a false wall. From there it seemed to run around the outside of the building, possibly to an old service exit, and from there—freedom. A tingle of anticipation ran up my spine, and I smiled widely at the thought of being back in the outside world again, where everything felt normal. I looked over at Rebecca, who looked wistful. I bet she thought as I did. Getting out of here would be a dream come true at this point.

"So, half an hour and then we can head out," said Jodi. "I strongly suggest you two get your things together and have any private conversations you want to have with each other, just to be on the safe side. You never know what might happen and the last thing I need is for you two to wind up in a tough spot and go all soft and sentimental on me, when you need to keep your mind focused on the goal, whatever comes."

She hastily cleaned up the table and wandered into the dining area of Rebecca's place, leaving the two of us alone. I got up and offered a hand to Rebecca, and we went into the garden where we could have a bit more privacy.

I wrapped my arms around her and held her near to me for a while.

"If something happens to us to separate us, or we otherwise end up apart and not able to get back together Becca, I want you to know that I love you. I don't regret a moment of the time we've spent together, and if I had to do it over, I still hope I'd find you, even if it meant going through hell all over again."

I felt her nod against my chest and then lean back so she could look at me.

"I love you too, hon," she said simply. She didn't need to say more than that. She wasn't the one who had the "burden of proof," per se.

"Anything you want to add, hmm?" I teased.

She looked up at me again. "What do you want me to say that you haven't already, Jon? I love you, I'd go through hell to be with you, more than what I've already done? That I also don't regret a single moment we've been together, and I want to spend my foreseeable future with you?"

I rolled my eyes. "Only if it's true. I've had enough of being lied to by someone close to me."

Rebecca reached up and ran a hand along the side of my face, watching me with a smile and something else in her expression that said more than she probably wanted it to.

"Jonathan Walsh, you are silly sometimes, you know that? It's part of what I love about you. I don't think you ever really grew up—and that's a good thing."

She tiptoed up and kissed my nose. There was a polite cough from behind us. Jodi stood with her arms folded across her chest.

"If you're ready, it's time to get going," said Jodi.

Hand-in-hand, Rebecca and I walked back into her suite, and grabbed our bags, the batons, and the flashlights, and headed out into the night.

CHAPTER 17

*W*e headed out into the corridors at just past midnight and for once, the place was quiet as a church on Tuesday afternoon. It was cold out, and I felt glad I'd dressed in layers. Jodi lead the way with Rebecca and me following her down the corridors while still holding hands.

Not even now could I help feeling like a teenager around Rebecca, though nothing could be further from reality. Part of me wanted to take her into any corner I could find and shag her silly, as if I'd just discovered the massive amount of fantastic shagging could be. Really, it probably was that I'd rediscovered fun again, with the added dimension of actually being in love with the person themselves rather than just experiencing the brief flare of physical attraction. What we had felt like something that could last a long while.

We made our way through the passageways, which were unlit, like the night I'd arrived. The place was cold and quiet as a tomb, and it gave me the chills. We cut into the dining area, and Jodi motioned for us to stop. We did and she took off into the prep area. I pulled Rebecca in close and she laid her head on my shoulder. I glanced down at her. She stared worriedly across the room, towards where I was pretty sure we were heading.

"So, what do you want to do when you get out of here?" I whispered quietly to her.

She lifted her head and thought for a moment. "Other than dance like a fool that I'm free? I need a haircut. That is the first order of business for me. Okay, second. Sleep, haircut, and then going home to get my license renewed and maybe, just maybe introduce the new man in my life to my family."

The last bit was said with a smirk and a slight elbow in my ribs. Introducing me to her family cemented the deal. We were definitely an item.

Jodi returned juggling a few bottles of water. "Here, take two each. You might need them, for whatever reason." She held them out to us and Rebecca put them in her bag, which had more room than mine.

We headed back towards the secret passageway. Jodi rummaged around in her pockets and produced a set of keys. This end of the compound was rarely visited; you could tell from the lack of signs of human habitation, and the dust that had been collecting around the area. I sneezed as I inhaled it, and Rebecca looked up at me with red eyes.

"I'm sure we'll be there shortly," she said quietly with a squeeze of my hand. Light filtered in through the windows from the moon and signs of the town beyond this place, muted through the veil of dust that filtered through the air. We entered into a long-disused area, more so than the rest of it, mainly used for storage and things for the preparation area, seemingly for when the inn would be busier. I wasn't sure if that meant for a time in the past or the future.

Jodi noticed my searching around, and confirmed that this stuff had been planned for the ongoing expansion. You could hear the sarcasm in her voice, and she shook her head as she stared back down the hallway.

"They'll never get the chance to use it if I have anything to say about it," she muttered loud enough so we could hear.

We turned down another twist in the hallway, and where the wall ended seemed a bit odd, as if it should have been a few feet longer. Rebecca looked expectantly at Jodi, who nodded. We were there at long last.

Jodi fished the keys from her pocket again, after having put them back. She asked Rebecca to help her push the carts out of the way, and after the they moved them, the door was revealed. Jodi slipped a key into the padlock around the handles of the door, and with a satisfying click, the tumblers turned in the lock, opening the way to what I hoped was the path to freedom.

Jodi removed the lock and chain, and after gently tossing them aside, opened the doors to a dark, musty, unlit corridor.

"Well, here we are," she said, expectation high in her voice as she turned to both of us. "Let's face the unknown."

She turned, flicking on the flashlight, and without any further words, she went down the dark hallway.

Rebecca turned to me with a look of anticipation. "Well, you ready to take our first steps to the outside world?"

I leaned down and gave her a quick kiss. "Definitely."

We both flicked on the flashlights that Jodi had given us, and with a gulp and thoughts of mice running all over my feet, we both took our first steps into the dark hallway. Rebecca closed the doors behind us, sealing us off from the brightness of the hallway and plunging us into darkness.

The only illumination was the bobbing and weaving of the flashlights of our little trio. The place thankfully wasn't damp, because the desert of Arizona had kept everything dry. There hung quite a bit of cob webbing, and for once in my life I felt extremely glad I didn't mind spiders. Rebecca had dropped my hand as we walked into the corridor, but kept a close distance, never more than a few steps between her and myself, and no more than double that between Jodi and me. Though the place spanned widely enough so we could have walked two abreast, we all walked single file. It was a slow walk, almost a death march through the passage.

Try as I might, I couldn't help but shine my flashlight occasionally on the posterior of the woman of my dreams, my lover, my sweetheart. This did not go unnoticed, and after about the third time that I'd done it, she stopped short, and I almost ran into her.

"Hon, you do that again, and I'll have to hurt you, badly," Rebecca whispered into my ear with a giggle. "Keep your light on the floor; the last thing you want to do is step on a mouse."

Those were the words I least wanted to hear, and got me instantly back to sweeping the passageway with my light, trying to avoid the little buggers. A chuckle told me that was a part of her plan; however, I had been serious about being terrified of mice. The cobwebs made me jump as they brushed my head and hands. It was almost like a Hollywood horror scene setup on the back lot. Then I thought to myself that even Hollywood couldn't dream up something as totally fucked up as this place. Truth was definitely stranger than fiction.

We all walked in silence for a while, following Jodi like ducklings after their mother. We made a turn, and Jodi stopped suddenly.

Rebecca and I ran into each other, and then into our mother duck. Jodi dug the hand-drawn map out of her pocket, and shining the light from her torch onto it, she looked around. I did, too. We were in a t-shaped section of the long-forgotten area of the hotel. I swept my own torch into the dark outer areas, and could have sworn I saw something vaguely rodent-like tear off out of the glare of the light. I couldn't help but shiver, and edged closer to Rebecca and Jodi.

"I think we should go ..." —Jodi looked closely at the map—"... right here. I'm pretty sure the other one comes out near the court-yard and that's something we don't want."

Swinging her flashlight around as if to confirm the correct path, Jodi nodded, deciding on the corridor to the right. Of course, if all else failed, we could always turn back and retrace our steps back to this spot.

I kept my flashlight on the ground, sweeping back and forth, keeping an eye on what could be there. This of course, enabled me to walk right into a rather large cobweb. I let out a yelp and jumped back from it, more surprised than scared. Jodi and Rebecca both stopped short and turned back, trying vainly to get the webbing off me as fast as possible. After a few minutes of struggling, I was able to extricate myself from it, and with a frus-trated sigh, I tossed the last of it to the ground. Rebecca fought cracking up and I had to admit I must have been a sight, covered in cobwebs and thrashing around like my head was on fire.

"You ready go on?" Jodi asked, and I nodded.

We headed back into the steady pace we'd kept, and I had the urge to check my watch. Calling for Jodi to stop, I flicked the flashlight up to my wrist. We'd only been walking about ten minutes, even though it felt much longer. I went to step forward and swung my light down. I could have sworn I saw mice and resisted the urge to scream like a little child or climb the walls. I cleared my throat and tried to calm the ball of fear that twisted my gut by telling myself there was a cat here that caught mice, and I shouldn't see too many of them.

We resumed the same pace we'd been on from the start. I kept an eye on the shadowy form of Rebecca in front of me, as she was a good indicator of when I would need to bob and weave to avoid things—like more cobwebs and the crossbeams—that framed the area. Being the tallest of the trio by at least five inches meant I had the unwished-for task of dodging everything at the height that the original designer of the place never considered people would reach. I had to keep ducking and continually got crap in my hair. Thankfully I was prepared, and after the first few times, it became second nature for me to reach up and brush my hair clear every so often.

After a while we came to another junction, and Jodi again checked the map. She seemed worried and a bit off kilter as compared to her usual composed self.

"Jodi, why don't we stop for a while?" I suggested.

She nodded, and we all rested, tentatively leaning against the walls. No one trusted what was on them and I sat down on the ground, the fear of mice temporarily forgotten. Rebecca handed me a bottle of water, which I took with silent thanks, and guzzled down a deep drink.

"Your lack of confidence right now bothers me, Jodi," I said. "What's up?"

Jodi sighed and turned, the beam of her flashlight temporarily blinding me as it crossed my vision. Her hair was pulled back into a low ponytail, and covered with as much dust and cobwebs as my own and Rebecca's.

"I don't know. This map just doesn't seem right to me. It looks like the one that I'd drawn when I was speaking with you guys when referring to the plans, but something is off about it, and I don't know what."

My stomach dropped at those words. I didn't want to think that someone had managed to get a hold of that map and possibly redirected us by having carefully redrawn it. Jodi wasn't that careless of a person to have left it out in plain sight either. If anything, Jodi had been one of those people that you could count on to think things through before acting.

"I certainly hope that it's just something you'd drawn on it, Jodi. I don't want to think of the unending hell that could be waiting for us if that thing's been changed around by someone outside of the three of us."

I took another long drink of water, hoping to drown the sinking sensation now firmly entrenched in my gut. It didn't work. If nothing else, the knot, the distinct feeling that someone had bamboozled us, was getting stronger, and my mind only went to one possibility—Sarah. Whoever had said hell hath no fury was bang on. I'd seen it in my ruthless harpy of an ex-wife and in Sarah, when she'd tried to sink her claws into me. They reminded me of each other in more ways than one. Both bleached blonde, attracted to money, could be highly charismatic, but when slighted, they had the tendency to bring down the wrath of Hades in ways only women can.

"Um, Jon ... hon. You might want to get up," Rebecca said with a grin on her face as she swung her flashlight at me.

"In a minute," I grumped, stretching my arms above my head with a small groan.

"Jon, seriously, you need to get up. I know you well enough to say that. Please listen to me."

I looked down to where her line of sight was, and sure enough, there was a smallish gray-brown blob of fur sitting brazenly on my left foot, gazing up at me with beady eyes.

With a scream that only could be described as "girly" I leapt to my feet and tried to get away from the flea ridden pest before it bit me. All I could think of for about a full minute was getting as far away from that thing as I could. When I stopped trying to climb the nearest wall and began hyperventilating, I saw both women bent over with laughter.

"What?!" I said between wheezes. "Those little buggers are pure evil."

"I just can't believe that you didn't feel the poor thing climbing up on your foot. I also love that the mouse actually had the balls to get up there," said Rebecca, her voice choked with laughter. "Don't worry, Kismet will make short work of them. Problem is there's just too many of them here for one cat to keep up with."

She came over, still laughing and wrapped her arms around me in a tight hug.

"It's okay, you'll be fine. Just no more sitting down in this passage-way, okay?"

I nodded. I wouldn't sit down again in that corridor, even if my legs gave out. Quite frankly, I felt pretty sure I'd not sit on any floor in this place again if I could help it. Once my breathing had settled back to a relatively normal rate, we set off down the cata-comb-like passage, following Jodi once more.

We wound again and again through the dark corridors, dust and dirt flung around by our footsteps in a place unvisited by humans in an era—a veritable vermin nest. I forced back a shudder and kept steadily plodding on behind Jodi and Rebecca. Time seemed to pass in slow motion, and I began to lose track of where we were. How many turns we'd made were a pure mystery to me, but by this point I didn't care. I just wanted out of this mouse-infested hellhole and back into the real world. I desperately wanted Rebecca to come with me. I wanted so much, and for once in my life, I had so little.

We came to what seemed to be the last set of doors. With an expectant glance at the two of us, Jodi pushed against the door, putting all her weight against it, and slowly, with a creak and a moan that reached to the marrow of my bones, it opened.

With my heart beating a mile a minute and threatening to jump out my chest, I took Rebecca's hand again and we went forward through the door, Jodi coming out first. I snuck a peek at Rebecca, who trembled with anticipation, and she looked up. With a smile that seemed to light the area a few shades brighter, she squeezed my hand and then stepped forward to wherever this place ended. I followed her.

When I stepped out, I blinked hard, as the change in lights almost hurt. I couldn't see for a few moments, and when I could, my heart sank to my shoes. We were deeper in the core of the place; in fact, we were in a well-lit basement area and not the outside world. What disquieted me more than that was the person who stood before us, casually attired, long blond hair hanging around her shoulders and a smug look on her face.

"Well, Jodi, I never would have thought you would pull something like this, but it seems you're in cahoots with our two little lovebirds here," said Sarah, watching from her perch on an antique desk.

I could see the outline of many bodies behind her, the "guards" of this place, the ones who played the role of enforcers—from what I could figure—portions of Sarah's inner circle. Jodi stared at Sarah with a combination of shock, amazement, and rage; the range of emotions cycled rapidly across Jodi's face, rarely settling on one for more than a few seconds.

Sarah turned her gaze to me and slithered down off the desk. Making her way across the floor, she stopped mere inches in front of me, and abruptly glanced at Rebecca. The venom in her eyes was palpable, and I pulled Rebecca close. This brought Sarah's focus back on me and with a sigh she smiled insincerely, which betrayed the depth of what machinations actually lurked beneath.

She reached out and cupped the side of my face. I fought hard to keep buried the shiver of revulsion that was threatening to make its way to the surface. If I ever showed any weaknesses or vulnerability, it would only be to the woman who was at my side, the woman I would protect with everything at my disposal.

"Oh, Jonathan. So much potential and you had to go throw it away with the rabble. What a waste. You could have done so much better."

"What, like you?" I asked, hoping my voice sounded hard, dripping in sarcasm.

"Why yes, or one of the many other women around here who would have loved to have gotten know you better," she cooed, running her fingers up the front of my shirt.

I could feel Rebecca's arm tensing around my back, and figured it was a matter of time before she knocked Sarah her flat on her ass.

"Yeah, well, I've never been one for wise decisions. Just ask my ex-wife," I said, knowing full well the sneer that was on my face. Reaching up, I took Sarah's wandering hand off my chest. "I'm not interested, Sarah. It's not even tempting."

Sarah's face was a combination of rage and amazement. The thought crawled through my mind again that no one have ever turned her down; she was entirely used to getting her way in everything she did.

"Fine, have it your way. You could've had it easy," she said, each word clipped in anger as she motioned to some of the faceless people who stood behind her.

Three of them moved forward, the first one taking hold of Jodi, who did not resist—there was no point in fighting it. Jodi simply peered over at us with remorse and mutely mouthed the words, "I'm sorry." Tears ran down her face. She was escorted out of the room and I had no doubt that Sarah would leave it to Kyle to extract whatever punishment he saw fit for the "crime" of helping us. Two more goons stepped forward and tried to pry Rebecca and me apart. Drawing myself up to my full height, I glared at the one closest to me and told him that we either went together to whatever fate was in store for us, or I'd take him on with every ounce of strength I had in me. Despite my age, he decided it wouldn't be worth his time, even though he could probably have turned me into a bruised puddle with a few quick blows. It had been years since I'd last been in a physical fight and I knew I wouldn't be on the winning end in any scuffle here.

As we were paraded by Sarah, she stared at me with a malevolent smile.

"We'll see, Jonathan, if a few days in the hole will change your tune. Maybe then you'll be more willing to entertain any offers I have for you."

"I doubt it, Sarah," I said over my shoulder as we were ushered out of the room into the waiting darkness.

CHAPTER 18

They ushered us through a dark passageway to someplace. I still had no idea where we were. We came up into the main area of the compound; I could tell that much, as the temperature jumped from cool to the dry warmth of the Arizona autumn.

We were still in a dark, under-lit portion of the Skylark Inn, and we had our bags with us. For some reason, we weren't being shoved down the corridors—just gently guided. Eventually, the two guards indicated for us to stop. When Sarah had said "holes" I figured we would be taken back to the same type place we had been imprisoned last time. This seemed almost civilized compared to where I'd been trapped. Maybe it was the lack of a hit on the head, because this was still dark and dreary, but at least we weren't being squeezed into a small box. It was large enough for two people, although still a prison-cell sized, windowless room without any amenities. They took our bags and ushered us inside. The guard on Rebecca's side leaned down and said something quietly to her, and then closed and locked the door behind us. The darkness enveloped us again, and I heard Rebecca crying.

As my eyes adjusted to the light, or lack thereof, I could see there were cracks allowing some form of illumination, just enough that I could make out her outline. I slid down on the floor beside Becca and pulled her shaking and crying form against me. She leaned into me as I held her and made comforting noises, running my hands over her hair to calm her down.

Rebecca didn't hold me as she normally would, and I realized the dam that had kept back so much was breaking. She wept for what seemed like forever, and I continued to hold her as close as I could. My heart broke for her and for our situation. I struggled to hold in my own tears, as two of us falling to pieces would do no good for either of us, and I felt afraid that my own sadness would trigger her in some way.

After a while, her sobbing subsided into body-shuddering hiccups. She re-arranged herself in my arms, so that her head rested against my shoulder and her back was to my front with my arms wrapped around her. I leaned my cheek against her head, and sighed deeply.

I never imagined I'd end up in a place like this, totally removed from the reality of the world, a black hole to normalcy. When I'd set out from Oakland over a month before, I had envisioned a simple trip to Colorado to visit my daughter, son-in-law, and newborn granddaughter for a few weeks, then I'd head back to work on my own, maybe taking off a few weeks at Christmas time to drive to New York to see Ryan and family before returning back to California for the foreseeable future. I'd never thought of finding love. Hell, I'd not been looking for it at all when it hit me over the head in the form of an impressive woman who, if I'd been somewhere else, I probably never would have given a second thought beyond: *Isn't she beautiful?* Rebecca seemed like the answer to an unspoken prayer—not the perfect woman, but a one with her own faults who'd be willing to put up with mine. She cared for me not because I was well-to-do; in fact, I was pretty sure that if tomorrow the money I'd worked hard to put away over the years was gone, she'd still be with me. It was refreshing to speak to someone who didn't turn themselves into a gibbering pulp at my feet, who wanted to discuss regular, mundane things that in my line of work were rarely spoken of. Someone who I could talk about something that mattered to me and not have them pretend to be interested in it. Rather, I knew Rebecca would tell me she either wasn't into it, or listen and ask for clarification if it was something that intrigued her but hadn't encountered before.

With the slim hope that we'd actually survive to live together in the outside world, I looked forward to taking her to things I knew she'd never had the opportunity to see and do. For me it was like getting a new lease on life, a breath of fresh air that I'd not had for years—definitely not in my marriage to Tricia. Tricia had been all about status: having the biggest house, the most money, the biggest and best car, and the daughter in the Ivy League school-things that didn't rate on my radar. Sure, I enjoyed the comforts that money brought me, but I'd just as soon have the car that I wanted, a smaller house, a nice yard and, as being with Rebecca had shown me, someone down to earth I could share it with.

My mind daydreamed in the darkness, and I could imagine the two of us walking hand in hand through the garden I'd put in, just chatting and enjoying being together. I could see taking her to industry events without worrying she'd act like a fool and say something embarrassing about us in public. I was sure I wouldn't hear complaints about the endless hours that sometimes needed to be put in while bringing an album to completion, or the length of time a tour took. Looking down on her now sleeping form, I could actually see taking Rebecca with me on tour. She wasn't pretentious and climbing; if anything, she came across as humble to a fault. I knew her father was a lawyer and her mother a teacher, so she wasn't penniless, but rather comfortably upper middle class—the same type of family that I'd come from. If my parents were still alive, I had no doubt that they'd be wholly accepting of Rebecca. She was the type of woman they'd hoped I'd end up with as a partner.

With a small wry smile, I could picture Dad speaking to Rebecca about his work in cultural anthropology, the places he'd visited, and things he'd accomplished in life. Dad had never done that with Tricia; both he and Mum had pretty much disowned me after the wedding. The only reason they had stayed in contact with me was for their granddaughter, Kristen. They had made no secret of their distaste for what they considered the overly loud and obnoxious Southern Californian I'd married, even though they'd loved Kristen with all their hearts. Tricia regarded them as "typically British" and had mostly stayed away from them, which in the end had been quite good for everyone involved. Mum had passed away six years ago, and Dad not too long after that. I made a note that when I got out of here that I should go visit their grave site, which I hadn't in years.

My mind finally stopped wandering and slowly I drifted to sleep. I woke when Rebecca moved, and once she'd settled back into my arms I quickly dozed off again. It was by no stretch of the imagination a restful sleep, but it was sleep in some form. The night dragged on, and without any way to judge the movement of the hours—it could have been minutes, hours or days—the door opened, and a slash of blinding light fell across the floor.

Jodi stood there, a guard at her side, and a tray of food in her hands. It was evident the day had come, and this time Sarah wouldn't be taking any chances of Jodi letting us out of here before Sarah was able to do whatever it was that she'd planned. Jodi came in wordlessly and with a look that spoke more than words could have, laid the tray down and then walked out. It was unnerving not to have Jodi speak when I was used to her boisterous laugh and almost ever-present smile. Both were gone and I had no doubt I'd probably never see them again.

Someone flicked a switch and suddenly everything was bathed in a yellowish light. Rebecca grunted her dissatisfaction and tried to bury her head on my shoulder. After a few minutes of blinking and cursing, we were able to see again, and Rebecca moved forward to investigate what had been left for us.

"Well, it at least looks like they're allowing Jodi to do her regular stuff in the kitchens." said Rebecca, poking at the food before handing it to me. "I can't tell if it's been drugged or not, and I'd not put it past Sarah to do something like that."

I shrugged and took a bite. If they were going to drug me, they were going to drug me; there wasn't much I could do about that. The food tasted to Jodi's usual standards and we both finished quickly. Rebecca happened upon something taped to the bottom of the plate, and with a quizzical expression, she pulled it off and looked at me in surprise.

She moved back over to sit beside me and opened the note so that we both could read it.

Dear Jon and Becca,

Well, you know I'm still out here. They handed me over to Kyle to do whatever he wanted with me, and I'm not going into what he's done so far. Jon, you'd be madder than hell about it, so I'll save you the time. They've put me back to work in the kitchens, and there is always someone watching over me now. I'm writing this note to you both in the few minutes that I get where Kyle or someone isn't monitoring my every muscle movement. Sarah has been speaking about what she wants to do with you Jon, and I hope that she doesn't get the opportunity. Keep yourselves steady for the next few days. Kyle keeps saying that she's planning something and Jon will be pulled out from where you are for it to happen. Becca, brace for things to get worse.

Love you both.

Jodi.

I sighed and laid my head back against the wall. I had no idea what Kyle did to her, but I knew it wasn't good. At least she'd managed to get us some warning about what would come down the tubes, which all things considered, was good. There wasn't much that I could do about it, but at least knowing that over the next few days I'd be facing the first of whatever propositions Sarah had in mind would allow me to steel myself against the onslaught.

The warning to Rebecca had been a little vaguer and I hoped it wasn't going to be anything seriously threatening. My mind had images of torture running through it and I hoped that it was only my overworked imagination going at full tilt rather than some form of premonition of what would happen to her.

Rebecca folded up the note into an impossibly small size and tucked it away into her pocket, then cuddled up alongside me. There was not much to do in here other than sit and chat. Anything else that might come to mind was not an option; the surroundings just didn't lend themselves to any type of romantic interlude.

"So, you want to talk?" she asked, looking up at me.

"Not much else we can do, is there?" I said with a smile as she shook her head with a bit of an ironic grin. It seemed her mind had been in the same place as mine. "What do you want to talk about, then?"

She shrugged. "Anything you want to discuss is fine with me. I just love listening to your voice. Plus, your life has been a hundred times more interesting than mine ever hoped to be."

"I'd say you've had a quite interesting life Rebecca. How many people in North America have traveled as far as you have? Most people rarely leave their home state, and you've traveled in two countries, countless states, and done things that some people would never do in their lives. I wouldn't say that you've lived an ordinary or boring life."

A slight rosy blush bloomed on her cheeks. "Well, when you put it that way, yeah, but your life, makes mine pale in comparison."

I laughed. "Yes, but those of us who are picked by whatever is out there to have the luck and talent to get anywhere in this field are few and far between. Comparing my life to yours up until this point is really apples and oranges. If you were to take me back to when I was in my early twenties, before the band, my life was rather more boring than yours, I'm afraid."

She laughed at that. "Jonathan Christopher, stop being such a liar. By the time you were my age you'd lived in three countries and had more experiences than I could only dream of!"

It was my turn to blush and laugh. "So, I'm supposing that now would be one of those times when you'd like to hear more about my boring childhood? I swear Becca, you're going to have enough information to write a tell-all book about me when we're out of here."

There it was again, that lingering feeling that we were going to get out of here that I just couldn't squelch out. It was like a flame deep inside my psyche that kept me going—that slim hope that this place would eventually become a thing of our past.

Rebecca giggled. "Like I'd ever do that. I'm a composer, not a writer. You tell all this to my sister Michaela though, and you'll have a best seller on your hands in a few months."

We sat there laughing, before settling down to a silent companionship again.

"You never talk about your family, Becca. From what you have said, you and Michaela sound like a right pair of fools together."

She looked away from me then, and her face went far away and contemplative.

"I've just never trusted anyone here enough to talk about my family. You're the first person who has gotten to know me this much."

She sat back and thought for a few moments. "Now, you want to know about Michaela? That's a story that'll take a while, so make yourself comfortable."

"I'm comfortable as can be." I said.

She laughed through her nose. "Well, Michaela and I are actually first cousins. She was adopted by my parents years ago when my aunt and uncle were killed in a terrible car accident. It was gruesome and gory and ugh, I'll just not go into it. Anyway, she came to live with us around the time I was twelve, I think. She's really smart, but never lives up to her potential. She's always in trouble—nothing serious—but enough to keep my parents constantly watching her, or at least that was what it was like when I lived at home. She's zany and crazy and just ... I don't think there are words in the English language to describe her to anyone who hasn't met her." She shrugged, but with a grin.

"She always said I was the "good one" in the family, the one everyone depended on, and everyone could look to. She was always the creative one, the silly one, the one who you'd expect to run through the center of town naked just because she could. I know her parents dying definitely had an effect on her. I mean, before she came to live with us, she was the quiet one in the family. You rarely heard a word out of her. Now you can't shut her up. I've asked her about it before and she said then that she learned to live for today, to hell with tomorrow and the past as well."

Rebecca sighed then and leaned against me "I miss her. Guess she is to me kinda like Ryan is to you."

She looked at me. "So, why don't you tell me how you and Ryan met. Fair is fair. I told you about my life for once. It's your turn."

I sat back and let the memories of over twenty years of friendship run through my mind.

"Well, you know that Ryan and I met when Torrent was looking for a permanent bass player. Ryan is one talented little guy … well, he's not so little anymore, but he'll always be the "little guy" to me. Chris talked me into running an advert in the newspapers up in the New York, New Jersey, and the Rhode Island area when I'd come home from UCLA for the summer in '75, just before Torrent got signed. I can't remember how many auditions I sat through. There are reasons they say bassists are expendable; there's so many bad ones out there that you can afford to work your way through a fistful before you get to the good ones. I was about two steps from giving up and just signing with the guy we had—a total asshole that couldn't get along with Mike if you paid him to—when Ryan called me up and asked if he could audition. I was kind of shocked. A fifteen-year-old kid, I mean, how good could he be? So, I called up Mike and we got together for an audition in Newport. Hell, Ryan didn't even have his license! When we got there and sat down, I was prepared to be disappointed. Here comes this geeky little redhead, looking like you could knock him over with a stiff wind, and a five-string bass. Anyway, we get to auditioning him and Mike decides to throw him a few challenges, and lo and behold the tyke can keep up with him. Two hours later, Mike and I are headed up to New York, and it's decided, we'll bring Ryan on and see how he does. So, we recorded the demo and the rest, as you know, is history. I promised Ry's Dad that I'd keep an eye on him and keep him out of trouble, and I paid for his education. I started out as Ryan's on-the-road guardian. Then as the years went by, he became mine, and he could tell you some stories about trying to keep my ass on the straight and narrow."

I sat up a bit straighter and wrapped my arm around Becca. "Through it all, both of us looking out for each other, we just became good friends. When he met Heather, he didn't take her home to meet his Mum and Dad until he'd introduced her to me. Not that my judgment on women was anything to go by at the time, but he felt I was his family and she deserved to meet the people he spent most of his time with first. I don't know when it happened, but the two us became like brothers. Our tour manager used to say it was fun keeping track of us—wherever I went, Ryan was sure to be right there with me. Chris was always in the bar and Mike was usually in the first place that sold anything caffeine-infused. I think you'll like Ryan, Becca. You two share a lot of things in common and I can't wait for you to meet him and his family."

She nodded, and we sat in silence again. I listened for the sounds of what might be going on out in the hall, but it was mostly quiet, save for the noises of an old building settling during the course of a day.

The door opened again, and Jodi returned. She barely glanced at us, and I noticed the guard standing right behind her, close enough that he would notice if she did anything suspicious. She took the tray without a word and disappeared into the hallway. Then they turned off the lights and we were plunged into darkness again.

"I feel like a prisoner of war," Rebecca said, as she felt around for me, and moved so she was could hear my voice more clearly. "I just don't want to think about when they'll begin the torture."

The finality in her voice led me to think that yes, Sarah would be vicious enough to do something like that, and what I'd seen from Kyle's violence towards Rebecca definitely left the impression that we might not get out of here alive. The niggling doubt and fear hiding in the bottom of my stomach acted up again, and I tried to bury it deep. It wasn't working, and my mind once again began to imagine numerous scenarios that wouldn't end well for both Rebecca and me.

Time once again ran slowly, and with nothing to judge the passage of it against, I wasn't sure of the duration of anything. Rebecca got up and wandered around the room slowly for a while, and then tried to alert whomever kept watch over us that she needed to use the facilities. Someone opened the door, grabbed her roughly, and removed Rebecca from our cell. When she came back, they threw her into the room, and in the dim and quickly receding light from the hallways, I could see red marks on her arms. She looked up at me, her eyes brimming with tears, and quickly made her way over to me, enveloping herself in my arms. Then the dam broke once more and she sobbed with abandon.

Eventually Rebecca wore herself out and fell asleep on my shoulder. I drifted in and out of daydreams and sleep, the former bringing some escape from the mental boredom, the latter because there was nothing much else to do.

After what seemed like an eternity, the door opened again, and someone, a tall someone, showed up.

"Jonathan Walsh?" A deep and somewhat frightening voice asked. I blinked a few times, trying to focus on the face that went with the voice, and failing.

"Yeah?" I asked, groggy from sleep.

"Come with me."

I gently moved Rebecca off me and she moaned her displeasure. Standing up on unsure feet, I wobbled along behind whomever it was, blinking and rubbing my eyes against the searing brightness. The guard lead down a hall, and into a large room. My eyes were still adjusting to the marked difference between where I was and where I had been, so I was unable to make out any features of my surroundings.

"Well, Jonathan. How has the night treated you?"

I groaned. That voice belonged to only one person. Sarah.

"Fine, Sarah. As fine as being kept in a windowless box without a loo and lights can be," I said, my eyes finally beginning to focus.

Sarah sat on the edge of her large, heavy wooden desk, long tanned legs crossed, wearing a dress hiked up quite high. She leaned forward towards me, her hair falling in long blond waves over her shoulders. Steel blue eyes stared me directly in the eye and a grin filtered across her face.

"Might you be willing now to entertain some of my requests?" she said, uncrossing her legs and slithering off the desk to walk up towards me. The more I watched this woman, the more she struck me as snake.

"Sarah, I could be dying of thirst, and if you offered me a sip of water I'd turn it down and die a happy man," I said, meeting her eyes. "I feel like hell, I'm stuck here, and quite frankly, I'd rather die than entertain any of your requests."

The resentment flickered across her face.

"Have it your way, then." She turned and walked away, and the guard who had so kindly seen me here grabbed me and pushed me back along the way that I had come with more than a little force. I staggered and fell more than a few times, to be picked back up by the scruff of my neck and pushed along the hallway, tripping and falling repeatedly until I was pretty much thrown back into the place where Rebecca sat waiting for me.

"Where were you?" she asked, as I picked myself up off the floor and made my way over to her.

I told her of the few minutes I'd been with Sarah, and that I'd refused to take on any of her offers as I was pretty sure they included getting sexually involved with that snake. I didn't care if she told me it would buy my freedom; I'd still be unwilling.

"So, I guess that means we're going to die here after all?" Rebecca asked, her voice showing the wear and unhappiness as to our situation, and it had been less than one day.

"Becca, she's trying to break us. She wants us to do whatever's in her twisted brain, and that's not going to happen as long as I can help it."

Rebecca sighed then, a soul shuddering sound that seemed to come from her shoes, and I could just barely make out her outline leaning back against the wall. Her hair, which had been so neatly braided back a while before, wildly escaped its plait in certain spots. She probably felt as filthy as I did, and in this place, things would get worse before they got better—if better even remained an option.

I settled down beside her, and talked about random things to pass the time. After a while of hearing my own voice without comment from Rebecca, I went silent and sat back with a sigh.

"Why did you stop?" she asked.

"Unlike Chris, I can't take listening to my own voice for hours on end. I didn't think you were listening."

I could hear the chuckle and as it had become so dark that not even her outline was visible anymore, I was forced to picture the smile I felt sure accompanied it.

"I'm usually pretty quiet when I'm listening. I didn't have any questions or anything to contribute to the conversation, but I was listening!"

I heard her shuffle around until she sat beside me, and then I felt her take my arm and wrap it around her shoulders. "Right now, all I want to do is just be. Not talk or anything." Her head found my shoulder, and her own arm wrapped around me.

All of this had not exactly been what I'd expected in a relationship, but when you were trapped in one of the circles of hell, what was normal? I'd never had a relationship with someone who just wanted to sit and be together, and even in this bizarre setting, I welcomed it. I had my worries and doubts about our immediate future, but I tried to look for the silver lining. My mind wandered again, thinking of what would happen on the outside. My past track record when it came to women wasn't spectacular; most would spend a short time with me and then move on for greater pastures.

Rebecca was the first so-called "fan" I'd ever gotten into a relationship with. Throughout my life I'd made sure to give them the widest berth possible—some of them needed very little motivation for their cheese to go slipping off their crackers—and I'd heard some horrible stories through the grapevine. If fans thought their antics had never been spoken of by their adored artists, it was the furthest thing from the truth.

News of what people to avoid spread like wildfire, and most of our crew had been briefed on who wouldn't be allowed near the band. But Rebecca had admitted she was a fan only in the sense of she enjoyed the music, and hadn't an ambition to be in a relationship with any of the band members.

What happened between her and me had grown on its own; in fact, the matter of my fame had kept her from moving on what she'd felt. I had found this out from one of the long talks we had during our time together. Not that I considered myself to be "famous" in any sense of the word anymore. I had my moment in the limelight and now I was an old rock star trying to hang on to what had been there years ago. A part of my mind worried about us, but after having gotten to know Rebecca over the past little while, I realized there seemed to be nothing highly unusual about her or unstable. Unlike Tricia, who to be honest, had been a fan as well, but not the good kind. That had been a relationship I never should have gotten into, right from the beginning.

My mind finally fell silent again, and I drifted in and out of a restless, dreamless sleep. When I managed to stay asleep long enough, I dreamt about falling and woke up with a start. Rebecca groaned, the poor thing woken up by a jumpy, half-asleep musician who should have been able to sleep standing up, from years of traveling in a tour bus.

The next day came and went in a blur—a repeat of the day before —with Sarah asking me if I'd entertain her ideas, and my refusing them. The day after that was the same and so was the next day, or what I'd judged to be the next day. For all I knew it could have been the same day or maybe a day later. Finally, two of the goons came and got both Rebecca and me, almost literally dragging us down the hall, and threw us into a well-lit room. Blinking hard against what felt blindingly bright, I tried to ascertain where we'd been taken, but I only saw blurry blobs, dark against a light background.

I could hear footsteps around us, and I struggled to get some vision back, blinking hard and squinting to see what was there. My vision swam, and things eventually came into focus. We were in the same room I'd been taken to each time that Sarah wanted to talk to me.

"What the," I muttered under my breath, wondering why the hell the two of us had been brought here. I couldn't make out any of the faces yet; my eyes had a hard time adjusting to the light, which I could've sworn had been turned up to infinity.

The blurry figures kept moving around and I closed my eyes and bowed my head so I wouldn't have to focus on them. The more I tried to make them out, the harder it became and the more nauseated I felt. After a while, someone approached us and bound our hands behind our backs. I could've sworn from the sound of the voice and the gentleness of the touch that it was Jodi, but she wouldn't willingly assist Sarah in anything like this —would she? I dismissed the thought and just submitted to whatever they were doing. Trying to fight a losing battle wasn't worth expending the energy just to end up back where we'd been ... or possibly worse.

I heard Rebecca struggling to the left of me, and I lifted my head just in time to see her being removed from the room. I tried to get to on my feet, but without my hands and arms for balance, I was like a turtle on its back. All I could do was watch in horror as they took her away, unable to do anything other than be highly vocal over it—which I was in spades, until someone knocked me up the side of the head with something hard to shut me up. This garnered a single comment from me about their obsession with knocking me in the head with heavy things.

After the dizzy feelings subsided, all I was left with was a huge headache that roared like a lion behind my eyes. Another person entered the room. Looking up from the corner where I'd been placed, I saw it was Sarah. The room had a few people, mainly the goons who had been tossing us around for the last little bit. Sarah sat down on the floor in front of me. She reached around my back and undid the bindings. I'm not sure why she did that because my first urge was to throttle her to death with my bare hands. She judged correctly that at this point in time I had neither the strength or ability to do so. The most I could manage at the moment was to give her a glare I hoped would melt steel.

"So, Jonathan. Are you finally going to be a little more willing to listen to me?" she asked, in a voice you would typically use on a child who had been naughty.

"Where has Rebecca been taken, and is she okay?"

"If you answer my question, I'll answer yours," she said, leaning down so she was in my face. "I think that's only fair."

"I'm not promising anything, Sarah. Now, tell me where the hell Rebecca is and if she's not okay, I swear to God—"

"You'll do what exactly, Jonathan? It's not like you're in charge here. See these people? They all are my followers. I'm the one who teaches them what they need to know. I'm the one who makes sure there's a roof over their heads, food in their stomachs, and that they get their religion in terms they can understand. You just happened to stumble into this place. I'm not sure yet how you managed it that one fateful night, but you're here and that's that. I did at one point think you might make a great addition to our little clan here, but you've proven repeatedly that you're too ... oh, what's the word I'm looking for?" She paused in thought. "Well, I'll use stubborn but it's more than that. I offered you a position of status and importance and you threw it away for that little whore. I should have dealt with her a long time ago, but I kept my word to Jodi. Now I find all three of you in cahoots with each other, which just makes my day in ways I can't tell you. Now. For the last time ... I'm giving you a chance to redeem yourself. We'll start out with small things and see how that goes from there. Would you be agreeable to that at least?"

"What is in it for me?" If I was going to be forced into a situation, I would take as much with me as I could when—not if—when, I left here.

"Well, I'm feeling a generous today. I'll release Rebecca back to her rooms. You'll be free, for the most part to go about your business within this compound. However, I do not ever want to see you two together again. You will be under watch as many hours of the day as I can manage someone to keep an eye on you. Yes, don't think for a moment you're getting your freedom back. Cross me again and I'll have you drawn and quartered. I don't take dissent lightly."

Sarah stood then, dusting off her knees and offering me a perfectly manicured hand to help me up.

"Do we have a deal? Or should I just throw you back into the holes for another week, alone this time with no one to talk to?"

I sat back and weighed the options. Life without Rebecca in both of them, but only one with the slight chance of seeing her again. I sighed. In choosing love, I had definitely chosen the path through hell. This path was the uphill, both ways, a bramble and bracken one.

I sighed deeply again and nodded my agreement to the terms. I felt like I was being torn between two poles—one of love and the other of necessity. I had no doubts that this would probably end my relationship with Rebecca, which had been just getting off the ground. I wanted desperately to find her and explain my choice, but I knew the terms I'd agreed to meant I'd rarely see her without someone watching over our every move. If this could even buy us a short while to regroup and get ourselves together for another escape attempt, it might just be worth it. At the same time, I felt sure I wouldn't be able to stay away from the woman I loved, and we'd be back in solitary before too long.

I ignored Sarah's hand and lifted myself up off the floor and walked unsteadily out the door. I felt like I'd just sold my soul, that my whole world was going to end, and everything I'd worked so hard to keep alive was about to die.

I wanted to die, too.

CHAPTER 19

I'm still not sure how I made it from where I was back to where Sarah had arranged for me to stay. It wasn't the suite I'd occupied when I first stayed here, and I knew for certain it wasn't anywhere near Rebecca. The closest I'd been to her in the past few days had been in the dining area. Sarah insisted I stay at the main table and converse with her and Kyle and the group as if nothing had changed—that I was still the same, accepted, and happy. The only person I felt glad to see at the table was Jodi, and even there Kyle kept her at a distance, lest we start nefariously planning to escape this nightmare again.

I saw the familiar brunette enter into the dining area and when Rebecca turned, she stood still for a moment while our eyes locked, before she broke contact and scurried back to wherever she was headed. With a sigh, I turned my attention back to my food and tried to ignore the incessant babble that spewed from Sarah.

When the night fell, I stayed in my quarters, not daring to risk being caught looking for Rebecca. She had taken over my heart, my soul, my very being. For once I knew what it felt like to have your heart break, and the pain that felt like my entire world ended was unbearable. I couldn't sleep at night, I spent most of the day either just sitting and waiting to be told things to do, or staring into nothingness. I felt like a total failure. The only thing that kept me from getting completely pissed drunk once more was the fact that there someone usually hovered over me when I wasn't in my room. Even then, there had been someone keeping an eye on the door, watching all my comings and goings.

The days passed, and by the time a week had gone by, I was getting tired of feeling so damned lovesick. I'd never been one to moon around over someone, and even though I felt like my heart was being stomped to death, I knew I had to do something about it or go insane. So, keeping an eye on the person generally assigned to guard me, I noticed he'd usually been scheduled to go on break at night. Taking the chance that the person who watched over Rebecca would be prone to taking their break around the same time, I decided to wander around to see her. God knows what she'd say to me once she saw me, even if she would speak to me, but for my own sanity I had to find that out.

Sitting in my room, with the half-finished apple pie I hadn't been able to finish for dessert, I bided the time between sundown to when Chuck—whose name I'd come to learn from simply talking to him—would head on his break. I remained just behind my door and off a bit so that if he opened it, he'd find me resting casually with a book borrowed from Jodi in one hand and a fork-full of pie in the other. Truth was, I was far from relaxed. I listened to every little sound in that hallway. Checking my watch, I noticed it was getting mercifully close to midnight, which was when, like clockwork, Chuck went off the clock for about eight hours. Seemed I hadn't been considered a threat between midnight and eight in the morning.

I got up and put the contents of the plate in the garbage and left the book by the door. Having seen one too many prison escape movies, I'd made sure to make the bed up so it looked like I slept there. I wasn't sure it was wholly convincing, but I hoped it would be convincing enough to buy me the time to get to where I was going, and back before being discovered. I knew they'd taken her to her rooms, and after a week of being too and fro from the small suite I stayed in, I knew she was no more than a few minutes away from me. Cutting through the courtyard would have shaved a bit off the time, but it was too public of a place for me to be seen in right now, and saving time versus actually being able to see the woman I loved didn't seem like a fair trade-off.

I leaned against the door, listening to Chuck talk to the other men who made up the goon squad around here, and heard him mentioned it was quitting time. Apparently, the job of guarding Jonathan Walsh had been a pretty easy one. Counting footsteps, I watched the minutes tick by on my watch. When it was about five minutes after the hour, I slowly cracked open the door and peered around.

The hallways were empty, the place practically silent. Knowing the door would lock behind me, I made sure I propped it open with the book, leaving just enough room that to the non-discriminating eye, it looked like the door was closed. Checking my work before I headed off, I nodded in satisfaction when the door almost shut, but stopped and stayed open.

I quietly walked down the hall. *Nice and steady. Don't give anything away. If anyone sees you, act like you're out for a walk and not skulking around.*

I felt once again like an adolescent sneaking out for a late-night tryst with a girlfriend. Wasn't too far from the truth, except I was twenty-six years past my teens, and I wasn't even sure if the girlfriend in question would be willing to speak to me at this point.

No one was in sight, and I made record time across the

compound to Rebecca's place. Checking down the hallway where someone should normally have been stationed, I saw no one and offered a silent prayer that I'd had the kind of luck that seemed to only show up in movies. Taking a few cautious steps around the corner, I came to her door. Noting that the light was on, and hoping that meant she was still up, I quietly knocked. There was no response. I put my ear to the door and could hear the strumming of a guitar. She must be out in the garden, and the force of the knocking I'd have to use to be heard out there would attract more attention than I dared risk.

Reaching down, I tried the knob. To my surprise, the door was unlocked. Opening it carefully, I saw the place was empty, the lights on, and out in the garden, a familiar dark-haired beauty sat with a guitar, looking off to the horizon while strumming random chords. Knowing better from the last time I'd tried to sneak up on her, the thought of which still made certain areas of my body hurt immensely, I closed the door behind me and made my way as quietly as I could over to the large French doors, which separated the garden from the living room.

I called her name softly at first, and slowly increased the volume to a point where I felt sure the rest of the residents would hear me. At the last, she sat straight, without moving, and then turned cautiously in the chair to see what or who was behind her.

The look on her face as she saw me was one of relief, and when she stood, she dropped the guitar with a clatter. I winced at the clang of the strings and wood on the flagstone that lined the garden but didn't have much time to think about it as she grabbed me in a passionate embrace.

"Jonathan Christopher Walsh. I don't know whether to kick you in the nuts or shag your brains out," she said, breaking the embrace to look at me. "What the hell did you have to do to get us into this situation?"

Taking her hand, I led her over to the sofa and sat down. Once she was seated, I told her of the deal I'd had to strike with Sarah to keep both Rebecca and me from certain harm.

"Luckily so far, it's not been much other than keeping away from you, which I have to say, has been one of the most difficult things I'd ever have to do in my life. I'm pretty sure the proverbial Sword of Damocles is hanging over my head, and Sarah's just about ready to drop it. I just couldn't take another long, lonesome night without you. I mean it when I say I love you, Becca," I said, finishing off the story. "So really, after hearing all that, it's your choice as to what you want to do with me. I'm furious with myself for taking her up on her offer, but it was the only way that I could ensure you would be safe. You mean more than the world to me and the thought of you in pain ... it's beyond what I can handle. I can take pain myself, but couldn't bear it if you got hurt."

The images that had been running rampant in my head for the past week of what possibilities lay before us in Sarah's vicious mind resurfaced with that one thought and I shuddered.

Rebecca sat back then, still not letting go of the hand I'd guided her over to the couch with and looked contemplatively at me. It was a while before she spoke, and I braced myself for what I was almost certain was coming.

"I probably should be so angry with you that I'd never speak to you again. Hell, I'm pretty sure that would be the perfect punishment, considering what you've just told me. Part of me wants to hurt you for how I'm feeling right now. The other part of me knows you did this for a reason and that I was at the center of your decision. The crazy things we do for love." She smiled a bit then, but in her eyes I could see the conflict that fought in her mind.

She looked away from me then. "If it weren't for the fact that I've gotten to know you quite well, Jon, I'd be out of "us" like a shot. But, I honestly believe that in your heart, you actually do love me, and you're willing to be here for the long run. That scares me as much as it amazes me. It's kind of frightening to be loved that much. For someone to sacrifice everything for someone else." She looked back at me. "That's a love that I've never experienced."

"Neither have I," I said simply. I didn't know if she felt the same way as I did about her, but deep down I hoped she did. I didn't want to think my love for her was unrequited.

"You're not asking if I feel that same thing with you," she said, once again reading my mind and watching me carefully. "Would I sacrifice everything for you? Would I go to outrageous lengths, sell my soul to the devil just to make sure that you're okay, that you're safe, at a cost to me that's incalculable? I'm not sure if it's just because you're scared to hear a negative to that question, or if it's just that you love me enough to know the answer."

"How about a little of both?" I asked, my voice cracking with emotion. *Damn it, she knows what things to say to get a reaction out of me.*

She let go of my hand then and leaned in so that her face was mere inches from mine.

"You're right," she said and kissed me.

Without knowing quite how we got there, clothes were removed in short order and we were clinging to each other in only the way that two lovers who are frightened of never seeing each other again can do. We made love several times that night, never knowing when each embrace might be our last. Lying together with limbs intertwined as the sun rose, I vowed to myself that I never wanted to willingly leave this woman's side, no matter what the costs.

I watched her as she slept, peaceful and snug in my arms, and wanted to burn every curve, every imperfection into my mind, so that I would never forget what she looked like at this moment. I reached up and softly ran the back of my hand down her cheek, still amazed that she wanted to be with me for me, rather than for the million other reasons she could have picked. Slowly leaning over to kiss her temple, I saw her eyes flutter open, and her gaze locked with mine.

"Hey," she said sleepily as she stretched, then laid back in my arms, turning her head to face me. "Did you get any sleep last night?"

"Enough. Don't worry about me. I've learned over the years to function on about two hours of sleep when I need to. Being with you right now is more important than getting eight hours of sleep."

She looked over at me, and with a smile on her face, reached out to rumple my hair. "Shouldn't you be heading back to your room soon? I mean, not that I don't want to keep you here permanently, but for safety's sake ..."

"Yeah, I probably should," I said, sitting up with a wince and a groan. I was used to being the one leaving, but for once, I didn't want to. I wanted to stay with her.

Getting out of bed slowly, I gathered my things together and dressed in the early morning light, just enough to see shades of gray and the beginnings of color. As I finished dressing, Rebecca emerged from the bedroom, attired in a red dressing-gown, her hair tousled by sleep and a contented smile on her face.

"So, are you planning on making this a nightly outing, hmm?" she asked as I stood, wrapping an arm about her waist as we walked to the door of her suite. "Or should I try and meet you at wherever they've put you for now?"

I thought for a moment, as much as I needed to be with her, daily trips back and forth were the quickest way to arouse Sarah's suspicions and I wanted to keep up these visits for as long as we could, until we got out of here.

"Hon, you know I want you with me every moment, but right now I'll try and come back as often as I can. We just don't need to tip Sarah's off to how we're actually able to see each other."

I pulled her to me for a kiss and the held her tight. "I know that sounds like a feeble excuse, but it's not. I don't want to put you in any more danger than I have to, and Sarah knows that hurting you will kill me."

On that note, arm-in-arm we walked to the door. We spent a while saying goodbye before finally parting, not without the long, tender glances back over the shoulder, as I made my way quickly and quietly back to my room.

Opening the door, I breathed a sigh of relief that the book was still there, and checking in the first light of the day, which slowly coloured the room in pastel hues of yellow, pink and violet, I saw there was no one in my room besides me. I quickly stripped to my shirt and underwear and crawled into the cold, empty bed and wrapped my arms around one of the pillows, holding it close to me as if it were Rebecca. Checking my watch before tossing it on the bedside table I noted that it was six in the morning, just before anyone but Jodi and her crew were up and running. Usually Chuck pounded on the door around nine, after arriving at eight. From what I could tell, he finished his breakfast in the hall, talking with other people who filtered out of this place to work, like the women who took their offspring to the rooms nearest the dining area where some adults—who, in another life had been teachers—instructed the children in the reading, writing, mathematics, history, and of course, religion.

I closed my eyes and tried to drift to sleep. Thoughts filled my mind of Becca and I together, and I smiled. I looked forward to a time when we'd test the waters of our relationship outside of the compound.

I heard the usual knock at the door and groaned, pulling the pillow I wasn't hugging over my head and muffling curses about how I'd just sodding well gotten to sleep and couldn't someone find something better to do with their time than wake me up at an ungodly hour. The knocking persisted, and after the fourth bout of it, I finally managed to get myself up, dressed, and ready for the day. One thing I noticed as I brushed my teeth was a smile I couldn't wipe off my face. I had my worries about that attracting Sarah's attention, but brushed it aside that she'd hopefully chalk it up to a good night's sleep, even though I was practically a walking zombie today.

Heading out the door, I was shocked to find Sarah standing there, across the hall from me, inspecting her fingernails. Once she saw me, a bright smile lit up her face. Internally, I worried over responses like that. Usually the next thing that happened was quite unpleasant.

"You look like you had a good night, Jonathan. Pleasant dreams?"

Better than pleasant dreams. I spent my night in the arms of a woman I'm wholly in love with. I laughed. "You could say that, I guess."

"Join us for breakfast?" she asked in a sunny cheery voice.

Knowing I had no real choice, I allowed her to take my arm and guide me away from my room, towards Kyle and Jodi's place, on the other side of the compound—near Rebecca's. Sarah kept up the usual stream of chitchat that I'd learned to ignore for the most part. When she knocked on the door, a surprised Jodi answered, wiping her hands on a towel she had with her. I had no doubt the expression Jodi sported was in regard to the insanely happy look on my face coupled with Sarah hanging off my arm.

"Hey, Sarah ... um, hi, Jon. C'mon in and make yourself at home." Jodi gestured us inside and titled her head at me as Sarah escorted me in.

Kyle was already seated at the table, his feet up on the chair across from him, plans for something laid out across his area of the table. Sarah let go of my arm to give her brother a hug and sat down beside him. The two of them discussed random things while I followed Jodi into the small kitchen area, where she prepared breakfast.

She pulled me in as discreetly as possible and loudly declared that she needed my help in preparing a full English breakfast, which was greeted with dismissal from the two seated at the table; they appeared to be deep in conversation about topics that were not clearly audible from where we stood.

"Why the hell did you have that shit-eating grin on your face with Sarah on your arm? From what she's been saying, she's separated you and Becca for good. I was down to see Becca last night she because was so low. She thought you'd never speak to her again."

I laughed quietly. "Jodi, you were there before midnight, weren't you?"

She nodded, working on omelettes, breaking eggs and whisking them in a large bowl. Then looked up at me. Catching my grin, she was quickly able to put two and two together and she laughed, the first time I'd heard her do so since the day she'd dragged us down that passageway.

"Ah, you managed to sneak your ass in there ... and I'm guessing from that stupid grin, you definitely scored."

I smiled and grabbed a spatula to flip the omelet she had left in the pan. I refused to say a word, the look on my face probably told more to anyone who knew me more than I could've by saying anything.

"I notice not a word of objection," said Jodi, handing me a plate. I slid the cooked omelet onto it.

"Nor word of confirmation. I for one, do not kiss and tell."

She laughed again, and slipped by me, taking the plates over to Kyle and Sarah, who were still engrossed in their discussion. When Jodi returned, we headed into topics that were not as light-hearted as before.

"So, what are you planning?" Jodi said, barely above a whisper.

"I'm not sure anymore, doesn't look like anything short of a miracle will get us out of here."

She nodded again and poured more mixture into the frying pan. "Leave it to me then."

I didn't get a chance to ask her what she had in mind as Sarah came up and took my arm, holding a glass of something; I wasn't sure what.

"Jonathan, sit, eat. You're a guest here today and you shouldn't be working in the kitchen! Jodi, why did you let him help?"

All Jodi could do was mutely shrug. Sarah dragged me with her to the table, my plate in hand. Jodi followed along shortly and then joined the rest of our crew. For the next few minutes, everyone ate in silence.

Then Sarah looked up. "So, Jon. Things have been going well for you here. It's good to see that you've forgotten about that little unfortunate incident with the, um, shall we say, less desirable girl?"

Less desirable? I'd never thought fall in love with the antithesis of what I used to think was the perfect woman. Becca is tall, dark and just bloody-well gorgeous.

"Hmm? What, Sarah? Sorry, just a little distracted this morning."

She gave me a stony look, and but then turned her attention back to her breakfast for a while. Seems my faking brain fog had worked.

However, the silence didn't last long. "Jon, would you care to join me today? I could use an extra set of hands."

Kyle shot his sister a look. "Sarah, I wanted Jon to join me and work with the guys. We're a bit short-handed."

"Well, I need him more, my dear brother," went her stilted response.

It was obvious Sarah had something up her sleeve—a test of loyalty or something I really didn't want to think about. I wasn't sure exactly what she planned, but it's not like I had much choice in deciding my fate.

I finally answered her question with. "I guess, I mean, what else is there for me to do?" I gave a little shrug. I wouldn't be able see Rebecca until after the sun had been gone below the horizon, anyway.

"Well, then let's get going," Sarah said, standing up from the table.

I glanced over at Jodi and Kyle. They stared back at me with a little shock, and with another shrug, as I followed Sarah out of the room.

For the most part, all Sarah had me do was follow her around. Well, it was more like she paraded me about the place arm-in-arm, for all to see, as if she'd won the battle between Rebecca and herself for who had custody of me. Little did Sarah know she was still the loser. When it came down to it, I'd be finding my way back into the arms of Rebecca as soon as I possibly could.

I followed Sarah back to her place at her insistence, and once we were behind the door, she turned to face me. I was trapped between the her and the door, with no place left to go.

Sarah's blue eyes reminded of me of a stormy ocean. I had no doubt as to what she wanted, too. I also knew the likelihood of her getting a willing, smitten Jonathan Walsh to be added to her stable of men was about as slim me willingly remarrying Tricia.

"Jonathan ..." she trailed in a wanton voice, reaching for me. I tried to step back, but realized that I was trapped with no options but to resist.

"Why have you been ignoring me? What is it that *she* has that I don't? I want you so much I could taste it, and I would do anything to have you." She reached up and put her arms around my neck.

I stiffened. I wasn't sure how to deal with this diplomatically, other than to gently explain why I wasn't interested, which would most certainly blow the top off the little secret that I'd been out to see Rebecca.

"Sarah, really, I'm flattered, but I just can't," I said, removing her arms from around my neck and holding her hand. "You're just not my type of woman. I'm sorry." *Oh great. Here comes the acerbic look.*

"And that little whore is your ideal woman?! No one, and I mean no one turns *me* down more than once." She pulled her hand from mine in a quick motion, and if looks could kill, I certainly would be dead.

"I've tried being nice, I've tried being patient, I've tried everything

I can think of to get your attention. And every time, I lose out to that little harlot, who just has look at you and you're like putty!"

She stalked about the place. The hair was rising on the back of my neck, and I tried to inconspicuously turn the door knob and exit the room. Unfortunately, my attempts to leave unnoticed were not successful. Sarah turned on her heel to glare at me.

"Don't even think of trying it. I've got you here and I'm going to get my way one way or the other."

She took two steps towards me, and I tried the door handle again. My hands were slick with perspiration, but I managed to get a hand hold on the handle and with a quick twist, I opened the door and slipped out.

I ran down the hallways, appearing like I had no any idea of where I was headed, but I knew definitely where I wanted to go. I'd get Rebecca first and then take her wherever we could find someplace safer around here, as I didn't trust that Sarah, who had gone off her nut with my refusal to accept her advances. Goddamn, the more days went by here the more I wished I could have conquered my fear of flying. I wasn't sure what I'd done in the past to deserve this punishment, but I'd rather atone for whatever it was in more pleasant ways than being stuck in the middle of nowhere in a situation that was worse than my worst nightmares.

I rounded the turns, running into people as I pushed through the hallways, single-mindedly veering towards my goal. I didn't even stop to apologize to anyone. I knew that I was attracting attention, and at this point, I just didn't care anymore. Yeah, sure, we'd both probably be tarred and feathered by Sarah, if not killed, but I was not going to sit back and bide my time any longer.

I finally made it to Rebecca's suite, and with a considerable amount of apprehension that I was too late to effectively do anything, I pounded on the door. After a few moments silence, I pounded again, this time yelling for Rebecca to get her backside to the door.

The door opened and a stunned Rebecca stood there in the doorway.

"What the sweet hell is going on?" she said as I blew by her into the room and slammed the door behind me.

Leaning up against it, I listened for sounds of pursuit, and luckily, I didn't hear any. I still wasn't moving from the door. I panted, trying to catch my breath, and sat down, my back still against the door. If nothing else, running from crap in place had done more than a gym membership, with providing ample exercise.

I gently grabbed Rebecca's hand and pulled her down to my level. Between heavy breaths I explained what had happened. At each statement, she blanched paler and paler until she was as white as a sheet and trembling. She collapsed in a heap on the floor beside me, and I instinctively moved to stop her from passing out.

"Jon, anyone ever told you that you attract trouble like flies on shit? I swear, over the past month I've seen you walk right into it."

She laughed half-heartedly and looked away from me, her hands on her face, like she was trying to figure out what our next step would to be.

"I never thought I'd die in this place," I said.

She looked at me and sighed. "Well, I'm also going to die because the man I've fallen in love with managed to send the neurotic nut that runs this place into a fit. God help me, because I'm certain that I'll die because I love you."

She curled up, bringing her knees up and resting her chin on them, then wrapped her arms around her legs as if to make herself into the smallest ball possible. I guessed she was losing hope as every day went by and the events of today must have added to that hopeless feeling.

"So, what are we going to do?" I asked, my breath finally back, and gently prodded her with a toe.

She sighed deeply again. "I'm not sure Jon. I really don't know what we can do. Jodi would be our best bet, and I'm not sure she can even do anything. We might end up back in the solitary confinement areas that are apparently all over this compound. I never knew what they were doing during those renovations, until the first time I ended up in there. Seems you and I are destined to spend our time in the dungeon, doesn't it?"

There came a knock at the door. Both of us froze. The knock came again, and Rebecca slowly stood up, finger on her lips, and opened the door.

I could only see Rebecca's side of the conversation, though I could hear both sides. It was Jodi, and after a brief questioning, Rebecca let her in.

"Jesus, Jon, you really know how to light a fire under people don't you? I swear I could hear the explosion from my place. Sarah is steaming like there is no tomorrow over your refusal of her. Let's just say that the last guy who managed to piss her off that much, well, he's not alive anymore. Kyle's got her calmed down enough that she's not calling out the goon squad right now, but you're going to have to walk on egg-shells from now on," Jodi said, walking around, her hands gesturing wildly. She was quite red in the face and looked like she wanted to slap me into tomorrow.

Once she finally settled down, I got up off the floor and we gathered in Rebecca's living room. Rebecca, made sure the door was locked tight before joining us. Then she curled up on the sofa, putting her legs up on me and leaning back against the arm.

"So, Jodi, what do we do now that Jon has awakened the dragon?" Becca asked with a sigh and a pointed look at me.

"Hey!" I barked. "What did expect me to do? Let her take me to bed? I'm sorry, but I just can't even feign interest in that woman. She reminds me too much of my ex-wife, and any libido I could have just shrivels up and dies." I shuddered, imagining the many things Sarah had planned to do to me.

"No," said Rebecca, "I expected you to handle it better than running like an axe murderer after you got away from her." The crossness in her voice was clear.

"Whoa, listen, I'm sorry, but I'm not staying in a room with someone who tells me that they're going to have their way with me *no matter what*. Doesn't that sound like rape to you? I've watched too many obsessed fans go that route with Torrent, and other friends and acquaintances of mine. If I can fight and run away, I'll take it."

I threw my hands up in frustration. There was nothing else I could say. If Rebecca wanted to take further issue with what happened, then that was her choice. Jodi had sat there watching the argument between Rebecca and me like someone at Wimbledon, but once the two of us had finally simmered down, Jodi found she could speak.

"Okay, I get it, I do. I'm sorry," she said. "Look, you two have to figure out a way to keep everything low key and on an even keel. I know you can't keep apart from each other, but you know as well as I do Sarah will come down on you again, and it's not going to be pretty. You need to be prepared when it happens. Your things, well, they're in Kyle's possession, so I know where they're hidden. When the time is right, you'll be able to get out of here, both of you. I need you to trust me fully on that. If you don't, this plan won't work."

Jodi sat back then, her hazel eyes watching both of us closely. I nodded my agreement and saw Rebecca nodding as well. Silent tears ran down Rebecca's face at the thought of having to leave behind one of her closest, if not *the* closest friend she had in this snake pit.

"That's great, just leave things to me," said Jodi. "No planning. Keep to yourselves. I know you two are going to be seen together in public and that's going to irritate Sarah and her flunkies. Just don't put yourselves in a situation where the wrath of the madwoman who has this place in her grip is going to react. If you have to see each other, make sure it's when Sarah won't be around. Becca, you know those times, so I expect you to keep Jon to them as well."

With that, Jodi and made her way over to the door. "I'll try to keep things calm with Sarah as best I can, seeing as she treats me like the hired help around here. In the meantime, have faith. You will be out of this place. I promise."

With that, she left the two of us together, sitting silently on the couch.

CHAPTER 20

*a*fter Jodi left, we sat there for a while without talking, then went to bed. I joined Rebecca for the night, and it was a restful sleep. The kind of peace that only settles over the damned before the sword falls and the world goes black.

The next day I headed out alone to judge the waters. Rebecca left after I did and engaged in her usual performance in the courtyard, wearing a light sweater, keeping an eye on the sky. Sarah ignored me for the most part. She acknowledged my presence occasionally while putting a distance between us, and the blue eyes that had once been full of things that I didn't want to contemplate were like sapphire lasers now. I wanted to make sure I stayed out of their way. Jodi kept the peace between everyone involved, and was invaluable when I made the mistake of showing up in the dining area hand-in-hand with Rebecca.

We'd been out in the garden, wandering around and talking, when the sky opened up and dumped water down on the two of us. We made a mad dash into the building, laughing like fools and deciding on the spur of the moment to seek out Jodi for a hot cup of tea, before heading back to Rebecca's place to dry off. We'd come in, still dripping from the rain, feeling pretty good about the day and how things had been going for us. The misunderstandings of earlier had been put aside. Calling out to Jodi as I stepped into the prep area sopping wet, I felt Rebecca stop suddenly and stiffen. I looked away from her for a second and saw what had caused the reaction. Standing there alongside Jodi was Sarah, glaring reproachfully in our direction, almost as if our crime was dripping water on her precious floor. Ignoring the ice blue eyes that bored anger into my skull, I asked Jodi if she could tell me where I could find some tea.

Jodi gestured to her left, and I went over, shaking my head, trying to shed some of the water out of my hair. Unfortunately for me, I picked the wrong time to do it, and from the yell that I got from Sarah, I'd tossed a good deal of it on her. I apologized, and quickly poured two cups of hot water, throwing in a bag of Rebecca's favorite white tea in each mug. Rebecca stood with her arms crossed, waiting for me with a panic-stricken expression. She took the tea and with a frightened glance at me, then Sarah, Rebecca walked away. I put my free arm around her waist and guided her gently out of the danger zone.

Something in my gut twisted, and I tried to ignore it; I wanted to stay on the high of the moment where we'd been enjoying ourselves out in the garden. I knew Jodi probably dealt with a somewhat irate Sarah right now, and I'd broken a cardinal request of Jodi's—that Rebecca and I not appear together around Sarah as a couple.

We headed back to Rebecca's room, where I finished off preparing the tea, and after drying off and changing from the damp clothes, we sat, watching the rain cascade down the patio doors. I could see a blurry gray shape streak across the flagstone of the small garden, and Rebecca advised that was Kismet, trying to find a way back into the place to get out of the torrential downpour.

There wasn't much to do with the compound being drenched into the next life. Exploring was pretty much out of the question during the day with Sarah about, and after being caught in the downpour, I felt rather sleepy and wanted to put my feet up and relax for a while. Jodi came by before that evening's dinner, bringing with her some things for Rebecca and me, but left quickly, advising us that Sarah was in a right mood and wanted both her and Kyle with her, probably to keep Sarah in line and from killing Rebecca and me without compunction.

Rebecca curled up on the sofa, looking drowsily out the glass of the doors. Lightning shot across the sky, briefly lighting up the room an eerie bluish-white and then plunging us back into the normal life. I moved into the kitchen, by this time I knew where most everything was and how moody the stove could be at times. After peeking at Rebecca, who gazed at the weather out the window, I prepared supper. I checked my watch, which I'd found the other day in one of the bags that I still had with me, and realized we were coming up on the end of November. I wanted to be out of here before Christmas, preferably with Rebecca. As I made dinner, I thought about where we'd possibly spend the holiday season—California didn't strike me as a great idea—no snow, too many people, and too many damned management parties to go to and smile at. No, I wouldn't subject Becca to that. New York didn't rate that highly either—too many people, snow—but the press of New Yorkers in the days leading up to Christmas barely made it worth taking her skating at Rockefeller Center. I knew she hailed from the New England area, and running over the possibilities there, I thought of only one place that would work.

"Becca ..." I called as I turned off the stove and dished out the meal I'd prepared.

Her back was to me, but I could tell from the steady rise and fall of her back that she'd fallen asleep, her head resting on the arm of the couch. With a quiet chuckle to myself, I left my plate on the counter and made my way over to her. She'd been markedly better in the past few weeks since the incident where she'd suffered a nasty knock to the head, but I knew from watching her that she still had moments of dizziness and her memory was still fuzzy from time to time.

I made my way over to where she sat, sound asleep on the couch. I wasn't even sure that she'd heard Jodi come into the room and leave. Bending down beside her, I gently shook her shoulder, and she awoke with a start. Confused and bleary ebony eyes looked at me with a bit of reproachfulness at having woken her, but a thankful smile quickly appeared as she took her plate, sat up with a smile, and stretched.

"You're too good to me, you know that?" she asked, getting up from the couch and heading toward the table to have dinner.

I wandered back into the kitchen and picked up my own plate and sat down across from her.

"Not sure what you mean by that, Becca. I love you, and I'm pretty sure that being nice to the person you love is pretty common."

She shook her head and laughed.

"I'm not talking about just being nice, Jon. You just do a lot of little things, things that you don't have to do, but you do anyway." She reached out and put her hand on mine.

As I always had when she touched me, I felt that thrill that shook me right to my core, that sensation I'd never felt with anyone else. It was like there was an unspoken connection between the two of us on a level that I didn't even begin to comprehend. When I'd described to Jodi back in my first weeks in this place my ideal woman, at that point I had no idea that she was sitting in the same room, and that Rebecca would become the first person I would willingly sacrifice everything I had for. I kicked myself mentally for having been so involved in my own self-pity that I almost missed out on what could possibly be the relationship I'd been searching for my entire life.

I looked down at her hand, and then up at her. She gave me that certain smile I was always glad to receive but didn't get to see too often. Her brown-black eyes sparkled in the light, and I couldn't help but return the smile. I leaned in to give her a kiss when suddenly all the lights went out.

Rebecca cursed, and quickly got up. I couldn't find her but I could hear her rummaging around. Then the rough sound of a match being struck and a brief quavering light broke the darkness with yellow glow, and I could make out her face yet again.

"Lightning must've hit one of the transformers around here. It'll be a few hours at least before the electric company gets to fixing it. C'mon, give me a hand with the candles." She gestured to me and I made my way over.

Finding an old plate, she tipped the candle to make a small puddle of wax, and then pressed the bottom of the candle onto it. Placing it just above the junk drawer, she pulled out a handful of the textbook emergency candles, the type I could remember from my childhood. Lighting them promptly from the already lit candle, I placed them in the candle-holders that had been buried in the drawer. Spreading them around the room, the wobbling light threw creepy shapes on the walls. We took the last few candles back to the table and in their glow we finished our meal together in relative silence.

After we'd finished, Rebecca took the dishes back to the table, and I wandered aimlessly around the living room. There were many pictures on a side table, and one caught my eye. It was a drawing actually, of who appeared to be Rebecca. She stared wistfully out a window, wearing a long flowing dress. It was a beautiful picture, and whomever did it was highly talented.

"Is this you in the picture?" I asked, picking it up off the table and holding it closer to the candle that I had with me.

She smiled wistfully. "No, that's my grandmother when she was young. My grandfather was completely nuts for her and drew that picture. He sent it to her as a way to ask her out on a date. He was quite the romantic." She looked at me questioningly. "You've been here for how long, and you're just noticing the pictures now?"

I put the picture down and looked back at her.

"In my own defense, every other time I've been here, there has been something else going on or someone else on my mind. This is really the first time that I've had a real chance to notice things like that."

She came up beside me then, the glow of the candlelight doubled from both our candles.

"So, what do you want to do then? This place gets really boring when the power's out. When it was just me I'd usually read or just sit and think."

I thought back to the last time the power had gone out when I'd been home. I had gone out for a drive, where ever the road took me. I'd ended up on the most beautiful stretch of beach that I'd seen in a while, and had written a song that I had yet to record. The stillness seemed to inspire me, I could compose my thoughts without interruption and daydream all I wanted.

"Why don't we just sit, talk, think—whatever comes to mind," I said, and noticed immediately the quirky smile. "I see where your mind is headed, my dear. You'd be a lousy poker player—against me at least. What you're thinking shows clearly on your face."

With a laugh that filled the still room, she pulled me to her for a hug, and we settled onto the sofa to just talk, which is something that we did quite frequently, and for once, it felt comfortable to bear my soul to someone and not worry about how much was going to end up being broadcast to the world.

The candles had dwindled down to almost nothing. Rebecca had curled up with her head resting on my chest after about an hour, and we'd spoken about anything and everything. She'd definitively answered the question of if she planned to stay with me once we'd gotten out of this hole, and I only could hope that the reality of the outside world and all the circumstances that went with it wouldn't break us apart. I knew I'd have more demands on my time and that I'd not be around like I was right now. I felt in my heart of hearts that Rebecca would understand; after all, she had lived on her own for three years now. While she missed me when I couldn't be with her in this place, I felt it was more from worry of what Sarah could do to me that drove Becca's feeling of desperation when we were reunited. We'd have to wait and see. Rebecca didn't seem like the overly clingy type, but you could never be sure. I also knew that relationships forged under circumstances like this one tended to fizzle quickly when they hit the real world, as they were based on a sense of closeness that was multiplied beyond normal in confined quarters.

After she extinguished the candles, leaving only our two burning, and had gone to get the last two replacements, we headed to bed for the night. Remembering that the lights had been on when we'd been up, I flicked off the switches for the dining and kitchen areas and followed the sleepy-eyed figure of Rebecca into the bedroom. Rather than look in the dark for nightclothes, I simply stripped off and crawled into bed. When skin touched skin under the covers, Rebecca started for a moment, then settled back comfortably against me. Neither of us was much accustomed to sharing a bed with someone else, and usually one of us would wake up cold in the mornings, the other having wound the blankets around themselves, and Rebecca had mentioned that she had a few nights where I'd rolled over onto her and simply stayed there, sound asleep.

I wrapped my free arm around her and pulled her as close as I could to me. I loved the feel of her body next to mine, the smell of her hair, the way that we seemed to fit each other perfectly. She sighed and slowly fell asleep. I stayed awake a bit longer than she did, watching her sleeping quietly in the little moonlight that was now able to break through the clearing skies. The last thing I could clearly remember was running my hand gently over her hair, and her stretching and rolling over to hold me in her sleep.

～

The next day dawned early, and I woke before Rebecca. She was sprawled across the bed, arms and legs taking up as much room as she could without pushing me off the bed. I decided to wake her with a kiss, or two, or three. Rolling over, I gently lifted the curtain of ebony hair that was splayed across the pillow out of the way, and gently kissed her shoulder. She murmured something in her sleep, and snuggled back against me. I decided to take my chances and nibbled softly on her neck, working up to her earlobe. She gasped softly, and taking that as encouragement, I gently turned her head, and kissed her. That woke her, and dark brown eyes slowly and sleepily fluttered open.

"Mmm ... what a sight to wake up to," she murmured softly. "A gorgeous Brit in my bed, naked as a jaybird and"— with a quick glance down the bed—"apparently very happy to see me."

She laughed softly then, and rolled over to face me, moulding her body to mine, and running her hand through my hair. She leaned in and kissed me, which I returned with some fervor I felt her tongue gently probing and returned the explorations while running my free hand down her body. Gently rolling her onto her back, I moved my attentions further south, lavishing gentle nibbling kisses along her collarbone and to her breasts.

As I was about to move the situation further forward, there was a loud knock at the door, and with a string of curses from both of us, I rolled back over onto my own side of the bed.

"You'd best go deal with that. There is no way I'm going out there right now," I said, climbing back under the covers.

"I'll try and be as quick as I can," she said, pulling on a dressing gown from the nearby closet. "It's probably just Jodi dropping of some stuff."

She came over and kissed me passionately, and with a wink, she headed out the door to answer the insistent knock, finger combing her hair into some semblance of decency as she went.

I laid there in bed and thought of the beautiful woman who had just left the room, and who was hopefully coming back right away. How I'd almost overlooked this meaningful relationship because I'd been so burned by my divorce made me want to kick myself.

When Rebecca didn't return and after checking my watch on the bedside table, which showed fifteen minutes had passed, I began to worry. If it were something trivial, she'd have come back to tell me that she'd be a bit longer, and the silence that greeted my ears when I listened to for her voice in the living room disturbed me more. Getting up out of bed, any sexual desire I'd had now gone and replaced with concern, I scrambled around the floor for my pants from the night before. After pulling them on, I headed out to the living room.

I found Rebecca there, sitting on the couch, a letter in hand, shaking like a leaf. She heard me come into the room and looked at me then, her eyes filled with fear. I practically ran over, then wrapped my arms around her as I sat down.

"What's wrong?" I asked as I tried to stop her from trembling.

She looked at me wordlessly, handing me the sheet of paper.

I took it from her quivering hand and studied the message. It obviously came from Sarah or Kyle. One simple sentence read:

You will pay for this.

I tossed the note aside, and pulling Becca to me, still shaking, I tried to soothe her the best way I knew how. For me that meant singing to her, and even as a part of me screamed it was the corniest thing to do, another quickly told me to shut up, because even babies were comforted by someone they loved singing to them. I held her in my arms and sang whatever song came into my head until finally, at long last, her trembling subsided and she relaxed enough to lean up against me, rather than clutching me in complete fright. I stopped singing, and she looked up at me.

"Why did you stop?" she asked, in a voice that sounded much younger than her years.

"I figured you didn't want to hear me sing all day, plus you seemed to be feeling a bit better now." I said, smoothing her hair back, away from her face.

She made some non-committal noises and snuggled up closer.

"What do you think that means?" she asked, finally moving away from me and leaning back against the sofa, trying not to read the letter again, which I had tossed on the table.

"I think they're just trying to scare us, to be honest. I've known bullies and they're all usually more bark than they are bite. Sarah and Kyle seem to fit that mold."

She looked at me then. "Jon, you still don't get it. You just don't piss off Sarah and walk out of here. No one's ever done it!"

The fear that had been gone and buried for a long time resurfaced at an alarming rate. She rose from the couch and paced the living area.

"How are we going to get out of here? She's probably sitting there waiting to pounce the next time we try. I just ... I don't want to die here and I'm getting more and more certain that's what's going to happen."

She finally stopped moving, her arms crossed across her chest, watching me with dark eyes filled with dread.

I stood to face her. Taking her hands from her chest, I looked her straight in the eyes and spoke as honestly as I could:

"Look Rebecca, I trust Jodi. I know you do, too. We have to let her handle the hows of getting us out of here. I know things got a bit bungled last time, but we've got to listen to her and have faith. She will find a way. Once we do escape, and I promise you we will, we'll find a place where we can be by ourselves for a while before heading back to the regular work-a-day world."

I reached up and ran my hand along her face. "I love you and I know this is frightening. If I said I wasn't scared, I'd be lying. As long as I have you though, I'll get through it. Sarah's not going to stop me, Kyle's not going to stop me. You and I will pull through this together."

She looked away from me. I knew that she wanted to believe what I said, and I couldn't blame her for having a seed of doubt. After all, our last attempt had gotten both of us thrown into solitary, and I'd had to make a deal with the devil to get her out of harm's way—of which I still wasn't sure she was clear. I had a feeling I stood right in the middle of it.

"Now why don't you go get into something comfortable, and I'll go see if they've gotten the power back on, hmm?"

She nodded numbly, and went back into the bedroom. I followed, on a search for wherever my shirt had ended up the night before. When I couldn't find it, I realized that it was on Rebecca the entire time.

"What?" she said with a lovely smile as she ran her hands defensively over the arms of the shirt. "It's comfortable, it smells like you, and I like it." She turned and rummaged in a drawer for a moment, then turned back with the Torrent shirt that I'd seen her wearing before.

"It was my favorite shirt. It's gigantic on me, so it should fit you with room to spare."

I took it from her and shrugged it on.

"Must kinda feel odd wearing one of your own band's old tour shirts," she said.

I looked down at the shirt. This was from the last tour we'd done in '81. I was pretty sure that Mike or Chris were the only people who possibly still owned one. Mine had gone to Kristen years ago. I had to wonder if Sarah would make the connection from this amazingly young image of myself at about twenty-six with my current self almost twenty years later.

"It's a bit odd, but seeing as Sarah doesn't link me with Torrent at all, it's probably okay. I can barely resist the urge to sign it, though," I said with a laugh. "When we get out of here, I promise I'll sign it for you."

With one last kiss, I headed into the bathroom to brush my hair and teeth before heading out on my own, to find out the source of the power failure. My first planned stop was Jodi, and if she didn't know, I'd have to speak to Sarah, which would probably thrill her to no end. Not.

When I emerged from the bathroom I found Rebecca in the kitchen with a glass of water. She'd gotten dressed, and the simple white button-down shirt that I'd been told looked good on me was fabulous on her—probably because she wore it open over a simple camisole. Though in my opinion she would look good in sackcloth and ashes. I came up behind her and wrapped her in my arms, resting my head on hers before reluctantly leaving, with a promise that I'd be back as soon as possible.

Once outside in the hall, I ventured toward the dining area—specifically the preparation area—where if there was some form of power, I knew I'd most likely find Jodi hard at work, dealing with the day-to-day idiocy she put up with in her job.

The room itself was still dark, but as no one was using it at the time, this wasn't entirely unusual. I could see a light on back in the prep area, so I took my chances to see if Jodi was there.

Pushing open the doors, I saw that indeed she was there, and that the electricity did not seem to be on.

Jodi glanced up as I crossed the floor to her. She looked tired, overrun with cares and problems. As I got closer, I noted the same bruises that Rebecca once had around Jodi's neckline. She stiffly smiled and faced me.

"Jon. Long-time no see," she said hoarsely to me.

"Jodi what the hell ..." I began but she waved me to silence.

"Don't ask me what I can't answer honestly. I know you're here about the power outage. Yes, it was because of the storm last night. They're still working on it. No, there was no ulterior motive for it happening. This is a small town, Jon, an inn like this isn't high on the priority list when bigger places are out of power."

"Then you know nothing about the note."

Jodi gave me a surprised stare as she shook her head. "It wasn't Kyle, he's been with me for the last twenty-four hours."

I was about to speak up about the bruises and again was waved to silence.

"I'll talk to you in time, Jon. Right now is not that time. There are more important things I need to deal with other than myself. Don't worry, though, I'll be okay. This isn't anything I've not been through before, so hush."

She gathered up the papers she'd been looking at under the blue-white glow of a lantern and went out the doors. I followed her. It was quiet, but in the way that a place full of people was quiet, not the tomblike silence that had echoed through the halls earlier. There were signs of life today.

It was mid-day and the courtyard was filled with parents and young children. The children splashed about playfully. Jodi stopped and watched them for a while, arms crossed over her chest, the papers held close to her body.

"I used to dream that would be me someday, but"—she shrugged —"guess I'm not destined to do that. Becca one day will have a family of her own with someone who cares for her."

She turned to look at me, and I couldn't help the chill that ran down my spine. It was like looking into the future.

"Jon, take good care of her. Just make sure she's happy, that's all I ask. You two are meant to be together. You're from two totally different worlds, yet you fit so well. It's as if something bigger than all of us reached across the night and put you two in the same place at the right time for things to happen. You'll have your ups and downs—don't get me wrong about that—but in the end, she's the woman who was meant to help you to begin again."

She turned away then, but not before I could see the sadness in her eyes.

"C'mon," said Jodi, walking way and wiping the tears from her eyes with the back of her hand.

I followed her down the hallway and around a few corners until we reached a small office-like area, where I'd never previously been. Jodi pulled a small thing of keys from her pockets, and rattled through them until she found the right one, then she opened the door and I went inside with her. The office was meagrely decorated with a desk, a lamp, and a few chairs. Papers were stacked on the desk, and she took the ones that she carried and tossed them on top of the pile. The biggest attraction in the office was the large windows, which illuminated the office with a significant amount of natural light.

Wandering off to the window, she stood there, watching the outside world. This was one of the few places that wasn't surrounded by the high fence that encircled the compound. Jodi had a beautiful view of a large field and the town beyond. Vision Lake was a small town, and from the looks of it, had been a larger one not too many years before. She seemed lost in thought. After a few minutes, she turned back to me.

"Sarah found the map, Jon. She found it and led us into that trap. I am so, so sorry. I didn't know it until well after. I broke the trust that you two had in me, and I can't blame you if you no longer feel I can help you get out of here, because right now I wouldn't trust myself to get me out of here."

She sat at the desk, and watched me. There was a chair on the opposite side of the desk, and I sat down in it.

"Jodi, we both still believe in you. We knew there had to have been something beyond your control that night. When you give the word, we'll follow it. Just don't give up on yourself, okay?"

With a small smile, she turned back to the windows. "It's late November, Jon. I want you two to be out of here before Christmas. You've been here since mid-September, haven't you?" she turned to look at me for the nod. "That's too long. Sarah has to have something up her sleeve for you or you'd be , well, you'd probably be dead by now. Rebecca is right on that. I've gotten too deep into this place to get out again ..." she trailed, turning back to the windows and watching the hustling and bustling that went on around the town, so near yet so far away.

"I swear, just a bit longer, Jon. You and Becca will be out soon," she said with a sigh. "You'd best get going unless you really want to talk to Sarah. I'll drop by later tonight with a light supper and if they turn the electricity back on before then I'll let you know."

I nodded and reached across the desk to grab her hand in a squeeze to say what I couldn't, then quickly left the room. I rushed back to Rebecca's, which had become *our place*, even though we'd been a couple for less than a month, if you took Jodi's wedding as the official start of our relationship. If you went with when we'd acknowledged we were more than just friends, then it had been almost two months. I had never been one to mark off relationship milestones before; however, with Rebecca, it was easy to remember without prompting.

Stopping by one of the gardens, I picked a handful of assorted flowers that caught my eye and headed "home" with them in hand. With a quick knock on the door, I came in, and found Rebecca stretched out on the couch with a book—likely Faust—in hand.

"Hey, hon," she said, stretching lazily before she got up to meet me at the door.

Keeping the handful of flowers behind me, I hugged her one-handed and nuzzled her neck. She smiled up at me, then wandered back to where she'd been on the couch. Catching her arm as she went, I brought forth the flowers, and let her know it has been two months since we'd first decided to take things one day at a time.

"Wow. I've never met a man who remembered things like that. The flowers are beautiful." She brought them up to her nose and inhaled their fragrance deeply.

"I've never cared enough for anyone to even think of remembering these occasions. Yeah, only two months but it feels like we've known each other forever." *And that we'll be together for a long, long time.*

She smiled at me, her eyes twinkling in the light. "Maybe I should've dated older men a long time ago. Matt certainly never treated me this well."

"You deserve to be treated even better than this, Becca," I said as she wandered into the kitchen and grabbed a vase from the cupboards. "You're everything I could want in a woman: smart, beautiful, sexy, musical."

"Half your age," she teased.

I came up behind her, put my arms around her waist, and kissed the bare spot on the back of her neck.

"I'll admit, it doesn't hurt matters any ... but if you were my age, I wouldn't mind either."

She brought the vase full of flowers up for another deep inhalation of the floral scent and then leaned back against me. "I still can't believe you love me. It's like a wild dream. I didn't ever think I'd end up with someone like you. I was content to go home and be with mister average, raise a houseful of kids, and just live life. To be loved by someone like you"—she turned to me, the flowers forgotten on the counter—"who is like my soul mate, who understands me, and wants only to make me happy every waking moment of every day ... well, if it's a dream, I don't ever want to wake up."

I smiled back at her. "I notice you left rock star out of that, thankfully."

"Yes, because it's your job, not a part of who you are. You're a recording artist. That could go away tomorrow. You could sell shoes and I wouldn't care."

She was right, in a way. She'd not known me for more than myself at Skylark Inn. Advantage to me: I was able to show who I was without having to throw around large amounts of money. I couldn't give her anything but my heart.

"So, what did you find out?" she asked, taking the flowers to the coffee table.

I explained what Jodi had told me . Rebecca shrugged and looked out the doors. The day had mostly run by. It was late afternoon, and most of the garden had dried out.

"So, we going to do anything or what?" she asked, facing me.

"What do you want to do?"

She turned back to the door. "I haven't really thought about it. I want to do something, though. I feel like I've been sitting around too much, and I need to move."

I walked over to the stereo and riffled through the collection of CDs she had. She'd shown that she was quite light on her feet at

Jodi's wedding. Maybe dancing would solve both the boredom and need to move without bringing us into the prying eyes of Sarah and her assorted goons. I found some classic Journey, and threw that on and turned up the volume. *Any Way You Want It* rang out and I grabbed her hands.

"C'mon. You want to move; this is the best way I know how."

She laughed but joined in. She was quite a good dancer, and not just to country songs and pop ballads. Singing along and bopping about with me, Rebecca finally let go of what had been bothering her, the sombre mood dissipating into cheerfulness. The threatening note seemed to have slipped her mind, for which I was happy. Finally, the song faded, and as the CD player was set to random, it moved to another disc, a slow song from a group I didn't recognize.

She stood for a moment, unsure of what to do, before I pulled her close to me.

"Time to teach you to waltz properly," I said.

I wrapped my arm around her lower back and took her hand in mine. Looking in her eyes, I started to dance, she followed my lead effortlessly, not once looking at her feet.

"You're a natural, you know. Even I had to stare at my feet the first time I was learning how to waltz."

She laughed. "What makes you think this is my first time doing the waltz? I just don't get to dance with many people my age who actually know how to dance it. C'mon Jon, be honest, I'll bet you were the one who taught your daughter."

I nodded. She was right. Kristen had learned to dance when she was a young girl, the way all young girls seemed to—by standing on Daddy's feet. I'd had the honor of dancing the traditional father-daughter dance with her at her wedding, and was surprised at the grace that she'd acquired, admittedly through lessons for the occasion.

We finished off the rest of the dance in silence, and the music segued into another slow song, this time one of the songs that had played at Jodi's wedding, the country song. She laid her head on my shoulder, and wrapped her arms around me, pulling me as close as possible.

"Hard to believe it's been about a month since that night, hmm?" I said, and felt her nod.

It had been a harrowing period—between the last time I'd heard this song, and now. We seemed to be in limbo, a calm that hung in the air like a slow-moving fog and sent waves of anxiety up my spine that the next hour, minute, or second could bring the world crashing down around us. I felt, rather than knew that Sarah had to be planning something huge. There was no other reason that Rebecca and I were still together and in relative safety. I'd pissed off the giant; it was only a matter of time before that giant squished us both, either together or separately.

Sarah knew my weakness: the dark-haired woman in my arms. I feared that whatever attack that snake would pull on us would have Rebecca at its core.

The song finished, and after my train of thought had been taken through a deep dark tunnel, I didn't much feel like dancing anymore.

I shut off the stereo and wandered outside to the garden. Rebecca followed me, confused. She didn't say a word, but placed her arms around my neck and rested her head on mine after I'd sat down. She could tell something had changed my mood.

"Penny for your thoughts," she said quietly.

I reached up and patted her hand. "Becca, I don't want to talk about what's on my mind right now. It's not good. I'll say that much."

She made a noncommittal noise and with a gentle kiss to the top of my head, she moved over to her own chair and sat silently for a while.

"I've got to see Jodi," she said suddenly, and with a kiss, she dashed out of the garden, leaving me staring in surprise as she disappeared inside to grab a light sweater.

I was able to make it into the room in time to tell her that she should be careful before trekking out into the halls, as I was aware there was likely something afoot for her if left on her own.

"Don't worry, hon, I'm a big girl. I can take care of myself," she said with a wink and a smile as she headed out the door.

Once the door closed behind her with a soft but solid click, the place settled into silence. I sat down on the sofa, and the grayness descended upon me. While Rebecca had generally been a quiet person, her personality lit up whatever space that she entered. Without her, things seemed to lose colour.

I picked up the book she'd been reading. Sure enough, it was Faust, and she was almost done. Placing the bookmark—a simple sheet of paper—where she'd left the book open, I flipped back to the beginning of the novel and read, trying to pass the time until she returned. I made it a few chapters in before the boredom hit, then I put the book down. Checking my watch, I saw that it was almost dinner hour and Rebecca should be back before long.

I wandered out to the garden and tried to meditate like I'd learned from Mike many years ago. It wasn't working. My thoughts kept sliding back to: *Why is Becca late? Where can she possibly be?* I kept trying to push away the ludicrous notions that something had happened to her and she was somewhere only

Sarah could have put Rebecca. My mind ran away with itself, and I felt disconcerted. Finally, there was a knock on the door, and I came inside, my heart skipping a few beats as I opened it.

Jodi stood with a basket in hand. "Brought you two some supper. Thought you'd enjoy this," she said as she came into the room. "Where's Becca? She was supposed to visit me earlier today."

She looked around the room, and I swallowed hard.

"She's not with you?" I asked.

Jodi shook her head so hard that I thought her hair was going to come off. "No, she was supposed to drop by this afternoon to pick up some things that I'd managed to ferret away for you two from the stuff that Sarah had taken, but I haven't seen her. I assumed she was with you."

I stumbled backwards and landed on the couch. Jodi came quickly to my side.

"Oh Jesus. I don't want to..." I buried my head in my hands. I had to learn to stop ignoring those gut feelings. "If she's not with you and she's not with me..."

"Sarah's got her." Jodi said with finality in her tone.

CHAPTER 21

I sat in shock for a few minutes, unable to do much but shake and go over many unfortunate situations in my head, none of which, hopefully, had come to be. I had no doubts she'd been taken just to get to me, and that anything Sarah tried would end poorly for Rebecca. Becca was the one for whom I would fight, and the one weakness Sarah knew I had. Once I managed to get my wits about me, I took a deep breath and headed to the one place that I felt sure Rebecca would be.

At Jodi's insistence, I stopped in the usual haunts where Rebecca and I had spent a lot of time together, but she wasn't there. Steeling myself for what I was certain would to be the biggest showdown since I'd arrived, I walked up to Sarah's place and knocked on the door.

No one answered. I knocked again.

There was nobody there, it seemed. I put my ear to the door and listened for something, any sign that either Rebecca might be in there, or that Sarah was there. Nothing.

The next thing that came to mind was that Rebecca might in the "holes" where we'd been before. I headed down there, keeping up hope that I could find her and get her out of there. Then it would be out of *here*, back to the real world where things were sane.

I walked down the halls, my footsteps echoing around me. Without Jodi, I was going on instinct as to where they could be. When I came to a corridor that seemed familiar, I knocked on the walls, trying to determine if I was in the right location.

I honestly couldn't tell. I began to panic; I didn't like not knowing if she was dead, alive, hurt, all right, or whatever else was going on. Taking one last quick walk around a nondescript block, like the last ten blocks of doors had been, I decided it was best that I find Jodi and at bring her with me on this wild goose chase. She knew the location where we were kept last time, and she could lead me to it, if Sarah hadn't caught up with her as well.

Turning back, I headed down the maze of corridors as fast as I could without attracting attention to myself. I arrived at Jodi's and knocked on the door. After a few moments of silence, I was greeted with the stern countenance of Kyle, who reluctantly brought Jodi to the door under the pretense of something going on in the kitchens. I waited until we'd gotten out of the main passage areas, and then informed her why I'd asked for her.

"Jon, you're playing a very dangerous game," she said, her voice filled with concern and worry. She didn't stop her quick pace as she spoke. "I haven't the foggiest where Rebecca's been taken, and it worries me silly. Kyle's being silent on the issue, which makes me really think that Sarah's done something to her."

She led me to where we'd been kept last time, and inspected the cells carefully, trying not to attract any more attention that the actual checking of them would bring on the both of us. Each time she emerged from the cells, she shook her head, and after a while, I was beginning to lose hope that I'd find Rebecca.

Finally, we had exhausted every possibility as to where she

could be that Jodi and I could think of. We headed, more slowly this time, back to Jodi's place, my heart alternatively in my feet and in my throat. As we passed the main courtyard, I stopped and stood, looking out over the gray expanse of concrete that was designed to replicate Roman columns. In my mind's eye, I could see her sitting at that piano, long dark hair caught in a slight breeze. I felt the burning in my eyes that I knew was tears that wanted to fall, but I managed to hold back. I'd never felt the urge to protect someone who wasn't mine by blood, but rather by free will and choice. Someone who chose to be associated with me of her own free will and not because I had been famous or had money or owned a large house. While I was quite aware these things didn't guarantee we'd have a successful or long-lasting relationship, we did have a better chance than any of my prior relationships, right from the get go.

Rubbing my eyes, I moved away from the courtyard, pushing back the urge to cry, and walked with Jodi to her rooms. Kyle stood outside the door, seemingly concerned, but with a single glance at me, Jodi headed to him and was ushered inside. I now faced two choices: go back to our suite in a depressed state and wonder what had happened to Rebecca, or take matters into my own hands and confront the person I felt pretty damned sure had a good deal to do with Rebecca's sudden disappearance.

With a deep breath, I turned down the hallway that would take me to Sarah's place again. As it was past the dinner hour, I should be able to find her there this time, and maybe, just maybe, find out where the woman who owned my heart and soul had been taken.

I marched across the compound with a sense of purpose and the simple fact that I wanted to smack Sarah into the next life if she in any way harmed a hair on the head of the woman I loved.

Never had I ever wanted to rain hellfire down upon anyone more than I wanted to on Sarah at that moment in time.

I arrived at the door to Sarah's palatial suite, and pounded on it relentlessly. I didn't care if my fist ended up on the other side of the thing. There was sort of silence yet again, but it did sound like someone was there. I listened for a while and walloped the door. Finally, it swung open and Sarah stood there, in a revealing negligée and a dressing gown that was wide open. Behind her stood one of the young guys from around the compound, in a similar state of undress. He pushed by her, pulling on his shirt as he left, not looking at either of us.

"Yes, Jonathan?" She glared at me, the venom in her eyes almost a living thing on its own.

"Where the fuck is Becca?"

She was taken back by that statement, and it showed, she shrugged the dressing gown back up onto her shoulders and tied the sash.

"What makes you think that I've done anything with your little whore?" she asked, meeting my eyes.

"Plenty, and everything points to you. I swear to God, if you've done anything to her, and she's hurt or harmed in any way, I will kill you with my bare hands."

She blinked once, but her face didn't change. She kept eye contact with me, and I was seething, shaking with both fear and anger. It took everything I had not to reach out and grab her by the throat.

"What if I did do something? Like you're in any position to threaten me. You're still here because of me, you're still breathing because of me. Whether or not you want to admit it, you're mine and there isn't anything you can do about it."

She turned away then, and without thinking, I grabbed her and forcefully pushed her up against a wall. The shock was evident on her face. Hell, even I was shocked at what I was doing. I was not the type to treat women this way. However, I knew playing by the rules wouldn't get me anywhere in this situation, and I was going to use being six feet four and not exactly a beanpole to my advantage. I might be past my twenties, but the manual labour they'd assigned me around this place had nicely brought me back into shape. I knew I could and would exert whatever strength I needed to get Rebecca back again, so we could flee this hell on earth and back to the semi-sane real world—together.

I looked Sarah straight in the face. Did I actually see a glimmer of fear? I bet she definitely wasn't used to being challenged over anything verbally, and much less physically.

"Look Sarah, let's just cut the bullshit here. I know you have something to do with where Becca suddenly up and took off to, and I'm going to venture that it's not exactly nice. She pisses you off, and let's be dead fucking honest with each other, you want her dead because she refuses to acknowledge you as her superior. I know you've wanted to sink your hooks into me like you've done to so many of the men around here, and the fact that I don't find you a turn on in the least, and that I chose her over you, bothers you right to your very soul."

I was shaking her ever so slightly at the end of every sentence and I could see the fear rising on her face, but I wasn't done yet.

"Now, before I get really pissed off, and if you think I'm not pissed off right now, then just try me—seriously go for it—try your usual shit. WHERE THE FUCK IS REBECCA???"

I slammed her hard against the wall with the last statement, which I bellowed at the highest volume that I could manage and with enough ire that people for miles around must have heard me. Sarah squirmed, trying to get out of my grasp, but I would not let up.

"Where the hell is she, Sarah? I'm not releasing you until I get her back, so it's just easier for you in the end to answer the damned question."

She stared at me, and I knew that look well enough—she planned to struggle more rather than reply to me. I also suspected she would attempt to kick me, but before she could, I moved to prevent her from doing so.

Again, I could've sworn I caught a glimpse of complete shock in her eyes.

"What are you going to do, Sarah? Scream? I'm pretty damned sure that no one will come running. They'll just assume you're meeting with one of your lovers, and no one wants to interrupt that, do they? That, and when I answer the door, they'll not wonder anything, other than what took you so long to bring the new guy into the fold."

Her eyes narrowed. She glared at me with a heat that would've outshone a million suns.

"Let ... me ... go," she hissed, and made yet another vain attempt to wriggle free of my tight grip on her.

"No."

The simple statement echoed in the room.

"No," I repeated. "You're going to take me to wherever you have Becca, and you're going to take me there right now. I am not letting go until I know she's okay and we're together again. Then, maybe I'll consider it."

I wanted nothing more than to throw her to the wolves, to rip her apart with my bare hands for everything that she'd done to both Rebecca and I in the time that we'd been here. I wanted to find Kyle and hang him out to dry with his sister. Nothing would have pleased me more than to bring on them what they'd done to others. But I knew I wasn't going to be the one to do it.

I wrenched Sarah away from the wall, and pushed her out into the hallway, not caring that she wasn't dressed in more than her nightclothes. She continually struggled, and I was past the point of caring.

"Now, let's go find Becca. Trust me, this will be less painful for both of us if you just take me to her."

I never knew I could be this much of an utter asshole, and downright abusive, which I swear was not in my nature. However, my entire mindset was about finding the woman I loved, and making sure she was unhurt and alive.

Sarah stood defiantly in the hallway, watching me with blue eyes that wanted to burn holes through my head. I met her gaze straight on. There was no way I would allow her to best me this round. She'd won by default at every other confrontation, and by my own surrender at the last one, involving Rebecca's freedom and my staying away from her, which hadn't lasted long. I wasn't in the mood to play games any longer. I really didn't care if it cost me my life—Becca meant that much to me. If she got out of here and could to live a long and happy life, that's what mattered. In this compound she was definitely not happy. She was a city person, and being caged in what had been a small hotel within what felt like an even smaller town—deprived of contact with family or friends for years on end—had to have taken its toll on her.

Sarah and I continued to stand in the hall, both of us defiant and unmoving. I wasn't going to give in on this issue, and I had the feeling neither was she. I didn't give a damn about what people thought about me anymore. Most of them, hell, all of them besides Jodi and Rebecca, didn't seem to have a clue as to who I really was. Sometimes being a washed-up rock star had its perks. Yet, people in the outside world still knew who I was, even if Torrent hadn't been at the top of the charts anymore. I was still used to being recognized, and the fact that people here never ... well, it didn't sit right with me. This "congregation" had to have been sheltered for a long time. However, it hit me deep down that Sarah did know who I was in the real world, and would somehow try to use that to her advantage.

"Would I be completely off in left field if I suggested to you that you're using the fact of who I am against me?" I said, trying to control the curiosity in my voice.

The disdain in her expression was intense. She *did* know who I was, despite all pretenses to the contrary. Even though I had suspected her motives, I was still somewhat shocked, and completely sodding-well disturbed by the revelation. I was also perplexed to have stumbled, unknowingly, into this small cult. Why the hell *had* I found this place? From all that I understand of its operations, the door should have been locked and the place dark, as the power had been out the night I'd gone through town, from what both Jodi and Rebecca had told me. Why had the sign been lit? Why had the door been open? Too many unanswered questions.

"If you think I'm that stupid, Jonathan Walsh, then you're dumber than you look. Of course I know who you are. I'm still not sure how you got in here, but I'm as sure as hell impressed that you did." She laughed bitterly and tried again to free herself from my grasp.

I held on to her still. She gave me a look again, and I returned it with one of frustration. I felt tired, ever more exhausted of this charade as the time wore on. I was also getting nowhere quickly.

"So, Sarah. Are we going to just stand here, or will you finally wise up and tell me where she is? Maybe I need to drag you from door to door in this place until I get what I want."

"I'm not telling you anything."

She tried to pull away, and only succeeded in dragging me a few steps down the hallway, as she caught me off guard. We came to a stop, and she glared at me, yet again.

"Don't think I can't hold on for a long time, Sarah. You'll be sorely mistaken if you think that."

Why she kept trying to fight was beyond me. I was probably just as stubborn as she, if not more so. Ryan had often remarked that when I dug my heels into something I wanted, there was no convincing me otherwise. Which, when it came to the band, was not necessarily a good thing. You could prove to me the reasoning for whatever choice you wanted me to make and I'd change my mind, but you'd have to make a great a case of it to convince me.

Finally, with a deep sigh, she stopped struggling. People walked by in the hall, giving us a quick look and then with cheeks reddened by embarrassment, they ducked their heads and increased their speed down the hallway and away from the two of us. Sarah looked anywhere but directly at me. Finally, after what seemed an eternity, she met my eyes again, cheeks aflame, as more and more people seemed to be coming by, and it wasn't doing anything good for her image to be held captive in the hallway by the man that she'd been trying to seduce since he'd shown up at Skylark Inn.

"Fine. I'll take you to where she is," she said with resignation.

I had no doubt that this was an entire act for my benefit. She hadn't given up on attempting to get Rebecca either killed or otherwise silenced since I'd been here, and more than likely she'd been trying to do it for many months before then, if not years. Why would she suddenly take me to her, unless there was either a trap or something that was to her benefit?

She straightened up and walked down the hall, her feet padding almost silently on the carpet. I kept my grip on her arm, following her down the hallway, trying to keep track of the amount of turns and twists we took. Finally, we ended up in a normal looking end of the compound that I recognized as close to Jodi's place. She opened the door, which was unlocked, and gestured with her free arm to enter the room.

I did so with trepidation, pulling Sarah along behind me. The room was dark, the sun having its languorous slide below the horizon, throwing only the barest light into the room. Curled in a corner, her hands and feet bound, and her mouth gagged, was Rebecca. She looked up, and I could see the glimmer of hope in her eyes.

Unthinking, I let go of Sarah's arm and made my way over to Becca. Carefully, I untied her arms and legs, then removed the tape gag over her mouth. She could barely move, but tried valiantly to hold me. Taking her hands in mine, I kissed each one in turn and then pulled her close.

"You alright love?" I asked, holding her out from me so I could see her and make sure she was okay.

She didn't say a word, just nodded, tears sliding down her cheeks as she tried to pull me to her. I turned to Sarah, who stood there defiantly, arms crossed across her chest. Rebecca clung to me like her world was ending and I was the last thing that was solid and that she could trust to save her. She had been gone from me less than eight hours. It made me wonder what Sarah had done to her in that time.

I turned back to Rebecca. She was still crying soundlessly in my arms. I picked her up like a rag doll, and moved towards the door. As I passed Sarah, I looked at her and stopped for a minute.

I went to say something but shook my head and continued past her. I had no doubts that when I was beyond her gaze that the goon squad would be called out on me, and that something monstrously bad would happen.

I walked down the hall, Rebecca cradled in my arms. She was still clinging to me, her head buried on my shoulder, not moving other than the slight shaking that told me she was still crying. I stopped at the part of hallway that faced the courtyard.

"Becca, hon, you think you're up to walking?" I asked.

She looked up at me, her face tear-stained, with red eyes. She nodded slowly.

"Not that you're heavy or anything. I could carry you all the way back to your room if you need me to."

"I'll be okay," she said quietly. I lowered her legs down until she was able to touch the floor.

She gingerly stood, still clinging to me. She took a few uncertain steps, and I could see the marks where the rope she'd been tied up with had cut into her skin. Whomever had done it hadn't taken much care not to hurt her, and my blood boiled.

Keeping my arm around her, we walked slowly back to her suite. Once we were safely inside, I pointed to the bedroom and instructed her to go in. She protested, assuming that I was after a roll in the hay. I shook my head as I guided her into the room.

"I'm not going to even dignify that with a response," I said, closing the door behind us out of habit rather than need.

Taking her hands in mine again, I looked at her wrists, and saw the same marks as on her legs. Cursing under my breath, I checked up her arms for bruises, finding none, I went to remove the sweater that she had on still. She flinched when I touched her and it was like a knife to my heart.

"I'm not going to ask what they did right now, because I'm pretty sure I'll want to kill whomever did it when I find out. Becca, love, as much I as I don't want to ask you this right now, I need to make sure you're not injured too badly. That means I'm going to need you to"—I searched for the word and found it—"disrobe."

She looked at me with tormented eyes. She nodded, and keeping her eyes on mine, slowly undressed. It was the most unarousing strip I'd ever had the misfortune to be present for, and it made the bile rise in my throat. As each piece of clothing was removed, I noted that whomever had taken her had taken great care to leave very few marks visible to the eye.

She stood there in front of me, eyes downcast, shoulders slumped and resembling a puppy who'd been kicked. Turning her around, I saw the line of welts that ran up and down her back. My hands clenched involuntarily, and I cursed louder than I'd intended to.

She looked up at me, her eyes brimming with tears, and my heart broke.

"Ah, Becca, you know I'm not upset with you," I said as I pulled her close to me and held her as tightly as I could without hurting her. "I just hate seeing you in pain and I want to make whoever did that to suffer in return. I love you so much..."

She stared sobbing again, and inwardly, my blood boiled. Whatever had been done, and whoever had done it looked to have broken down the last little barriers between her reserve of strength and bowing to Sarah's will in this place. There was nothing more I could do that would solve the situation, other than to hold Becca and tell her things would be all right in the end.

While I held her, I felt totally inadequate and lost at what to do. All I could think of was to comfort her as best I could. Well, truthfully, I was thinking I'd like to go kick someone's arse, but that wouldn't make our situation any better—probably much, much worse.

When she stopped sobbing, I sat her down and took care of her wounds. I'd been in her rooms long enough that I knew where most things were. Gathering some moisturizing lotion, rubbing alcohol, and cotton balls, I carefully cleaned the abraded skin and then rubbed some lotion on it. Once that was taken care of, I dressed her in her nightclothes and put her to bed. She was in no shape for me to ask her any questions.

I tucked her in and sat down beside her.

"If you don't want me in here with you, I understand, hon. I just need to know if you do or if you don't."

She laid there silently for a while, eyes focused on something on the wall, probably just thinking and not looking at anything. After a long while, I stood up to leave, and she suddenly came to life, grabbing my arm with a look of alarm and fear in her eyes.

"Please stay here with me, Jon. I'm scared to be alone, and in the dark."

I nodded and sat back down beside her. "Do you want me to just stay until you fall asleep or all night?"

I brushed back a lock of hair that had fallen forward on her face. I didn't want to push my presence on her if it wasn't wanted. I loved her enough that I'd gladly sleep on broken glass if she'd asked me to. She didn't flinch at my touch this time, and I was hopeful this meant she still trusted me.

"Stay with me."

It was a simple statement that under the surface, spoke volumes about how she felt. I smiled and gently patted her hand, then leaned over and kissed her on the forehead before getting up. I moved around to the other side of the bed, then stripped and slid into bed beside her. She lay on her side, and I curled up behind her. She snuggled back against me as she always did, out of habit, and I wrapped my arm around her, watching her as she settled in to sleep for the night.

She was so beautiful and peaceful looking, but I knew I'd not have a lot of rest tonight, as she probably would suffer nightmares. As her eyes fluttered shut, I reached over her and turned off the bedside lamp. She groaned a complaint about being moved, but thankfully stayed asleep. The last dying rays of the sunset filtered through kinks in the blinds and I sat up, watching her as she fell deeper into sleep.

In her sleep, she snuggled closer to me. For all the hell that was going on around us, this woman was the owner of my heart and soul, I knew of no words to tell her the extent of what she meant to me. I hoped that my actions thus far spoke loud enough to her —that I'd do whatever I could as long as she was with me. I loved her more than any words could express.

It frightened me how quickly I'd fallen for her; I'd been drawn to her from the moment I laid eyes on her when I walked into this place. I had never before believed in love at first sight. If someone had told me when I left Colorado that I'd fall for someone half my age inside of a month of meeting them, to the point that I'd willingly lay down my own life for them, I'd have snorted in disbelief and laughed them off the face of the world. Now that I laid here beside her, it all didn't sound so farfetched.

I leaned down and gently kissed her cheek, and then rested my head on the pillow. Her breathing was regular now and I inhaled in her scent—a soothing floral fragrance—and slowly fell asleep myself, holding her tightly.

CHAPTER 22

A heart stopping scream woke me in the middle of the night.

I sat up like I'd been shot, and rolled over to find out if it was Rebecca. She wasn't beside me. Panicked, I threw off the sheets and flew out of bed, pulling on a pair of pants and tripping over my own two feet in the process. I found her curled into a little ball in a corner of the living room, tears streaming down her face, staring at something. Slowly wandering over to the light switch, I discovered that the power had been restored. I saw nothing in the corner where Becca's gaze remained transfixed, and a quick check around the place confirmed that there was no one there. *A night terror, then.* This must be Karmic payback for being a sleep-talker for years, and for the effect Valium had on me. Ryan told me I'd let out enough bloodcurdling screams during the times I'd been sedated on planes to have taken more than a decade off his life.

Sitting down beside Rebecca, I wrapped my arms around her, and tried to calm her down. Knowing that my singing helped, I sang one of the lullabies that my mother had sung to me when I was terrified at night as a child. One of the advantages of having a mother who has half Scottish was that I'd been brought up with a lot of song—both English and Gaelic. Dad's family traced its roots to Ireland, and beyond that to Wales. Though he'd never been outwardly musical, he'd definitely been appreciative of music, and I'd found out a short while ago, despite how he'd seem disapproving of my career choice, he was actually proud as hell of me, and had often had praised me to his colleagues and friends.

Rebecca seemed to quiet down as I sang. Inwardly I laughed at the sight this must've been. I could see the critics crowing on how I'd fallen: Moderately Successful Solo Artist Reduced to Singing Children's Lullabies for a Distraught Woman in the Middle of Nowhere, Arizona in Nothing but His Jeans. I really didn't care; there was a good reason for why I did.

When I'd finished the last lullaby I could recall, the tears had stopped, and her eyelids were drooping. I knew she'd never really awakened, and would not likely remember in the morning what had triggered this episode. Gently guiding her to a standing position I took her slowly back to her room and into bed. When I went to turn off the light, I caught a glimpse of something in the patio area. Dismissing it as probably being the cursed cat who couldn't keep up with the damned mouse population, I closed the door behind myself, shedding my pants and crawling back into bed.

The morning came too quickly, the light cutting through the blinds into my eyes waking me at what probably was the crack of dawn. With a muttered curse, I rolled over and came face to face with Rebecca, who was wide awake and looking at me with a smile.

"Thank you," she said simply and kissed me.

"For what?"

She smiled. "For staying with me."

"I love you. Why would I leave you when you need me?"

She shrugged and rolled over onto her back, and I put my arm around her waist. The marks on her wrists had deepened with bruises and looked as nasty as they probably felt. I pushed away the thought of trying to take her mind off things by making love —I was pretty sure I'd have my nuts handed to me on a platter. It might distract me, but experience had been a great teacher that it wasn't so successful with women. No matter how tender or caring I could be, it would still amount to a wrongdoing, and that was the last thing I wanted.

She stretched, wincing as the areas where her skin had been bound and rubbed raw touched the blankets, then looked back over at me. I hoped that she'd tell me what had been done to her and by whom. Not knowing drove me bonkers.

"You're thinking something, Jon. You going to talk, or do I have to drag it out of you?" She smiled at that, and I laughed.

"I'm actually waiting for you to talk. You worry me with the fact that you're not really speaking."

She rolled over, away from me.

"I want to talk, Jon, but I'm afraid you'll go off half-cocked after the people who did it. You're very protective of me, and well ..." she trailed off, still looking at the wall.

I tenderly rolled her back to face me. Taking her chin in my hand, I lifted her head until we were eye-to-eye.

"Rebecca Nicole, you should know by now that even though I want to rain hellfire down on people, I'm not so featherbrained. I love you, and yes, I am protective of those that I love, but I'm not about to get us further into this mess than we already are. Now, spill it."

She sighed, and breaking her contact with me, laid back on the pillows and told me what had happened after she'd left the room.

She'd headed off to Jodi's suite, and feeling a bit cagey at having been inside for a long while with just me for company, she'd taken the long route to get there and had stopped in the courtyard to pay a visit to the piano. She'd been playing several minutes when someone, she wasn't sure who, had come up behind her and had grabbed her from the back. She also hadn't known what they'd used to knock her out, but there was a cloth covered with something that was put over her nose and mouth until she blacked out.

When she'd next come to a few hours later, she'd been bound and gagged, and left in a room somewhere in the compound. At this point in the retelling of her story, she pulled me closer, trying to wrap me around her as best as she could. I held her and let her rest her head on my chest.

"When I regained consciousness in that little room, there was just me. I was bound and gagged. I tried to scream and move, but, well, neither of those things worked. So, what could I do other than sit there and wait out whatever they wanted to do to me?"

She ran her hands up and down her arms as if she felt cold, but I knew that it wasn't from the temperature in the room. I ran a hand over her hair and let her take the time that she needed before moving on to the next part of her story.

"Anyway, I'm stuck in there, bound and gagged like a pig for the spit. I don't know how long it was, time stopped having any meaning when I couldn't see either my watch or the sun, so I just sat there, hoping that you or Jodi would realize I'd gone missing and that at least one of you would come to your senses and try to find me. I'm pretty sure I heard you go by earlier in the day, but I'm not absolutely certain."

She sighed deeply, and tears rolled down her cheeks. She was shaking. I kissed the top of her head and rested my head against hers as I continued to hold her close.

"Sweetheart, if it's too much, then maybe you shouldn't talk about it right now."

As much as I wanted to know what had happened, if it meant hurting her this badly, it wasn't worthwhile to me.

"I'll be okay, hon. I ... I ... just need a bit of time."

She rolled over to face me. Resting her head on my shoulder, she cried—the silent crying of the damned—for what felt like forever. I held her, trying my best to soothe her even though I didn't know the source of her tears. Eventually she stopped; however, it was to fall asleep, probably from sheer emotional exhaustion.

Not wanting to wake her, I kept her beside me. Eventually, I gave into the pull of sleep, and drifted off.

When I awoke a while later, Rebecca was already up, which had probably been what had roused me from a sound sleep. She was dressed and sat on the edge of the bed, watching me.

"Hello," I said groggily, with a grin.

She returned the smile and crawled up onto the bed beside me. I noticed that she'd wrapped some sort of bandage around her wrists, and when she noticed my staring at them, she let me know that Jodi had been over earlier and rather than wake me up, she'd let me sleep.

"You've been taking care of me for so long, I figured that it would only be right to allow you to get some rest without worrying about me." She smacked me playfully on the behind. "Now get your butt out of bed, showered and dressed, and we'll go have supper in the garden. It's a beautiful evening."

She walked off with a saucy wiggle and wink.

I got out of bed, and twenty minutes later, I was showered, dressed, and headed out into the garden. Rebecca stood there, her long ebony hair blowing about her as she looked out at the night sky. If it weren't for the fact that her wrists were bandaged, and I knew that dark and painful bruises lurked beneath the lovely dress she had on, it would just have been a normal dinner for two. The table displayed the nice feast that Jodi had brought, and the warm golden flames of candles flickered in the gentle breeze.

"Good evening sleepy head," said Rebecca, coming over to where I'd been watching her at the door.

She put her arms around my neck and gave me a brief but passionate kiss, before taking my hand and leading me over to the table. Once I was seated, she sat down and we began dinner in silence.

I gazed at her across the table; she looked noticeably withdrawn, and despite the sleep she'd managed, there were dark circles under her eyes. Any slight noise made her jump, too. She was clearly on edge. I only hoped that she'd be able to speak to me about what had happened—sooner rather than later.

Neither of us made small talk, nor did we need to. When we'd finished eating, we cleared the table together, and when that was done, we ended up standing there, completely unsure about the next step.

"So... what's on tap for tonight, my love?" I asked, pulling her close.

"I don't know. I hadn't really thought much beyond dinner. We could stargaze if you'd like."

I hit upon an idea. Taking the keys from the counter, I headed out the door with her. She hesitated as she got to the threshold, and looked at me with eyes almost wild with fear.

"Rebecca, I swear to you right now, if anyone tries anything with you, I will defend you with everything I have. I'd die for you if need be. I love you and I'm not going to let anyone hurt you. I promise."

Becca blushed a bit at that declaration but took a deep breath and came with me. She started as the door clicked shut loudly, echoing in the eerily empty hallway, but with my arm around her, she stayed by me, trembling with fright.

We walked down hallways silent as catacombs out to the courtyard. We'd not been here in quite a long while, and it was an almost refreshing change of pace.

Pushing open the glass door that separated us from the gray expanse of the courtyard, I was greeted by the chill of the night. Moving to taking her hand, I gently towed her out to the piano, which was still there—unharmed, untouched by anyone—and sat her down on the bench with me.

"Jon, what are you—"

I silenced her with a single finger gently on her lips.

"Just listen," I said as I opened the cover from the keys.

Taking a deep breath, I played, slowly at first, but building into a song that was familiar but not. I realized this was the tune I'd been playing absentmindedly shortly before I'd kissed her for the first time in the kitchens. She sat there, her eyes closed. I felt quite flattered that she listened to the music that intently.

When I'd finished up, I rested my hands on the keyboard and watched her. Slowly she opened her eyes and looked at me, a serene smile on her face.

"That was beautiful, Jon. Very haunting and ... wow. I've got chills." She ran her hands up and down her arms, where the skin was peppered with goose flesh.

"I think I'll call it *Becca's Song*." I said, and she blushed. "Every time I think of you, that's the music that seems to flow through my entire being."

"Wow. I'm honored." she said, looking at me.

I leaned in and gently kissed her. She leaned into me, and before I knew what was happening, we were locked in a passionate embrace. I never heard the footsteps coming up behind us or felt the blow that made the world go black. Again.

~

J came to in complete darkness again. I wasn't sure if I'd been blindfolded or my eyes just refused to see the light, but whatever the case, I couldn't tell where I was. Testing my arms and legs showed me that they'd been bound. I stayed silent and listened for any signs that Rebecca might be with me. I heard shuffling around the area and I tried to talk but found my mouth gagged and I couldn't say anything. Making a guttural noise I hoped Rebecca would understand as me trying to call her name, I vainly shifted in the direction that the noise came from. Eventually making the distance of perhaps a few feet, I reached out as much as I could to touch whatever lay out there. Praying I wouldn't feel the flea-bitten hide of a mouse or other rodent, I fumbled around as much as my hog-tied hands would allow me and discovered the hand of who I was sure was Rebecca. The hand was slender, like that of a lifelong pianist.

When my hand came in touch with hers, it jumped, and the sound of a muffled squeak came from its owner. Now I was positive it was Becca. I grabbed the hand in mine and gave it as much of a reassuring squeeze as was manageable under the circumstances. It squeezed back, and my heart soared.

Scuttling as close to her as I could, I took stock of how I felt. My head still hurt like the dickens, whatever had been used as a cudgel to knock me senseless had been hard, and from the texture of my hair, there was a sizable amount of congealed blood. I was definitely blindfolded; when I tried to open my eyes, the fabric caught my eyelashes. Other than the obvious—being tied hand and foot and having a head that ached like the national elephant tap dance finals had been held on my skull—I was in good shape.

Rebecca leaned up against me. Everything about her told me that it was her: the smell of her perfume, the scent of her shampoo, and the familiar weight of her head resting on my shoulder. I wished that I could free my arms to both check her state of being and to hold her close. I'd waited all my life for a love like this, and I wasn't going to let it be taken from me—or even injured—willingly. Wherever we'd been brought and by whom, they'd put us together for a reason. My heart sank. I'd let my guard down in the courtyard, as had she, and that moment where my senses had been filled with Rebecca, and hers with me, was used to our disadvantage. I had my suspicions as to the whom of the equation. There was only one person insane enough to attack us. Whether it was her in person, or by proxy, Sarah was at the heart of anything like this.

Hell hath no fury like a woman scorned.

I laughed wryly at that. I'd thought until this time, hell hath no fury like my annoying harpy of an ex-wife.

I leaned my head down on Rebecca's. I loved this woman more than life, and should they have done any harm to her, they'd have me, irate and protective, to go through. I knew why Rebecca didn't wish to speak of what had happened during that time; I had the distinct sensation that we would go through it again.

Time eventually lost its meaning. We stayed like that—leaning together, resting against each other—for what seemed an eternity. The sounds of the world around us washed over me, and I could tell from her breathing that Rebecca had fallen asleep. I longed to be able to reassure her as well as myself that we'd both be all right in the end. Unfortunately, at this moment in time, it didn't seem likely.

Finally, after what felt like eons had passed but was probably no more than a few hours, there was the distinct sound of footsteps in our direction, then of the door opening, and more footsteps. I felt myself being pulled to my feet, and the blindfold removed from my eyes. One of Sarah's goons was standing there, a firm grasp around my arm, as if there was any way I could make a run for it.

I looked down, and confirmed that Rebecca was indeed the owner of the hand that I'd been holding during our time of captivity. Another one of Sarah's bodyguards roughly pulled Becca to her feet. Looking around and blinking against the light that seared through my senses, I noted that we were in one of the suites that was being reconstructed into God only knew what.

They shoved us out the door and down a long-deserted hallway, being ushered, no doubt, to wherever Sarah currently waited. I'd never been in this part of the compound either, and being gagged, I didn't have the the ability to ask Rebecca if she'd been here before. Even when I turned slightly to look at her, the goon holding my arm and "guiding" me wrenched that arm around to the point where I wanted to scream in pain.

Finally, after a long walk without any conversation between either Becca and I or the two goons, we arrived in a room that seemed familiar, but after all the blows to the head I'd suffered in the last two months, I wasn't entirely sure that this was real or a part of a delusion or illusion created by my poor savaged brain. They again pushed us into the room, and, none too gently, removed the gags but not the bindings. Then they left us, collapsed in a heap on the floor.

"Becca."

My voice was no more than a whisper, hoarse and alien to my own ears. She looked up from where she lay and ebony eyes met my own. She smiled faintly at me.

"Jon."

Her voice was as raw and weak as my own. I crawled as best I could over to her and took a good look. She'd also been hit hard on the head, and I had no doubt she would suffer a relapse of the symptoms that she had been suffering from the last wicked blow she had received.

I tried to move my arms over her, but it was fruitless. Whatever reason we were brought here, we were alone right now, and that was all that really mattered.

"You okay?" I asked as I settled into the most comfortable position that I could, considering the circumstances.

"Yeah, my head fucking-well hurts though." She grimaced. "Love may be blind, but whomever conked us both over the head wasn't."

I couldn't help but grin at her statement. There wasn't much else we could do—either go mad with the possibilities that were piling up or try and find what minimal humor that there was in the absurdity of the situation.

She looked up at me and noticed the blood in my hair. Her eyes went wide and she opened her mouth to speak.

"I'm all right, Becca. I think it was you not so long ago that told me that head wounds tend to look worse than what they are. At least this time I'm not seeing double."

She nodded, and we lapsed into silence again. No sounds were audible in the room other than the two of us breathing, and the pounding of my own heartbeat in my ears. I felt sure this delay had been planned on purpose. Build the suspense and leave both of us wondering what was going to happen before the proverbial sword fell on our necks.

Rebecca and I sat there, unmoving for what seemed like forever. When she did shuffle about, I jumped, as I wasn't expecting it, and with a small laugh she made her way over to me. She laid her head against my shoulder again and arranged herself as best she could to get comfortable.

"I'm so tired, Jon." she yawned, her eyelids slowly fluttering shut. "It's ... just ... too much."

"I know, love, I know. Get some sleep. I doubt we'll have that luxury soon."

She shifted to rest her head on my lap, and fell asleep. I stayed awake, on edge and staying vigilant. There wasn't much going on, but I still wanted to stay alert and awake. I finally gave into sleep after a while.

When I came to, I was vaguely aware that I wasn't bound any longer and Rebecca was no longer by my side.

Blinking wildly for a few moments until the room came into focus, I immediately began to worry. I was in the same place as I'd been before, and Rebecca was simply stretched out on the floor. Someone had freed us from our bindings, and I saw that food had been laid out. There were no tables or chairs, but the food was served on trays.

Nudging Rebecca awake, I pointed out the food to her, as she blinked groggily.

"I don't trust it," she murmured as she wiped the sleep from her eyes. "This entire thing smacks of Sarah's touch."

She sat back against the wall, refusing to touch the food. My own mouth was watering at the smells of it, but taking her lead, as she'd been here much longer than I and knew the typical antics of Sarah, I stayed back from it, and instead reveled in the fact that I no longer was gagged and bound.

Rebecca snuggled back into my arms, and together, we awaited whatever fate had ordained for us.

We didn't have to wait for long.

The sounds of footsteps echoing down the hallways to us brought both of us from the state of semi-wakefulness completely alert in seconds.

Sarah entered the room with a brace of her goons surrounding her, and her brother bringing up the rear. She was dressed in what was barely more than a tank top and shorts that left nothing to the imagination. She glowered at Rebecca, and with a quick and subtle movement of her hand, two of the pack of goons descended on to Becca and pulled her away from me.

The scream that issued from Rebecca was bone-chilling, and I quickly rose to my feet to defend her. Sarah stepped forward, along with the remaining two of her goons, and before I could do anything, I was pinned to the wall.

I watched in horror, struggling against the two well-muscled young men who held me as Rebecca was taken away. Kyle followed them as they dragged her kicking, screaming, and thrashing from the room. To add to the insult as they left the room, he stopped them, and with a venomous look at me, he pulled Rebecca to him. The two men holding her held her still and grabbing her by the hair he proceeded to roughly kiss and fondle her.

Her scream of horror was muted, and when he pulled away, the look of terror on her face had increased ten-fold. Yelling in anger and fighting against the strong arms that held me to the wall like shackles, I made what attempt I could to come to her aid. Feeling utterly useless as she was dragged from the room, still fighting, I sagged against the wall. I felt like the wind had been kicked out of me, like the life itself had been dragged from my body.

"Well, well. We meet again, Jonathan." Sarah said with a wry grin. "I think this time may be a little bit different from our last meeting. Perhaps you'll be more, accommodating."

She ran her fingernail down the side of my face, and I grimaced.

"Bring him to my room, and make sure he's compliant," she said, turning and leaving the room through the same hallway that Rebecca had been taken down.

Before I could ask as to what Sarah meant by compliant, hands reached around my face with a rag covered in something, and the world danced before my eyes, then narrowed down into a tunnel that ended in a blissful darkness.

CHAPTER 23

The world spun and twirled around me. I curled into a ball, trying desperately to keep from retching up what I'd recently eaten. I jammed my eyes shut and concentrated on trying to stop the world from spinning. When the incessant whirling ceased, I slowly pried my eyes open, and looked around me.

The world refused to come into focus at first. Blinking hard against the wooziness that seemed to come in waves, I scanned my surroundings.

I was in a comfortable bed, somewhere within the confines of the compound. It wasn't the one I'd lain in when I'd first arrived, and it was most definitely not Rebecca's. Checking that I was alone, which I was, I slowly tested my balance by trying to roll over and sit u. Only when I put my feet on the floor did I notice I was bound to the bed. Even though the leather straps that held me were quite long, and allowed for a great deal of movement, there was no doubt I was still captive.

Unsteadily, I stood and glanced around, then stared down at myself. I still wore the same clothes as when Rebecca and I had last been together. I resisted the urge to check that I'd not been molested, and simply redressed.

With a sigh at not being able to move more than about a foot in any direction from the bed, I curled up in the center of it, displeased at having to sit and await whatever fate would come for me. My mind kept running over the possibilities as to what could be happening with Rebecca. None of the situations turned out on the good side for either her or myself. I worried for her and cursed the fact that they kept here, unable to pace the floor, building up energy that could go nowhere. The only way in or out of the room was the door, and I had no illusions that there would be—by some miracle if I got loose—at least two of the burly men Sarah called friends on the other side, waiting to pound me into another life.

Uncurling and lying down on the bed, I put my hand up to assuage the ache in my head, and found relief that the blood was still in my hair; it was an indication no one had done much other than cart me like a sack of potatoes to this room, wherever it was. I had vague recollections of Sarah saying that I was to be brought to her room and made compliant.

From what little I had seen of Sarah's suite, it was out of character for what her bedroom should look like. Spartan, empty save the bed and the door. I looked around for any indication of human life other than myself and saw nothing. Settling back onto the bed, I supposed I had no real choice but to unwillingly accept my fate.

Again, time seemed to drift by in slow motion. I had no watch on, no way to tell the time. All I could do was sit and wonder what lay in store for me, what had become of Rebecca, and more importantly, what had been she subjected to.

The silence of the room was almost crushing, in and of itself.

There was no sound of anyone from the outside, and that left my brain to come up with random combinations of noises that in turn made my mind wander more and more down strange and twisted paths. My own heartbeat seemed to echo in my ears, like a drum beating in the heart of a cavern.

As I lay there, contemplating the meaning of life and if I should start counting the bumps on the stucco ceiling above me, my mind continued to imagine various things, all involving what Kyle and Sarah might do to Rebecca.

After what seemed like an eternity alone with nothing but my own thoughts to keep me company, I heard footsteps. Someone entered the room. It wasn't Kyle or Sarah, and I was pretty sure it wasn't Rebecca or Jodi either, as the form was covered in black from head to toe, bearing a simple tray of food, which was placed on the bed beside me.

"You'd better eat. Sarah wants you strong and willing," they said, before walking out.

Willing for what? my brain asked me, then immediately jumped to the most likely conclusion. Sarah had wanted to add me to her stable of men since I'd shown up, and as Jodi had informed us earlier, that snake was not used to someone not giving her what she wanted. I had no interest in becoming a stud among her stallions, none whatsoever.

The smell of the food wafted over to me and I curled back into a small ball, as the aroma of what I'd normally considered good food now turned my stomach and made me retch. I was already weak, sore, and beaten down; being ill would only weaken me further and allow Sarah to try whatever she desired.

Pushing the food away with a foot, trying to get it as far as I could from myself before I threw up, the world began to whirl, and I felt like I'd been put through the spin cycle one too many times. I

closed my eyes tightly—trying to keep both my head on my
shoulders and my stomach contents inside my body, praying
silently for release from this hell hole and its torture, wishing I
could know what was going on with Rebecca—until I slowly fell
into the black pit of a drugged and dreamless sleep.

When I came to again, the food was gone, and clothing rested on
a chair that had been brought into the room, along with a basin
of water and some towels. Somebody felt I should change and
wash myself. Once I sat up, I noticed I had been unbound from
the bed. Rubbing my wrists, where the leather bonds had cut into
the skin, I stood, wearily, and looked around again.

Nothing seemed new in the room, save for the change of clothing
and the items for cleaning myself up. I saw that the binds had not
been removed from the room, but only from me, so that I was free
to move around. Checking carefully to see that no one overtly
watched me (though covertly could be another story, and I was
pretty sure that someone, somewhere knew what was going on in
this room), I decided to indulge whomever had brought the
clothes and water and at least try and get the blood out of
my hair.

The temperature of the water still felt quite warm, which spoke to
it having been brought into the room very recently. I poured
some into the basin, and hung my head over it, pouring water
onto my hair. The water stung my scalp. Hissing with the pain, I
clenched my teeth and gently worked on getting as much of the
guck out of my hair as I could.

I tried to dry my hair without further cursing or reopening the
wound on the back of my head. I was rather filthy considering
what I'd been through recently, and finally the urge to be clean
won out over the worry that someone monitored my every move.
A few minutes later, I was freshened up and changed into the
clothing that had been left for me. Sitting back on the bed, as

there wasn't much else I could do in the room, I resigned myself to the fact that unless a miracle happened, I would be stuck here for the foreseeable future. I wondered, yet again, about what was happening to Rebecca. I couldn't help predicting she'd come to a nasty and upsetting end, and that bothered me on too many levels. I loved her more than life, and being caged in this small room, I felt like a wildcat stuck in a zoo. All I could do was pace the confines of my cell.

After a while, I began to daydream again and drifted in and out of conscious thought. I heard someone approach the door to what I had begun to regard as my jail cell, but paid it little heed as the images in my mind caught more of my attention than anything else. It wasn't until someone physically touched me that I jumped, and almost clocked them in my surprise.

The person before me was shrouded in a dark cloak-like jacket, with a hood pulled over their head, which hid their face from view.

"Jon, relax. It's me," the voice attached to the person said, and pushed the hood back until I could see the familiar auburn hair and hazel eyes of Jodi.

I sighed deeply and sat, nerves still on edge. "How the hell did you manage to get in here? I was pretty sure only one person knew about this room, and that person wouldn't be you."

She pulled the cloak's hood back over her hair, so that it hid her face, and laughed wryly.

"There are more things about this place Sarah doesn't know— that I know—than there are stars in the sky," said Jodi, sitting gingerly on the edge of the bed. "I'm here to tell you about Becca."

My heart both plummeted and soared at the same time. If

Rebecca wasn't with Jodi, it was an indication that Becca was likely being held like I was, but it could also mean that the absolute worst things I could dream up hadn't happened yet.

"What about her?" I was trying to sound like I didn't want to go running to wherever Rebecca was and save her from whatever fate had befallen her.

Jodi sighed and looked away. It couldn't be good news.

"They've thrown her back in the pits. She's hanging on, but I'm not sure how. She, well, she's clinging to the hope that somehow a knight on a white horse will come to her rescue. Of course, that's not literal, but you know what I mean. She's holding out for a miracle, and I'm not sure you or I will be able to deliver it."

There was a sound of footsteps in the hallway. With a start, Jodi rose to her feet, and taking the soiled clothing and the basin of water, made her way out of the room. My one contact with the world disappeared without another word to me.

More footsteps milled around outside the door, and I could hear muted conversations, bits of which seeped through. Finally, one of the voices moved off, and the other came closer. I found myself sitting on the edge of the bed, leaning forward in anticipation of what might be on the other side of that door. I had no illusions that it could be something purely evil, but a part of my brain, however unlikely it may be, hoped that it would be Rebecca.

The door slowly opened, creaking on its hinges. Slowly, painfully slowly, the person behind it emerged. The sharp florescent lighting highlighted sun-bleached and over-processed blonde hair, and I groaned inwardly as she entered the room, followed by a rather large, muscular member of her goon squad. The door shut with a heavy thump, and the two of them stood there, identical postures—arms folded across their chests and eerily similar expressions on their faces. From Sarah, I had expected to see a look of pure hatred with evil dripping from every pore. The one she gave me seemed more calculating than I'd previously thought possible, and it sent a shiver up my spine.

"Well, Jonathan. I hope you're feeling comfortable ... as comfortable as is possible considering the circumstances that you've forced me to place you in."

I looked up at her, summoning every ounce of the raw, boiling hatred for her that existed within my being, and tried fruitlessly to focus it in the glare I fixed upon her. Her eyebrows flew up, then she laughed.

"Oh, you are amusing. I think I'll keep you around for a while."

I remained silent. I didn't want to bandy words with her; it was futile and a waste of time, energy, and breath.

"So quiet you are ..." she cooed, slowly making her way to the side of the bed, where she sat beside me.

It took everything I had to resist the urge not to wrap my hands around her throat and squeeze the worthless life out of her. I knew that if I dared, the silent, stoic and highly muscle-bound goon at the door would be on me before I had the opportunity to blink.

Sarah reached out her hand and pushed the hair back from my face. In the time I'd been here, my hair had become rather unruly; but because Rebecca claimed she liked it and the length made me look much younger, I'd let it be. I enjoyed having Rebecca spontaneously running her fingers through it as we just sat around talking or just being. However, with Sarah, I couldn't repress the urge to shudder in revulsion.

"Why do you insist on making this so hard for yourself?" she asked.

I looked away, anywhere but at her. The anger and disgust I felt winding into a ball in my gut could result in my saying things I'd regret mere moments later.

She sighed, and with one final caress of my face, left room.

"You will be mine, Jonathan. One way or another I will have you for my own."

With a smile, she left the room, then the door snapped shut again. I was alone, and for once I gave thanks. I got up and turned off the light, the blessed darkness blanketing the room and everything in it. Carefully checking my way to the bed, I knelt down along side of it, as I'd done many decades before with my mother at my side and bowed my head in prayer.

God, I don't know if you're out there, and it's certainly been a long time since we last talked. I know I've not been what you wanted of me. I've broken several commandments, repeatedly, and without any sorrow. But now I've found the woman of my dreams and I don't want to lose her. I love her more than I ever thought it was possible to love someone. I want nothing more than to make her happy, to take her away from here. If by some miracle, you could see to both forgiving me and getting the two of us out of this place, I promise she will be my only woman from here on out, and that I'll have no one, and I mean no one else, other than her in my life. I am ashamed of the things I've done in my past, I am sorry for them, and if I could have another go 'round on the carousel of life, I'd live the way you wanted me to, and you know what? I'd wait for her. I don't care that there is twenty some years between us. I love her, and I'd lay down my life for her in a split second, without any thought. Please God, keep her safe.

With a soul-shuddering sigh, I got up from my knees, and crawled into bed. I wanted to see the moon and the stars, to feel the warm body of the woman I loved beside me, to hear her softly breathing as she slept. I wanted her to be happy. I hoped I was the one who would be able to make her feel that way, but if it wasn't to be, then I'd have to live with that. But I'd go to my grave loving her, even if she stopped loving me.

Staring blankly out into the darkness, I waited for whatever rest that would claim me. Eventually a blissful feeling slid over me, and I slowly fell into the arms of Morpheus, towards a dreamless sleep.

~

I was awakened by the pounding on the door of my prison. Opening one eye, I saw one of the goons bringing in a tray and putting it on the small table where the basin and pitcher had been the day before. Then they left. I jammed my eye shut again and rolled over. The smells coming from the tray were tempting, but as far as I was concerned, I was on a hunger strike until I found out more about Rebecca. I could already hear Jodi lecturing me about this, but I wasn't going to give up my plans so easily. I had no intention of starving myself, but merely using hunger as a tool to get what I wanted.

I must have fallen asleep again, as the next thing I could remember was being woken up by a hooded figure. Unfortunately, I didn't remember who it was and screamed like I'd seen a ghost, then shot up in the bed like my ass was on fire.

"Holy shit," Jodi said with a gasp, and sat back on the bed, clutching her chest.

"Don't wake me up like that!" I croaked, my throat drier than the desert surrounding this place.

Once we'd both calmed down, and our breathing returned to normal, Jodi updated me on what she'd come to discover.

"Well, last night, I heard something going on. You know me, Jon, curiosity killed the Jodi, let alone the cat! So, I kept an ear to the ground. Kyle had some visitors last night. Guys I recognized from Sarah's goon squad. I couldn't quite overhear what they said but judging from what I could see of Kyle's face, something's going to go down, and if they were talking to Kyle, well, that lead me to only one conclusion."

I looked up at her. "Becca."

She nodded.

"But why?" I asked.

Jodi stood and walked away from the bed. Wrapping her arms around herself, she looked away from me to a blank wall with nothing on it. She sighed deeply and then turned back to me.

"Kyle and his sister aren't that far apart in their thinking. If either of them wants something, they'll work until they get it. And if it's another person, then they'll try to wear that person down until they give in. But if that person has too much spine and doesn't give them all they desire, then the siblings will try to eliminate them from the picture."

Jodi paced the room again. "If you think I'm who Kyle wanted, then you're very sorely mistaken. Kyle has wanted Rebecca since she set foot into this place almost two years ago. To him, she's his perfect match—beauty and brains for the golden boy. I can tell you Becca would rather slit her wrists with rusty knives than ever be with him. When you came along, you inadvertently gave Kyle some competition."

She sat back down on the end of the bed, and smiled.

"Don't give me that look—it was obvious you were struck by her from the first moment you talked to her. She took a lot longer to warm up to you then you did to her, which considering the things that I know have happened to her, and how she was even before then ..." Jodi shrugged. "She was afraid of being another notch on someone's headboard, someone that you'd use and throw away. Not that she was looking for a relationship, but she wanted to know you for you before she went any further than simple friendship. Once you'd finally crossed that line of trust with her, she could see that you were interested, but she's never been one—despite all the evidence that she's a feminist—to try and take the lead. Me, I saw how you looked at her, and how well you two suited each other, then catching her looking at you the same way, well ..."

Jodi laughed, and brought her knees up to her chin.

"I'm guilty of trying to throw you two together at every opportunity that came up. Neither of you were making a move, and it was obvious to me that both of you were meant to be. Once you two finally stopped acting like the world would end if you got together, and admitted, 'Hey I really like this person,' you were both changed. You, Jon, you were happy. I'd see you gaze at her and a smile would come onto your face that you couldn't get rid of; I'm not sure you even knew it was there. Becca, well, despite all this madness, she's not been this happy in years, and so balanced. You give her something to think about other than— well, I'll let her talk about that. It's her life, and I'm not going into things she needs to tell you herself."

She went silent for a few minutes, and then looked me straight in the eyes.

"Jon, I need you to still trust me. Things are going to get worse for you before they get better, But you have my word that I'll get you both out of here, safe."

She checked around first, but then quickly placed her hand on mine and offered an expression that was intended to reassure me. She pulled the hood back over her head, and almost bolted from the room. I had no doubts that Jodi would do everything in her power to keep her promise, but I doubted that her plan could do anything. She didn't seem worried about it, but I was, and I was pretty damned sure that it terrified Rebecca.

I could hear Jodi's footsteps retreating down the hall, then all was quiet again. The sounds of the day-to-day movement around the place didn't even seep into wherever I was. The silence was crushing, and slowly driving me insane. I had the distinct impression that it was meant to do that—drive me ever closer to the brink of insanity—to where I would do whatever Sarah wanted, to just make it stop.

I got up and wandered around the room, checking for where I could possibly find some route of escape, or possibly just do something to entertain my mind. Nothing. Finally exhausting my search for anything other than the small spiders that seemed to skitter into the dark hollows of the room, I flopped back across the width of the bed, stared at the ceiling, and tried to keep from counting the dots. The silence made so I could hear my heart pounding in my ears, and every breath that I took echoed loudly.

Closing my eyes, I concentrated on keeping my breathing steady and my heart rate calm, as Mike had instructed me many times over the years. As my breathing slowed, and my heartbeat joined it, I slipped into a semi-trance-like state. I was dimly aware of the world around me, but for once, I was more aware of my own mind, my own being, than I'd been, well, ever. My thoughts, rather than being scattered and seemingly random, were there for me, almost in physical form to examine and dissect. At the center of them was the ebony haired, dark eyed beauty called Rebecca. I smiled, and I could feel the warmth in my heart and mind when I thought of her.

I let my mind linger on that image, holding her at the core of my thoughts. She made every nerve in my body feel like it tingled with electricity. I avoided certain other aspects of her that made other parts of my body react. The last thing I needed was to be in a semi-conscious state where someone could take advantage of me with a raging hard-on.

Slipping slowly out of my trance, unsure of how much time had passed, I blinked and focused on the room in front of me. I was still on the bed; however, I was restrained once more, and sitting astride me was Sarah, looking quite pleased with herself. Quickly, I did a physical assessment of myself. No, I wasn't aroused in any physical way, but had I been, Sarah straddling me would have killed that in a flash anyway.

"What the flying fuck are you doing in here, and moreover, what the *hell* are you doing *on* me?" I cried, barely containing the venom in my voice.

She laughed and leaned down so that her straw-colored hair hung in my face, the ends of it touching my nose and making me want to sneeze.

"I told you, Jonathan, one way or another, I would make you mine. If that means tying you to a bed and forcibly taking what I want, then so be it. You've gotten more than enough chances from me—more than anyone ever should be allowed."

She leaned in and kissed me. As much as I could, I recoiled in horror. It was the only thing that I could pretty much do. Then she laughed, like one who thinks she's won the battle, who thinks that she's won the day, and like one who feels her captive had no choice to give in her.

"Why are you still baulking? You were meant to be mine, Jonathan, not that little slut's. I don't know what magic spell she cast over you, but I am damned sure that I'm going to ..."

There was a loud crash, taking her attention away from me. It was enough for me to be able to test my binds and find out they weren't done that tightly. Trying to keep my expression from giving away my surprise, I turned my attention back to Sarah.

She'd slid off me and made tracks for the door, to see what had caused the commotion. I breathed a sigh of relief that whatever she had in mind for me was at least postponed for the time being.

As the door clicked shut, I pried my hand slowly out of the strap that tied it to the bed, and then tried the other one. It came loose as quickly as the other, and once I was freed, I sat there rubbing my wrists, trying to get some feeling back into them, then I undid the ones that secured me legs to the bed as well.

Feeling somewhat adventurous and somewhat terrified at what lay ahead, I got up and tired the door. She'd forgotten to lock it. I opened it carefully and looked around the corner. I was in a hallway near Sarah's suite. I shuddered involuntarily, then stepped quietly into the corridor. Voices argued loudly somewhere else in the suite; it seemed to come from the direction of Sarah's bedroom, or possibly the room that I'd been at meetings in, what seemed like ages ago. I really didn't care, I just wanted out of here.

Taking quiet steps down towards where I knew the living room and the doors out of this place where, I kept one ear on the argument that went on in the other room. Something had happened; I couldn't tell exactly what, but something. Slowly making my way down the hall, half listening, and into the main room of the place, I hugged the walls, and found the twin glass doors that marked the entrance to this place. Never had two doors held so much significance for me—the exit of the hell I'd been dragged into, the possible gates to where love of my life might be, and the way out of this place.

Creeping across the floor, hoping that whatever had, thankfully, kept Sarah's attention would continue to hold it for as long as it took me to escape. My heartbeat, frantic and pounding hard in my ears, was the only thing I could hear clearly. The sound of the argument in another room was muffled as through cotton balls.

I reached for the door, knowing my hands were slicked with perspiration, and as I expected, my hand slipped on the first try at turning the knob. Cursing under my breath, I wiped my hand on the pants that I'd been given the other day and reached for it again. Cool metal met my hand, and with a quiet prayer uttered skyward, I attempted the knob again.

It moved with an almost silent creak, and holding my breath, I turned it as far as it would go and slowly opened the door, hoping that it was as well maintained as the rest of Sarah's place. I wasn't to be disappointed. The door swung inward on well-oiled hinges and the hallway stretched in front of me, heading toward freedom.

I took a step out into the hallway, the cool breeze of the air flowing freely blew over my skin, and getting my bearings, I turned to the north branch of the hallway and headed towards Jodi's suite. I didn't give two shits if Kyle was home; I needed desperately to find out where they imprisoned Rebecca.

Fortunately, I didn't have to go far before running, literally, into Jodi. With breathless joy, she hugged me, but when I explained what I needed and wanted to do, a dark expression clouded her face. However, she nodded and we flew down the labyrinth of hallways that made up the compound. I was never able to truly keep track of the amount of turns and twists we took, and was thankful that Jodi could distinguish between one set of hallways and the identical twenty others or so that we had passed through to get to our desired location.

Finally, coming to an abrupt stop in the middle of what seemed like an empty corridor, Jodi turned to a wall, and with a difficult push in and off to the side, she revealed a dark, sodden passage that led into the bowels of the compound. Ducking down, and following her through the passageway, careful not to touch the sides for fear of whatever may be hidden in the grime, I followed her, even though the light dimmed to the point I could simply move forward without knowing where I was going. If Jodi stopped, I would hit her out of sheer inability to see, which is what invariably happened a few moments later.

"She's in here," Jodi said quietly, as if trying not to wake whatever evil was in the place. I heard, rather than saw her search something, and she flickered into existence the barest of glows thrown by a lighter.

With a cry that I knew came from the bottom of my soul, I could see the form of Rebecca, curled into the fetal position not three feet in front of me, barely breathing, skin gray, and her long dark hair matted.

She reacted to the light, and with a voice that sounded more than five times older than she was, Rebecca croaked out my name, as if I were a part of a dream.

Silently, I made my way over to the sodden, begrimed figure that was the light of my life, the one thing that kept me going despite everything, and I lay down on the floor beside her, cradling her. She'd almost wasted away to nothingness; the svelte curves that had been there the last time I'd seen her were hard angles, and even through the grime, I could make out in the flickering light that her usually radiant skin had the lackluster pallor of someone who hadn't seen daylight in a while.

"How long have I been gone, Jodi? What day is it?"

"Two weeks. It's December now, December third."

I looked up at Jodi, who was cast in shadows from the small light she'd cast. "I don't care anymore," I said. "I've got to get the two of us out of here before it kills her."

I looked down on the still silent figure in my arms. She was still breathing, and with what energy she could muster, clung to me as if I were the last thing on earth. For her, I might well have been.

CHAPTER 24

odi left after a few moments, the light disappearing as quickly as it had arrived. Rebecca and I were left together in the squalor of the small area. I'd had more than enough of the strangeness of the compound, the fact that I'd almost been forcibly raped by the leader of a cult while being terrified that the woman I'd no intentions of falling in love with—but that I'd fallen head over heels with—was slowly dying. We had to escape, no matter what the cost to myself. If I could at least get Rebecca out of here, it was worth whatever price would be exacted from my own hide.

I listened to her breathing; it sounded ragged and difficult. I wasn't sure how she'd ever recover. Fighting tears, I pulled her closer. She rested her head on my chest, and I struggled to stay awake for her. The darkness, the lack of anything other than white noise of two people breathing, and the skittering noises of what I prayed were not mice made keeping myself awake difficult. I finally nodded off, Rebecca clinging to me, both of us still on the floor.

When I came to a while later, it was to the wavering of a flashlight. The person who wielding it was not Jodi, as I'd anticipated, but Sarah herself.

"*T*he cur and his bitch, together. No matter what I do Jonathan, you seem to find your way back to her. I'm not sure why you do it, or how you're able to do it." The sneer on her face made her features twice as ugly as they had been before.

Looking up through a sleep induced haze, I smirked at her.

"Love finds a way, Sarah. You'd know that if you weren't so desperately trying to bed every man in this place in search of God knows what. Higher powers? The next messiah?"

Those were most definitely the wrong words to say in my present circumstances, but I'd had enough, and quite frankly, there wasn't much left that she could take from me—only the woman I loved and my life—and I'd not willingly part with either.

Sarah just about screamed, I wasn't sure how to describe the sound that she made, but it was a noise I'd only heard from one other person before or since, and the similarity was uncanny. She turned on her heel and left the cell along with whoever tailed her.

I wondered if I were madder than a Morris dancer. I couldn't be sane for thinking that we'd ever be rid of this place and for falling in love in the middle of this chaotic mess.

Rebecca stirred at my side, bringing my thoughts back from the netherworld to reality. She slept and dreamt. Holding her a bit tighter while trying to bring some sensation back to my arm, I watched her carefully. She jerked in fits and spurts, not able to move fully as she was sound asleep, and the troubled squeaks that came out of her worried me. I reflected that this whole thing was no pleasant dream of running through fields filled with flowers and sunshine. Rather, it was a nightmare about a nightmare inside of a nightmare, of a surreal situation like nothing I'd ever experienced throughout the whole of my life. People say that fame and its trappings make for a strange life for those of us picked from the rank and file of "normal" people. Those people have never been in this place, this hell, this ... I don't know. This entire place lacked definition to me. It was a black hole to normalcy, almost as if a parallel universe had been created within the walls of what once had been a hotel, where the simple acts of human existence had been twisted and perverted into something else.

Rebecca stirred once more and with a start, woke up. For a moment, I could feel her moving around, trying to figure out her surroundings, and who was with her, as her hands fluttered quickly across my torso and chest. Pulling her gently to have her sit in my lap, I held her tight, and kissed her hair while whispering comforting words.

"It's okay, Becca. It's okay. It's me, Jon. I'm here for you."

She let out a ragged sigh of relief and I felt her body sag against mine.

"Thank God," she croaked, her throat dry and scratchy. "How long was I asleep? I try not to in here ... the thought of things getting to me." She shuddered involuntarily.

"For a while. I couldn't tell you how long you'd been out, my love, but you were asleep a long while."

I ran my hand through her hair, gently picking out the tangles and mats as best I could. She leaned against me, rested her head on my shoulder, and wrapped her arms around me. There was nothing but time for the two of us now, until whatever punishment Sarah wanted to rain on us came crashing down.

During my life, I'd waited for plenty of things—planes, trains, concerts, paychecks, my divorce to become final—but the waiting that was forced on us in that small, dank, cramped place was beyond anything. It was in and of itself ... torture. Every little sound seemed to echo in this hellhole, and the constant trickling somewhere behind the walls made my skin crawl, not because it was simply a sign of poor workmanship, but also because of other things it could be—mice, chief amongst them. I half prayed it was water, because at least then I could keep myself semi-sane. Full sanity wasn't going to be an option in the position that we were in.

After what seemed like an eternity, a wavering light in the distance grew until it was a bluish blob, and behind it was the familiar form of Jodi with lantern in hand. Like Father Christmas, she carried a sack full of things for us.

"Becca, hon, are you okay?" Jodi asked, as the pallid and frail form of Rebecca looked up from her perch on my lap.

"No, Jodi, I'm not. I've not seen the sun in weeks, I've barely eaten or drunk anything, and until the other day, I've been in here by myself. I'm so not okay."

Rebecca laid her head back on my shoulder and sighed. Jodi's eyes caught mine in the ghostly blue glow of the lantern and between the two of us, we shared a look. Both of us knew that Becca wasn't lying, or even trying to make the situation better for once. From what I could tell, she'd given up all hope of actually getting out of here alive.

"Becca, hon..." I whispered in her ear.

She barely murmured a reply to me but as she looked down, I could see sable eyes meeting mine. She looked more worn, exhausted, and thinner than I'd seen her in the entire time we'd been here. Even when she'd been unable to keep food down from the dizziness caused by the multiple head injuries that she'd sustained within a short period, she'd not looked as wan and sickly as she did now.

"You've got to keep up hope. I have no doubts Jodi will be able to figure out a way we can leave permanently."

Rebecca looked away from me then, and emitted a sound that could only remotely be called a laugh. It completely lacked in any humor. I sighed deeply. The worst had happened, and Sarah had apparently gotten her wish; she'd finally broken down the stubborn confidence Rebecca had that she's get out of here alive, and that she was worth something.

"I'm going to go check on a few things," said Jodi. "Becca, you need to listen to what Jon says while I'm gone. Listen to him, you hear me?"

Jodi reached out, grabbed Rebecca's chin in her hands, and stared right into the eyes until Rebecca nodded. Then with a look at me that told me I'd better keep Becca focused, Jodi took her lantern and headed back down where she'd come. The solid sound of the door to our prison clunking shut behind her.

The sigh that escaped Becca echoed off the walls, and I held her.

"Becca, it's going to happen," I said, and she looked up at me, the single lantern casting a ghostly glow on her face. "I have faith in Jodi, and I need you to as well. Sarah isn't going to get her way, not with me, not with you, not in any way, shape, or form."

"I only wish I could believe that, Jon, but I just can't. Too many things have gone wrong since, well, since you showed up, for me to keep believing."

She sighed and looked away. Sighing myself, I reached out and turned off the light. I figured it would be best that we both conserve what energy we would need to get out of this hole, should the opportunity arise.

"Try to rest, Becca. You need the rest. Tomorrow may be one of those days when you need your strength."

I held her close to me as always and tried not to feel I'd failed her, or I'd run out of something meaningful and intelligent to say to her that would brighten her world. She was my everything; why couldn't I find it within me to be her rock in this storm? I felt something wet on my face, and reaching up, I found that it was my own tears. I wept without even recognizing I was crying. Wiping away the tears, I rested my head on hers and prayed that sleep would take me from this horror.

"Jonathan Walsh ..."

I groaned and turned in my sleep, trying to ignore the voice that called my name, unsure if it was within the dream or in the outside world.

"Jon, I love you. Please don't leave me."

I shrugged and tried to turn from whatever was talking to me. I wanted to sleep damn it, and things kept me from it.

"Have I done something wrong? I'm sorry. Really. I am. I'm ... I'm just ..."

A sob echoed.

I opened my eyes slowly and could barely make out that Becca had, sometime during when I'd been asleep, managed to work her way across the cell from me, and was curled up into a small ball against the wall. It was her voice that had cut through into my sleep and reached me. I turned on the lantern—on low as not to disturb her—and crawled over to her. Trying not to wake her, I brushed her hair back and ran my hand down her face. Even asleep she wasn't at peace and I couldn't say I was surprised. This place had become my own personal hell, but it had been hers for much longer.

Gently kissing her, I stood as best as I could in the small area where we were confined, and paced about. It didn't help my mood, but the small bit of exercise I gained from it helped my mind flow again. No doubt about it, being stuck in this little hovel did nothing for either of us. I began to formulate a plan when sneezing and the annoying itch that felt like a parade of ants crawled across my eyes and down my throat threatened to overwhelm me.

"Holy sweet Jesus," I croaked, running a hand across my eyes, trying to clear the tears that covered my vision.

"Jon? Wh ...what's up?"

Becca's voice seemed to come from some distance away. All I could concentrate on was the constant itch and the feeling that my throat almost closed up on me.

"Allergies," I wheezed, reaching out to grasp the wall lest I fall down from lack of oxygen.

Whatever might have been going on, Rebecca hopped to feet and held me up as best as she could. I tried to think of what could possibly be in here that could set off an allergy attack this severe. Unfortunately, the feeling that my head would burst from the sheer amount of sinus fluid that wanted to escape through my eyes and how the air seemed have been turned into liquid sand, prevented me from remembering the list of things I was allergic to. Fortunately for me, I suppose, I suddenly became able to answer the question when a small meow issued from around my feet.

"KISMET!" Becca crowed and picked up the bundle of gray and

white fluff that caused my head to simultaneously implode and explode. "How did you get in here?"

I sneezed repeatedly and violently, and sagged back down on the floor, trying to contain the veritable flood that streamed out my nose and eyes. Her questioning was greeted by a quiet series of chirps and gurgles from the flea-bitten mop she so lovingly called Kismet. Becca got down on the floor where I was, I had to put my hand up to stop her.

"Don't bring that evil thing any closer. I'm already nearly dying from the fact I can't breathe. Any closer and my skin might just decide to break out in hives, and we just don't need that right now."

With each word, I gasped for air. My ears itched, my throat felt like someone had taken sandpaper to it, my lungs gurgled like a fish tank with each breath, and my eyes were undoubtedly red and itched like the desert sands had been deposited on their surface.

With a look at me, she cuddled the cat one more time and put him down on the floor.

"You realize what this means, don't you?" She said, the first gleam of hope that I'd seen in a long time poured from her eyes.

I shook my head. Right now, thinking wasn't high on the priority list. Keeping that cat away from me, getting some antihistamines and hopefully living to see another day rated higher than imagining what that fucking cat being here meant—the cat who seemed to want to become a permanent part of my clothes. I swore the little bugger knew I was allergic and just had to try and become one with me to get some form of perverse pleasure out of it. Fucking cats.

"If Kismet got in here, that means that, somehow, we should be able to get out of here."

I looked up at her, sniffling and sneezing and desperately trying to hold back the urge to scratch both my ears and eyes out of my body.

"Love, I hate to break it to you, but I'm probably a hundred times bigger than that ... thing." I said, trying to keep the wheezing out my voice and suck in what air that I could manage.

She laughed, and gathered Kismet to her again. The diabolical feline responded with more chirps, purring and almost inaudible meows. Part of my brain wondered if I was feeling jealous of the cat, upon which Rebecca showered with love and adoration. The other part of me would've given anything at that moment to be the cat.

"Silly Jonathan. It means that there is another way out of here. If Kismet had gotten in the same way as Jodi had, one of us should've noticed the door opening. It means that this place isn't half as secure as Sarah thinks it is."

She put the cat back down, and thankfully shooed him away from me every time he came over to try and be friendly. With no one paying much attention to him, Kismet turned and walked away, and Rebecca, the most animated I'd seen her in the time we'd been imprisoned, got down on her hands and knees to follow him.

"I've got it! Is there a flashlight in the things that Jodi brought?" Becca called, her voice echoing strangely.

I moved silently, still sneezing and snuffling over to the small bag of things that Jodi had brought. I rifled through the things: some food, mostly in the form of snack bars, and bottled water; a change of clothes for both of us; and near the bottom, a flashlight. I took it and handed it over to Rebecca, who had her hand outstretched behind her body. She took it, switched it on and went back to what she was doing. A few minutes later she emerged from her activity, covered more, if that was possible, in dirt and other grime.

"There is definitely something there, I just can't see it too well." she pushed some hair that had fallen into her face away, leaving a trail of grime behind.

Despite my wheezing, sneezing and all, I laughed, and was greeted by the most confused look I'd seen in years. When asked what I was laughing at, I was struck by a coughing fit that took away my ability to explain.

Once the spasms had passed, the fact that I'd been laughing like a fool at the streak of dirt on her face was forgotten, in the midst of planning and scheming. Rebecca had come back to life, perhaps not completely, but she was more animated than she'd been since I'd holed in with her these past maybe two days.

She sat back and discussed with me about ways to get out of this place. What she'd found was a small hole, about the size she could fit through. There was no way that I could get out that way, but to her and to myself, it offered at least a glimmer of hope. I listened as best I could, between the sneezing and snuffling; coughing and scratching at my eyes. I probably looked a right mess on top of being covered in grime and filth from having stayed in this place for more than a few minutes. I half-heartedly wondered if the compound still contained asbestos, but dismissed the thought. I'd been a regular smoker, like a little bit of asbestos was going to change the end point of my health.

"God, I could so go for a smoke and a drink right now," I said, half joking.

I could almost feel Rebecca's eyes boring into me.

"What?!" I cried. "Old bad habits die hard. Not that I'm going to do it, but I'm just feeling the urge."

"That's good. The last time that you gave into that urge, it didn't end well for many parties—you included."

I could hear a bit of laugh in that statement and I could feel the smile creeping across my own face. I'd been told that it had been quite the stunning display of just how disgustingly someone could projectile vomit all over one person. I felt relieved I barely had recollection of it and had passed out afterwards. I knew after that experience I'd not be drinking to that extent again in the foreseeable future. The only good things that had come of it were that Rebecca and I had become closer, we'd finally become a couple, and my life had taken a change for the better—despite our clearly being in hell and desperately looking for any escape.

I felt something on my hand, and pulling it away quickly, it followed me. When it grasped my hand again and was neither furry nor slimy, but soft and warm, I realized it was Rebecca reaching for me. I grasped her hand tight in mine, and we descended into a comfortable silence.

I wondered what my life would have been like had I not stopped here in this town, and inadvertently stumbled into this place. I'd probably have made it home to Oakland, called up Chris and politely declined reuniting Torrent until I could think it through, gotten myself drunk in the garden, and just generally have spent my life wasting my time being bitter, angry and unhappy, far from friends, family, and anyone who cared about me.

What did I plan on doing after we got out of here? Besides treating the woman beside me like the special gem of a person she was and ensuring that she got the best of everything, which was less than what she deserved, I actually would take Chris up on his offer to get my life in order. If Rebecca stayed with me, I'd introduce her to the people who actually did matter to me—Ryan and Heather; Kristen, Erik and Kathryn—and show her my world. If she let me, I wanted to meet the people who mattered to her, who were close to her heart. Anything she wanted, I'd gladly do. If she asked for the moon, I knew I'd try to find a way to make it happen.

Time seemed to become fluid, there was no day, no night. The only thing that punctuated the day was when one of us fell asleep, someone came to take us out for short, closely-watched bathroom breaks and then threw us back in, and when Jodi visited, which was a rare occurrence.

From what I could figure two more days had gone by, and things still hadn't changed. Sarah hadn't returned, and we were left alone. I began to think that we were possibly forgotten in this place, but when Jodi did visit once more, she brought with her news that things were not well, and that someone, though she refused to say who, had challenged Sarah's leadership of the compound.

"This might just be the opportunity you and Becca need to get free, Jon," Jodi said. "Everything is up in the air, the infighting right now is horrible, and if something doesn't happen soon, this place will implode on itself. Then it'll be anyone's guess as to who will leave here alive."

No matter how much I pried, she refused to reveal the name of the person who had openly challenged Sarah's authority. She eventually bid us a somewhat tearful farewell and took off at high speed back down the small tunnel from our cell.

Once I was sure she was gone, I myself tried that same passage and found myself at a door, which, from what I could surmise, might have been well-hidden in the wall, as there were no people standing guard in the tunnel. Checking for any weaknesses or chinks of light coming through, with a sigh, I had to admit I came up empty-handed. Turning around, I returned to the small, revolting room Rebecca and I shared. She had the lantern on, and the blue color of the light cast her black and white features into an even more stark contrast. As I walked towards her, she looked up at me, and I could see many emotions flitting across her face, finally settling on acceptance.

"No way that we can get out, hon," I sat back down beside her. "We're going to have to rely on Jodi's promise that things will happen when it's the right time."

Rebecca leaned over and rested her head on my shoulder.

"I just hope that comes before we both lose our minds."

I sighed deeply and took her hand, before turning off the lamp and then resting my head on hers.

"Me, too, love. Me, too."

I felt her sigh and wriggle closer to me, and slowly I drifted towards what I knew would be a restless and dreamless sleep.

CHAPTER 25

I woke with a start. A light shone in my face, and no matter how much I tried to swat it away, it remained. Something shook me as well, and again, no matter how much I told it to go away, that I didn't have to be anywhere today and that I wanted to sleep, it kept rattling me until I finally woke up and leveled a glare at the source of the disturbance.

"Jesus, Mary, and Joseph. You don't need to give me a look like that," said Jodi, turning the lamp away from my face. "You were out pretty soundly, Jon. I pity anyone who tries to wake you up from a deep sleep."

I rubbed my eyes and muttered, "Be thankful it's only a look. I can be a right asshole before I get my morning coffee."

"C'mon, then."

I stood and followed her. It was nighttime and without seeing the moon or the stars, I couldn't say for sure what time it was. Rebecca lay on the floor coated in grime and barely able to stand up on her own. I got down on her level and tried to lift her to her feet, with Jodi's help. Rebecca's form appeared practically emaciated; having not eaten for almost an additional a week.

"I can't keep you out here for long," said Jodi. "Sarah's on the warpath again, and if you think you're out of sight, out of mind, you're more delusional than she is."

It was the first time I'd really heard Jodi speak out against her sister-in-law, whether by choice or not, and it brought me to a complete standstill.

"You act like that's a surprise," she said. "You two are very much on her mind. You're just being kept for the right time, the right moment, and then the axe will fall."

The stark turn in Jodi's mood amazed me. She had been the person who I could count on to be happy, sunny, and always the optimist in pretty much any situation. The dark, gloomy Jodi who stood before us was someone who I wasn't sure I knew. I confronted her about the change in mood and she shrugged.

"After a while, only the fools have hope. I've pretty much given up on everything except getting you two out of here. Kyle's cold and distant, and you know as well as I do he's practically got a harem of young things around the place who are willing to placate him sexually, so at least he doesn't generally come looking for me unless he's drunk and in a bad mood."

She sighed deeply and turned, starting down a familiar hallway. She was taking us back to the original suite where I stayed when I arrived here.

"Sarah wouldn't think I'd take you back there. No one would be that stupid in her opinion, so she'll likely not think to look there for a day or two, and it's safer for everyone. She knows I'm one of the dissidents around here, and despite the help Sarah gave me when I first came here, I can't take her anymore. I just can't. She's obsessed with being the next messiah, and she's so not. I can't stop her, but I can definitely slow her down."

Jodi closed the door then, and I found myself alone with Rebecca again. Under normal circumstances, I'd probably have tried to romance her, but with the current situation, those thoughts were the furthest from my mind.

Becca leaned against me, almost as limp as a rag doll, her long dark hair matted and pale skin coated in enough dirt and grime that it gave her a sick, gray color, more than not eating had done. The first order of business: get the two of us cleaned up.

I flipped on the light with my free hand and saw that while our belongings hadn't been brought here (no doubt that bringing those would have required some super-human feat I doubted anyone was capable of), Jodi had managed to scavenge away the basics—some food, clothing, and toiletries we needed. With a sigh and a gentle kiss on her cheek, I guided Rebecca into the bathroom. She didn't resist; she didn't seem to have the energy to fight.

Talking gently to her, I peeled her out of the soiled rags, and sitting her down on the toilet, I stripped and turned on the shower. I had no doubt that it would take more than a few washings to get the layers of dirt off both of us.

As I was adjusting the temperature of the running water, I felt something on my leg, and I saw Rebecca had grabbed a hold of it while staring vacantly into empty space. With a small smile, I turned back to what I was doing, and prayed silently that everything she'd been through—the mental, physical and emotional torture—hadn't caused her to retreat into a catatonic state. I hoped that her bahaviour was simply attributed to malnourishment, fatigue, leaving her without the stamina to verbally respond to anything right now.

Pulling the knob to turn on the shower, I gently removed Rebecca's grip from my leg, and guided her into the tub with me. This was as far removed as could be from the shower we'd shared before. We were not two lovers whispering sweet nothings to each other after lovemaking. While still lovers, this time we were people who shared the same nightmare, with one desperately trying to take care of the other as best as he could.

I held her to me, let the water run over us, and closed my eyes. Listening only to the patter of the water as it cascaded down and feeling her body against mine, I tried to center myself as Mike had taught me years ago, when I'd kicked several different habits pretty much cold turkey. I focused on slowing my own heartbeat and breathing into a mirror of hers.

When I'd managed to get myself calmed down enough to be rational, I noticed that she'd wrapped her arms around me, and while still staring off, she at least acknowledged my presence. Trying to gently get as much dirt off of her that I could without holding her too far apart, I found myself simply letting the water do most of the work.

When it came time to wash her hair, I looked down at her. She had closed her eyes and was grinning slightly. She'd fallen asleep, head on my shoulder.

"Becca, hon ..." I shook her gently. Beautiful dark brown eyes slowly fluttered open.

"Hey," she muttered quietly. "I was just dreaming I was under a waterfall with you. It was nice."

She smiled up at me, and it was infectious.

"You okay to stand on your own hon?" I asked.

Rebecca nodded sleepily and I let her go. She stood on her own, shoulders slumped, the image of exhaustion. I was beginning to see that she'd been essentially asleep on her feet. Changing places with her under the shower head, I grabbed the shampoo that was in the shower and pouring some directly onto her head, which got me a look which made me smile more and laugh, despite the circumstances that we were under. Once I'd washed and rinsed her hair to the point that the water ran clear, and scrubbed her from head to toe, which had been observed with a grin, I kissed her gently and traded spots and washed myself. She made a move to help me as I'd done to her, but I stopped her with a hand and a look.

Once we were both clean, I turned off the shower. I grabbed the towels that had been neatly piled on the counter and trying to be as gentle as possible, I dried Rebecca off, then myself. After tossing the towels aside, I carefully picked her up and took her over to the bed.

Tenderly placing her down on the sheets and then crawling onto the bed beside her, I stared at the defenseless and unclothed form of the woman I loved. Under any other circumstances, I would have made love her then and there, slowly, to help her forgot the outside world. Right now, however, wasn't the right time. I lifted her legs and pulled the sheets up over us. Rolling onto my side, facing the door, I felt her turn over and put her arms around me.

"I love you," she whispered quietly, and I laid my arm on hers.

"I love you too, Becca-bear."

She snuggled in closer to me. I wished the night wouldn't end and the daylight wouldn't break the serenity of the simple moments in between this tempest.

～

*T*he dawn came quietly, and Rebecca woke me when the sun climbed steadily higher into the sky. She seemed more energetic, and it set a feeling in the air like a thousand bees buzzing at once, an anticipation that put everything on edge. It was like being a child again, waiting for Father Christmas on Christmas Eve. Only, in this case, I had no doubts there wouldn't be a jolly gift giving fat man in a red suit. No, it would be a psychotic blonde female version of David Koresh wielding that proverbial sword. It had been an inadvertent kick in the ass that the son of a cultural anthropologist would end up in a situation where his father's knowledge might actually have come in handy.

While we dressed and kept an eye on things through the blinds and the still sealed door that lead to the courtyard, there was not much for us to do other than sit there and wait for the hands of time to click down to the end of this chapter. We'd wait for the fire—that for some unknown reason had been kept at bay throughout my entire stay, for almost to two months from what I could figure—to consume us in its rage.

We watched the comings and goings of the people in the courtyard, like a couple of voyeurs. It was clear that people had splintered into two groups, of roughly equal size. It wasn't clear as to whom lead the rebellious group, but I cheered them on silently. Any resistance to the seemingly wild whims of Sarah was a boon to them, in my books. They left no illusions that there was something separating them.

The groups in the courtyard were smaller, and when I snuck out that night, I found the groups by the dining area clearly splintered into two halves. Jodi had made herself scarce, and a few days passed before we saw her again. When she showed up, she was decidedly on edge, very twitchy, and always checking over her shoulder. I had my suspicions that she led the movement against Sarah, but shook my head and quickly dismissed that possibility. It was too out there to be truly possible. I knew Jodi had not been a huge fan of that bitch, that she'd rather have a rattlesnake as her sister-in-law, because at least then you knew how it could react when it wanted to kill you. With Sarah, the threat was always there, but I'd yet to have seen it come to fruition — and I hoped I never would while I was here.

"So, Jodi?" I asked on her second visit to us in the room where I'd started out here, "When are we going to have to head back to the holes?"

Her eyes clouded over with disappointment. "Tomorrow. No later. She's already suspicious of what I'm doing around here, and with you two free, there is just too much for me to handle right now. I swear, this place is a powder keg, and it's going to blow. When it does, I want you out of here and I want her safe." She gestured to Becca, who watched from her perch on the desk.

Rebecca had taken to sitting high off the ground lately—not that I could blame her—there had been vermin in that hell hole where we'd been held captive, and having been forced to sleep on the dirt covered floor where they would take random bites at her legs. The small bites still showed as red marks on her skin.

I nodded. Jodi's main concern was the happiness and well-being of a long-time friend who had been with her through the good times, the bad times, and the downright shitty times. Jodi had campaigned hard in her own little ways to get the two of us together, and now that it seemed like the end was near and Sarah might actually win, Jodi's spirits were depressed.

With a hug to both of us, she headed back out. Rebecca, usually moody and brooding in circumstances like this, acted relatively sunny. She felt bored, as did I, and the activities that came to mind I wasn't up to doing.

So, we sat, and waited for the time to pass. Becca curled up next to me and slept like a kitten most of the day while I tried to keep awake and thought of what might happen to us, what needed to be done, and what lay ahead. Occasionally she awoke, and after a small smile, she would usually curl back up and go back to sleep. I had no doubt that she'd been sleep deprived in that hole, and we were headed back there again.

My mind wandered and eventually I fell asleep myself. When I awoke with a start, the room had gone dark, and the sun slid below the horizon. Rebecca was not by my side, and a sense of panic set in when, with a few quick glances around the room, I couldn't find her.

Getting up and searching about the room, I couldn't see any signs of a struggle, and despite the fact that I knew I slept soundly, I tried to reassure myself that if she'd been taken from me, I'd have woken up. I needed to stop panicking, to stop my heart from hammering in my ears. When I finally managed to get my racing pulse to normal levels, I noticed the door to the courtyard, which had been sealed with something since shortly after I'd shown up here, was open again, and a cool, gentle night breeze blew in and ruffled the blinds that separated the courtyard from the room. Listening carefully, I heard the quiet, almost inaudible tinkling of the piano.

Für Elise. Becca... I held back from running out into the courtyard and possibly drawing more attention to myself than I'd ever intended to, and peeked out from behind the blinds.

Sure enough, she sat there, at the piano. The moonlight illuminated her in its meager light, like a scene from a fantasy or dream. In the still night with no one around to interrupt, it was almost too perfect.

I stepped out into the courtyard and made my way over to her.

She was in almost a trance. Rebecca had been without music for so long, I felt sure she suffered withdrawal symptoms. Hearing her play gave me goose bumps. This was more than talent; she played with such feeling, I could believe that music was a part of her being, her very soul.

She finished the piece and sat there, staring out into nothingness, her hands resting lightly on the keys. I came up to the dais quietly, trying not to startle her and break the moment. She seemed to sense my presence there, and turned to face me, a dreamy expression giving an almost otherworldly quality to her features.

"Took you long enough, sleepy head," she said with a soft laugh as she turned back to close the lid on the keyboard.

"You have no idea how much you panicked me by not being there," I said, taking her hand, which she'd offered me. "Moreover, I want to know how the hell you managed to get that door open."

She shrugged, looking up at the sky. "I know a few tricks, thanks to Jodi, that is."

We went back into the compound, rather than taking the door into the room where we'd been staying. We took the long route because the place was well and truly silent for once. We even wandered through the gardens, which had once been lush and vibrant but were now painted with shades of ocher and yellow, and were withered, shriveled, and dried up. It was like this would be our last day here, our last day that we'd see the outside, the stars, the clouds, the sun and the moon.

It could very well be our last day alive if Sarah had her way, and I had no doubt that the clock was quickly clicking down on that. Or, it might be our last day here, if the fates lined up for us in that manner.

We walked through the garden, and Becca stopped beneath the trellis that separated the vegetable garden from the flower garden.

"You know what?" she asked, turning to take my other hand in hers. I shook my head no, afraid of ruining the moment by speaking. "No matter what happens after tonight, I want you to know that I love you and that the time I've spent with you has given me some of the most incredible days in my life."

She leaned in to kiss me and I couldn't help but think this also was still too perfect. Something had to go wrong, and disastrously so.

How right I was.

If I'd not been so absorbed in how I had a beautiful woman who I loved cuddling with me in the middle of a garden on an overly flawless night, I might have heard the footsteps coming up behind us. The last thing I remember happening was the cloths pulled over our faces and the grayish-blackness seeping in, once again.

CHAPTER 26

*U*gh.

I wasn't sure if I'd just thought that or I'd actually said it. Every part of my body hurt, and I felt like I was trying to think through molasses. Trying to lift the lead weight known as my head was nearly impossible. When I cracked open my eyes, I was blinded almost instantly by several million candlepower units of light, right in my face. If I'd not known that I'd been sober up until what could only be called "the kidnapping" last night, I would've sworn I'd just taken on Chris in a head to head drinking challenge and lost pitifully. Not that I would lose to Chris, but, even there, I felt worse now than I'd ever had from a night of drinking.

As my senses slowly came around, I realized I sat on a chair, was tied to said chair, and the light actually burned that damned bright. I heard someone in the room but moving my head or opening my eyes more than a slit was impossible. Clenching my eyes shut, I prayed fervently the person in the room with me wasn't Sarah, but deep down I knew that the likelihood of that being true was slim to none. That woman didn't understand "No, bugger off, I can't stand you," as an answer. Whomever it was stayed silent, and eventually dimmed the lights enough so I could open my eyes.

Blinking furiously against the still-too-bright-for-my-vision light, I looked up. It was almost impossible in my current state to figure out who it could be; they appeared only as a silhouette, dark against the blinding background.

"So, it's come to this. I finally have you where I want you, and nothing, nothing is going to stop me now," a voice purred from the side of the room.

I tried to laugh, but it sounded more like a dry rasping noise rather than a chortle.

"You find that funny, Jonathan?"

I'd never heard my name spoken with such hatred, even by my ex-wife, who I felt sure would enjoy seeing me in this situation. Tricia would have give anything to ensure I would suffer a punishment fit enough for the slights I'd done to her over the years.

I turned my eyes upwards, and sure enough, there was Sarah, hovering mere inches away from me. I swallowed, my throat as dry as the desert outside of this hell, and tried to speak.

"You ... you're insane," I croaked, lips parched and cracking.

She laughed then, a sound that made me shiver with the sheer rabidity of it.

"You'd think that, wouldn't you? Stuck here in the middle of nowhere. But I'm not. Oh, far from it. I've got a purpose, a plan, and you and your little whore aren't going to keep me from it any longer—oh no."

She wandered off chuckling under her breath.

"What part do I play in this little plan of yours, Sarah? Huh? What part of your glorious plan do I take? Fool? Troubadour? What?"

I could hear her stop and turn, and within moments she was a hairsbreadth from my face.

"*You*, are out of the way. That's what part you're going to play. You and that little bitch, are out of my way, and when the time is right, you'll both find out what else I've been dreaming up for you two. Ah yes, the lovers ... entwined beneath the moonlight. Such an idyllic picture. Too bad that true love only exists in children's stories and cheap romances."

She pulled away from me and I heard her footsteps retreat into the distance, and then a door closed with a metallic thud.

I was alone again. No respite from the bright lights, and no way to move. I knew this was a last-ditch attempt to break me, to make me bend to her will. I'd managed to pull through them so far, with a combination of sheer bloody luck and the help of one insanely crafty woman named Jodi, but this time it appeared my luck had finally run out.

My mind wandered to what they had done to Rebecca and where they had taken her. Again. I quickly turned away from that before my overly fertile imagination dredged up scenarios I didn't want to contemplate, no matter how true they might be. I hung my head again and prayed the prayer of those who are condemned on death row with all appeals denied, even though I was beginning to feel, once more, there was no one out there listening to the prayers of the damned.

I couldn't sleep, I couldn't do anything. I was stuck in a seated position, and I knew soon my muscles would begin to twitch with the stress of both the situation and the single position that I was bound in.

Seconds felt like minutes, minutes like hours, and hours like eternities. Time, while often standing still out in the old hotel, dragged like a prisoner's chains in this minuscule cell. I began to consider chewing off my arms, and then collapsed into helpless laughter at the sheer insanity of that thought. I wanted to scream, yell, to get someone—anyone's—attention, but I knew it was useless. Sarah had probably booby trapped this place more than I, Becca, or Jodi could've ever imagined.

I settled for leaning back in the chair, turning my head from the brightness of the light, and stared blankly into a darkened corner. My mind, deprived of any entertainment, drifted randomly, dredging up images of my childhood, my family, and Becca. Those memories I clung to, and let them dance in front of my eyes like an old movie.

Becca.

The woman I'd fallen hopelessly for, almost the minute I'd walked in that door. The woman that it took a madwoman's insane religious fantasy to bring me to meet. Rebecca was the only reason that I held any hope of getting out of here.

I was becoming delusional, I knew it, and desperately tried to fight it. If I was going to get out of here alive, I needed to be mentally in one piece. Of course, it would likely be Sarah's plan for me to be mentally sliced and diced as possible; that way, she most likely would be able to use me according to her will.

Except ... she didn't know me, and understanding me would've told her that trying to break me was futile. She'd never come up against the Walsh stubborn streak, which both Chris and I shared. It was one of the few things that I had in common with the man I most often called a scum-sucking asshole. If he weren't family, I'd have nothing to do with him, but he was, and somewhat co-worker, too, so that meant circumstances forced me to spend time with him.

The sound of the door opening again pulled me from my reverie. Part of me hoped Jodi would come to rescue me from the insanity. The other, more rational part of myself guessed it was either Sarah or one of the nameless lackeys she employed throughout the place to do her dirty work. Looking up, I discovered it was the latter—the snake with two of her trademark goons in tow. She stood back, cowering like a small dog, acting terrified that I might do something to her. I wondered what malarkey Sarah had been spreading about me in the congregation of people that lived in the compound.

The two goons undid my binds, and all but threw me into a corner. My legs felt weak, and there was no way I could stand on my own, let alone fight. A young girl placed the meal in front of me and backed away timidly, gray-blue eyes filled with horror. I looked up at her; she couldn't have been more than thirteen if she were a day. I shuddered, thinking Kyle would probably be the type to have wet dreams about girls this young. Now, some people might have problems Rebecca being twenty-one-years younger than me; however, Rebecca was an adult when I met her, fully capable of making her own decisions, and she had lived out in the real world.

The girl skittered away and the goons closed the door. I sat there in the corner, trying to stretch my aching limbs. I glanced at the food and my stomach rolled. I doubted Sarah had a major pharmaceutical cache at her disposal, even though I'd been drugged with something similar to ether or chloroform, and I knew some of the people worked in pharmacies. So, I convinced myself nothing had been put in that food. Still, I didn't feel like eating it. I just wanted to sleep until the Second Coming, but those damned lights would make it impossible. Even though my family and friends pegged me as someone who could fall asleep pretty much anywhere, I needed some form of darkness to fall into the embrace of Morpheus, and that wasn't likely to be happen before hell froze over.

Curling into the small ball that my body need me to be in, I leaned against the nearest wall. The smell of the food made my stomach pitch and roll, and I closed my eyes, fighting back the seemingly endless waves of nausea that threatened to overcome me. I wanted out of here, but escape would be improbable at this rate.

I wondered what Sarah had up her sleeve for me now. It was obvious I'd gone from being the piece of ass she'd coveted since I'd shown up here, to something more sinister, but exactly what she had in mind evaded me.

Time seemed to stand still while I lay alone in the room. The only thing that demarcated when time had passed was the return of one of the goon-squad, to remove the uneaten food with a sneer and a laugh, and then to leave the room again, the solid metal door slamming shut with a definite thunk.

I was alone.

Alone in ways I'd not been for as long as I could remember. While I'd been by myself in Oakland, I always had the comfort of reaching out through the telephone, letter, or electronic communication—be it email or instant messenger—to Ryan, Kristen, or Mike. Here, there was no way to make contact with anyone who might have cared. The two people in the compound who might have given a fuck as to what happened to me were somewhere I didn't even know, and it left me feeling very small, cold, and solitary. The only spark I held close was a belief that Rebecca was alive and unhurt, even though I had my doubts. I desperately wanted to be back with her. Then I wanted the hell out of here. That desire was the fire that kept me alive.

I nodded between sleep and wakefulness as my body fought to stay awake and plan ways to break free of the cell. I was in one of those in-between states when I heard the door open.

My eyes couldn't focus, but I could've sworn I saw Jodi enter the room with a limping and obviously injured Rebecca in tow. I laughed and brushed it off as my own wishful thinking, closed my eyes, and leaned back against the wall.

I felt something shake me and ignored it. Maybe if I played dead, it would go away and leave me alone and let me die in whatever little peace I could manage to scrounge up in this hole. The shaking continued, and it got to the point that I thought that my teeth were going to be rattled out my head. Still, keeping my eyes closed, I played possum as best I could, until the person eventually left me alone and exited the room.

I was alone yet again. I closed my eyes and leaned my head against the wall. My mind fought to stay awake while the exhaustion of my body felt like lead weights that dragged me down into the bottom of the pit of sleep. I certainly wasn't a young man anymore, and even with the turnaround in my physical shape, I still fought a losing battle over remaining alert. Finally, giving over to exhaustion, I let myself slide headlong into a dark, comforting numbness.

When I awoke, it was with that jolted sensation you get when someone or something wakes you suddenly. The blurriness of sleep still hung on me like morning fog in London, and as much as I tried to shake it off, it stayed on me and made each movement, no matter how slight a gesture, as if I'd attempted it underwater while the cares of the world weighed me down. I wasn't

Atlas and I knew I would break. I wondered if this was again part of the after effects of whatever I had been drugged with.

Turning my head slowly in the direction of what I assumed had woke me up, I saw a blurry form. I couldn't make out what it was. It was darker in the room now, as dark as it could get , as there were still lights on. Some poor soul had turned them down to a bearable level, for which I gave many silent thanks.

Through the mental fog I realized what had startled me from my slumber was the calling of my name. Not by just anyone, which normally I would've slept through without stirring once, but by a voice I had a deeper connection with. Blinking my eyes to try and focus on whoever it was, as they were now rather silent, I still couldn't figure out who they were.

"Hello? Who the hell are you? I can't see a thing here, really. If you're there, and you can answer me, well, that would be nice."

I cringed. My voice sounded so spineless and unlike me it was hard to believe that it had come out of my mouth. I moved slowly across the floor to the fuzzy blob I assumed was a person, and as I got nearer, could make out more clearly. The person was curled up much as I'd been when I'd been loosed from the chair, head resting on their knees, arms wrapped around them. Long, dark hair laid in tangles over their shoulders and their head lolled against the wall.

I hadn't been hallucinating. That had been Jodi. This had to be Rebecca. There was no one else that Jodi would bring to me.

I picked up a limp hand and checked for a pulse. Weak. Thready, but still there. She was still alive. I looked at her arms and saw a myriad of bruises, which colored her skin a dark blue and purple. Her wrists showed signs of rope burn, and I cursed quietly. Someone had taken quite the time to inflict these wounds, and I only hoped that Rebecca hadn't also been assaulted sexually; it would be the last straw that would keep me from dismantling this place piece by piece until I got to Sarah and loosed my wrath on her. Pushing the hair back away from her face, I saw that she had long red lines radiating into her hairline. So, Sarah had been a part of this. At least someone female, but I had no doubts that it was Sarah.

Running my hands over her face, I bit my lip to keep back the tears that threatened to flow—tears of anger, of sadness, of a million emotions that I didn't want to admit to. I'd been a fucking fool in my life. Too much so. I wasn't going to let Becca slip away from me if I could do anything about it. I'd not give up on this one chance at love that I'd been given again after so many years of following physical desires in an attempt to fill that void within me that I'd not known had existed until I'd met this woman. So unlike every other woman I'd had in my life, I could've passed her on the streets a million times and not have noticed her.

"Oh, Becca. I'm so sorry I've dragged you into this. That you've been hurt because of me. I swear, we get out of here, if you'll put up with me, I'll make everything up to you. I promise, and I won't break that promise to you." I ran my hand over her hair and held her unresponsive hand in mine.

Beyond the feelings of hopelessness and betrayal, and the consistent sense of being in a place reality had abandoned long ago, strong feelings rose within me—determination, anger, frustration —fueled by how I'd been treated first as a stud horse, then as a criminal without trial. And now the woman I loved more than my own life lay injured and possibly dying, beside me. I didn't care who I took down anymore; we were leaving.

Afraid to move her, I set myself at her feet, and rested against the wall. I watched her breathe slowly, steadily. It was one of the few constants in this sideways hell.

She eventually woke, her dark eyes fluttering open. When she tried to focus on me, and recognition set in, a smile crossed her face. Then she winced—no doubt caused by the scratches on her face—and her eyes clouded with pain.

"Hey," she croaked, her throat dry and likely sore. "You're alive."

"I could say the same thing for you."

I reached out again, and she leaned her face against my hand.

"Just barely. What Sarah has planned for you requires you to be intact for it. Me, not so much." A sardonic laugh.

"When the hell did you get in here?"

She blinked at me; she had no clue as to how out of it I'd been.

"Jon, it was about three days ago. You watched Jodi bring me in. You don't remember?"

I told her what I could recall. The after-effects of whatever had been used to drug me were stronger than I'd thought. Becca's eyes went wide at the tale, and she sighed deeply.

"I've wondered what she's had in mind for a long time. I knew she wanted, hell, *wants* me dead. You I thought it was merely a case of her getting into your pants. If I didn't feel I'd been put through several title bouts, I'd make the joke that knowing what's in your pants, I can't blame her, but ... this is more than just her wildly rutting with every male in sight."

I shuddered. The worst had been realized—Sarah had finally made the small leap from simmering nut job who either thought she was the next messiah or could try to fuck her way into conceiving said messiah, to all out madwoman. So, the likelihood that we'd ever see out of this place officially went to nope.

"I'm not going out with a whimper," I muttered under my breath, and sat back against the wall.

Rebecca flitted between sleep and wakefulness, her head nodding and the smallest snores escaping her every now and then. There wasn't much I could do around here. The chair I'd been bound to had been removed, along with the ropes that had bound me; however, the marks were still on my skin. I truly been out of it more than I'd realized, which infuriated me. Waiting and not knowing what was happening combined to make me half mad. I sat and inspected myself for further marks. Unlike Rebecca, who was a walking bruise from almost head to toe, I was left pretty much unscathed, which added credence to her thoughts that I was the target in this place, of whatever Sarah had dreamed up.

Time continued to drag in the confines of that room. People came in at random times to feed us or haul us to and from the loo. Usually the day ended whenever the two of us fell asleep in each other's arms It wasn't the most comfortable position for me, but as she suffered ongoing nightmares and didn't want to be alone, in almost any sense of the word, I was willing to endure a minor bit of irritation to make her life easier.

Days had gone by without either of us eating, and it really showed on Rebecca. Normally a woman of voluptuous curves without being overweight, she had become stark angles and dark hollows. Knowing that we had to drink to stay alive, we did as sparingly as possible, and finally, it got to the point where both of us were on the verge of dehydration.

It occurred to me that our starvation was something that could work to Sarah's advantage, both to harm Rebecca and to make me more pliable. I managed to coax Rebecca into eating and drinking a bit the next time food was brought to us. We had to resist gorging ourselves, but the thought of being sick was more than enough for me to reign it in, and Becca admitted the food didn't seem that appetizing at all.

We ate and when the girl who usually came in to take our food entered to collect the plates, she seemed surprised that we had actually eaten the food. That raised the hairs on the back of my neck in alarm, but other than panic over it, there was not much I could do. The axe would fall one way or the other and we'd either make it out alive—which was my hope—or die by Sarah's ruthless hand.

I'd not seen the evil bitch in a few days, and that in itself worried me. She'd been gone since before Jodi had brought Becca into the room and left her here. But it didn't make sense. Sarah should've known ...

I stood, holding myself up by leaning against the wall, and took a few hesitant steps. Things were topsy-turvier than I was used to —even for this place. Someone else was keeping us here. Someone else was keeping us fed, someone else ...

I stopped my pacing. Becca looked up at me, curiously.

"What, Jon?" she asked, her voice barely audible.

"There is something just too fishy here ... just not right."

She snorted, which was within her rights; she knew just as well as I did that this place didn't run under the normal rules of the world. It was a microcosm unto itself.

"It's not just that," I said. "Think on it. If Sarah knew you were in here, she'd be all over it, trying to separate of us. She's not been 'round. Only one or two of her goons have shown up with the girl who brings the food, the same ones who drag us out of here for piss breaks. Becca, that's just not usual for what goes on here. Something is up, but I'm not sure exactly what the hell it is."

She looked away.

"You'll only drive yourself mad if you try to figure out this place, or anything having to do with Sarah," Rebecca said with a sigh. Sorrowful brown eyes met mine. "I've tried, Jon. I've tried to leave before. I'm still not sure what happened that night that you showed up. That door is always locked. How you got in, I don't know."

I made my way back over to her and flopped down on the floor. *Bowed, bent, but not broken.* I had to keeping reminding myself of that.

"Fate. Maybe this was required for the two of us to be together? Maybe I was supposed to go through hell on earth before finding my own bit of heaven, and an angel to go with it?"

She blushed and looked away again, coloring right to the tips of her ears. "I don't believe in fate. I'm not sure what I believe in anymore. I have a hard time believing that loving God would allow this to happen to any human being that he cared about."

She stared off into the corner, her mind on other things. I turned her head back to face me.

"Becca Nicole. I'd face hell, firing squads, my ex-wife, even the Queen naked if it meant finding you again. You're worth more to me than you'll ever know."

She tried to look away again, but I kept her facing me with a gentle hand on her chin.

"You're not running away this time," I continued. "I know you've done it before, but not this time, love. I'm not letting you run away. I've done it all my life, and it's gotten me into enough shit to last me forever."

She sighed and leaned her head against my shoulder. After a few moments, I felt her tears, and could hear her softly weeping. I pulled her close. She was the one, the only constant in my life right now. To see her hurt, physically and mentally, tore me to shreds. I wanted to comfort her, to soothe her wounds, and at the same time rain hellfire down on those who had brought this pain into her life, to make them hurt the same, if not more, than they'd done to her.

She clung to me like I was a life preserver in the middle of a raging, perfect storm.

I let her cry, simply holding her to me and running my hand through her hair.

Then, the sneezing resumed. Rebecca looked up at me, an expression of amazement crossed her face.

"There's nothing that you're possibly allergic to in here. What are you sneezing and wheezing over? Unless you're allergic to more than cats?"

"No, I'm not. Cats only," I replied, my voice thick and almost cartoonish sounding as the searing pain of nasal passages swelling and lungs closing took over me.

"There is only one cat around here, and I'm not sure ..."

A round gray head poked itself in the room through a small hole in the wall. With an almost silent meow, it crossed the room, wove itself between my ankles briefly before running over to Becca and covering her in both cat hair and protestations of love.

"Kismet!" she cooed and once again held the cat closely. It seemed the cat was as much a lifeline for her as I was. Of course, between the cat and myself, Becca and Kismet had been together longer.

Kismet, luckily didn't stay long, and after giving Rebecca a cocky look, he took off back down the hole where he'd come from. Shortly after he left, Sarah made her first visit to the room in ages. It went exactly as I'd expected.

She stalked in, took one look at Rebecca, and with flushed cheeks, Sarah stalked out, leaving the confused and worried goons in her wake. I heard her hiss something to one of them as the door shut with a heavy thunk, and knew it wasn't good.

We sat in silence once more.

Becca decided it was best that she try and walk and I helped her, as she was much weaker than I was; years of abusing my own body's limits as to what I should do and should not do had taught me to conserve energy. While I wasn't going to be running any marathons any time soon, I did have more than enough drive to keep her moving, and mentally, the strength to keep her with me.

I had no doubt that when (and not if, I kept reminding myself) we got out of here, her personality would be quite different from what I'd known. I hoped I'd have the chance to see her turn into the person she'd let me see in the rare moments where her guard was down. A person who had a creative streak a mile wide, who not only played piano like an angel, but who was the artist who had painted the watercolors in the lobby; a person with a sense of humor just as twisted as my own; a person who despite a load of shit that had been thrown on her plate, was a strong woman, deeply loving and fiercely loyal to those whom she let into her inner circle. As I watched her concentrate on walking, I couldn't help but feel deeply in love with her. Every moment I spent with her made my life better—even in the depths of hell.

After a while she tired, and we settled back down. There was no bed, nothing but four walls and a door, and a few small holes that Kismet thankfully did not come through again. We settled against the furthest wall from the door, and she cuddled into my side, head against my shoulder, a slight weight against me.

We slept on and off throughout the night. When the girl came in for the morning breakfast and bathroom break, we both felt exhausted, and stumbled around before falling back together, her in my arms, fitfully sleeping.

CHAPTER 27

a rather large explosion that blasted out of nowhere rocked the air. It was as if a bomb had gone off—the building itself trembled and the earth shook. Rebecca sat bolt upright, her eyes wild with fear, like a deer who had been caught in oncoming headlights.

"What. The. Hell," she said as she got up and looked around, moving tentatively.

Several smaller explosions followed, and I got to my feet cautiously, following her, to see if we could find out what had been their cause.

After a few minutes of quiet, we prepared to settle back in. Then the screaming began. I could only guess what had happened. Rebecca looked at me with an expression that combined both fear and curiosity. It was as if the world itself were ending, and the "world" we knew here, no matter how fucked up, had turned on its side yet again.

She made her way to the door, which had been locked tight for the duration of the time we'd been incarcerated. I'd tried it each day between visits.

Placing her hand against the door and trying the knob, Rebecca jumped back in surprise when she found that it moved. She turned to me with a look of apprehension.

"Oh my God ... Jon ... Jodi," she said in almost slow motion before running out the door.

I had no doubt Becca's ultimate destination was the kitchen areas. It would be the only source potent enough to cause the explosions. The abundant supply of natural gas that fed the fryers, the grills, and pretty much everything—from food to hot-water heating—was located in that area of the compound.

I followed Rebecca, my mind working over the possibilities as we ran down the endless maze of hallways and against the people who streamed away from whatever had happened. About half way there, it dawned on me: Jodi had always maintained she would get the two of us out of here, even if it were the last thing she did. I bit back the thought that this was part of her plan, as it meant that she sacrificed herself and the entirety of this place ... for us. I also pushed away the notion that she had been the one who had challenged Sarah's authority, the one who had started the rebellion within the ranks, the mysterious leader who was able to pull together a coherent group that challenged Sarah's in both loyalty and power.

Jodi never struck me as a leader. She, for all intents and purposes, seemed more of a follower. Knowing that she'd come here from a bad relationship, where in essence she'd been left at the altar by a man she'd fallen deeply in love with, and then how she complied with the marriage to Kyle, I never expected her to pierce the heart of hell from deep within it.

Of course, I also once thought Ryan couldn't be the person with the strongest will. He came over quiet, almost effeminate, a shy geeky person. Cross him however, and you'd see the red hair belonged to a raging, roaring lion, who didn't take kindly to his family, his pride to so speak, being hurt in any way or form. When Tricia and I had divorced, he had flown down to Oakland and stayed with me during the far too long division of assets, and had helped me out in infinite ways.

Rebecca seemed to know where she was going, and I trusted her judgment. As we tore through the halls, I noticed we'd passed the courtyard, the place where everything here seemed to be centered, and for once, it was empty, save for the people who used it to shorten their flight from whatever terror toward which we were now headed. It was like running against the current of a stream, fighting against the flow of bodies away from there. The place was in chaos and no one was around to quell it, perhaps no one really cared to.

As we rounded a corner that brought me into more familiar territory, I saw great plumes of gray smoke coming from around the bend. It billowed out of the compound, and I was totally unprepared for what I saw next as we entered the prep area.

The place was on fire, flames licking up the walls and cross the beams of the ceiling, dropping on occasion to the floor, and setting off more fires. In the center of the room, the center of hell, stood Jodi, burnt, battered, and bleeding. She resembled some strange goddess of the underworld. Her hair was mostly burnt off, and her face partially disfigured with horrific scratches. The hazel eyes were as sharp as ever, and when she recognized the two of us, a smile spread across her face as best as it could. Rebecca, unthinkingly, ran across the room towards her friend, her companion of many years, and stumbled as she got there, tripping over something on the floor.

Looking down at Jodi's feet, there lay the bleeding and severely battered body of Sarah. It was obvious to anyone with half a brain that Sarah was dead, and I felt confident Jodi had been the one to deal the fatal blow. Sarah's too-light-to-be-real blond hair was streaked with blood and her neck was bent at a pretty damned unnatural angle. I retched, trying to keep down the flood of bile that threatened to make its way up my throat. Rebecca, too stunned to do anything other than fumble blindly backwards into me, looked wildly from Sarah's corpse to Jodi and back before running to a corner and vomited what little she'd eaten in the past few days.

Jodi had one of the large fire extinguishers in her hands, and when Rebecca turned back from the corner, Jodi watched her with weary eyes—eyes that had seen too much in this life, eyes that had suffered, and were still suffering.

Rebecca's hands shook and tears fell down her face. She made her way over to Jodi, stepping over the prone body of Sarah as if it weren't there, yet I knew that Becca had seen it. The corpse had now become just another part of the place, something that was no longer a threat to Rebecca or her sanity and could be, under the circumstances, safely ignored. Jodi was more important to her, and to myself.

Without regard to her clothing, she grabbed Jodi in a hug and pulled her close. Jodi winced but returned the hug. Once Rebecca let her go, Jodi smiled weakly at the two of us.

"Your stuff is in the dining area, I'm pretty sure it's not on fire yet." Jodi rummaged around in her pockets and tossed a set of keys at me. "That's for the front door. If it's locked, try them or just bust it down."

She let go of the fire extinguisher which clanked to the floor with a heavy noise. "Go, get out of here before this place consumes you, too."

Flames were beginning to tear through the room and the groaning structure around us told me, even with my limited knowledge of construction, that this building would collapse and ignite whatever remaining gas and oil were left.

Rebecca grabbed onto Jodi's one hand that wasn't scaled with burn marks and tried to pull her along with us.

"Becca, no. I'm not going with you. There is no way I'd be able to keep up with you both. Plus, for what I've done today, I'd spend a good portion of my life in prison. You two, go on, get out of here."

She pried Rebecca's hands off her and made her way over to me.

"You made the right choice, Jon. No matter what anyone else might say. Take her and get out of here," Jodi said quietly to me, and I hugged her tight, knowing this would be the last time that I ever saw Judith Clarke alive.

"Jodi…" My voice caught in my throat, and tears fell. She reached up and took my face in a hand, then brought me down to her level.

"Jonathan Christopher, you two were meant to be. You might think your paths were never meant to cross, that you're from two worlds a million light years apart, but you're actually the other half of the wandering soul that the other has been looking for in the night. For me to have had a part in bringing you two together, in bringing two halves of the same heart to the realization that they love each other, well, in my mind, that's absolution from what acts I've committed today."

Jodi let go of me, and again, a soul-shuddering moan issued from the building around us.

"Now go, before it really is too late," she said.

She turned me towards the door, and with a hefty push, sent me on my way, followed by Rebecca.

The door clanked shut behind us, and Rebecca, out of her mind with grief and panic, flung herself against it, crying, and screaming for Jodi to let her back in.

Pulling Becca away, my own heart in my throat, I headed towards the dining area. Jodi had been right, this place was barely smoldering, the flames just starting to lick around the hallway that joined it to the prep area. Jodi had left a door open, as they were heavy fire doors, meant to keep in a blaze. She'd meant for this place to be taken and razed to the ground—that this bit of hell on Earth should be never seen again.

Just as Jodi had told us, our belongings were safely left at the other end. I grabbed both of our bags, as Rebecca was still preoccupied with trying to go back for Jodi. As the flames licked higher and the dining area burned, filling the air with thick, acrid smoke, I took a hold of Becca by the shoulders, and turning her to face me, I inhaled deeply and tried not to sound like I was lecturing her.

"Rebecca Nicole Taylor, we can't return for her. I know you love her like family, and so do I, but you have to listen to me. If we go back, it means putting our own safety in jeopardy. It might mean that we die in this inferno. We must leave, and right now. This compound is going up like a Roman candle, and we need to get moving if we're not going to burn with it. I care for Jodi too, but love, we've got to save ourselves."

She refused to meet my eyes for a few moments, and then slowly, her dark brown eyes overflowing with tears, nodded her understanding.

I handed her the backpack I knew was hers, which she shouldered, and taking her hand tightly in my own, we went back out down the hallways. I pulled her behind me, as I was the stronger of the two of us, more able to navigate through the press of people who were flipping out and milling about the hallways in fright. It was like the panics at concerts, riots in Los Angeles, things that would make you glad to live somewhere else and only be watching them on the evening news.

People crushed in around us, and some grabbed at Rebecca and me as we moved through. I turned to keep an eye on her and saw the petrified look on her face. Her usual pinkish yet pale skin was white with anxiety and her eyes wide with fear. I wasn't sure if there was anything I could say to her that would make things any better. I just squeezed her hand tightly and she squeezed back, which reminded me once again that we didn't need to talk to communicate with each other.

Thick billows of smoke began to choke the air as more and more of the place went up in flames. I gripped Rebecca tighter by the arm and we ran faster. Fuck everything I'd ever learned in my life about fire safety; all I knew was that I wanted out of there, and that I wanted it now.

Everyone in the compound ran around us confused and bewildered. Keeping my eye on Rebecca, I wasn't looking where I was going, and ran square into Kyle. I stumbled back a few steps and looked him in the eye. He stared unblinkingly at me for a moment and then moved out of my way. I stood for a moment, aghast. He had to have known what was happening, or had suspected it.

He no longer blocked our way. Kyle would stay and go down with the ship, for lack of a better term. He gave a look of, something—I wasn't sure what—to Rebecca, but moved even further back out of her way as we bolted for the front door, to escape to the real world.

We pushed past Kyle, as he took up most of the hallway, through to the lobby and then found the front door. Taking the keys Jodi had given me, I tried one, and it refused to move in the lock.

Trying another and then another in rapid succession, panic mounting, I cursed and shook the door in frustration. Why the fuck had we come so far to fail at the last step, the final moments?

Cursing under my breath, I turned and headed to the furthest area from the fire that I could think of, which was Rebecca's suite.

"We're doomed, aren't we, Jon?" Rebecca called as she trailed along behind me, still holding tightly to my hand.

I slowed down in the hallway and stopped.

"Not if I have anything to say about it." I said, dropping her hand, and tossing her my bag.

"Hon, check and tell me if the keys are in there for my car, they should be on a BMW key fob."

She rustled through the bag, digging through the main pockets with the fervor of a dog after a bone. Meanwhile, I discovered a fire extinguisher right in front of me. Grabbing it with both hands, I gave it a few good yanks and it came free from the wall.

"Got them!" came the triumphant cry from Rebecca who held my keys up in one hand while giving me a quizzical stare. "What are you doing?"

I hefted the weight of the fire extinguisher onto my shoulder. "Taking a page from the Book of Jodi. Are you coming?"

We headed back to the lobby, where I'd come in that fateful night.

The smoke began to roll down the hallway, and I knew when it reached the fryers or any of the areas where the natural gas was piped into this place, it would be a huge fireball that would take the lives of anyone in its path. I'd fought too damned long and hard to get out to be a part of that.

Quickening my pace, I came back to the lobby. No one was here.

Kyle was gone wherever; I wasn't sure and I didn't care. The smoke was just starting to reach this area. I wondered why I didn't hear the drone of sirens of the local fire department, but figured they'd probably not take the fire seriously until the flames licked through the ceiling, which had to be happening somewhere in the compound already.

Telling Rebecca to stand back, I swung the fire extinguisher at the glass of the door. Time seemed to move in slow motion, and I worried I'd never make contact with the door, and if I did, the extinguisher would bounce off the glass harmlessly and I'd be left looking like the old incompetent fool I still occasionally felt I was.

The thing hit the glass, though, which broke with a wholly satisfying crack, but the pane did not shatter. Cursing, and then taking another deep breath, I threw my weight into another swing at the door, and this time, when the metal hit glass, it shattered, splintering into a million little pieces that flew back in my direction, catching in my skin and hair. Fuming under my breath, I took one last swing at the door, and the majority of the glass in the frame fell away.

Stepping through the empty space, I turned and held out my hand to Rebecca.

"Coming?"

She hesitated for a moment, and then, after one final glance back at the compound, Becca took my hand. As she stepped through the door, a roaring, deafening explosion ripped through the air, and the world tilted on its axis as the once beautiful Skylark Inn burst into a disjointed puzzle in a cacophony of sound that shook the neighborhood to its foundations, and threw us into the air.

EPILOGUE

"*A*CHOO!"

The sneeze echoed throughout the room, and so did the whinging that accompanied it. Becca, myself, and that hairy ass of a cat called Kismet had managed to survive the destruction of the compound. We were now kept in high style by the local sheriff's department until the investigation was complete—high style being the local *Journey's End* type of motel, which came with deputies outside the damn doors.

This new confinement had forced the three of us into closed quarters, and my allergies were having a field day. No matter how many antihistamines I downed, the annoying scratchy feeling at the back of my throat and the constant drip of my sinuses were beginning to convince me my nose was nothing but a faulty faucet from a hardware centre.

I implored Becca to find a home for the furry bastard, but she wouldn't hear of him going to the humane society. So, she'd been telephoning friends from her days at university, hoping to find a pace for the little fuzz ball.

The only break I got from the itching and sneezing were the

wonderfully escorted visits with various assorted law enforcement types, who asked me questions for what seemed like days on end. Lucky for me, I'd managed to get in touch with Ryan who had contacted my attorneys, so it wasn't as bad as I knew it could be. I kind of felt sorry for my lawyer, because he'd been privy to some crap that attorneys generally wouldn't see. Mind you, I didn't dole out that much sympathy, because I pay the man good money. Being legal counsel for a rock star for any length of time would be good water cooler talk for anyone. For this case, however, he and his staff would need a water cooler that could hold Niagara Falls just to keep hydrated while gossiping over the entire story.

As for us, we had enough of this chapter from the *Tales of the Creeps* at Skylark inn. I personally looked forward to what lay ahead for Becca and me, as we set out to build a future together.

Without that bloody cat.

ABOUT THE AUTHOR

Amy M. Young was born in Miramichi New Brunswick, and lived her young life between New Brunswick and NorthWestern Ontario, before returning to the east coast for her post-secondary education, where she met her husband.

She currently lives in the National Capital Region of Canada with the aforementioned husband, young daughter and their small zoo.

A Desert Song is Amy's first novel.

Find out more about Amy at:

facebook.com/amymyoungwrites

twitter.com/amymyoung

instagram.com/amymyoung

goodreads.com/amymyoung